Praise for *Dark Enough* by Lauren Belski

"An exuberant, fiercely funny novel that peers deep into the dark heart of adolescence, illuminating its secret joys and sorrows." – Jenny Offill, *Dept of Speculation*

"Belski's *Dark Enough* is an absolute love song for the euphoric growing pains of youth. It is so funny and heartbreaking and page-turning to follow Emily Banks through her life that a person could almost miss how ferociously smart this novel is about the danger that runs tandem with becoming a sexual being and the kinds of wounds that don't hurt us any less for going unnamed. I left these pages full of joy and hope and the certainty that I was already missing these characters I loved so much." – CJ Hauser, *The Crane Wife*

"In *Dark Enough*, Lauren Belski evokes the particular loneliness of adolescence, the questions and contradictions that arise on one young woman's journey toward adulthood. With keen attention to the complexities of human relationships, this ultimately heartwarming debut novel is a raw and honest exploration of a teen's summer of transformation." – Helen Phillips, *Hum*

"Urgent, atmospheric, and effortlessly profound, *Dark Enough* is a story of girlhood and growing up that is both universally resonant and strikingly original. Emily Banks will have a long life in the minds and hearts of readers." – Caeli Widger, *Mother of Invention*

Dark Enough

By
Lauren Belski

Under the BQE Press
Brooklyn, NY

PUBLISHED BY UNDER THE BQE PRESS
Brooklyn, NY

underthebqe.com

ISBN: 979-8-9911220-1-6
LCCN: 2025934657

Cover design and art by Loni Gaghan
@lovetoloveyouclothing

Cover photo by Ed Belski

Interior design by Brian Russ
campersrule.com

Manufactured in the United States of America

For Brian, who makes all my dreams come true <3

“So let me be clear, I wrote this poem with a very specific intent. I have a 15-year-old daughter. It is important to me that I throw every part of my experience, whatever wisdom I’ve gleaned from that, every part of my backbone, toward her, to sustain her, to offer her language that lifts her up and keeps her up.” – Dominique Christina

“At the very moment that humans discovered the scale of the universe and found that their most unconstrained fancies were in fact dwarfed by the true dimensions of even the Milky Way Galaxy, they took steps that ensured that their descendants would be unable to see the stars at all.” – *Contact*, Carl Sagan

- 1 -

Bathing suit weather had hit early that year, starting in May, and since I was 15 with nothing better to do, I'd spent way too much time loitering in the pharmacy on Main Street, looking at various tubes of sunscreen and analyzing their SPFs. Even though I was a seriously fair-skinned girl of the freckly Irish and English variety, I somehow deluded myself into thinking I was also the sort of person who could get a tan. This was mostly because of Deb, who had inherited her olive skin from her mom. Since the summer after seventh grade, Deb had become a devotee of an even tan, and so, by proximity, had I. But unlike Deb, whose goal was to turn a deep, beautiful brown, my goal was basically to see proof that the sun had changed the color of my skin without burning it—to go from white to less white. This required the exact right sunscreen. Too high an SPF, I feared, would result in no change at all, but that SPF 8 coconut-smelling oil meant ouch. I was suddenly purpley red and peely.

The summer before, I'd made that mistake at Deb's shore house and could barely enter the shower. I bathed in nothing but a cool, sticky layer of aloe for a week, and my skin bubbled and shed itself in long translucent strips like a snake. My mother turned her own shade of red when she saw it. "You're going to kill yourself," she said. "You're going to ruin your future. Do you want melanoma?" My mom was staunchly against the idea of a tan. She hid underneath wide brimmed hats and umbrellas. To her, the sun was nothing but a cancer-causing ball of skin-aging wrath.

This year though, Mom would have no reason for dismay, and Deb would be impressed. I would get a healthy tan. I chose a brand named Glow. I bought two bottles. One of SPF 15 and one of 30 and made sure to slather myself with one every time Deb asked me to lay out in her backyard after school so that we could be ready for Memorial Day.

Track season had just ended. School assignments were finally beginning to slow down, and I'll admit that I felt whiplash from the sudden languidness of the Stevens' patio. I'd spent the entire school year, from the break of dawn until I collapsed in my bed, working towards the prize: straight As, record-breaking times, test scores that validated my analytical strengths. My body was a machine. It ran the courses. It lifted the five pound weights in reps of eight. It stretched and hydrated and ate and held a perfectly sharpened number two pencil that filled in the answers on the PSAT scantron sheets. And now, it reached for a grape from a bowl of fruit, swatting away a tiny fruit fly.

Deb always wore a bikini and I always wore a one-piece, my "Baywatch suit," Deb called it, though I lacked the voluptuousness of *Baywatch*'s red-suited star, Pamela Anderson.

"You've got to up your boob factor," Deb told me. I was still an A cup. She had somehow graduated to a B and all of her bras and bikini tops were "push up" style. Her chest kind of gushed up out of her suit, like a waterfall of boob.

"You've got enough boob for both of us," I said back.

Jenna, though, had us both beat. We called her a B+, or a C -, depending on our mood.

"Em," Jenna triumphantly declared to me once when we were comparing our anatomy, "This is the only thing we've both got you beat in." She was teasing me, trying to get under my skin. It was working. Everyone knew I hated to lose. It didn't matter at what. My ambition was like a disease, and the three of us had played enough games of Monopoly for them to know that.

"That's cool," I said back. "At least I still get an A." Which, I have to admit, I took a strange solace in.

Behind her back, at a sleepover a few months before, Deb had told me that she thought that Jenna's boobs were too big and that they made her look fat when she wore the wrong kinds of shirts. But in person, on those lazy May days when school was over and there was no practice and Mom and Dad were still at work and I suddenly could join in the afterschool ritual of snacks and gossip, I noticed Deb was all syrupy sweet to Jenna, saying things like, "That top is so hot." "You are so pretty it's not even fair." Or, "You are totally going to get a boyfriend, I know it."

"I already have a boyfriend," Jenna would remind her. She was still technically dating a guy from her country club outside of Minneapolis, where she'd moved from last year. Deb rolled her eyes. We knew where she stood on this subject. Long distance relationships did not count because how would you ever lose your virginity?

"Another boyfriend then," Deb would correct herself.

For some reason, every compliment Deb gave to Jenna felt like a backwards insult directed at me. I had no hot tops. I was not pretty, or no one ever told me I was anyway. I may have been a straight A student and the reigning NJ state champion in the women's 1500 and cross country, but these accomplishments held no weight in teenage society. I was a disappointment to Deb. Too freckled and brainy. Too comfortable in a one-piece.

I was no match for Jenna's midwestern blondeness and charm. She called brownies, "bars," and soda, "pop," and had this perfect laugh that managed to be both innocent and devilish at the same time.

Her bounciness brought out a moodiness in me. I couldn't help but scowl at her easy joy and complete dismissal of schoolwork, which made her seem even more spoiled than Deb. Her dad was some sort of executive for a company called Target that was "expanding to the northeast," —her words. And her family had three houses. One on Lake Michigan, one in Florida, and one here in town.

She also liked to act as if the three of us had always been besties despite the fact that she'd only lived in our town for a year and a half. She didn't have the history Deb and I had, the past part of the "forever" in "BFF." Still, she memorized our stories from elementary school and repeated them back to us so easily it was almost like she had been there, her Midwest accent sounding as wholesome as a glass of milk. Sometimes, it seemed like maybe she should have been there. Like it would be better for everyone if we just edited me out and replaced me with her. I saw how easily Deb and her clicked, and I knew that all those days after school for all of freshman year, while I was at practice, they were at each other's houses or loitering downtown sharing a plate of French fries. It caused a twisting ache in my gut, sort of like the ones you get from running. A friend cramp. And it had the power to make me act out of character.

Like how I started doing hilarious things to elevate my cleavage grade to a B or C+. One time, I shoved socks into the top of my bathing suit. Another time, tiny donut peaches that I found in a bowl on the kitchen table at Deb's house. Why I thought this was hilarious is beyond me now. I think it reminded me of the end of *Austin Powers*, when Elizabeth Hurley was naked and kept picking up random things in the apartment and holding them in front of her boobs at the exact right time so that the audience couldn't see anything.

Anyway, with fruit lodged against my nipples, I pranced down the deck stairs like a kitten, gestured towards my chest and said, "Boys...peaches," like an overly jubilant stay-at-home mom from a 50s sitcom on Nick at Nite. But as Deb and Jenna turned to look, gravity caused the peaches to slide a bit further down my bathing suit. It looked like I had a few goiters growing out of my abdomen. Then I pushed them down to my groin.

"Look, I have testicles," I said.

"Gross," said Deb.

"Your chest is so flat you actually kind of look like a man in a bathing suit," Jenna said flippantly. That made the two of them laugh. Not in the way I'd been hoping for.

Deb claimed to have read somewhere (or probably actually seen on MTV) that sometimes to give actresses cleavage, costume and wardrobe specialists would duct tape their breasts together. One Friday, when I was inside Deb's house going to the bathroom, I saw some duct tape near a clutter of tools and couldn't help myself. I cut long strips and placed them under my little boobs, binding them together. The results were quite buoyant. I suddenly had two swollen water balloons levitating towards my chin. When I presented myself outside, I got the laugh I was after. Our faces hurt from smiling. Tears and pee leaked from us in joy.

The duct tape hurt coming off, and it left a sticky film on my skin for days. Still, at the time, I'd have said it was worth it.

Deb's backyard opened to a big, public park. Her family chose not to put up a fence around their property—partially because no one really used the park—so it just made the entire expanse look like an extension of their yard. The other neighbors had picket fences around their properties with doors that opened to the park, except for a tiny, old building a few houses down that was set further back and surrounded by dandelions and wildflowers.

"What's the deal with that tool shed down there? Did someone buy it yet?" Jenna asked at some point.

The "tool shed" was actually a house, or it had been. An old woman had lived there for a while when we were little. She used to wave to us. Then at some point, we never saw her again. She got moved to a nursing home. Then she died.

Now the house was for sale. It drove my mom, and many of the other adults in the area, crazy. They wanted the town to buy it, knock it down, and turn it into a parking lot for the park. Or a playground. But another group of neighbors had started a petition. The house had been built in 1672 and was actually one of the oldest standing structures in the state of New Jersey. Now, it was an official historic landmark that was slowly crumbling.

"Oh please," Deb said to Jenna. "You know it's not a tool shed. Little Rita used to live there before she died."

"You're right, it's not a tool shed. It's a love shack," Jenna giggled. "Who's losing their virginity in that palace over there tonight?"

"Ewww! Can you imagine a naked butt on whatever sort of gross rug is still on the floor in there?"

"Stop," I said, "I'm going to throw up."

Our banter was performative. It was as if we thought of the bright bulb of the sun as a sort of spotlight. Within the power of its glow, we communicated in high-pitched squeals and whispers. We analyzed the concept of erections, wondering just how much bigger did a boy's penis get. We questioned the logistics of blow jobs and penetration, fingers and tongues, condoms and birth control.

In hopeful, reverent whispers, we retold the stories we'd heard about older girls in our school, wondering if we too would share their fate.

Deb was obsessed with being popular. She wanted to live the East Coast version of *90210*. Now that both of her older, bookish brothers were out of the house, no one was around to mock her close readings of *YM* beauty tips. Jenna was on board too. She packed hot rollers when she went to sleepovers so she could set her hair. She knew how to apply make-up professionally and had a bag full of very expensive brushes for eye shadow and blush. She liked to lean over me and play with my hair, saying things like, "We could do so much with your look." And so, by default, I too dreamed popular girl dreams. I too had a quiet wish to be prom queen. I pictured myself in the world that we gossiped about the same way I imagined myself in the outfits from the glossy pages of our magazines.

One of our favorite Tonley legends was about Mandy Gladstone, who'd supposedly been caught in the locker room last October with Beau Ryder, a senior headed to Notre Dame on a football scholarship, who'd apparently had nothing on but his backwards baseball hat. Beau was a future NFL star. He was the kind of guy where you already knew you'd be at a bar someday and people would be gathered around cheering at TVs and that he would be the guy who scored the touchdown, and you could casually mention that you knew him. Or, if you were Mandy, I guess you could also quietly think to yourself, I fucked him in my high school locker room. For some reason, with most of our freshman year of high school behind us, this seemed like something a girl would be proud of.

Mandy's much talked about escapade with Beau had supposedly ended her relationship with Doug Ryan, king of the juniors-soon-to-be-seniors, and number one on my list of Tonley boys I'd hook up with if they ever realized I existed. In other words, by fucking Beau, Mandy had "set Doug free."

From my outer orbit, like a fan girl, I'd been observing tiny things about Doug all school year, like how he always wore Abercrombie and Fitch t-shirts or collared shirts with a polo crest, Adidas shell tops, earbuds in the hall, one always firmly implanted, the other dangling by his Adam's apple, so you could hear the sounds of whatever he was listening to, "Who Let the Dogs Out" being the most memorable one because it caused his friends to howl at him as they passed. Why I didn't find it offensive, intimidating, or just plain cringe-worthy when they all ruffed together in the hallway, I can't say. My high school brain was half-hatched. For some strange reason I found it cute. I saw those testosterone-and-protein-shake filled, well-sculpted, young men as a bunch of strays from *Oliver and Company*. Their scrappy danger was adorable.

Besides, Doug also read books. I knew he was one of the best students in AP European History. People talked about how he always got 100s on all the tests. This was a big deal because Mr. Hudson was Harvard-level hard.

Doug was an Eagles fan, like everyone in South Jersey, but he also had an affinity for the Packers because of their quarterback. I heard him discuss this at length in the hallway during football season, flexing his arm back and forth and rubbing his muscles, though not in a way that struck me as particularly vain. As an athlete, I could identify with living in a body that was always asking me to bend and stretch at odd moments.

These were the sorts of details Deb, Jenna, and I explored in great detail. We'd fill in the narratives overheard in the hall with our own crazy theories and assertions, like we were the authors of a town gossip rag to rival *Us Weekly*. We heard that he'd started hooking up with a girl named Kelsey, a teammate of mine from cross country, who was also one of his ex-girlfriend Mandy's best friends.

"Can you believe it?" we'd gasp, affirming that we'd never stoop to such levels. Hoes before bros was our obvious mantra. We didn't think anything of using "hoe" to describe ourselves, just like we didn't think anything of referring to Mandy and Kelsey and whoever else as "sluts". These words came out of our mouths freely: "Did you see that slut in the cafeteria yesterday? She was like begging for attention," or, one time when I smiled at a cashier at an ice cream place as he handed me my change, "You are such a slut. You like him.

You want him to undress you with his eyes." Or the way Deb talked about Parker, Doug's best friend, her chosen love: "If I had a chance, I would totally give him a blow job." This declaration required the follow up question, "Even if it was in the locker room and Mr. Bonanno might walk in?" For some reason, this was the true test of love: taking the risk of being caught like Mandy and Beaux. Of course, none of us had ever given a blow job. We only knew what one was in the abstract, and I don't think we had any real plans for that to change anytime soon. At least I didn't. I thought about all of this stuff as some sort of big, silly joke.

Then a Friday sunbathing sesh morphed into a sleepover, and after Deb's parents had gone to bed, we watched a porno on one of the pay channels that was half-coming through her television in wavy lines.

"Oh my God!" Deb said. "Gross!" But she didn't change the channel.

We were in her sunken living room, which was set off from the kitchen by a few stairs, a little hallway, and some swinging doors. We loved it because it was so private. Her parents kept to the kitchen or the living room near the front of the house, and now that they were asleep upstairs, it was truly our clubhouse. I was sitting where I always sat, that same corner of the couch, my head resting against the overstuffed arm, my legs curled under me. Deb was on the floor, her head resting against the seat cushion on the other side of the couch, her hands on the remote.

Jenna had gone home. Her mom had some reason why she couldn't stay that night. But if I were to edit her into the story, I'd imagine that she would have screamed that it was disgusting and demanded we turn it off. For whatever reason, Deb and I did no such thing.

I sat up from my reclined position and squinted at the

screen. "I can't even see it."

"I can," Deb said, moving towards the screen and using the remote control as a pointer. "See, there's her butt. She's like bent over something and he's standing behind her."

"What?!" I shrieked.

"Shhhh," Deb said. "Listen."

I obeyed. Quietly, I attempted to see what she was seeing—the butt and the man behind it. But it was just indecipherable wavy lines to me. As my eyes gave up, my ears seemed to focus on the high-pitched yeses and ohhs. The oohs were mostly the man, the yesses the woman, though sometimes her yesses became yeahs and the yeahs became the high-pitched screams people let out on a roller coaster.

Her voice shocked me. I felt a squirmy sense of discomfort, not physically aroused exactly, but curious, confused, unable to imagine my own wail, wondering what it would sound like, whether I would also say yes, and who it would be I'd be saying yes to, and what exactly would I mean by it? Like, yes, this is ok? Yes, I like this? Yes, keep going? Or would I be talking to myself? Like yes, this is what I want, or yes, this is happening, or yes, I did it, the way I celebrated a hard-earned A on a test or a win on the track.

The wavy lines continued to moan towards a climax. On the TV, there was concern that someone outside the door could hear them. But then, the person opened the door and joined in.

"In my mouth," the woman directed the newcomer. Her yeses dissolved into moans.

"Gross!" I said.

"Perverted," Deb agreed.

But neither of us moved to turn it off. We let it run for another couple of minutes. Maybe a full 15, who knows. I only know we didn't watch the whole thing. It got boring and we turned it off.

The living room had sliding doors that lead to the patio, the scene of all our sunbathing. Now we were under the moon, except I couldn't find the moon, but then I did, a blackened ball with the tiniest little strip of light. The lounge chairs felt different in pajamas. I picked strands of pollen from the crevices near the buttons of the cushions. Above us was the gray dome of the suburban night. I watched the flight pattern of a plane headed towards Philadelphia International Airport, and then saw the flashing lights of other planes waiting behind it, the sum of their headlights a modern constellation. I wondered if anyone aboard any of those planes was a part of the mile high club, and then I decided that no one was actually a member of the mile high club, at least anyone who flew commercial. The mile high club was just something horny high school boys liked to talk about so that they could talk about sex while also bragging about going on vacation.

I guess Deb was having her own silent porno reflections, because out of nowhere she said, "Why does sex always sound like dying orcas?" which made us both laugh hysterically, probably because we were very tired and also because we were weirded out by what we'd shared. Still, the sound of orcas became code for getting nasty. And for whatever reason, whenever I happen to see planes in the sky lined up to land at night, I still connect the dots along the curve of the horizon and think of them as a humpback whale, which even though I know is not an orca, somehow makes more sense.

- 2 -

It was like some sort of animal that had been sleeping inside me all my life was suddenly waking up from hibernation, and by Memorial Day Weekend, she was hungry, though I still didn't know what I was supposed to feed her.

I threw a toothbrush and a few things in a duffle bag while my mom hovered hawk-like over me, offering commentary on every item I chose.

"I know how to pack for the beach, you know," I told her. "I don't need your help." She was looking at me with her crazy mom eyes, the ones that were so full of aggressive love that it felt a little like she'd be willing to eat me, to crunch and swallow my bones, just to keep me close.

"Are you sure you don't want to go to Nanny's picnic? Dad and I are going to be lonely without you. Everyone will be asking where you are."

"Mom," I said defensively, trying my best to keep the annoyance out of my voice for fear she'd accuse me of being disrespectful and then try to take the weekend away from me. "You hate going to Nanny's. You never let me eat anything there or touch anything there anyway. Why would I even want to go?" Mom was extremely judgmental and ashamed of Nanny, criticizing the sugar and oil-laden store-bought plastic trays of baked goods and the appetizers filled with mystery meat that her mother bought from the freezer section of the discount grocery. I thought they all tasted delicious but understood that the forty-lettered chemical additives on the ingredients lists were either cancer-causing or made you fat, or both, and so I only dared nibble a small portion. Nanny's furniture was also cheap and covered in plastic. She wore house dresses and slippers and her hair was usually in pink, plastic foam curlers. She was like the "old lady" costume you found prepackaged at costume shops around Halloween. Some people had cute, cuddly relationships with their grandmothers—not me and Nanny. I think she sensed that my mom didn't want her coming too close. She kept the television on when we visited and spent most of her time watching it. Sometimes, she tried to give me jelly donuts or something to show she knew I existed. When she slipped me one of these treats, wrapped in a napkin, she would say "eat it quick," and then wink at me, practically shoving it into my face. It was hard to tell whether she really wanted me to have it or if she was trying to give a quiet fuck you to my mom. Either way, I ate them, usually in one gulp, like a snake swallowing a mouse whole.

Mom sighed. "I just worry. Nanny's your grandmother. You never get to see her."

"But I never get to see her because you never take me to her house."

"You could go to Deb's another weekend."

"Or," I said, "I could see Nanny another weekend. We could have her over for dinner. You and Dad could pick her up and we could cook for her. It'll be easier to spend time with her that way anyway, without a whole bunch of other people around and Uncle Tommy's dogs." My mother's oldest brother, Tommy, still lived with Nanny even though he was at least 50, and he had two loud and muscular Doberman mixes that always kept my mom on edge. Actually, everything about Tommy, a permanently-disabled Vietnam vet with a bad leg full of shrapnel and a two-packs-of-Newports-and-a-twelve-pack-of-Bud-a-day habit, put my mom on edge, but that was a different story, and yet another reason why visiting Nanny's was far from relaxing or fun.

Mom paused for a moment, knowing she had no legs to stand on, and then relented. "Fine," she said. "I'll ask Nanny to come over one night." But I knew she'd never make arrangements. That was the way it worked.

The next day, Friday at 2:42pm, right at the dismissal bell, Mrs. Stevens met us at the doors of the school and we made our way down the Atlantic City Expressway to exit 7S, then took the Parkway down to Exit 0. Deb's shore house was literally at the end of the earth. It was on a dead-end street in a little village of houses clustered around a still operational lighthouse. No one was ever driving by and you could pretty much walk in the middle of her street whenever you wanted.

After we unpacked our clothes and rode our bikes into town for ice cream, back at her house, in the shower I noticed I had the ever-so-faintest tan line. I ran to the bedroom to show Deb, my still-wet hair dripping and clumpy, sticking to my back.

"It's right here, see?" I said, pointing to my shoulder where I could see an obvious demarcation where my bathing suit had been.

Deb's mouth, which had just received a fresh coat of pink gloss, puckered as she examined me. "But it's not a tan line." she declared. "It's just a line."

I stuck my tongue out at her. "Yes it is!"

She went back to pulling clothes out of the huge suitcase she'd brought with her for our three night stay.

"A new family bought the house across the street," she said. "Did you see? The sale sign is gone and they painted it like a coral color, which is kind of too Key West for my taste, but whatever." Whenever she said "for my taste" she sounded like her mother. It was an expression I'd heard her use about movies, menu items, and appliques on shoes. I thought of my own mother, how nothing she did was anything like Nanny. What made some people embody their parents and others reject everything about them?

Money, I realized. Or at least in this case. Deb held up a little sundress with three yellow buttons at the chest, pulling a thread from the neckline before tossing it over a chair. "I heard the new neighbors have sons. Maybe they're cute, or maybe they're going to rent their place out, which means there could be different cute boys staying there every week!"

"But I thought you said you weren't going to be here all summer," I said.

"Off and on," Deb said. "Two weeks in July. I think another in August. And most weekends. That's plenty of time to romance the neighbors."

"Ha," I said.

"You should try that on." She motioned to the dress she'd tossed on the chair.

I was still wearing a towel, fresh from the shower, so it was easy to comply. I put my arms through the holes and pulled it over my head, feeling the fabric strain a bit as I pulled it down over my chest. I wasn't busty at all, but I was taller and wider than Deb, so even though I didn't exactly fill out the top of the dress, it still clung to my body, showing the outline of my breasts.

"Ha! You can see your nips," she said, pointing to the eraser-sized nubs below the floral pattern.

"Oh my god!" I said, covering them protectively, as if there was anyone in the room to gape.

"But the dress looks hot," she said, approvingly. "It shows off how narrow you are. You just need a bra."

I reached my arms up to the ceiling and then down towards my toes, feeling the hem of the dress tickle the bottom of my butt cheeks.

"No way, this thing is too small," I said while wriggling out of it.

I was a fashion minimalist, an athlete first, prone to breaking into a trot and playing a sport at any second. I liked to feel cute, but I valued feeling comfortable, so I packed predictable attire, except for one thing: a new bikini I'd bought with my mom the fall before. I think the only reason Mom let me buy it was because it was on the sales rack and she assumed I'd never wear it. Since I'd purchased it, it'd sat in my underwear drawer where I'd shoved it, but for whatever reason, after Mom had left my room the other night, I'd snuck it into my bag, returning my Speedo to the dresser. The bikini was basically triangles and strings that were bright pink, with tiny white polka dots. It was the most revealing thing I'd ever worn. When I put it on the next morning when we got ready for the beach, for the first time ever, Deb gushed over me with an enthusiasm she usually reserved for Jenna.

"Oh my god, you are so skinny and toned. It's not fair. I'm so fat. Look at your abs. There's like muscle there. You almost have a six pack. You should bleach your hair. You'd look like Gwen Stefani. We should cut all your t-shirts so that you're always showing your abs. They are totally your best feature."

For the record, Deb was not fat. She just wasn't an athlete who ran and did strength training almost every day. Her body was less muscular, thin but also soft, more feminine and attractive by glossy magazine standards. Mine, on the other hand, was kind of ropy. I sort of bulged in weird places, like my arms and the tops of my thighs, and then became spindly and sharp in others, like my shoulder blades and elbows.

It feels lame to admit, but I felt elated by her recognition. I looked in the mirror and attempted to see myself the way she described me. I touched my abs with my fingers. I probably could rock a crop top if I actually had the guts. And if I never had to be seen by my mother.

People never really looked at me when I had regular clothes

on. I was just a normal person, part of the crowd, another ponytail and t-shirt in a desk. But that Saturday, after we had laid on the beach blanket and let the sun warm our skin, after I had fallen into such a beach haze that I'd even forgotten about my new revealing bathing suit, as we walked across the sand past other beach blankets towards the water for a swim, I felt strangers' eyes trailing my wake, the power of my bare skin radiating from every pore.

It's not that I had any desire to capitalize on this power, I just noticed it, the way you sometimes notice all at once that you're one of the only ones in the class who is keeping pace with the math teacher as they explain how to calculate the period of a sine wave. I took note of it, and was simultaneously pleased and embarrassed. But Deb noticed too.

"Oh my god, that grandpa was checking you out," she whispered.

"No way, he was looking at you," I hissed.

"So glad you lost the Speedo," she said. Then she ran into the water, screamed about how cold it was, and ran right back out. It reminded me of a scene from a movie or magazine. Deb was in the mood to draw the eyes of beachgoers, and because I was under the spell of my new bathing suit, I went with it. We splashed and screeched together in a particularly girly way, kicking the water and running away from each other, giggling in exaggerated pitches.

Once we were bored of that, we played paddle ball together, running and diving for the little ball along the shoreline and then tip-toeing past blankets when it flew out of reach, accepting the ball from strangers, some of them cute boys our age, with whom we exchanged shy glances. One in particular kind of caught my eye. He was reading a book and wearing bright green sunglasses. After we returned to the blanket for water and a snack, as I flipped through a copy of *Seventeen* magazine, I concocted an entire fantasy in my head involving Green Sunglasses Boy. I imagined us riding bikes by each other later that night and saying hi to each other, and then parking the bikes and doing something together in the grass, maybe badminton or frisbee, then we'd spend the whole next day talking on a beach blanket. I decided that he was definitely from one of the Pennsylvania suburbs, not the Jersey ones like us, maybe Lower Merion. I bet his family had a boat and he knew how to sail. I imagined how by the end of the weekend we'd have exchanged phone numbers and that we'd call each other every night and plan to somehow see each other again at the beach. The relationship would continue to grow; by junior year, he would be my prom date. Afterwards, we'd come down here and party on his parents' boat. I'd lose my virginity on the deck under the stars. He was a year older than me, so he'd graduate first, but we'd go to the same college, probably Yale. Get married. Travel Europe. Get in a big fight and somehow lose each other in Paris and then find each other again and reaffirm our love.

The cover stories on my copy of *Seventeen* were "25 Ways to Perfect Your Summer Look," and "When your best friend has a boyfriend and you don't." The summer look article was a combination of ways to stay slim and become blonder. Smoothies for breakfast was number one. Tip 10 was "try squeezing lemon juice into your hair before you head to the beach to get some natural highlights." I'd seen some lemons in a grocery bag that Mrs. Stevens had carried into the house when we'd arrived. Maybe I'd give them a go tomorrow, I thought.

I eyed my future husband on the blanket. He was deep into his book. I stood up. "I'm boiling. Let's go swimming."

Deb shook her head. She was locked into the historical romance novel she'd found in the free library of books by the entrance to the beach. It was about a knight stumbling through a time warp and falling in love with a New York City fashion designer. She'd showed me one of the pages with a sex scene about the knight's "swelling cock." She couldn't tear her eyes away. She'd tried to convince me to pick up a Danielle Steel novel from the pile, but I'd chosen a paperback copy of *The Prisoner of Azkaban*. The fourth Harry Potter book was due out in a couple of months and I thought it'd be a good idea to refresh my memory. But the wizard world wasn't really doing it for me at that exact moment.

"Please can we go to the water?"

Deb's eyes did not stray from her page. "No way! The knight is about to walk down the runway! And that water is like an ice bucket."

It was true that it was pretty cold. It was early in the season, but I wasn't one to sit out a chance to swim, so I dove head first through the waves, every hair on my body standing up with the chill, though eventually I did get used to it. This was the moment I discovered the major problem with bikinis, which are designed to display your body more than actually stay on it while you swim. The first time I dove through a wave, my bottoms slipped down to almost my ankles. Quickly, I hoisted them back up under the water before anyone noticed. While treading water, I re-tied the strings at each hip super tight, double knotting them so they felt secure. I wanted to do the same with my top, but was afraid to do it alone, so I decided to go back out of the ocean and ask Deb to do it.

When I came out of the water, the air felt freezing too. I hid under my beach towel, ate a peanut butter and jelly sandwich, and slowly warmed up. Deb double knotted my bikini top behind my back and at my neck. I felt the muscles in my shoulders and my neck flinch against the pressure of the knot, but I had no choice. I rolled my head around from side to side as I chewed my sandwich, feeling particles of sand crackle in my teeth. The oppressive waves of heat called me back to the water. I nudged Deb's leg. She was sprawled out, holding her book, her face behind sunglasses. "Come on," I said. "Will you please swim with me?"

"Do you think men were more chivalrous in the Middle Ages?" she asked, looking up from her page.

"I have no idea," I said.

"Well, this one really cares about how this lady feels," she said.

"Isn't he supposed to be a 'knight in shining armor'?" I asked. "That's not like a real thing, right? Wasn't that always a fairytale?"

She closed the book and moaned at the sky. "I hope not," she said.

"Don't worry," I joked, "Somewhere out there, there's a Heath Ledger waiting to serenade you with the help of a marching band, during soccer practice in front of the whole school." We'd watched *10 Things I Hate About You* before we went to sleep the night before.

"Ha, ha," she said.

I pulled off her sunglasses.

She writhed, covering her eyes and crying, "Ahhh."

"Play with me," I said. "I'm bored."

"Play," Deb snorted, retrieving her glasses, and giving me a look that said, Stop being a child, before putting them back on her face. "What do you want to play?"

"Let's dig a hole big enough for someone to sit in. Let's bury your dad or mom or something."

Her parents had taken their beach chairs a few blankets over and were sitting with another couple, drinking wine out of little plastic cups.

"There is no way my mom is going to go in a hole, but fine,

let's dig." When we got up to walk towards the coast, my eyes strayed towards Mr. Green Sunglasses's blanket. I noticed he was no longer there. I scanned the coastline and water for him and saw him holding a boogie board with a smaller kid, maybe his brother? Did he go into the water because I'd been in there? Probably not. I mean, we were at the beach. The ocean was pretty much the main event.

Deb and I used our hands as shovels and got to work. We worked silently until we'd created quite a chasm in the sand. Little kids were drawn to the hole. On three sides, the sand towered around it like the hills of Kilimanjaro.

"This thing is like a tomb," Deb said.

"Let's play a paddle ball game after this and whoever loses has to get buried in here," I said.

"Fine," Deb said, "but let's do best out of three because you always win the first one."

I was smiling to myself, imagining what Deb's head would look like sticking out of a pile of sand, and wondering whether or not the spectacle would draw my imaginary boyfriend from the waves, when all of a sudden, out of nowhere, Doug Ryan, Parker Finney, Scott Kane, and Rick Henderson appeared at the bend of the coast by the jetty, which is to say that pretty much all of the popular guys we gossiped about were now in our sights, shirtless and running and shoving one another while taking turns on a skimboard that they slid on along the coast. They were like a stag of wild horses. The sun was so bright in their direction, I had to squint to see them, making the light bend around them like they were the shadowy figures of a developing Polaroid. Their presence sent a bolt through me. I felt their force.

These were the stars of our "blow job" conversations. There was Doug, bare chested. (I wasn't surprised to discover he had a chiseled torso. He was the captain of the soccer team, after all.) Our pictures were featured, along with a few other scholar athletes, in the showcase outside of the athletic office by the gym, like a shrine to our future love, or so I pretended sometimes when I passed. Though he was allegedly smart, he emanated zero nerdiness. He was about 6 ft tall and broad, already a man. I'd sat in the stands during soccer games and seen him play. His arms were strong, and he could throw a soccer ball almost halfway across the field. That, along with being in the top 10% of his class, made him, as my mother would say, "the full package."

"Oh my God," Deb squealed under her breath. "What are they doing here? I thought Doug's house was like two miles down the beach. Do you think they'll say hi to us? I'm going to faint."

I usually fed off of Deb's unbridled confidence in social situations. Her sudden declaration of nervousness was like a call to abandon ship. All that sexiness I'd been feeling in my bikini promptly vanished. I wanted to cover up. I felt too exposed, caught being an imposter version of myself. But we'd already been spotted, and our blanket was too far away. It'd be too obvious to retreat to it now. My body felt fuzzy. I didn't know what to do with my arms, legs, nostrils, teeth. I was unprepared.

It was obvious something monumental was happening. A collision of teenage tectonic plates. On an average day, these guys would have never acknowledged I was alive, but now, here, at the beach, 90 miles or so from our town, here they were racing towards us, overloading my nervous system into a panic zone. And unless I was hallucinating, Doug Ryan was running directly at me like a Spanish bull.

"Banks!" he yelled as he approached me at full force. It was at that moment that I suddenly understood that blurry woman's porno wails. Before I was even aware of it, a shriek of pure delight came out of my mouth. I felt ashamed by it afterwards. He scooped me up and threw all five feet, seven inches of me over his shoulder.

I'd never been touched by a boy like that. My bare stomach was literally against his bare shoulder, skin on skin.

He threatened to carry me out into the ocean and throw me in the waves, but I wriggled and protested, so he dropped me in the wake. I landed on my feet and caught my breath, both mortified and intensely alive, conscious in every pore, my face open wide in a large, confused and searching grin.

The other guys and Deb gathered around us. Parker jumped on the skimboard and stood on one foot, then flipped off of it, landing on his ass. As he sprung up to chase the board out of the waves, a round of dude insults ensued, strange references I couldn't quite keep up with.

Thankfully, Deb sprung to life and held the conversation together, discussing where Doug's family's house was and where he usually went to the beach. Before we knew it, out of nowhere, Deb and these older, popular guys and I were digging an even deeper hole together, and instead of one of us girls, it was Rick, who was always pretty much stoned and a little out of it, whom they eventually pushed in and covered with sand, leaving only his head exposed to the elements.

While all of this was happening, I felt like a half version of myself, incapable of speaking plainly or even thinking a full thought.

Doug, I noticed, was different close up. He was kind of meaner than I expected. Once Rick had been fully submerged in the sand, he looked towards the guys and said, "Give me a snood."

Snood? Scott reached into the backpack in the sand and pulled a crumpled stick from a soft pack of Camel Lights. Cigarettes? It was broad daylight. Everywhere around us were families. Grown ups and little kids. I was scandalized. I looked around for Mr. and Mrs. Stevens, but they must have gone back to the house. I tried to search Deb's face for a sign of concern, but I didn't see any. She was just watching the action. Neither of us smoked. I personally considered a cigarette scary enough to run away from, but I was taking Deb's lead. If she was going to be cool, I had to be cool too. I took a deep breath to quiet the alarms in my chest and tried not to look at Deb's face, for fear she would criticize me for looking as afraid as I felt. Scott tossed the snood to Doug, who went up to Rick's head and stuck the end up his nostril. All the guys laughed. Then Doug took a lighter and pushed down to spark it. There was a little knob on the end that adjusted the size of the flame. Doug moved the knob all the way to one side, so that the flame was an inch high and started carrying it towards Rick's face.

"Ready dude?" Doug said.

A second of panic flickered across Rick's face before he snorted a laugh along with everyone else.

Parker took the cigarette out of his nose and set it in his mouth as Doug crawled towards his buried head and approached with the torch-like flame. I turned my head. I couldn't watch. I was sure Rick's face was going to melt. The dude laughter hit a pitch, like a herd of hyenas, so I turned back, and there was Rick, his chubby head resting on the sand like a bowling ball, or the ghostly remains of a decapitated jester. Smoke billowed from his mouth like a chimney. I wondered how he could breathe with all those carcinogens billowing directly up his nose. But he was smiling, delighted by himself. He actually smoked that cigarette down to the filter. I was both horrified and fascinated. Eventually, when it got close to the end, he spat it into the sand. I quickly grabbed it and stubbed it out, afraid someone might try to stick it back in his mouth. I wanted to free him from his grave.

"Are you ready to get out?" I asked him. I didn't wait for an answer. I just started digging around him until he broke through and climbed the rest of the way himself. He had dark circles underneath his eyes and there was something off about him that I couldn't quite place, but when he smiled at me, his face rearranged itself so that I saw a glimpse of something good inside, so I smiled back.

After all that digging, I was covered in sand, so I went to the ocean to wash off and just to swim. The chill of the water took my breath away at first, but I decided to commit to the cold again, diving through and treading water on the other side of the breakers. The waves were pretty rough that day, large and loud, and it was nice to hear them hiss and crash instead of having to navigate the rules of conversation in Doug's world. I floated for a minute and searched for dolphins on the horizon, but my wildlife quest was short lived. I saw Doug enter the water and cut through a wave and soon he was right next to me, close enough that his toe grazed my calf. I said nothing.

"It's fucking cold out here!" he yelled.

"You get used to it," I said, and then I smiled, but it was a forced one, an attempt to look happy and playful and in control.

"I wish I had my wet suit, these waves are gnarly," He shook his head back and forth, maybe trying to get water out of his ears. It made the short, wet dark locks on his head flop back and forth. "I should go get my board."

I took a deep breath and attempted to speak back without stuttering. "Yeah, I think surfers go further down the beach. I've seen them here before."

"That's where I usually go," he said. "The end of Beach Ave. I might head there in a little bit."

I said nothing.

"Do you surf?" he asked.

"No," I said. "I never tried."

"I bet you'd get up first try. I could teach you."

A new fantasy flashed through my mind, involving surfing

lessons that turned into true love, prom dates, etc.

"Maybe tomorrow," I said. "We're here all weekend."

"Alright. Let's do it. Get Banks on a board."

I wished we could talk about something else. Like marine life or sand castles or how close he'd have been willing to carry that lighter torch towards Rick's face just to get laughs from a crowd, but I wasn't one for starting conversations, especially not in a scenario like this.

He had the sort of nose that looked like it'd been broken once. There was a flat spot right in the middle that was the size of the end of a thumb. I felt an impulse to reach across the water and touch it, but I stopped myself. I watched his head and neck hover above the surface of the water. His eyebrows were thick and straight and dark brown and they framed his clear blue eyes just like Jagger's in *General Hospital*, except Jagger's were brown. Was I visibly swooning? I hoped not.

"Cool," I said. I swam a bit towards the breakers and caught a wave, figuring the best way to show that I'd be good at surfing would be to try to body surf, momentarily forgetful of my bathing suit, but then pleasantly surprised by the strength of the new knots at my hips and neck, and also by the way the ocean made my body feel both attractive and strong. Doug took my cue and caught his own wave, and so for a while we just bodysurfed, acknowledging each other's triumphs and flops with laughs and nods that felt more than just friendly, laced with flirtation and lingering eye contact. I was moving in fast forward, charged by a nervous desire to impress. Swimming was an easier way for me to communicate than attempting a real conversation, so I just kept going, wave after wave.

At one point, a huge one was coming towards us, and I made the mistake of deciding to ride it. I managed to catch it right before it broke, and for a moment I caught sight of everyone else on the beach—Deb, Parker, Scott, and Rick sitting on the sand, shooting the shit—and I felt like I was soaring above them, some spirit who had left them, a murdered teen in a Christopher Pike novel returning to haunt them from the ocean where they'd drowned me the year before, ready to show them how the ghost world had made me an even more unstoppable force. It was an infinite and empowering surge that lasted a split second—soaring like a mermaid on this enormous wave—before the wave dropped me and I tumbled like a sock in a spin cycle. The next thing I knew I was slamming into the sand. I felt my bathing suit jam up over my chest and my breasts pop out. My bottoms had ridden all the way into my butt. I had an enormous wedgie. Also, I was in pain. But vanity prevailed. Quickly, I tucked myself back inside my bathing suit, attempting to scrape the clumps of sand out of the triangles as I did, but as I turned around I saw that the entire crew had witnessed my wipe-out. Humiliation stampeded through me. I touched the side of my head. Deb ran up to me.

"Oh my God," she said. "I thought you broke your neck. Are you ok?" She picked a piece of seaweed out of my hair.

"Am I bleeding?" I asked.

I moved my head back and forth. She squinted at me closely. "I don't think so," she said.

"Did everyone see my bathing suit fall off?" I hissed between my teeth as I pushed my hair out of my face.

She smiled and shrugged, her eyes twinkling with laughter. Before she could say anything, Doug walked over with a grin on his face.

"That was some ride."

"Ha ha, wipe out," I said, looking at the sand. He walked back towards the sand where everyone was hanging out. I looked at Deb. "Oh my god, kill me now."

"You stripper," she whispered to me, giving me a teasing shove. "All the popular boys have seen your boobies." She looked delighted by my fall in a way that felt like betrayal. Sometimes it was unclear whose team she was on. Usually, I just ran home when we had one of these moments. But I was staying at her house, and we were hours from my home. There was nowhere to run.

"I hate you," I said. Burning with embarrassment, I dove back into the waves. I needed to stay far away from the coast and the upperclassmen boys who had just seen my butt cheeks and nipples.

I went out deep past the breakers again. There was no way I was going to body surf this time. I just wanted to be alone. I swam back and forth in the water, doing laps, my arms and legs on fire from the workout. With each stroke, my anger dissipated a little. I imagined myself dissolving like a tablet of Alka-Seltzer until I was nothing but ocean froth. This exercise of becoming one with the universe calmed me. I floated on my back and looked at the clouds. The lifeguard blew his whistle at me for drifting too far out, so I swam back a bit, but still, I kept my distance.

The next thing I knew Deb was standing at the water's edge yelling my name and waving me back in. The guys were gone. My fingers were raisins.

"We have to go," she said as I pulled my body back to land. "My parents are taking us out to dinner, remember?"

The air felt alive with particles of sand. They were like teeth against my salty skin. I crossed my arms over my stomach and ran back to where our blanket had been set up, looking for a towel, but the blanket was gone.

"Here," Deb said, fishing one out of the beach bag and tossing it at me. I took it silently, and wrapped it around like a shield.

"Are you mad at me or something?" Deb said. I hated the inflection she gave the word "mad." Of course I was mad at her and she knew it, but she also knew that I would not bother to bring the subject back up, so her asking this question was her way of telling me to get over it and move on. But I didn't feel like getting over it.

I shrugged. "I'm cold," I said. "I want to take a shower."

"The guys are getting a 30 pack and going to the beach by the lighthouse," she said, smiling at me. "I told them we'd meet them there."

"I don't want to."

"Oh stop it," she said. "You'll change your mind. Besides," she pulled down her sunglasses and waggled her eyebrows at me. "Doug Ryan specifically said he wanted to party with Banks."

I rolled my eyes. "I'm sure he did," I said, inwardly pleased, but also doubtful.

We walked the little trail through the dunes and exited onto a quiet street of beach bungalows. It didn't look like anything fancy to me, but my mom and dad were constantly reminding me that the Stevens were millionaires, and that everyone I was surrounded by down here was rich. The fact that this was the same in Tonley was not relevant to the conversation for some reason. I guess they felt like even though they'd managed to buy a house there, to "get me in," so to speak, it was imperative to remind me that I wasn't of this breed. That I was something lesser because my parents hadn't also grown up vacationing in this exclusive beach community, the way that Mr. Stevens had.

If Deb's parents had ever had a similar conversation with her, essentially explaining to her that she was slumming it by entertaining my friendship, it never came up beyond the obvious comparisons of our houses. Hers was way bigger. But she had a bigger family, so in a way that made sense. Of course we didn't have a second house (or a third one), but who was counting? Deb wasn't, she was conspiring about how to get on the beach to party.

"I think Mom and Dad are going to the new neighbors to hang in their yard. They're lighting a bonfire or something. They said we could come, but we'll say we just want to walk on the beach. Their kids are way older than us anyway. They're not really kids. I think one of them is Eric's age. He has like a job in Philly and lives in his own apartment. They're both out of college."

"So they're yuppies," I said, as we walked into her front door. I had recently learned that the y-u-p in yuppie stood for young urban professional and was excited to discover an applicable use for this noun.

"I guess."

I felt a cold chill run over my body. I thought it was just adrenaline and nerves and the air conditioning from inside the house, but when I got in the shower I discovered that it was more than that—sunburn. I was bright red. Like a lobster fresh from a boil. Apparently Glow was not as waterproof as advertised. Naked, I saw that my "tan" lines were now well pronounced. My breasts and the little triangle of my crotch and butt were like the only nutrient-rich remains of a scorched earth. I struggled out of the shower and into my underwear. I pressed my fingers against my thighs and watched the white finger marks turn back to crimson. The air on my skin made it tingle. This was a medical emergency. Plus, my mother was going to kill me.

I had to cover up. Evenings were always cooler at the beach anyway, so it wouldn't look that suspicious if I wore jeans and a long sleeve t-shirt. I didn't have jeans though. I only had a pair of Adidas snap-up pants, my warm up pants from track. As I exited the bathroom, Deb frowned at my outfit choice from her spot on the bed, her chin tilted to the side to cradle the weight of the telephone. She was talking to Jenna.

"Doug Ryan swam with her in the water for like three hours

and invited us to party on the beach, and do you know what this bitch is wearing?" she said into the phone. "A track outfit! She looks like she's going to practice."

I rolled my eyes and curled up on the bed, every inch of me pulsing with heat.

Deb looked at me. "Jenna says you should wear my polka dot sundress. We both think you should."

I flinched at that phrase: We both think.

"I can't wear that dress," I said, raising my shirt so that Deb could see the damage. She screamed a horror movie scream. Her mother ran into the room, and I dropped my shirt.

"What is it?" Mrs. Stevens asked in a worried voice as she slipped a gold hoop earring into her ear. She was wearing a short, sleeveless dress with a sparkly sequined collar. Her make-up was colorful and bright. She had on a dark plum lipstick. Her tanned legs were thick and slightly pocked with cellulite. It was something my mother liked to comment on, so now my eye was trained to notice it and judge.

"Emily has sunburn!" Deb said.

Mrs. Stevens looked genuinely concerned. "Oh no! Not again! I saw you put sunscreen on. Are you ok?" Mrs. Stevens asked me. "We have some aloe around here somewhere."

"I'm alright," I said.

"Emily," Deb said, like a worried mother. "That looks so painful. Does she need a doctor?"

"I'm fine," I said defensively. "It'll go away. I mean, I could use some aloe if you have it." Then I looked at Deb after her mom left the room in search of aloe. "I just don't want to wear anything too tight on my skin because it freaking kills."

Deb announced to Jenna that we would have to call her back.

Mrs. Stevens came in with a bottle of green goo. "Hope this helps," she said to me kindly. Then she looked at us both. "Will you be ready to go in 15 minutes? The reservation at the club is for 7."

We nodded. I peeled off my clothes and gooped the aloe on my skin. It felt both soothing and gross.

Deb was holding a fashion solution in her hand. It was a long hippie shirt and a black top. "I bought this at the surf shop last summer, but it is totally not my style. It's not really yours, either, I know, but it won't cling to your sunburn! And you can probably even get away with wearing your track hoodie over the top." The last bit sold me. "Not at the club, though. You have to just wear the shirt." The shirt had ruffled, poofed out, sort of poet's sleeves that made me feel a little bit ridiculous, but I was too weak to argue. Also, I found the skirt to be surprisingly comfortable, even more so than my snap pants. It probably would've covered Deb's toes, but it hit at my ankles. It was sort of like a curtain, with long panels that alternated mismatched floral patterns. I liked the way it moved when I walked. I felt a little like a witch.

Deb came up to me and took the t-shirt and folded it up inside itself so that my bright red belly was out. "See?" she said. "This is what I'm talking about. You look like you could be on MTV. I'm packing some scissors in my bag so we can cut this shirt before we meet the boys. You need to flaunt what you got."

"What I've got is partially cooked flesh," I said, unconvinced.

"It's going to be dark on the beach. You won't look that red. You'll look tan. Also, we need to get your belly-button pierced. Stat."

"Oh, sure, Frankie will love that." Frankie was what we called my mother. Her name was Frances.

"Frankie won't ever have to know."

I didn't have the energy to state the obvious, that there was no hiding anything from Frankie ever. She was like *Nancy Drew* meets *Murder She Wrote.*

The yacht club was right on the bay and you could watch the sunset from every window. Our table was on the deck, and from there you could watch little kids play in the grassy lawn that led towards the dock where members kept their boats. One little girl was doing cartwheel after cartwheel in a line, her little dress bunching around her legs each time and threatening to expose her underwear. Her mother kept telling her to stop in an embarrassed, hushed voice. But the girl had no reason to feel ashamed of her body. Who cares if someone saw her butt?

Mr. and Mrs. Stevens said she made them feel old. "Even you guys are teenagers now. Stop growing," Mrs. Stevens said. They wished for Cody and Eric and the old days when everyone was little. Eric, who was 22, had taken a job in San Francisco. Cody was 19 and still in college. He went to Swarthmore, which was close, but he'd decided not to come down for the weekend because "he had his own life," Mrs. Stevens said with disdain. She still hadn't forgiven him for deciding to sublet a place in West Philly for the summer with his friends instead of living at home.

"He could get to Philly from our house in no time," she said. "What's the point? He won't even come to the shore. It's because of Maura. He says she isn't living in that house, but I know she is." The way Mrs. Stevens said "Maura" told you everything you needed to know about her opinion on the relationship. Maura was Cody's first real girlfriend, and he'd changed in big and small ways since they'd met. His hair was different. He spoke a little differently, and—most significant to the Stevenses—he'd changed his major from econ to philosophy. None of these seemed like horrible decisions to me. But in a way, I had to side with Mrs. Stevens, just because I missed Cody. I'd always felt close to him, like he was my brother too, and the fact that he wasn't home made me sad. It made the shore house feel different. I'd never been down there without him before, and I missed the sound of him strumming his guitar and the silly way he navigated his sister's temper and gave her a reality check.

I'd met Maura over Christmas and found her to be intimidating. She had a nose ring, and her forearm was sprinkled with tiny star tattoos. She was beautiful and beyond cool. Her eyes felt like x-ray beams of judgement. I felt lame in her presence when Cody introduced me as the town superstar. Compared to her, my achievements were not real achievements. They meant nothing. Maura was only five years older than us and had already started a non-profit to reclaim open space in cities to turn into farmland. She wanted to eliminate food deserts in urban areas. I didn't even know what a food desert was. When I'd asked her, she'd laughed and looked at Cody. "Don't they teach anything of value at that nationally ranked public high school of yours?" she'd said. It stung. Wait, I wanted to say. Really, I'm interested! Teach me! I don't want to be clueless about the system in which I thrive! But it was too late. Or at least that's how it had felt to me. I'd been humbled by that conversation and thought about it often. I'd even done a research paper on food deserts for our Humanities Seminar. And while writing the paper, I became acutely aware that I had never stepped foot in a food desert. Wherever I was, I could think of a nearby grocery store with fresh vegetables. Not to mention the fact that I was sitting on the deck of a freaking yacht club as I entertained these thoughts.

"Mom, if Cody doesn't want to come to the beach anymore it just means that I should be allowed to bring more friends down for the weekend," Deb suggested. More friends, meaning Jenna, I thought to myself, and felt happy that for at least this moment, I was still the only one with an automatic invite. I imagined what this dinner scene would look like if Jenna were part of it. Deb would have even more make-up on her face. My abs would definitely be exposed.

After dinner, the Stevens hung around the yard of the club and mingled with other members while Deb and I lounged and played bocce and talked to a few girls that Deb knew and I'd met in summers past. Moving around felt good. A few hours in the hippie skirt helped me acclimate to my throbbing body.

"If I bend my knees slowly," I explained to Deb as I settled into an Adirondack chair facing the bay, "It doesn't feel like the skin is being torn from my bone."

"Stop. I'm going to throw up."

"It's the truth."

"Do you think those guys are into us?" Deb asked, referencing the Doug crowd while she twirled a piece of her dark hair around her finger. She liked to do this thing with her forehead where she wrinkled it up when she was having a thought. I told her once that she looked like Alyssa Milano when she did it, which I think encouraged her to do it more.

"Well obviously they like you," I said. Deb's attractiveness was a universal truth. She was approached by boys everywhere we went—bowling alleys, movie theaters, boardwalks, food courts. That was just how it went. All of the attractive guys from our grade had been her boyfriend at one point or another in middle school, but their relationships hadn't been real relationships. "Training wheels," Jenna called them.

"I think they all like you," she said. "You're the one who's in the paper for running and everyone knows you're smart. You're more interesting." She didn't sound pleased by what she was saying.

"I was like hiding in the water the whole time. I didn't even talk to anyone. They are way more interested in you. You're the one who knows how to have a conversation like a normal person. And you are prettier."

"You're pretty too," she said. But I knew she said it because it was the right thing to do.

"No I'm not," I said. "I'm weird looking. I'm like Molly Ringwald with all of her quirky parts amplified: lankier, frizzier hair, bigger teeth."

"But boys liked Molly Ringwald," Deb said.

"But I'm not her," I said. I felt my tone betray the desperate truth behind those words, but Deb was blind to my suffering. She couldn't access the empathy required to connect on that level. She didn't know what it was like to have no confidence in her natural beauty.

"Oh shut up," she replied. She pushed against the cuticle of a fingernail. "Why weren't you talking?" she asked.

"I don't know," I said honestly, "they make me feel weird."

"Why?"

"Well, first of all, I don't even know them. They've never even talked to me before and then they were suddenly acting like we were all best friends just because we go to the same school, which seemed kind of strange."

"You just have to roll with it," Deb said. "They'll act like they know you when we get back."

I gave a cynical laugh in response and watched Mr. Stevens from across the lawn as he socialized with another 50-ish, gray-ish man. Whatever they were talking about, they were deeply engaged. It was an impossible thing to even contemplate most days, them ever being us, guys our age, walking down beaches, conspiring to have parties, instead of dads in button downs with gin-and-tonic breath, but for a second, I caught sight of it. Something in the eyes. A knowing look. I looked at Deb, her forehead with the Alyssa Milano crinkle arranged in deep thought. She would be ready with a rejoinder no matter what I had to say.

"Then there was the cigarette thing, with the lighter."

"Oh my god, don't be such a prude."

"I thought Doug was going to burn Rick!"

"Rick could have jumped out of the sand if he wanted to."

"Really? I've never been buried in sand like that before. It doesn't look easy. I had to like dig him out. Also, Rick kind of makes me sad."

Deb laughed. "Sad? You're so mean."

"No, really," I said. "There's something wrong with him, I think. I don't know what it is."

"He's just dumb," Deb said, dismissively.

"I'm not talking about math scores," I said.

"Neither am I," she said. "I think he takes a lot of pills or drinks too much or something and his brain is fucked."

"You don't think that's sad?" I asked.

She rolled her eyes. "Doug was like all over you today. If Mandy Gladstone knew, she'd be so jealous."

"Jealous of what?"

"He was swimming with you." I had to smile, thinking of how he'd followed me into the ocean.

"He told me he wanted to teach me how to surf," I said.

"What?!" Deb squealed. "You didn't tell me that! When?"

"When we were in the water."

"No!" She gave me a little shove. It activated the tender nerves of my scorched skin.

"Ouch!"

"Sorry, I forgot," she said, brushing off her tiny crime so we could get back to the important stuff. "When is he going to teach you?"

"I don't know. Tomorrow?"

"So first he invites us out tonight and then he's already

making a date for tomorrow? Watch out Mandy Gladstone."

"They broke up like months ago, didn't they? Besides, none of that means anything." I was a superstitious athlete. I never said what I wanted out loud. I decided to change the subject.

"I wish I didn't get so fried," I said, sighing and taking my hair out of its messy bun and then twisting it back up. "Then I could put some lemon juice in my hair and try to get highlights tomorrow."

"I wonder if it would really turn your hair blonde." She gave my auburn heaps of frizz a squeeze.

"Probably not, but it would be fun to try."

Across the lawn, at the bar, I saw Mr. Stevens signing the bill. It was almost time to head back to Deb's house and then out to the beach. I felt a combination of excitement and dread.

- 3 -

It was crazy to me how easy it was to get away with this adventure. As nuts as Mrs. Stevens was about the whereabouts of Cody, she didn't seem to mind what time we came and went. She said goodnight to us as she left and told us not to stay on the beach "too late," and then she and Mr. Stevens walked across the little street with two bottles, one of wine and one of scotch.

We took two bikes from the shed and pedaled them down the darkened streets of the quiet beach village, the sounds of people's television sets and conversations leaking onto the street through their screened porches or windows. We zig zagged from one narrow street to the next towards the only tall structure in sight. Technically the state park was closed, but there was no gate or guard to stop us. We pedaled silently through the parking lot, past the revolving, watchful glow of the lighthouse's eye, and rested our bikes against the fence that lined the dunes. Night noises brought a hush over us. This was not your classic New Jersey beach town with bars and beach rides lighting up the coast. It was bordered by nature paths that cut through maritime forest. We silently traveled along the beach trail while the crickets and frogs and birds called out to one another from the tall grass.

"Remember when we saw those foxes out here last summer?" Deb whispered. I smiled, remembering the little family skipping through the tall grass.

"They were so cute!" I said. I felt the buzz of a mosquito in my ear and swatted it away as the narrow sandy path expanded to reveal the ocean and the abandoned beach.

For some reason, it was like I was watching myself on a camera that was rolling. The story of my life in real time. The sand was the stage. The water, the audience. What I was to perform out there I was still not sure, but I felt a bolt of jitters flash through me that told me it was showtime.

On this particular stretch of sand, with no buildings at all beyond the lighthouse in sight, I felt disoriented, forgetful. Who was I? Where was I from? What year was it? And did that number even mean anything? What was the point of counting? Surely it all meant nothing to this ocean.

My heart, my stomach, my lungs, my gut. They were all one big ball of tangled yarn beneath my skin. Life was happening to me. I felt a need for the universe to acknowledge this reality.

The ocean surged and retreated, unimpressed.

We were standing on the very part of the coast where one of the earliest explorers, Captain James May, first pulled ashore and made friends with the Indians, a fact Mr. Stevens told me again and again every summer.

I never thought about Indians in Tonley. The cobblestones and historic pubs only conjured George Washington, Quakers, and runaway slaves. But here we were, standing on an eternally clean slate, an untouched strip of sea and sand. Even the sky was different, the stars as clear and expansive as the water they shined down on. Two abysses framing the landscape of the unknown.

We could hear their voices down the beach before we could see them. The sound of the crack of a can somehow drifted in the wind. Then there were Doug and Parker, two shadows throwing a darkened orb back and forth to one another in the moonlight. I got cold feet.

"Maybe we should turn around," I said to Deb.

"Are you kidding me?" she said. "No way. They already see us."

She ran a few steps ahead of me. I was forced to follow.

"Deb and Banks showed," Scott said from the blanket. I

guess that was his way of acknowledging us, and also letting us know he was unimpressed. Rick greeted us by reaching into a backpack and extracting two beers and handing them to me and Deb. Then he offered me a fist on which I delivered a pound. We were friends now. I could feel it. His eyes looked a little wacky. He was probably already wasted.

"Does anybody ever walk by out here?" Deb asked.

"The only people who we've ever seen walk by are some old people who were trying to fuck on the beach," Rick said, laughing hysterically.

"No way," Deb said. I wondered if she was thinking about her parents.

"Gross," I said.

"Dude, once when we were down here, we were walking back up the path and actually walked up on two people doing it! No lie! They jumped off of each other and were totally naked."

"Ewww," Deb said. "Oh my god! Did you know them?"

The football Parker threw whizzed past Doug and flew close to the blanket. He was jogging up to retrieve it as Rick said, "I think Doug did."

"Did what?" Doug said.

"Knew those old people who were humping on the beach path that night when we were freshmen." Then he pretended to cough. "Your mom."

Doug made a disgusted face and shuddered. "Why are you talking about that? Now I'm going to have to live with that image in my head for another summer."

Rick shrugged. "It just came up."

Doug just looked us both up and down and gave us a nod, "What's up," before he ran back to the water with the ball. I wondered why they couldn't just sit down and talk to us since they'd been the ones to invite us in the first place. Maybe Scott and Rick felt the same way. It took a few minutes for us all to adjust to one another's presence.

"How do they even see that ball?" I said.

"Night vision," Scott said. "If you let your eyes adjust to the dark you can see more than you think. Plus," he gestured to the sky, "the moon is pretty bright." He said this to me as if he were lecturing a two-year-old who overused the word "why." It was how he seemed to treat everyone. He even gave off the air that his friends bored him, but my insecurity left me feeling particularly burned by his scrutinous eye. It was as if he were trying to let me know how unworthy of his time I was without directly saying it.

I felt both defensive and diminished. What was his problem? We'd been invited! That's what Deb had said anyway! I looked towards Deb for guidance. I could see her searching for something to talk about, then her eyes lit up with a topic.

"Oh my god," she said to the guys, "You know how Em wiped out on the beach earlier?" she said. "Now she has sunburn too!"

"Shiiiiit," Rick said, laughing. "I forgot about that wipe out. Dude, you were torn up! Are you alright? I thought you were gonna get helivacked off the beach!"

Annoyed at Deb's subject choice, but too self-conscious to engage in a fight, I gave her a dirty look before I wedged my index finger under the tab of the beer can and cracked it open, remembering that Deb had forgotten to cut the t-shirt I was wearing into a crop top and feeling grateful at least for that.

"I'm still standing," I said, and shrugged. I took a few huge gulps from the can and tried not to retch at the taste. I'd drank beer a few times before, both times at Deb's house with her older brothers, but those ones had been ice cold and straight from the fridge. These were crusted in sand and sort of sticky. It was like swallowing bad breath. But I was thirsty. And this was what we were supposed to do, right? Still, after managing to keep it down I couldn't help but make a face, my body rejecting the warm bubbles inside. The carbonation brought a hot burp up my throat that I redirected through my nose, making my eyes water. Everyone was looking at me still, so I figured I'd say something.

"This stuff tastes like shit," I said.

That made Scott and Rick laugh. "Fucking Doug took it from the back fridge earlier in the day and hid it in this cooler in his side yard, but the thing had no ice in it, so this shit is all skunked."

Skunked was a new word for me, but I nodded my head as if I understood what he was talking about. Somehow, luckily, the skunked beer was an easier topic than my overcooked flesh and the conversation between Rick, Scott, and Deb began to flow easily. They seemed to be picking up old conversations that they'd started sometime before, and I realized that while I was in the ocean they'd sort of become friends.

Despite their level of comfort, I sadly still suffered from the same awkward and silent curse I'd had earlier in the day. It was like becoming afflicted. I lost all ability to speak, or even formulate the beginning of a thought that could be translated into words. They say that boys' brains go straight to their pants because that's where all their blood flows. I knew my blood was not in my brain, but it wasn't swarming towards my clitoris either. Still, my body felt especially alive. I was hyper observant, aware of being looked at in a specific way, like I was one of the rabbits in the grass on the nature paths through the wetlands, frozen mid-munch at the sudden sound of a foot on the trail. But unlike the rabbit, who wisely just remained motionless until the foot vanished or she saw an opportunity to scamper away, I sat next to Deb and drank heartily so that I could relax under the hunter's gaze. I wanted something to happen. I'd brought myself here, after all.

Having brothers, Deb was more at ease in the presence of older guys and seemed to know exactly when to insert herself into their banter. Eventually, Doug and Parker joined the circle, sitting close to Deb and me. One beer became another. The second one tasted better. Everything started to numb. Even my sunburn seemed less painful, or maybe I just forgot about it. Then someone opened a two-liter soda bottle that had vodka mixed with a red powdered pack of fruit punch flavored Kool-Aid. I took a few sips as it came around and felt the initial sweetness burn through my throat all the way to my stomach before I lurched forward with a gag. Thankfully, I didn't throw up. But it tasted terrible, the way I imagine turpentine might. It occurred to me then that liquor actually was poison, which was funny because it actually tasted like poison, but that didn't stop me from sipping it anyway.

You'd think all the booze would have helped, but something was still wrong. I couldn't keep up with what the guys were talking about. Even though I was a runner, I wasn't an ESPN viewer. I didn't know who the Eagles were supposed to draft. I also couldn't catch the lines they zinged back and forth to each other fast enough. They were always making fun of each other in some cruel way. They had weird nicknames like "Crumbs," which seemed innocent but also secretly perverted, sort of like Deb's and my orca joke.

I wanted to feel happy, like Deb, who was giggling and wrestling with Parker over his hat, which she'd knocked off his head, but I didn't feel ready to do something like that. I didn't want to knock anything off of anyone else. I just wanted to disappear and observe, to have the power of omniscience, like the ghost girl I'd briefly become atop that enormous wave before my boobs fell out of my bathing suit. But I wasn't a ghost. I lived in a body. My tangled-up organs pulsed against my skin, delivering an urgent message to my nervous system. Something was going to happen. It felt as large and powerful as that wave, and I couldn't stop it. I didn't know whether I should try to ride it or dive through it and drift further out to sea. Doug's breath was on my neck. The rawness of my skin caused every atom at the surface of me to clamor. A shiver shook my spine.

"You wanna take a walk over there," he said, gesturing to the darkened dunes around the bend of the coastline.

"You mean where the old people go to fuck?" I said, as he pulled me up. The words came out of my mouth without me processing their meaning. Once they caught up with me, I felt my entire body, already burned, blush. What the hell was I talking about? Who says that? What was I trying to suggest?

He locked eyes with me and laughed. "I have no idea what sort of bullshit Rick's been telling you." Then he took my hand.

I was holding his hand. It was big, like a bear's paw. His fingers were rough and wide. I was tall but he was taller, and wider. I shrugged and laughed with him. It was a stranger's laugh coming out of my throat. I noticed this in passing. The other me, the ghost girl sitting on the wave, saw me on the beach holding this boy's hand and thought, "she's drunk."

Ghost girl was critical of the drunk me, wondering why I said, "I can't believe you stuck that cigarette in Rick's mouth," while laughing, when in fact I hadn't found that moment funny.

Walking on the sand was harder than I thought. Not because my burned thighs throbbed under the flowing hippie skirt that was like a flag flapping in the wind—they did, but their pain was abstract. The liquor was working against my coordination. Dry lumps of sand gave way in twisty directions with every step. This was not solid earth. It was too easy to shape and contort. You could mold it to look however you wanted it to.

I stumbled into him, my forehead bumping into his chest. Suddenly my face was near his collar. I could smell his deodorant. Old Spice. Did he forget his own and have to borrow from his dad? His tongue was in my mouth. I opened my eyes and saw the stars in the sky. There were so many. How many? I tried to count them to stay in my head, but I couldn't get past six. Was this kissing? This was what it was? I was on the sand. It was like a pillow. My skirt was bunched up in his hand like a tissue. There was his penis, a shockingly long, large pendulum in my face, his head high above it, blocking out the moon, all shadow. Scott was right, my eyes had adjusted. I could still see his face. He was smiling. He was happy.

In the porno, things were scrambled, and they were here too. I didn't touch his penis. He bent over me again. His tongue swirled like a tornado. Earlier, when he'd picked me up out of the blue on the beach, I'd felt aroused. Maybe even a little wet, my nipples a little perked. I'd screeched in joy. But now I found I had no instinct to release a random call of pleasure. In fact, I wanted to stand up. He put his dick in my face again and said, "Do you know how to kiss it?" I said, "No." "I can help you," he said and he pushed it against my mouth so that I had to clamp my lips together and turn my head to the side. "Not right now," I said. Then he laid on top of me again and put the tornado back in my mouth. He pulled the elastic of my skirt down and hoisted my sweatshirt up and began rubbing himself against my torso.

"You are so hot," he said, as he moved back and forth against my stomach. I thought he was talking about the temperature of my body. "It's because I'm sunburned," I said. It hurt. I imagined a Brillo pad on a dirty pan. I thought my skin would split open.

But I didn't do anything. I didn't tell him to stop. I was just glad his penis had moved away from my face. I didn't make any noises at all. The words "He's dry humping me" appeared in my head. I thought of other people's pet dogs and couches. Mom never let us get a dog. Too much hair. Think of all the poop in Nanny's backyard, she always said. I could not see Doug's face. I only felt his chin tapping the crown of my head. I turned my face to get more air. The gasp may have suggested pleasure. Somehow, through this sliver between sand and chest, I saw the handle of the Little Dipper. I connected the dots and held the handle, and watched the Ghost Girl in the waves dip the ladle in the Atlantic Ocean. She poured the contents over Doug's head, shocking him with a deluge of cold water.

He came on my stomach with a moan. I felt a warm squirt and a pool of wetness that ran downwards in trickles towards the sand. What was next? I waited. He rolled off of me and lay quietly in the sand for a minute. Then he pulled his boxers and basketball shorts up and started laughing. "Banks," he said, "You are so insane." Insane? Was this good? He was touching my hair. The statement hit my ears as an insult. I was ready to run.

"I need to go find Deb," I said. I pulled her black shirt down over the blob of come on me and tried to stop gravity from letting it run towards my crotch. I felt afraid that it could seep through my underwear and get me pregnant. I'd read crazy stories in teen magazines before. But it was already on its way. I sprang to my feet and shimmied the shirt off underneath my hoodie and attempted to pull it over my head so I could use it as a rag to clean myself, but as I pulled it up over my face, some of the cum got on my chin and hair. I thought of Cameron Diaz in *There's Something About Mary*. I'd never gotten that joke in the movie, but now I realized it wasn't funny.

I used the dry parts of the shirt to scrub away the evidence and threw the shirt into the dunes. I never littered, but there was no way I was carrying this soiled fabric back with me; it was too embarrassing. What would everyone think? Doug said nothing and did nothing to help.

"Let's go swimming," he said.

"I need to go find Deb," I said again. I stood up and then fell down. Then he stood up. He extended his hand over me. I couldn't tell if he was as drunk as I was. "Banks," he said. "Get up."

I stood up, and he kissed me again. This time with his hands on both of my cheeks. It was a sweeter, less aggressive gesture. "The fastest girl in school," Doug said.

"What's that supposed to mean?"

"It means I like you."

My face felt like it was made of silly putty. The hippie skirt blew against my red legs. "Ok," was what I said.

He took my hand. The ocean roared. I noticed that the buzzing in my ears was impossible to drown out. This time it wasn't from mosquitos. It was more high pitched. Almost as if my brain could no longer broadcast a clear channel, but instead had to operate through a dog-whistle.

"I guess that's why they say feeling buzzed," I said out loud.

"What?" Doug asked.

"Nothing."

The water surged and retreated with its eternal poker face. I felt the ghost girl's eyes from the ocean. Something was wrong. My body began trembling. My teeth began to chatter. My sunburn became prickly with goosebumps. I was shivering like I'd been suddenly transplanted to the Arctic. The funny thing was, it was a hot and muggy night.

"We should go back," I said. "It's getting late."

"Come and sit down here," he said. "We can chill a minute." He was touching my hair.

"Deb has a curfew," I said through my chattering teeth.

Once again, my mouth disappeared into the vacuum of his. I pulled back. "I have to go. I have to go." I began the slow trudge back towards everyone else, Doug not far behind me.

I wiped the saliva from my mouth and cheek. I heard Deb yell, "There they are!" She started making orca noises from the blanket. When we got close enough to actually see their faces, I noticed their eyes had changed. They were lit up and wild looking. Their voices slurred. I slurred back. "We have to go," I said. We all decided to leave at the same time. The boys were walking down the beach back into the town. We were going to the parking lot by the lighthouse to get our bikes. We said goodbye at the path by the dunes. That was it. The night was over.

We rode our bikes back silently. I almost crashed mine twice, and Deb did end up falling from hers because she swerved to avoid a stick and then tipped her bike over, scraping her hands and the side of her knee on the pavement. "Fuck!" she cursed as she hobbled back onto her seat and began to pedal again. Would we make it? The distance, probably less than half a mile, felt impossible. Eventually, her driveway appeared, and I turned gratefully into it, coasting past the end of the pavement along the bumpy patches of grass to the shed in the back. But when I got off the bike, everything started swirling, fast as Doug's tongue in my mouth, like a boardwalk ride I couldn't get off of, and a huge wave of vomit frothed out of my mouth and splashed against the door of her shed.

"Fuck!" Deb said for the second time. We left the bikes on their sides right outside the shed door, positioning them in a way we felt disguised the puke. I could barely walk on two feet. I crawled towards her bedroom, which was luckily on the floor below her parents, so they couldn't really hear us. I puked again off the side of the deck by the door.

"I need to take a shower," I moaned. The water was terrible.

It cut through my sunburned skin. But I washed all the sand, vomit, and cum off of me. After several attempts, I managed to get my legs through the holes of my pajama pants and stumbled back into Deb's bedroom. She was already snoring. I crashed next to her on her double bed and was asleep in 30 seconds.

The next thing I knew, her face was two inches from mine. It was daylight. The sun penetrated the blinds on the windows like a million eyes watching me.

"Oh my god, you reek like puke."

"No. I don't want to wake up."

"You need this," she said. She held a cup full of juice with a straw under my mouth. I took a sip. It felt soothing as it went down, actually, cooling my throat.

"What happened to you? Where did you go? You were gone with Doug for so long?!"

With my eyes closed, I told her everything. The kissing and humping and the cum on the shirt. And, of course, the part about how he said we should hang out again and that he "liked" me.

"Oh my god!" she said. "Doug Ryan likes you and you touched his penis!" She said this like it was a good thing, so I forced a smile with my eyes closed.

"I mean, like, my stomach touched it," I moaned. "My hand didn't."

"Was he a good kisser?" she asked me. I thought of his helicopter tongue, and the way he'd used the power of his mouth to muscle me to the ground. Then I thought about how he was the best-looking guy in school. What did I know about what a good kiss was? I had nothing to compare it to. So I said yes. It was easier than exploring the other answer.

"Totally," I said. "It was like Jagger on *General Hospital*. He held both my cheeks with his hands."

"Oh my God!" she squealed. "You're going to be Doug Ryan's girlfriend!"

The way she seemed so happy and excited about it all was reassuring. It made it seem like what had happened was okay. So I laughed when she said I'd be Doug's girlfriend because at that moment it seemed like something that was possible.

"I'm in love with Parker," Deb declared with dramatic agony. "Do you think he likes me? He tried to hold my hand! Like this!" She reached out her fingers and grazed them lightly over mine.

"What did you do?" I asked her.

"This," she said, taking her index finger and running it up and down the back of my hand.

"He totally likes you," I told her, feeling a little jealous. I'd have taken quiet hand holding.

It felt wrong for me to have an experience that Deb hadn't already had. I was used to her doing everything first. She'd drunk a beer first and had been kissing guys since the sixth grade. So why did I have to be the first person to be ejaculated on? And why did it have to happen the night of my first kiss? Something about the situation wasn't right. It wasn't just my pounding head and hangover that was telling me this. I wanted to take the truth I'd told her back and lie and say nothing happened. But it was too late. I could already imagine her rushing off to report it in excited whispers to Jenna.

"Please," I begged. "Don't tell Jenna about this."

"What? How can we not?"

"I don't want her to know all the details."

"So we can tell her you kissed him though, right?" I sensed in her answer what I already dreaded: that there was a part of this story that was not quite right, that probably should be edited out. That was wrong.

I considered the fact that Deb would not be able to keep her mouth shut. I considered the fact that maybe if she just told Jenna about the kissing, that might satisfy her need to gossip. I considered the fact that Jenna would be calling in a few hours anyway to get the details of the night, since she'd known that we were going to the beach with them.

"I don't know," I said. But that seemed to settle it. Deb held the juice straw to my lips again and I took another tiny pull of liquid into my mouth.

"Let's get breakfast," Deb said. "My parents gave me money."

I somehow managed to summon the strength to get dressed and pedal my bike downtown to the pancake house. I ate everything that was put in front of me: pancakes, eggs, bacon, potatoes, and washed it all down with three refills of coke. A few tables away was the same little girl who'd been doing cartwheels last night at the yacht club. She was eating silver dollar pancakes with her hands. She spoke with animated gestures to her parents, wiggling the bits of pancake as if they were puppets. Now I was the one feeling the sort of nostalgia that Mrs. and Mr. Stevens had experienced the night before at the club, but for myself.

After we paid the bill, Deb insisted we go to the same beach we'd hung out with the guys on the day before, hoping to run into them again. I protested. My red body throbbed, my head pounded, and my soul writhed restlessly. But Mrs. Stevens let me borrow this hilarious outfit from her closet. It was like an old lady cover-up, with long baggy pants and a long baggy shirt. She even gave me a huge floppy hat and some oversized sunglasses. "I look like Jennifer Aniston hiding from the paparazzi," I said. But I didn't care what I wore as long as the evil sun was held at bay. I refused to play paddle ball or swim or participate in any beach games. I needed to recover. The boys never showed up anyway. I opened *Harry Potter* and tried to disappear to Hogwarts, but it didn't work. Flashes of Doug—in the ocean, on the beach, with his pants unzipped in the darkness—persisted like the pulse of my skin.

- 4 -

Mom was waiting for me where she always waited for me, in the arm chair in the living room right by the front window of the house, where she could pretend to read as she stared expectantly out the window in anticipation of my return. As soon as Mr. Stevens' car pulled into the driveway, she sprang to her feet and opened the front door. Mr. Stevens put the car in park and got out to retrieve my duffle bag from the trunk. I was opening one of the rear doors, when I heard Mom ask, "Did she behave herself?"

As far as I could tell, the Stevenses had no idea that I'd been hungover, or if they did know, they pretended not to. Still, I held my breath, afraid of what Mr. Stevens' response would be. He handed me my duffle bag as he patted my head.

"This one?" he said. "She keeps Deb out of trouble. We're always happy to have her."

"Thanks so much!" Mom said.

"It's our pleasure. See you soon, Emily," he called as he got in his car and backed out of the driveway. Mom ran toward me to give me a hug and a kiss, but as soon as my face came into closer focus and she took in the red, bubbliness of my nose and began to see the extent of my sunburn, I saw her face harden and flash between concern and outrage.

"Oh my God!" she said. "You've got sun poisoning."

"It's not so bad anymore," I said, keeping my eyes down, but I knew that I was in for it.

"Anymore?" she cried. "You mean it was worse? You look like a burn victim! This is horrific. Your poor, beautiful skin. We need to give you an oatmeal bath."

"Can I eat first?" I said. "I'm starving." They'd gone through a Burger King drive-thru on the way home, but my mother forbade me from eating meat from those kinds of places. I'd only had a small order of fries, and my stomach was growling.

"They didn't make you wear sunscreen and they didn't feed you?" Mom said, incredulously. Part of me believed that she liked moments like this. They were opportunities for her to affirm to me that she was the most trusted person in my life, the only person who knew what I needed and could provide those things to me.

"They fed me," I said. "It was just Burger King, so I only got a small fry, and I'm hungry again."

Dad came downstairs and we ate salad and pasta while I offered tiny details from the weekend: the body surfing, the boat club, while obviously omitting the most important event. "How was Nanny's?"

Mom laughed and then sighed. "It was alright. A lot of gross cigarette smoke as usual. Uncle Tommy is still obsessed with the TV show *Cops*."

"Bad boys, bad boys, whatcha gonna do, whatcha gonna do when they come for you," I sang.

She groaned. Dad, as usual, provided the upside. "It wasn't so bad, Fran. There was Jell-o. And horseshoes. And I came in second all around, which meant I won a bottle of Jägermeister," he waggled his eyebrows like this was a joke.

"You say it like it's a good thing," Mom said.

"What's Jägermeister?" I asked. Dad stood up and walked to the freezer and extracted a rectangular-looking bottle with a gothic looking deer on the label and a cross hovering above its antlers.

"It's a German liquor."

"It tastes disgusting," Mom said.

"Can I try it?" I asked. I was kidding, trying to keep things light, but I felt Mom's eyes on me, soaking in my aura with her x-ray vision, trying to determine how the weekend had gone by the way I carried myself in our family conversation.

"Is that what the Stevens do?" she asked, skeptically.

"No!" I said, perhaps too defensively.

"You can try it when Dad opens it, which most likely won't be until your twenty-first birthday because he doesn't like the stuff either."

"It's true," he said. "I'm definitely more of a beer guy. But I'm not going to promise to keep it for six more years."

"So you're telling me I may be able to drink before my twenty-first birthday," I said, smiling.

She made a disapproving cluck. "Are you finished?" she asked me, gesturing towards my plate. "Let's go upstairs. Let me see this sunburn."

I sat on the edge of the toilet as she filled the tub with an oatmeal mixture that made the water look clumpy and brown.

"Take off your clothes," she commanded. I didn't really ever get naked in front of her these days, but I obeyed. When I peeled off my clothes, she gasped.

"Oh my god! My baby!" she said. For a moment, I felt like she was reacting to more than just my sunburn, as if there was some way that Doug's cum across my stomach had left a permanent stain. I didn't like being called a baby, especially in the wake of the sort of weekend I'd just had. Couldn't she see I was not a child? I had hair in all the places babies did not.

"Did you even put sunscreen on?"

"I did," I said. "I just forgot to reapply."

"Poor baby. Why didn't anyone remind you?"

"Mom, I am not a child, let alone a baby," I said, my tone annoyed.

"Of course you are. Look at yourself." I looked in the

medicine cabinet mirror.

"What's your point?" I said.

She made a noise of exasperation and then commanded me into the tub. "It might be uncomfortable at first, but it will help soothe your skin." I stepped in. The tepid water sent a wave of goosebumps rippling across the surface of me, but I kept inching myself into the water until I was fully submerged except for my face and the bundle of hair piled on the top of my head.

Mom left me to do her normal chore hustle. I could hear her scurrying from one room to the next, folding things and carrying things from one place to another. I wasn't focused on her movements though. I was focused on the feeling of my own skin and flinching at the memories each patch of it evoked as my singed nerve endings winced against the murky water. There was a slideshow of groans and yelps and wipe outs in my head. Fragmented scenes that made me cringe or shake my head and roll my eyes, unaware that I was even doing it. I must have been moaning audibly at some particular flashback when Mom, walking by, mistook this for physical pain and opened the door with her hands on her hips.

"What do the Stevens even do at that house? Do they even look at you? Do they even ask you if you put on sunscreen? They don't even care. Meanwhile, my daughter is going to get melanoma because she's been fried in direct sunlight. How could they do this? Nobody even called me!"

"Mom, it's not Mrs. Stevens' job to make sure I put on sunscreen," I tried to say calmly.

"Well, then whose job is it? Yours? Because you clearly failed at that. How can you be trusted to do anything alone when you can't even take care of your own body?"

I knew that her angry hysteria was the product of worry, but it caused me to feel defensive. Anger flared inside me. How dare she question my ability to care for myself? I hated the fact that she did so with such a demeaning voice, and worse, I hated that she was partially right.

"Can you just get out and leave me alone?" I screamed. "Jeez. It's just one sunburn. It will go away. I will survive."

"But the damage is permanent. You can't treat this like it isn't a big deal, or you'll do it again."

"Mom," I said. "Go away."

She shut the door but continued to speak through it. "You are 15 years old. You are my responsibility. If I trust you to go away for the weekend with another family and you come back looking as if you escaped a burning building, that's room for concern!"

"I don't look like I escaped a burning building!"

"Sunburn is a serious deal! Your uncle has had entire sections of his back removed! Have you seen his scars?"

I held my breath and went under the thick oatmeal water. The glug, glug against my ears gave me a momentary sense of calm, but eventually I had to come back up for another breath and when I did I heard a knock on the door.

"What?" I said, annoyed.

"It's me."

"Dad!" I said. "I'm taking a bath! Leave me alone!"

"Just wanted to say we love you," he said from the other side of the door. "Your mother loves you. She is yelling at you right now and she shouldn't be yelling at you." I could tell he was looking at my mom, who was probably doing her best not to pounce on him, because she hated to be corrected. "But the reason she is yelling at you is because she loves you. We all love each other. Let's all just relax for a little bit. We'll talk in a few hours."

Mom reached her arm through the crack and dropped a green bottle of goo and a clean towel on the floor. "Put the aloe on when you get out and your skin is still a little wet. And don't get dressed until it's dry. I laid out a clean pair of long-sleeved pajama pants and a long-sleeved t-shirt. It's good to keep your skin covered."

My parents' peace offerings worked a little. I breathed deeply and tried to calm my rage. The truth was, despite their nagging, I was happy to be home, in my bathtub, with the pink and white tiles and the white curtains and my favorite big fuzzy towel. Once I was in bed, I could exist by myself, alone, behind a closed door.

I applied the aloe, let it dry, put on my winter pajamas to protect my tender skin and opened some folders to review the next day's assignments, making sure I had all my work completed. The weekend was over.

The days shed themselves like the peeling, translucent layer of my healing sunburned skin. My redness faded to a slightly more pigmented version of its original color. On the surface, things were back to normal.

June came. The countdown to summer break began. Freshman year was disappearing the same way the fabric of our shorts crept up our thighs as we walked. Soon, we were going to be sophomores—"wise fools," as my English teacher explained.

Only half of our school was air conditioned, and on the A wing, things were smoggy and ripe with the smell of adolescent sweat and the manufactured scent of deodorant. Our school really smelled like Teen Spirit.

Meanwhile, the C wing was like an ice box. When you traveled across the little indoor bridge that was built to connect the old building to the new one it was like entering the mall on a sweltering summer day after trekking across the humid sunscape of a parking lot. The warm wet of your body crystalized, which felt good for maybe one second before your lips were blue and you were covered in goosebumps.

I had more than one reason for my hair to stand on end. The other side of this bridge was my only guaranteed daily spotting of Doug Ryan. He had chemistry 6th period; I had biology in the neighboring classroom period 7. And his chemistry teacher, Mr. Klastinkski (Stinkski, as he was known to the student body), was notorious for keeping his class after the bell. Meanwhile, I, programmed at an early age by my mother, was incapable of being late. So often, really always, I rushed the long voyage from my English class (a trip most of my classmates chose to stretch out) and arrived outside his classroom door just as Doug burst out.

Devoutly, or perhaps pathetically, I tried my best to catch his eye or brush his elbow or run the soles of my shoes against his. But whether we met closer to the door of his classroom or further down the hall, whether my hair was up or down, whether I was wearing a skirt or shorts, or whether he was alone or with his friends, I might as well have been the ghost girl from the wave. He would walk by, looking right through me. I actually felt myself become invisible. Had he actually killed me that night?

Because it's not like he was blind or mute or shy. He said hello to friends who were behind me. And it's not like they were all guys. I'd seen him speak to girls too. Once, he'd even given Deb a high five. Meanwhile, I was left perpetually hanging.

The next week, I watched him represent the debate team in a district-wide tournament hosted in our school's auditorium. He was wearing a collared shirt, light blue tie and navy jacket over cargo pants with Nikes. Next to the opposing team's polished leather shoes, this fusion of professionalism with his classic jock style made him look laidback and confident as he delivered a passionate argument against altering our trade policies with the Chinese. "American workers are being displaced and laid off in record numbers," he'd said, addressing the student body and the panel of history teachers serving as judges. "The rust belt states are being affected the worst. If we don't do something about this today, the entire landscape of our nation's economy is going to shift in unpredictable and potentially dangerous ways. It already is." This was the first time I'd ever thought about the question of products being manufactured overseas. It was also the first time I'd ever seen a debate. I knew our school had a nationally ranked debate team, but I hadn't joined. I needed extracurriculars besides sports to complete my college application portfolio, but Mom and Dad had agreed to let me use freshman year just to suss them out and see what would be a good match.

Debate looked good on college applications. A lot of politicians and leaders cited it as the inspiration for their career, but it also seemed sort of exhausting, arguing all the time—sometimes for a side you didn't even agree with. Plus, there weren't many girls on the team, and the idea of intellectually jousting with all the A+ guys in every grade as an after-school activity seemed like a club that required an invitation. I liked to research interesting subjects and I enjoyed a good conversation, but I hadn't attained the level of confidence necessary to speak with such authority, if confidence was even the word for the frenzied back and forth I was witnessing. Chutzpah? Arrogance? I mined the thesaurus in my brain. What was the word for the sort of person who was so enamored with the sound of their own voice that they would happily argue for hours, publicly, with a stranger about a topic they barely knew anything about—not because they actually cared about resolving the complexities of the subject matter at all, but because they wanted to win points?

I was beginning to think that maybe I shouldn't spend all my extracurricular time trying to win. If there was some sort of ranking system involved in the activity, I knew I would not be able to control my impulse to scramble to the top. There had to be activities that weren't just about keeping score.

Maybe I was a future yearbook editor? Or maybe student council, which would involve an election—that would be stressful, of course, and involve winning, but after that, just brainstorming and organizing behind closed doors. Or maybe Habitat for Humanity? I liked helping people and the idea of building things seemed cool. I'd never held a hammer.

The auditorium seat's rough fabric scratched against the exposed part of my legs. Doug's face twisted in condescension as his opposition gave statistics in favor of shipping factory jobs overseas: trickle-down economics, a growth in the market, retirement portfolios. Then Doug had his turn for his closing argument.

A hush fell over the audience as he approached the podium. He cleared his throat. Then the boy who'd gyrated his erect penis against my sunburned stomach until he came all over me addressed the entire student body, all 550 of us, plus some spectators from the competing school and parents and teachers and whoever else had decided this was a good way to waste the hours of their precious life.

He spoke with such remarkable ease. Despite myself, I was impressed. But I wasn't stupid.

It was during this well-researched argument that won him regional acclaim in the high school debate world that I decided, though I was desperate for his attention, that I also despised him. He was so obviously putting on a show. He was a fake. He didn't give a shit about the Rust Belt. He just learned that phrase from a book. One day, he'd probably make his fortune off importing goods from China. I scanned the crowd and mentally rolled my eyes at every teacher and parent gazing at Doug as if he were a beacon, pride shining in their eyes. I wanted to stand up and boo. But I didn't. I just stuck my thumbnail into my thigh and watched it make an indentation before picking it up and choosing another spot of exposed flesh to stab.

My trust in the system had developed a leak. I felt a jostling inside me, like an earthquake, a rebellious lurch. What if it was all an elaborate charade? What if checking all these boxes really was meaningless? Honor societies, extracurriculars, athletic trophies, straight A's. Or maybe they were only part of it? There was something else. A tacit code. Doug finished his final argument and the audience whooped. The tiniest smile escaped his lips, which were arranged in a tight and serious line. In other words, he smirked.

There were only a few days left, but summer still seemed like it would never come, and every day was just one long trek to science class. I was either waiting for the moment to come, or it was happening, or it was over.

I'd never experienced heartburn like the sort they talked about on television ads, but each day, during those seconds I had to pass him in the hall, I felt like I needed a Tums or Pepto-Bismol. Something to coat my ribcage in bubblegum colored pink and build a barrier between my physical body and my memories.

Then the moment would pass. Doug would turn down the hall towards the C-wing bridge, and my body would materialize. I would enter the classroom and slip into my seat in the front row on the far left, feeling the cold burn of adrenalin in my veins, the thud of my heart evoking a flood of flashbacks and longings. Like an invisible leash around my neck, these secret moments kept me chained up in a fairy tale world where I told myself that he liked me like he said he did, that there was still a chance that he was ignoring me because that's just what boys did. Then the bell would ring, the rest of the class would hurry in, and I would experience a momentary reprieve from my agony. Or maybe I should say that I traded one sort of agony for another.

Mrs. Dreckford was the least zany of the science teachers at

Tonley High. The fetal pigs we were forced to dissect had more life in them. Her lessons came from the textbook. Her students were seated in alphabetical order. Being Emily Banks, that meant I was awarded a seat right in front. This was probably a good thing. I'd heard rumors in middle school that Dreckford's class was impossible. No one got an A. Listening to her teach was about as exciting as watching a slug drag itself across the cracked-up pavement of the sidewalk by the soccer fields near my house. Actually, less so. Because the truth was I experienced a strange pleasure from watching slugs. The way they moved so slowly threw the entire world off balance, leaving me to contemplate time and space. Were the slug and I actually sharing the same moment on earth in the space-time continuum? If you moved slower, did that slow down time? Even though slugs didn't live as long, since they moved slower, did that mean that their life felt just as long? Is that what Einstein said? What did things even look like down there? How did those antennas work?

I was less inspired by Dreckford and her gummy smile, which wasn't designed to offer empathy or inspire passion in her students. It was just a face she made, like a giraffe baring its teeth as it went about the monotony of plucking another bunch of leaves from a tree. The key to getting an A in Dreckford's class was basically figuring out how not to fall asleep. This worked in my favor. Being an overachiever with a general fear of authority, sitting in the front row made it impossible for me to zone out, which made me stand out as a student who "cared," unlike the other unlucky kids whose last names alphabetically landed them in the front row and who did not cower at the thought of breaking a rule or getting a B. Their heads nodded, their eyes rolled back in their heads, and Dreckford called them out publicly, labeling them as slackers while the others behind them visibly roused themselves. My shoulders, on the other hand, were always straight. My pencil was always sharpened. And so, she lavished me in accolades.

"When Ms. Banks is delivering her valedictorian speech and then waltzing off to Stanford or Harvard or wherever she chooses, I want you to think of this moment," she said once, during a particularly miserable lecture. "Exceptionalism isn't something that happens in spurts. It's the accumulation of average days of hard work." Even I groaned at that one.

Cowing masochist that I was, I earned the impossible A+, not once, but for all four marking periods, despite the fact that I remembered almost nothing of the lessons.

Even though I had broken the New Jersey state record for cross country in the state tournament that past fall (the first freshman in the history of the state ever to do so), my A+ in biology seemed to be the feat my classmates were most in awe of, though not all of them were awestruck in a good way.

"You're such a fucking dork," Jake Freelander whispered in my ear from behind me when Dreckford loudly applauded my 100 percent on a pop quiz after placing it on my desk.

"Good thing you waited until the end of the school year to say that to me," I hissed back at him. "I hope you're better at Physics. Because your days of copying my homework are over."

He opened his eyes wide and let out a fake whimper. Dreckford dropped his quiz on his desk. He got an 81. "Some people just turn off too early," she said under her breath as she breezed by him and finished handing out the papers.

Dreckford did the giraffe thing with her teeth and then said something that actually got everyone's attention. "So next year, as sophomores, most of you will be taking Ms. Celestino's Introduction to Physics, and, since Ms. Celestino has a free period now, she asked me if she could address your class and talk a bit about the course—and also explain a summer assignment that she needs you to complete."

Normally, hearing about a summer assignment would generate a murmur of protest from the class, but since Celestino's visit meant a vacation from Dreckford, we remained alert.

I was excited. Ms. Celestino's reputation was the opposite of Dreckford's. Her energy reminded me of those plastic glow sticks that they sell at carnivals and skating rinks, the kind that create a fan of colorful light when you wave them back and forth really quickly,. Celestino moved quickly and she wore a lot of gemstones and sequined appliques, so passing her in the hallway sometimes created this effect. All those necklaces, along with her wild, short, gray bush of hair and her oversized cat eyeglasses, made her look like she was wearing an elaborate costume. I'm not sure I could accurately identify her face without all her accoutrements.

We waited a few minutes, talking and goofing off before she burst into the classroom with a stack of stapled papers in her hand. She immediately started handing out the papers to the row closest to the door and furthest from me.

She was not a small woman. I watched her big fingers count off the stapled stacks of papers. She handed them to the first person in every row. "Take one and pass them back."

When she got to me, she only had three, but there were four people in our row.

"Shit," she said, which made us all laugh.

"I can look on with Jake," I said.

Jake rolled his eyes at me. He pretended to sneeze and said, "Goody goody" into his hands.

"God bless you," I told him solemnly. "You should pray for some ass-kissing skills. They would get you far."

He snorted and then made this crazy, psycho-killer face he liked to make, where he set his mouth in a straight line and opened his eyes until they seemed like they would pop from their sockets. But his bottom lip wiggled. I spied a few, rough, mustache hairs sprouting from his upper lip, on the same side of his face as the little freckle he had near his nose, which was also rippling a little as he attempted to contort his features into a zombie face. But he didn't scare me. There was an obvious, good-natured smile lurking beneath.

Three months ago, after tiring of his disruptions for the first two-thirds of the school year, Dreckford had broken her own seating code and made him switch seats with Gina Conroy, moving him up and over. Slowly, day by day, being classroom neighbors had kind of made us cool with one another, despite the fact that he was of the floppy haired, fuck-the-system, same-shirt-every-day grunge variety and my life was a practice in placating authority. Jake was the only sophomore in our class. He hadn't failed the year before. The state of New Jersey only required students to take three years of science in high school to get a diploma. For most kids that meant opting out senior year, but Jake delayed his science requirement for a year because he dreaded Dreckford. Some people were of the get-it-over-with mentality. He was of the put-it-off.

I looked at the packet. "Searching for the Night." The gist was that we were supposed to keep a stargazing journal all summer. The project was going to be like 25 pages long. Just what everybody felt like doing over summer break.

"Hello!" Ms. Celestino said, smiling. Then her smile collapsed and her eyes became a little glazed. She pushed her springy bush of hair down against her scalp and then released it to reach again towards the cosmos. "Ok," she said. "ok, ok, ok."

She turned and extended her arms towards us with her palms open to the ceiling and waved them from one end of the classroom to the other like she was showing us all an invisible treasure.

"Do you believe we are alone in the universe?"

"Alone?" someone said.

"Yes," she said, pacing back and forth. "As in, the only planet with life in the entirety of the universe?"

"Like," someone else said, "Are you asking if we think aliens exist?"

"She is totally an alien," Jake whispered.

I laughed. Everyone turned and looked at me.

"You," she said, pointing at me.

"Me?" I said, my newly-calmed heart thundering again in my chest.

"Yes, you. What is your name?"

I was relieved that she didn't already know me. It was nice to know that there were teachers at this school who didn't have a clue about the athletics department. It seemed I'd spent the entire year discussing upcoming races with random teachers in the hall.

"My name is Emily."

"Emily, do you believe that we are alone in the universe?"

I considered the question, my mind a reel of *E.T.* following Reece's Pieces and little blobbish cyclops on *The Simpsons*. I had no scientific information to base my opinion on. I felt everyone's collective gaze waiting for me to speak. I tried to read Celestino's eyes through her cat frames. What did she want me to say?

"Um," I said. "I don't know."

"You don't know?!" she said in a prodding and exacerbated voice.

I shrugged, showing her I had nothing further to offer. "No," I said back, slightly dismayed, worrying she would remember my lack of an opinion next year.

Then she smiled at me. "Me neither," she said. Everyone laughed. "But isn't that one of the greatest mysteries?" Then she launched into a soliloquy about the night sky and how for as long as people have been alive on earth it has served as the window into what lies beyond. She delivered her lecture while slowly spinning in circles as she looped around the desks in our classroom, as if she were a planet herself and we were a collective sun. Our entire class was entranced by her. Maybe any teacher would be entrancing after a year of Dreckford, or maybe Celestino was the real deal.

"The night sky is filled with the stories of gods and goddesses, the ancient soap operas of civilizations past. They are also the foundation for scientific thought. Explorers used the sky to navigate the oceans and calculate distance. You may think you see everything during the day, but think of everything the light from the sun blocks us from seeing. If night didn't exist, how would we even know that we lived on a planet in a solar system in the Milky Way in a galaxy in a universe in a—" she threw up her hands. "What?!"

I thought of my night on the beach with Doug Ryan and the way I'd imagined myself picking up the Little Dipper and dipping it into the sea. It was the only constellation I could ever identify. I wrapped my hands around my body and tucked my legs up in a ball.

Celestino began explaining and demonstrating the simple instruments that would be needed on a stargazing expedition. She recommended bringing a reference book or star chart to use as a way to judge what we were observing and recording in our journal. "It's ok to be wrong," she said. "I want to see what you do with the tools you're given and how you are able to judge." She also recommended taking red colored tape and putting it over the end of a flashlight if consulting a book. "The human eye reacts differently to red light," she said. "It won't ruin your night vision as you go between reference materials and staring at the sky." Each session, she said, should be about an hour long. "I know not everyone will give themselves this amount of time," Celestino lamented, "but the truth is you'll be cheating yourself out of an amazing experience. We live in a world of endless distraction. Sometimes taking a pause is all you need to realign your consciousness and remind yourself that you are a lifeform living on a planet with the means to sustain life—a crazier story than you can find on any television program!"

Her eyes lit up like a stage performer searching her audience for a connection. I wanted to meet them, but I felt shy. I didn't want her to see how inspired I felt because I wasn't sure I could live up to her expectations. She reminded me a little of an English teacher, the way she swayed when she spoke, like she was reciting poetry. And so, even though her assignment sounded like a lot of work, I was excited. Her energy had my hand scribbling notes in the margins of the packet Jake and I were looking at together, circling and highlighting specific items, lost in thought imagining future entries.

"Some will find this exercise addictive," Celestino had written. "And to those, I encourage you not to let 10 entries be your limit." I smiled to myself, thinking of how Celestino seemed so confident someone would want to go beyond 10 entries. It was like she was asking someone to do more than 10 entries. I underlined this line then wrote, 15? forgetting for a second that Jake was looking on with me.

He leaned close to my ear and whispered. "Always trying to get ahead." The warmth of his breath hit the nape of my neck and gave me a little shiver. I shot him a dirty look and continued listening.

In addition to our field reports where we recorded a page or so on our nightly observations, we were also supposed to write a reflection explaining what we learned throughout the summer as the result of our stargazing. The packet said the paper could take any form. It didn't matter, Celestino said, "as long as it shows your thinking and learning process." Easy enough. Again, I started writing notes in the margins without thinking: Stevens' beach house,

Poconos, Lander's Pond? Soccer Field? Pine Barrens?

"Nice to meet you," Celestino said to the class. "Have an excellent summer and I'll see you in the fall. Happy stargazing." Then just like that, she turned and walked out, leaving that sparkly glow in her wake. We all sat there for a moment, stunned.

Dreckford seemed unfazed by being so obviously outshined in her own classroom. Her face was the same as always, dull and wide. I think she was as ready for summer as we were. Who could blame her? We'd tackled the body one system at a time, and now it was spent. She didn't say anything to us. Instead, she kept her focus on whatever it was she was staring at on the computer at her desk. Our class interpreted this message as permission to pretend that she didn't exist, and so we burst into a million conversations at once, some about the assignment, but mostly not. There were summer jobs to discuss, beach houses and vacations, tv shows and whatever else.

Jake had turned around to talk to some of the people behind him about a baseball game. I contemplated getting out of my seat and going over to the other end of the classroom, where some friends were sitting, but my mind was still churning from the lecture, and the bell was going to ring in one minute anyway, so there wasn't much of a point. In fact, it rang before I even really processed it, and before I knew it, Jake had walked away with the packet in his hand. I got up to chase after him—since I had taken all the notes on the thing, technically it felt like mine—but I bumped smack into Deb, who was waiting with Jenna for me at the door. We all had 8th period study hall and usually walked down to the cafeteria together.

"Do you have any change?" she asked. "We want to buy a Diet Coke from the vending machine, but we only have 60 cents."

"Um, I think so," I said, "but come with me first." I grabbed Deb's hand and tugged her down the hall in the direction I saw Jake go. I was pretty sure he had an 8th period art or shop class.

"I'll just meet you guys downstairs," Jenna called, her tone dismissing my adventure as a chore.

"Come!" Deb called, looking back.

"No thank you," Jenna said.

I could feel the way the condescension in her voice made Deb question the voyage.

"Where are we going?" she asked skeptically as I tugged her along.

"I need to chase Jake Freelander!"

"What?" she said in a voice that let me know she was uninterested in our subject of pursuit. "Why?"

"Just come on."

I knew she wouldn't argue. Even though she didn't consider Jake Freelander cool enough to be on her radar, she also wasn't one to turn down an invitation to run through the halls, which opened up the opportunity to run into other people too.

We raced like we were in a teen movie, dodging our classmates and catching whiffs of their lotions, shampoos, deodorants, or lack thereof, giggling the whole way. My laugh was quiet and Deb's was loud. Her joy was always more pronounced. It echoed in the stairwell. We got to a narrow, empty stretch of hallway in front of the auditorium, and I jumped up and grazed my fingers against the banner that said "Congratulations Class of 2000," saying my silent goodbyes to the seniors who'd never really known I'd existed. The fact that I would one day be one of them, that my days in these halls were numbered, was not a thought that occurred to me. High school was four years long. I still had three left. That equaled forever. No one I knew was going anywhere yet. The only kids I'd known who'd become college students were Deb's older brothers, and they'd already left high school before we had arrived.

Deb stopped to examine her reflection in the display case glass outside the auditorium, her reflection transposed over the smiling senior portraits of the valedictorian, salutatorian, and class president. "Well, I know where your face goes in this line-up," she said.

"Salutatorian. I'm not ranked number one right now. That's Derek Gladstone." Doug Ryan's ex-girlfriend Mandy's little brother was in our grade and also happened to be my rival for top of the class.

Deb smiled. "We have plenty of time to take care of that," she said in a comedic, dark voice, rubbing her hands together.

"Yes," I agreed, my own voice turning devilish. "Murder. Murder is the answer."

"Poison," she said.

"Hemlock in the ear," I said.

"What's that?" she said.

"From *Hamlet*."

"We didn't read that in regular English," she said. Deb was proud to be in zero AP classes.

"All you need to know is that it is poison and it works while you sleep," I said, in a creepy voice. Murdering each other to knock off the competition for valedictorian was an ongoing joke between Derek's friends and mine.

I grabbed her elbow. "We have to keep going..." I said. We ran down the stairwell and burst into the narrow basement hallway that smelled like turpentine and paint. The art and shop floor. Why it was housed in the basement, I don't know. The classrooms did have windows, but the hallway lacked ventilation. I choked at thc air as it hit my lungs.

"This is like a ghost town," Deb said. "There's nobody here."

I poked my head into one of the classrooms. Mr. Hager, one

of the art teachers, looked up. "Hello?" he said.

"Where are all the classes down here?" I asked.

"The art and shop classes are closed for the school year," he said. "Seniors have dress rehearsal for graduation and juniors have a senior orientation."

"What about freshman and sophomores?" I asked.

"They have study hall."

"Thanks!" I said and then I took off down the hall.

"I'm starting to sweat," Deb said, stopping and smelling her armpit. "Can you slow down?"

"Meet me on the second floor," I called behind me. "I just need to catch Jake before he leaves."

"But Mr. Hager said he has study hall!"

"Then just meet me in the cafeteria!" I yelled, on my way to the second floor anyway.

"But what about my Diet Coke money?"

I stopped, reached in my pocket, and ran back to deliver her 35 cents before continuing towards the stairs.

If there was one thing I knew, it was that Jake Freelander would not be attending study hall. Sitting in front of him for the past few months had taught me that he was a master at making the rules work for him. He knew that if Dreckford was giving us the long stare for the final minute of bio, there was no way in hell anyone would actually be taking attendance in the cafeteria. There was nothing stopping him from walking out the door. I didn't care if he cut. I just wanted that packet! If that packet made its way out of the building, I'd never see it again. Sure, I could get another copy, but I didn't want to bother Celestino. Plus, I was anal and superstitious about notetaking. My freshman year of high school had shown me a direct correlation between studying from original notes and scoring well, and I knew Jake would probably be happier copying from me later anyway.

Sophomore lockers were located on the second floor of the A-wing, the sticky swampland of no AC. I took the stairs two at a time, passing sophomores, juniors and seniors walking leisurely in the opposite direction. None of them were Jake. The tardy bell rang as I poked my head through the stairwell door. My four minute window had expired. The floor was totally abandoned except for Rosalind Hickory, who was my sophomore twin, not by looks, but by books. Currently ranked number one in her class, she was class secretary on student council and a reporter for the school newspaper. She'd actually interviewed me for the paper after I'd beat the state record in cross country at the state championship in the fall. That was when I sensed the eerie synchronicity of our beings. The way she reviewed her notes before asking me questions reminded me of my own method of psychotically tracing my strides around the course in my mind in the moments before a race.

We were ladies who liked to be prepared. I recognized the skill. I knew Rosalind had study hall in the cafeteria too. She must have already checked in with the advisor and told them she needed to organize her locker. She was completely engrossed, meticulously sifting through the papers in a folder. Watching her gave me a visceral desire to reorganize and purge, a beloved activity for me, but I quickly snapped back to action. The empty, quiet hall meant that Jake had definitely left the building, along with my packet.

This prompted me to do something stupid. Or maybe not stupid exactly, but bold. It was something that made me very unlike Rosalind Hickory: I walked out the school doors without a pass for early dismissal.

I pushed against the long aluminum button that unlocked the side door and walked straight out into the sunshine, feeling an adrenaline rush from the fresh air. So this was how easy it was to cut school? You just walked out the door? It wasn't like I was doing something wrong, I reasoned with myself. I was chasing an assignment! And I wasn't missing any classes. There was no point in going to study hall. You could study outside.

That I cared so much about pursuing some stupid notes on a packet seems silly, I know. The wildness that I felt inside seemed ridiculous and excessive. But I was new to testing boundaries.

The hot glare of the sun against my skin hit me like the eyes of God, the principal, my parents, all of them judging me. But the fear of retribution wasn't strong enough to stop me from basking on the other side of the school's walls. I went into runner mode. I let my legs lead the way. They trotted me across the cool, green, freshly watered grass of the schoolyard. Each blade rubbed against my bare shins like an itchy tongue.

There was Jake with Travis, his best friend. Alone, Jake's grunge look just seemed like the clothes he was wearing, but next to Travis, who was a little taller and whose hair was even longer, more tangled, and dirtier looking than Jake's, and whose pants were handsewn with anarchist patches, I felt the gulf between them and me. We were like two different shops at The Cherry Hill Mall on opposite sides of the food court. Actually, not even. These guys were the Army Navy store, which wasn't even in the mall, though it was on the same highway. The two of them were walking towards Lander's Pond, the nature preserve at the end of the street. I knew those woods well. They were where the cross country team trained, and where others shaded off to smoke or make out or just screw around and waste time.

"Jake," I yelled as I ran towards them, "Jake!"

Perhaps my voice was louder than I intended. I had a mission and had momentarily lost all sense of everything else. "Yo, Freelander!"

I was now just a few feet from them. He and Travis both turned at the same time. Under their collective gaze, I suddenly felt the magnitude of my nerdiness. Why did I chase him out here for a science packet, an assignment that I'd already memorized and was unlikely to forget? Who does that? Travis had a cigarette tucked behind one of his ears. I remembered Jake's voice in my ear when the quizzes were returned, Fucking dork. Maybe I'd misinterpreted that as a joke. Maybe it was what he actually thought. I felt flustered for a second, blushing. Travis looked baffled, but Jake was smiling. I tried to explain myself, but kept tripping over my words, "I-ya, I-ya, um."

"Spit it out, Banks," he said.

I took a deep breath and held my hand up to my forehead to block the sun from my eyes so I didn't have to squint.

"The packet," I said.

"The packet?" he said.

"Science. Celestino."

"I don't have it."

"Yes you do! You left with it. I saw it in your hands."

"Can't you ask her for another one?"

"I took notes on that one."

"Notes?"

"Yeah. Remember?"

He considered this fact and tilted his head to the side, as if he was trying to remember into the distant past, even though what I was talking about happened all of 10 minutes ago. "Maybe it's in my locker. I can give it to you tomorrow, ok?"

You know how sometimes your body just feels someone's eyes on you and you turn in that direction without even consciously choosing to look? Right as I was processing the information in Jake's answer, my head subconsciously turned and I saw Doug Ryan sitting shotgun in Parker Kane's car, both of them watching our encounter with the windows down. The spell had been lifted. Apparently I was visible as long as I was standing outside the school doors doing something I wasn't supposed to be doing. The world went wonky. A heightened state of alarm coursed through me. A heavy lump appeared in my already stuttering throat. I struggled to swallow it.

"Yeah," I said slowly to Jake. "That works. I just didn't want to lose it."

"Her lecture was cool," Jake said.

Her lecture? I struggled to focus under Doug's gaze. I was like an ant under a magnifying glass. I grasped for the threads of conversation and attempted not to self-combust.

"Celestino's?"

"Yeah. I like her."

I realized that maybe Jake Freelander was actually capable of doing his own homework provided he found the subject interesting. I smiled at him in agreement and made a little wish that we'd be in the same class next year while my foot found a pebble on the pavement that it began to rub back and forth under the sole of my shoe.

"Me too," I said to him just as Doug decided to shout from his window, "Banks!"

Banks. My name. Aloud. After three whole weeks of walking past me as if through a mist. Again he yelled it. "Banks!" It didn't sound the way I wished it would in the weeks I had waited for his attention. There was a hint of amusement or sarcasm in his tone. Did he really want to talk to me, or was he just playing a game with his friends? Was he laughing at me or saying hi? I couldn't tell. I took the safe route.

I turned and glared at him. "What?" I said back in a thorny voice that surprised me.

"Come here," he said, waving me towards Parker's car. He

seemed to like that I sounded angry.

I had no time to think. Again, I surprised myself. I rolled my eyes at him and yelled, “Leave me alone,” and then I looked at Jake and said, “I’ll get the packet tomorrow, don’t lose it,” before tearing off in a dead sprint for the safety of the cafeteria, where I hoped to listen to Deb and Jenna gossip about the last episode of *Friends* while I stole sips of our collective Diet Coke, trying my best to ignore the aspartame.

- 5 -

We were wrapping up our second-to-last English class when Coach B called and asked my teacher to send me down to the athletic office.

"Emily," Ms. Bartovsky said as she rested the phone back onto the receiver, "Coach B."

Her inflection was equivalent to a subtle diss, and I felt her pain. This was the sort of thing Coach B did. He plucked me from my classes, right in the middle of a period, just because he was free and had something he wanted to talk about. As if running were the only thing in the world.

Ms. Bartovsky put her hand on my shoulder as I walked to the door. "Just in case tomorrow is too hectic," she said. "I wanted to make sure you know that you're a good writer. And to loosen up a little on the page. You're the best when you forget to care about sounding smart."

I looked at the floor, embarrassed, and barely mumbled a "Thanks."

I walked the hallways slowly, savoring the energy of those last days of school before summer, and taking my time descending the stairs and cutting through the gym to a set of double doors that opened onto a small hallway known as the Athletic Department. The last door on the left was Coach B's. "Burt Lauer," the placard on the door read. Outside, in a framed case were newspaper clippings: pictures of me and other track and field stars. The door was already half-propped open. I gave it a tap.

"Come in," Coach said. I opened the door. "There she is," he said in his friendly, yet firm manner. He was a kind man that never smiled. He pointed at an empty chair. "Sit down."

Kelsey Kramer was already sitting in one of the other chairs.

Consumed by a chip in her pink nail polish, she barely looked at me when I walked in the door. "Well," Coach said. "Let's get down to it." He handed us both a stack of papers stapled together. "These are instructions for summer training. Now it's not required. Technically, according to the laws of the league, we're not allowed to start practicing until August, but I'm assigning everyone on the cross country team buddies, and I expect you to complete the workout schedule that's here. I know people have summer travel plans and you might not be able to make every single day. I get it. It's fine. But there's a log here that shows the dates you should be meeting, and another column to record the days you make up if you miss a meeting. Of course, it's not required, but I need you to commit to me that you'll do it."

I looked at the papers. There was a weekly regimen of exercises and suggested meals for sustaining energy on long run days. On the top corner of the first page was Kelsey's home phone number. On the top corner of her front page was mine.

Kelsey looked at me and shrugged. I shrugged back.

"So it's not required, but we have to commit to it..." Kelsey said.

"Exactly," Coach said.

She gave him a confused look.

"It's illegal to make you practice when it's off season," he said. "But we want to win. And in order to win, you need to stay in shape over the summer. I'll be in touch in July to make sure everything is running smoothly." He gave us a forced smile. "Think of it as an opportunity to get to know each other."

We looked at each other skeptically.

"See ya," she said to me as we walked out the door. We went separate ways down the hall.

Grades came out on the last day of school. The A+ I'd

earned in Dreckford boosted my GPA .03 above Derek Gladstone's, which secured me the top rank in the class of '03. I found the synchronicity of these numbers pleasing. It felt like a sign.

The news was met with overwhelming euphoria by my mom and dad, though Dad tried to be less insane about it. He was proud of me, obviously, and probably also a little of himself, seeing as he represented one half of my gene pool, but he let me know with a gentle smile that told me he'd never doubted this would be the outcome from the start. Mom, on the other hand, screamed like she was watching the Eagles game in a Donovan McNabb jersey at Connoley's on a Sunday afternoon. I shriveled a bit under the intense heat of her happiness. I was a raisin version of myself—sweeter to those around me because they were so pleased by my actions, but exhausted and drained by the effort. She rattled off all her dreams for me like the longest to-do list ever. It ended, of course, with me as President of the United States.

This surge to the top also earned me a "death threat" from Evan Rikowitz, Derek's best friend, who drew a hangman in my yearbook. We all laughed. It wasn't a real threat, but when one of the history teachers caught wind of the situation I was sent to the guidance counselor—on the last freaking day of school—where I was questioned about who drew it and whether or not I felt "safe."

Violent jokes were not considered funny. The echoes of the bullets of Columbine were still ringing in every teacher's ears, so everything required investigation. If I admitted that Evan had drawn the noose, he would end up being suspended or start the year with a month's worth of detention or something, so I just played dumb.

"I have no idea who drew it, we were just passing the books around. But I'm fine," I said defensively. "It's a joke. I'm really good at hangman and Wheel of Fortune."

"What about Derek Gladstone? I hear you guys have a

serious competition for number one ranking in your class."

"It's not serious," I said. "Derek is my friend. Seriously, everything is fine."

And everything was fine, though if they'd actually done real research and read Derek's entry in my yearbook, which suggested we meet in a dark alley at around 2 am because he had "something he wanted to discuss," they may have been even more concerned. Luckily, they either weren't smart enough or were too lazy to do the investigating considering it was their last day of school too.

The guidance counselor looked up from her computer screen, where she was entering in the details of our conversation and sighed.

"I'm going to have to tell your parents about this," she said.

I shrugged, pretending that it wasn't a big deal but knowing that I now would have to endure an even longer and more torturous interrogation. There was nothing I could do about it though, so I decided not to care. Besides, it really was a joke, and the reason it was even happening was because I'd done it! I'd ended the school year ranked number one! Plus, I was the fastest female long distance runner in the state! All those nights of flashcards and afternoons of practice had meant something after all.

I busted out of the office and into the fresh air, feeling the unplanned days of summer stretching before me like unexplored trails through woods I'd never run. There was a green burst inside me. I felt conscious of the expansiveness of the world and the fact that I was young, that everything was just starting. I realized those corny posters in classrooms were actually kind of true: Anything was possible.

The problem with this feeling, however, was that even though I was 15, my parents still thought of me as 12.

"I got us tickets to Wildwater Palace to celebrate!" Dad said when he came home from work that night. "I bought four, so you can bring a friend. I figured Deb. Mom and I are going to take off one day midweek so we can avoid the weekend crowds."

Wildwater Palace. It had been a favorite family day trip for years. My dad and I had a mutual affinity for water parks: the crazy, looping slides, the huge drops into deep pools, the group rides on enormous rafts, the water mazes that felt like human car washes. For years, probably since second grade, our family had gone with Deb, the three of us going on slides while Mom stayed with the cooler at a lounge chair by the wave pool. She was not a water slide lady. "Too many germs," she always said. I was never allowed to go on anything without my water shoes, though sometimes Dad let me slip them off when we were out of her view.

Those trips had always been fun, but this year, for some reason, I just didn't feel like it. I didn't want to make all the decisions that going would require: bikini or one-piece, water shoes or Mom's wrath. I knew Deb wouldn't want to go, or if she did go, all she'd want to do is ditch my dad and follow a group of cute boys from one slide to the next, which was not the sort of day that my parents were after. But the look on Dad's face when he held up the passes made it impossible to say no. "Cool! Thanks, Dad! I'll ask Deb."

But I stalled. Besides the fact that I doubted she wanted to go, I wasn't even sure I wanted Deb to come. She was only half present any time we hung out anyway. She spent most of her time hovering by her family's computer, signed into AOL Instant Messenger waiting for the animated sound of a door opening, the notification that someone new had signed online. She kept the volume turned to the max so that no matter where we were in her house, she would hear the sound. When she heard it, she would sprint to the living room to see who had signed on. If it was Parker, that was it, I might as well have just opened her actual front door and gone home because the only purpose I seemed to serve was to provide fodder for the two of them to type about. One time she told him I was reading a book on the floor next to her.

"What book?" he'd asked.

"*Dubliners*," she'd typed back. I'd picked it up off of her brother Cody's shelf.

I was standing on a street in Dublin, living in the head of an Irish boy wondering about a dead priest, when I heard Deb giggle at the screen. "What?" I'd asked her. "Nothing," she said, trying to cover up the computer, but I hopped up in time to see his response to her: "At least it's not flashcards though."

The flashcards comment stung a little. It was evidence that she complained about the way I carried vocabulary words or historical dates around in my back pocket, perpetually inculcating my brain with minutiae. I felt betrayed and exposed. It put me on guard and made me second guess inviting her into my infantilized world, where my mother still micromanaged my existence. The last thing I needed was for her to report a full day of bonding with my boring family to Parker, who would cherry-pick the worst of it to pass on to Doug. That would compound my dorkiness exponentially. She'd already told him the story of the noose and Evan Rikowitz.

This frivolous sharing of my personal life hurt my feelings, but I didn't know how to express this without exacerbating the rift I already felt between us. Deb had a way of speaking impulsively. She had no filter. It was just how she was. And the closer she got to Parker through their AIM chats, the further I felt her loyalty stray from me. It was like she was constantly throwing me under the bus with her too-cool disses and stories from the past that always managed to cast me as a doofus. Like the time I cried at *The Lion King*. Or how when we were in sixth grade, I ran back to my house to be with my mom because I was scared to be home alone with her because Cody and Eric had convinced me their house was haunted. Why were these details that Parker needed to know?

Of course, not all the details she shared about me were cruel—many of them probably came out of love for our shared history and friendship—but it didn't feel that way. There was just a difference in the way we were alone together after that Memorial Day Weekend—a decision on her end not to see the way that I was suffering, to not recognize that I was the kind of person who needed to be asked about my pain. Instead, she glossed over the fact that Doug universally ignored me, only focusing on her own budding romance. Whether she was totally oblivious or just didn't care, the way she mentioned me in these chats as if everything was totally normal scarred me to the bone.

On top of that, whenever she spoke of Jenna in the chats, the details were different—less personal and more universally appealing. Like how her house was huge, and how there was a game room in the basement that included a collection of antique pinball machines, and how her dad had access to a private jet, and how she'd ridden it with Jenna after Christmas to go skiing in Vail. This, of course, was not my life. I'd been invited to go on that Vail trip too, but my parents had declined. "I've never even had a conversation for more than one minute with Jenna's parents," my mom said. "There's no way I'm letting you get on a plane to just fly away with them. What if there's an emergency? How will I even find you?" I'd been devastated then and reading Deb type about it made me feel devastated again.

The walls between us seemed to always be expanding. She may have driven me crazy sometimes, but Deb had always been my automatic best friend. It was weird to be sitting next to her but to also feel alone.

This feeling of rejection haunted me everywhere I went. I

even felt that way at 11 o'clock Mass at St. Mike's, stuck in a pew between my mom and dad, wearing what I argued was my "Sunday best," a long cotton skirt with a drawstring waist and a too-small t-shirt from middle school that said, "Tonley MS Tigers," my hair in a messy bun.

Sunday Mass was a strange thing. It wasn't like the whole school was there—not everybody in Tonley was Catholic—but there were enough peers present to keep it interesting. Even though I'd attended CCD from kindergarten through the 8th grade and completed all of my sacraments (except marriage and death,) gone were the days where I approached Mass as a place to commune with God. When I was little, the size of the church impressed me. So did the stained glass and the incense, the chants, the statues of Jesus, the blue of Mary, not to mention the way everyone stood up and sat down at the same time and mumbled the same words all together, creating a sort of drone. This mysterious behavior from all the grownups used to make me feel like I was a black cat at a cemetery seeing ghosts, but puberty had blinded me to whatever holy spirits were flitting through.

Now I mostly thought of Sunday morning as an opportunity to quietly analyze everyone else's families. Like Parker Kane, who was sitting a few pews ahead wearing the same cargo shorts he had on at the beach when we were drinking.

Deb's parents always arrived late and stood close to the back. After Confirmation, Deb never even went to church anymore, her parents didn't make her—until I told her that Parker was always there. Then, miraculously, by the grace of God she appeared. And that first Sunday of summer break, when I was returning to my seat after receiving Communion, I noticed her brother Cody was also there. His hair was longer and kind of flipped up around his face, which reminded me of Dave Grohl. We made eye contact, and he waggled his brows, making me smile. Visiting for the day, I guessed, from Philly, appeasing his mother who was so sad he'd rejected her to live in "the ghetto," as she liked to say. I noticed his nose-ringed girlfriend wasn't present. Probably also at the request of Mrs. Stevens. After church, he was excited to see me. While Deb snubbed me and pretended to use the bathroom so she could get a closer glimpse of Parker, Cody waited by the door to ask how I'd been and complimented me on my class rank and track record. I noticed he had the faintest hint of stubble shadowing his chin. I felt like it made him look both a little older and a little more like himself, as if this version of him had been hiding somewhere inside him all those years when we played together in his yard.

"You're killin' it," he said, giving me a huge smile. "It's awesome. You're going to get to go to any college that you want."

I knew he was genuinely happy for me, so I gave myself permission to let a simper of pride slip across my face. "I guess so," I said.

"Do you know where you want to go?"

"Hell no," I said, honestly. "I don't even know what I want to study. It's all, like, years away. Who knows. I could like break my leg or lose my mind before then anyway."

"Ha!" he said. "I hope not! You gotta protect those skillz. They're gonna help you get out of here." He gestured to the families congregating on the lawn and slowly dispersing to their cars. "Coming back here is depressing."

I looked around and tried to see it from his eyes, but I couldn't. It just looked like it always did: people happy to see each other, discussing the Phils and the Sixers now that the Eagles season was done, though there were the drafts to pine over. And trades. And whether Andy Reid really had what it took to take them all the way. Plans were made for picnics, playdates, and happy hours. It all seemed familiar and appropriate. I had no problem with any of it. Yet this didn't make me assume that Cody was wrong. I yearned for his vantage point. What did he see that I couldn't? I gave a sigh that I hoped would suggest contemplative agreement and shrugged at him. He laughed.

"You look pretty," he told me. Me? Pretty? I was mortified by his compliment. I felt my face turn beet red. Just as he said it, Deb reappeared.

"Are you flirting with Emily?" Deb said, dismissively coming up from behind. "That's gross. I'm going to tell Maura."

"She'd agree with me," Cody said. "Emily has style."

"Did you score any meaningful eye contact with Parker on the way to the bathroom?" I asked her, feeling brave enough to tease her with Cody by my side. "Gotta follow up on those late night IMs."

"Parker? Mr. Kane's kid?" Cody asked, referring to Parker's dad, who owned a well-known real estate company called Kane and Kane whose sale signs with his face on them we'd all grown up around. "You like that dude?" He was talking to Deb but he was looking at me to get information. I just raised my eyebrows and gazed at the sidewalk, hoping my gestures conveyed all he needed to know.

"Where's Doug?" she asked me. My face went from red to white. I prayed she wouldn't tell Cody about that night at the beach. My eyes conveyed my panic. I looked back at the church doors in a silent plea to God.

She made a face at me and stuck out her tongue. Then she pulled at her brother's arm.

"Let's go to brunch," she said. "Mom promised we could go to Old City. Then I want to go to Rittenhouse and shop before we drop you off at your broken-down mansion."

"It's a Brokedown Palace," he corrected her. Then he looked

at me. "You guys should come check it out one day. I'll come pick you up."

I would have liked that, but Deb looked at him like he'd suggested we pick some sort of trash off the street and eat it. "Yeah right," she said. She adjusted to her sing-songy voice. "Bye Em," she called as she pulled Cody away. It gave me a sour stomach. Cody saluted me as he disappeared down the lawn towards his parents' car.

The echo of Cody's compliment buzzed in my brain. Pretty. Why did a word like that matter more than being congratulated on school and track? I'd like to say it was because it was praise I wasn't used to hearing, but I know it was more than that. I was 15. There was just part of my brain that was wired to value male approval of my looks above all else. Blame it on society. All those glossy covers and MTV. Or just the centuries of patriarchy before me. After all, even Elizabeth Bennett was bruised when Darcy wouldn't ask her to dance because she was only "tolerable," not "handsome enough to tempt" him. Those lines were the world's truth. Being called pretty was the real reward. And I was a perfectionist.

- 6 -

For a few days after I'd told Doug Ryan to leave me alone, I'd lived in fear that there would be repercussions for my outburst, but it seemed my public declaration for him to leave me alone prompted him to do just that, which I guess wasn't so hard to do considering school was out and that's what he'd been doing for most of our shared existence anyway.

This was a good thing, I told myself, over and over again, whenever the flashbacks bubbled up, which was always. Logically speaking, never talking to him again was the right thing for me to want. Yes, he was good looking and popular, and his opinion mattered in our teenage world, but I knew he wasn't actually a good person. Still, my obsession was biological. Being ignored and avoided or maybe just forgotten, after being picked up and carried on the sand, after being followed into the ocean and flirted with in the waves, after whatever you wanted to call what happened on the beach—the startling nature of these events in succession created an endless battle of tug-of-war in my brain. I wanted to just forget him. I wanted to not remember so clearly everything about that night. There were so many awful details, the cum, the shirt I'd thrown in the dunes, the stupid shit I'd said. I'd been so drunk! Weren't drunk people supposed to forget things? Why was I cursed with such a clear memory? Of his tongue and his skin and my own stupid voice? Replaying these memories was a physical feeling. It was shame, shame, shame. But I had to pretend it was something else when I was with my friends.

Jenna saw Deb and Parker's IM romance as the window into the Jersey version of the *Sweet Valley High* dreamscape she'd been waiting for. Which was a great excuse for her to buy things on her parents' credit card. One of the last days of school, we went over to her sprawling mansion of a house and tried on a heap of clothes that'd just arrived from a Delia's catalog.

"Your turn," Deb said, tossing a micro mini skirt at me.

"I cannot wear that," I said. "I like long ones, remember?"

"Oh come on," Jenna said, "It's just us." She liked to pretend her room was the set to a show called *Who Wore it Best?*

"Fine," I said, consenting begrudgingly and slipping my legs through the micro skirt. Immediately, both of them started hyperventilating.

"Fold up the tank top!" Deb demanded. "Show the abs."

"The abs," I snorted.

"Don't be a prude," Jenna said.

"It's freezing in here. Your parents are like blasting the AC." Still, I obeyed because we were in a bedroom, all alone. Instagram did not exist. Everyone's internet was dial up. Cell phones didn't have cameras. The only eyes that could see me were Jenna's and Deb's, and my own, which warily examined my almost-naked body in the mirror. I put my hands on my hips and made my mirror face, a frowny expression of disapproval that Deb and my mother both separately scolded.

"There is no way I'd ever wear this anywhere," I declared. "I look like Julia Roberts in *Pretty Woman* before Richard Gere takes her shopping."

"In other words, you look like a prostitute," Deb said.

"Exactly. I can't move. When I walk you can see my butt cheeks." I demonstrated, pointing at my butt. It was true. There were my cheeks. Their appearance was a comic hit. I had "butt cleavage." We were all doubled over, gasping for air as we guffawed.

"I just can't wear stuff like that," I said as I put my loosely fitting clothes back on. "It's just not comfortable."

"For some reason, it is comfortable for me," Jenna said,

defensively. "It's stretchy. I don't have to suck in my gut like when I button and zip. I just pull it up."

"Suck in my gut," I repeated, making a face. "That's why I like drawstrings." I said this intending for it to sound as if I agreed with her. Though she liked stretchy clothes and I liked loose ones, we had a similar purpose. We wanted our clothes to feel like they fit, instead of feeling like we had to fit into them. But she didn't take it that way.

"Well, we can't all look perfect in everything we wear like you," Jenna said. "Some of us have to perform optical illusions." I was baffled. Jenna was far more attractive than me. We all knew this.

"Me?" I said.

"At least you don't have a muffin top," Jenna said.

"And you're basically destined for an Ivy or some fancy college," Deb said, chiming in.

"You're the one who is Ivy legacy," I told her. "Besides, what are you talking about? You don't care about that kind of stuff,"

"Yes I do," Deb said. "Why wouldn't I care? Just because I'm not ranked number one in the class doesn't mean I don't care about college."

I felt a fight brewing and was suddenly alarmed, but I was saved by the sound of a door creaking open on the internet. Our consciousness was swallowed by Scott, whom Jenna was now suddenly and conveniently in love with, signing onto AIM.

I walked home for dinner. The next day we were supposed to go to Wildwater Palace.

"Did you tell Deb to be ready by 8?" Mom said. "We want to get there right when it opens at 10. That way, we have time in case there's traffic."

I'd never even bothered to tell Deb about the trip. I cleared my throat. "Oops, I forgot to tell you. Deb can't come. She's busy helping her mom. Plus, she doesn't really like to go on the tall slides anyway, so it's just us. I didn't really feel like asking anyone else."

"Are you sure?" Mom said. "Is everything ok with you guys? Did you have a fight?" Mom could never conceal her feelings when she asked these types of questions. I could see that she was both concerned for my feelings and a little happy at the report. She thought Deb was spoiled and bossy. She was always trying to push me towards other, more ambitious girls like Diana Henley and Desiree Moss. And yes, I was friendly with those girls and they were nice and we got along great during group projects and all of that, but Deb and I were different. It was its own thing.

"Everything's fine, Mom. I think it'll be fun. Dad and I will go on all the rides and then we can go somewhere really good for dinner after."

"Sounds good to me," Dad said. "Can we go to Umberto's?"

"Yes!" Mom said. "Let's get the fried mushrooms."

And that was that. And I have to say, the day was much more tolerable. I wore the one-piece and the water shoes without a second thought. Dad and I went on the Tidal Wave, the tallest water slide in the Northeast, six times. I laughed and screamed and didn't give any gaggle of kids my age a second look. I ate a huge soft serve with a chocolate dip. And Dad and I talked about the stuff we liked to talk about best, how things worked.

"How do you think they built this slide?" I asked him. And he got a twinkle in his eye.

"It's incredible right?" he said. "This thing is a serious feat of engineering. Just think about the size of each panel of plastic..." and then he launched off on a thoughtful analysis about shipping, manufacturing, trade, and building permits.

I liked watching Dad talk about what he was interested in.

He made building water slides sound cool. His real job, making sure cans of soup were shipped all over the country, seemed less exciting. Perhaps he'd missed his calling. He certainly enjoyed going down the slides.

Dad was nearing 50, but he was still fit and pretty young looking. "Some people age out of this stuff," he said. "But I'm definitely going to be the oldest geezer on this thing one day." I believed him.

The mushrooms at Umberto's were as good as ever. We ate them on the deck and rehashed the craziest rides from the day. Then the entrees came. Dad and I got stuffed shells for dinner and shared a side of meatballs. Mom had a salad with broiled salmon. "One day, when you're not running a million miles a day, you'll have to change your diet if you want to keep your trim frame," she said to me. "All that cheese makes me feel bloated just looking at it."

"Not me!" Dad said.

"That's what you think," she said. "Until you fart in your sleep under the covers."

Mom had cracked a joke, and it was actually kind of funny. We all laughed. The temperature had gone down to a pleasant 70-something. The food tasted good. My teenage troubles and triumphs both seemed far off. I was just a girl with her parents eating at a restaurant, and I liked it that way. But the feeling, of course, was short lived.

Mom cleared her throat. "What's this thing I heard about from Mrs. Carey?" she said.

"What?" I asked.

"Someone drew a noose in your yearbook?"

They were both looking at me with concern. I sighed. I couldn't believe they'd let us have such a pleasant day while harboring this panic inside of them. A wave of annoyance blossomed from my stomach into my throat until it contorted my face into a scowl.

"Was it Deb?" Dad asked. "Is that why you didn't want to invite her?"

"No!" I yelled loudly, forgetting that I was in a restaurant. Other diners actually turned their heads. But honestly I didn't care.

"Who was it then?" Mom asked. "And what's it all about?"

"It's a joke," I said. "Don't worry about it. It's just something Derek Gladstone and my friends do back and forth to each other!"

"What's a joke?" Dad asked.

"Deb and Jenna pretend they're going to murder Derek and Derek's friends pretend they're going to murder me, so that we can secure the number one class rank. They pretend to be our henchmen."

Dad laughed, looking relieved. "That's actually pretty funny." Mom still looked concerned. "No it's not!" she said to him. Then she looked at me. "Threatening someone's life is serious."

"Look, none of us want to get in trouble," I said. "We're not going to do it anymore."

"Did you ever feel unsafe?" Mom said in her overly concerned voice.

"No!" I said loudly again, though this time not as loud as before. "It was funny. We all thought it was funny. I think Deb is the one who started it. I can't even remember. It's been going on all year."

My parents exchanged glances with one another. I wanted to flip the table over, to hiss at the look of worry on my mom's face.

"Ok..." she said. "I just feel like you've been acting a little strange lately, and I wanted to make sure this didn't have anything to do with it."

"Strange how?" I said defensively, searching her face for what she could possibly know about the last month of my life.

"Just..." she chose her words carefully, "quieter."

I wanted to cry, but I couldn't. Crying would have set off a serious alarm. We were not an emotional family. Nobody ever cried. We were even tempered and logical. We thought things out and worked hard and so we were rarely surprised. And besides, this conversation just let me know that she had no idea what was actually going on, which was good, because if she did, what would she say? What would she do? Ground me for life? And what problem would that solve? Why did she have to notice things about me anyway? Why couldn't she just live her own life and let me figure out mine in peace?

I took a deep breath, trying to smooth my tear ducts into submission. There was still a glob of cheese next to my back molar. I swallowed it down and took another breath. "Mom," I said. It was the only word I could muster and within it contained all of my frustration and grief. It was one syllable, and it lingered in the air like one of those white fluffy seed puffs that drift by in the summer, that kind you're supposed to capture, then release with a wish. If I could have grabbed the word and then let it go, I'd have wished that it would leave me the fuck alone, but I couldn't. So it just drifted there, incapable of being bent to anyone's will.

Time passed. Probably just a few seconds. I took a bite and chewed the stuffed shell, suddenly overly aware of how cheesy it was, and so freshly angry at my mom for robbing me even of that pleasure. There was only one way out of this. It was the same way, every time.

"You're right. I was acting weird because I knew Mrs. Carey was going to call you. And I knew that you were going to make a big deal of it. And it's not a big deal. So can we just drop it?"

There was a moment of stillness. I watched Mom consider her response and prepared for my rebuttal. But then she surprised me. She just leaned over and squeezed my shoulder. “I’m just glad you’re ok. Yes. Consider it dropped.”

I was relieved. But when the waitress came and cleared the plates and asked if we wanted to have dessert, we all said no. The conversation had taken the wind out of our happy, drifting, kite-of-a-day.

- 7 -

Summer settled over us all. At night, I sat on our back deck after the sun went down and attempted to see the stars. I knew this wasn't exactly what Celestino had in mind when she'd challenged us to stargaze, but I wasn't ready to commit to a larger adventure just yet. Tonley's streets were lined with streetlamps. And even though there was no nightlife on Main St., there was a 24-hour train station in the center of town, part of the commuter line to Philadelphia, which meant we were officially part of that glowing grid that was visible from space, while also blinding the earthbound in a reflective haze.

Dad came outside and sat with me for a while as I attempted to record what I saw of the night sky in my observation journal. I threw down my pencil after a few minutes, having written nothing.

"I see the moon," I said. "That's it."

"Well, what's that?" he asked, pointing up at the sky.

"I don't see anything," I said. "Where?"

"Right there," he said, "those three little dots."

"I see nothing."

"First look at the tree," he said. "Now go straight up and over a little towards the Biondi's yard."

I did see something. Barely. Three slightly lighter gray dots the size of pinholes surrounded by darker gray.

"Those are stars right?" Dad said.

He was right; they were. We contemplated them silently.

"Why does Mom always have to act like everything is the end of the world?" I said.

He didn't get to answer. Mom opened the sliding door to the back deck. She was in her pajamas. "See anything?" she asked.

"Dad discovered three stars. They are definitely part of a

constellation. But we don't know what."

"Where?" she asked. "I want to see too." We walked her through the process. "Ooh!" she said, "found it!"

We quietly thought a moment, perhaps searching for something to say about the stars, discovering we had nothing. I didn't even know what direction we were facing. It didn't seem like Dad or Mom did either. There was no need for celestial objects to serve as navigational guides. Just get on Route 70 either east or west and then you knew where you were based on green road signs and whatever fast food chain was on the corner. The old stories of the constellations had faded into the gray of our collective memory, replaced by the neon signs of our three lane roads and their fluorescent-lit houses full of waffles, pancakes, burgers, and chips.

"If we were in the middle of nowhere, nothing would look like this," I said. "We'd see way more. It's light pollution," I spoke these words with all the passionate authority of a person who'd sat through one brief lecture on the subject but had also been greatly moved.

"Light pollution?" Mom asked. I explained to her how all the streetlights and the high-rises and the lit-up signs and marquees on the roads impeded upon the darkness and made baby turtles walk the wrong way on stretches of beach after they'd hatched from their eggs, away from the ocean. How migrating birds grew disoriented and sometimes went off course. How some plants and nocturnal animals' cycles were disrupted. And how it even messed up the circadian rhythms of humans, and some doctors believed increased a person's likelihood of getting cancer. She wrinkled her nose and gave an exaggerated sigh. "Even light is bad? Is there anything that we do that is good?"

Dad laughed. I thought the answer to her question was no, which made me sad.

The back deck wasn't especially large. It fit a small table and four chairs. I had my feet resting on the fourth chair. Dad was sitting on the steps that led to the yard. Mom stretched her legs forward, so that her whole body was a straight line, like one side of a triangle.

I hated the rigidity of her posture. It seemed too symbolic of all the ways that I found her to be intolerable. I took a deep breath and released it slowly, careful not to sigh or alert anyone to my inner rage. I tried to keep my focus on the sky.

Celestino was right. The longer we looked, the more we saw. Muted white orbs through a purple polluted veil of night. I readjusted my eyes the way I sometimes readjusted my ears in a crowded restaurant, filtering out the din to focus on a conversation. No, the sky wasn't actually just a darkish purpley gray. There were some stars breaking through the reflective dome of our urban glow. But their light was the equivalent of a whisper in a basketball stadium. It was like hearing a song you liked on a staticky station and being incapable of getting a clear signal.

I started writing these ideas down, about the stadium and the whisper, and also a question about the stars. Were they closer to us? Is that why they were visible through the polluted haze? Or was it that they were hotter or bigger, which made them burn brighter? Even though I'd turned off the porch lights, it was still easy to see the page on the table with the lights from my neighbors' yards.

"Why do we all have to have so many lights on all the time?" I sighed, looking at my sad observation chart. "It makes doing homework impossible."

"It makes doing this homework impossible," Mom said, "But think of how much other homework you do with a lamp on."

"Most homework is useless busywork," I said.

"It makes a difference though," Mom said.

She didn't even understand what I was talking about.

I let a few minutes pass, hoping to create a silent buffer that put an end to the conversation about homework, and then said, "Could you ever see the stars out here? Like when you guys were my age?"

"Where I lived you could definitely see more," Dad said, but he was from Bucks County, the more farmy, Pennsylvania side of suburban Philadelphia. "You still can. Probably not as much as back then, but I can't say for sure. It's not like we were out there stargazing. Everyone was crowded around the TV fighting over which channel to watch."

"My dad knew all the constellations," Mom said. This was a rare mention. I'd never known my grandfather. He'd died in a drunk driving accident when my mom was twelve. He was the drunk one. He was alone in the car and it crashed into a tree. All I knew about him was that he'd never really recovered from the shock of fighting in World War II.

Mom never said anything about her childhood. I only knew the one story: that she'd been dirt poor and only managed to escape Nanny's house by getting a job at Macy's when she was 15, where she still worked today—many promotions later—as the Regional Sales and Store Marketing Manager of the Home Goods Department.

I'd known my grandfather died in a car accident—I'd asked why she didn't have a dad when I was a kid—but Dad was the one who eventually told me that he was drunk. I was in 7th grade and had to do a family tree for homework and was complaining about how Mom was always so weird about talking about her father and where he was from.

"He died," my dad had told me, "when she was your age. And the whole time before that, he wasn't happy. He stormed Normandy and was the only one out of his five best friends to survive. Or that's what Nanny told me at least. It sounds crazy, but sometimes people don't feel happy when they survive, they feel guilty. He never got over that guilt and it made it hard for him to be a father. Mom doesn't like to think about that."

Out on the deck, Mom spoke softly, like she was traveling into a part of her memory that required you to hush. "He grew up on a farm in Illinois and he hated living in the city, which is why he made Nanny move to New Jersey from Philadelphia, but even in Bronner he was always complaining you couldn't have any privacy. Tommy and Johnny used to say it was Mom's fault he was so depressed because she wouldn't leave Philly, and he wanted to go home to Illinois. Rose and I never said anything. We'd just pray with our rosaries if he was out too late and Nanny started to worry. But it's not like he was really doing anything wrong. He used to just drive his car down the White Horse Pike until you got out past all the towns into the farmland and then he'd pull his car onto the shoulder and lay across the hood."

The White Horse Pike was an old two lane road that connected Camden to Atlantic City. Nobody really drove on it that much anymore because of the traffic lights and the fact that it was way faster to take the Atlantic City Expressway. I wondered what that road was like back then, in the 60s when so much more of South Jersey was farmland, before the explosion of suburbs and strip malls. I knew that Walt Whitman once had a country house off of that road. Maybe the grandfather I never met was a bit of a poet.

"That's cool," I said.

"Sounds cool," Mom said, "but Nanny didn't like it. She was always looking out the window, saying, 'Where's your father, where's your father.'" She was quiet for a moment. "There was a VFW out there that he'd hang out in. We didn't have a phone back then, but sometimes Nanny would walk to the neighbors just to call and tell him to come home."

"You didn't have a phone?"

"It got turned off. Nanny said it was the phone or the lights."

"According to Emily," Dad said, "you chose wrong. Should've cut the lights. Then you could have seen the Milky Way."

Mom snorted out an unamused laugh. "Funny," she said. Mom did not find any part of her unglamorous upbringing funny. She was bitter about it. She felt screwed by the universe and determined to collect whatever it was she felt she deserved—anyone who worked for her at Macy's, or served her at a restaurant for that matter, could pick up on this vibe. She was a woman who frequently sent her food back. She did not permit you to let her down. I knew this first hand. But still, I loved her for who she was. She could be loving and kind and funny, too. You could see it sometimes, the joy inside her, fighting to be seen, the same as the stars.

I was drawing a crappy picture of our observations, sketching a compass in the corner, assuming I was facing west. Mom was staring into the memories in her head. "He would have loved the moon landing. I remember watching the astronauts on TV, thinking about him."

"Maybe he was there," I said, suddenly not feeling as mad at her as I'd been a couple moments before.

Mom smiled at me. "Maybe," she said. She gestured towards the sky "He's up there somewhere." She stood up and let out an exaggerated sigh. "Welp, that's enough stargazing for me. I'm going to bed."

"I'll go in with you," Dad said.

"I'll be in in a minute," I said. "I need to finish my notes."

"Just make sure to lock the back door," Dad said.

I listened to them shuffle through the kitchen until they disappeared into the front of the house and I was alone.

Sometimes I felt so obviously like their child, like I could connect the similarities between us the way stargazers saw pictures by drawing lines in the spaces between stars. Other times, I felt completely untethered, alone, a single star exploding into a void.

It was weird to think the only reason I was alive was because my grandfather survived an unthinkable circumstance during a global war. That all those other men had only ghost granddaughters. And here I was, alive.

A steward of this time period. This millennium. The year 2000, a number that only existed because it hovered around the birth of a single character, good old Jesus. But what did it all mean? Did I owe the world something by existing?

Was every little thing we did unfathomably important? Should we agonize over all of it, every perfectly tucked-in corner of the perfectly-made bed? Did it all add up to something better? Or was it all empty and meaningless?

Were there actually no choices at all? Because the truth was that life just happened to you, right? So how could you be in charge of the outcome of a story you didn't even start?

I felt an existential ache. A feeling of being tied to a wheel. Were we all a part of a constellation, or just single, burning bulbs?

I consoled myself with nihilism—though I didn't actually know there was a word for that feeling just yet.

Maybe one thing didn't become another. Maybe everything was just what it was. Shit happened. Then it passed.

It was only our need to explain what existed, to make use of our memories, that made us draw lines between things, to connect them—to make pictures in the stars.

- 8 -

Daylight pierced the blinds of my windows and brought with it its daily moment of panic as I shot up assuming I was late for school, before remembering that school was out, that it was summer, that I could miraculously just be still for a while, just lie in one spot, wiggle my limbs and breathe.

The day was a clean slate. Mom had threatened to make me get a job on the Macy's sales floor, but I had held her at bay by promising to memorize all 500 vocabulary words from the SAT list and dedicating 2 hours a day to math test prep. There would be timed practice exams every two weeks. If my scores weren't going up, she'd sign the working papers, and I'd be forced to stock blenders and place mats and attend one of those torturous test prep academies.

I thumped downstairs in my shorts and tank top and filled a bowl with cereal and milk and chewed at a leisurely pace, letting the milk fully saturate each cinnamon square until it squished under my teeth with a sugary burst. As I chewed, my eyes wandered across the kitchen, with its centerpiece of fake flowers and wallpaper border of green vines and purple bunches of grapes. "I live inside an upside-down eggplant," Dad sometimes protested, but you couldn't mess with a woman who had worked her way up from a salesclerk to the Regional Display Manager for the Home Department of Macy's. Frances Banks née Reilly was a champion of country cottage decor.

Mom had started working at Macy's in high school because after her dad died, Nanny could barely afford to buy her clothes. "Even when you let the hem down on Aunt Rose's old uniforms they still hit me above the knee," the story went. "The nuns made me kneel in front of the Virgin Mary every day before school and say an entire rosary for showing too much leg."

Finally, she decided she'd said the Hail Mary enough. She

had an idea. Or, the way she told it, the Virgin Mary spoke to her as she prayed and told her to get a job. She took the bus to The Cherry Hill Mall and applied at a few stores. Now, 30 years later, she drove her Audi between thirty-five malls in the tristate area, making sure every Home Department in every Macy's looked cozy enough to settle down in, so that after you decided to sit in one of the model living rooms for a few minutes to take a load off, you were scheming on how to take all the accoutrements that surrounded you home.

Mom was proud of her rise through the ranks but embarrassed that she'd never gone to college. "Who knows what I could be doing right now if I'd had the opportunities that you have," was what she was always saying to me. "The only difference between the people higher up on the corporate ladder and me is the fact that they went to business school."

"Why don't you just go to business school then?" I would respond.

"It's too late for me. I'm too old," was always her answer. But she was only 45. Maybe she was waiting for the Virgin Mary to intervene.

Because she'd built a career fiddling on showcase floors, Mom treated our home like her personal display. Dad and I were not just her family. We were living models inside her masterpiece. And if we acted in a way that went against her design—watch out. Forget the fact that it was impossible to live inside a perfect house without making it imperfect.

At that moment, chin dribbling milk as I lazily chewed, I was a living example of how her perfectly set kitchen table was not actually set for people to eat at because you weren't actually supposed to use any of the bowls, spoons, or cloth napkins on the table. They were for display only. But I'd gone and done it anyway.

She looked frantically at my dad. "We screwed up." She

gestured towards me with both hands, "Look at her. She's just going to sit like this. For months."

I felt my countenance shift, once again unable to enjoy a meal in her presence. I was just trying to eat breakfast! What was her problem?

Dad had my back. "Give the girl a rest, Frankie! What about that stack of test prep books in the living room? Isn't her job trying to get a 1600 on the SAT?"

At the same moment Dad invoked the test prep, I also announced defensively, "I have summer assignments. And don't forget that I'm training every day."

Saying "Frankie" was Dad's way of drawing attention to Mom's obvious lack of chill. To the world, Mom was Frances—she did not welcome any sort of nickname with "Frank" in it. But somehow, Dad got away with it. Maybe it was true love. I guess it had existed in some form since the moment he entered the Macy's men's department as a business student in search of suit pants for a job interview. Mom didn't know anything about men's suits. She was subbing for someone who'd called out sick. But Dad followed her around the whole floor and finally bought the pair she picked out for him. He even wore them the next time he went to the store looking for her, to tell her he'd got the job. When he asked someone, they told him she actually worked in the home department, so he had to pretend to want to buy some curtains to match a bed spread. Meanwhile, Dad can barely match a pair of socks.

Anyway, the point is, Dad knew how to talk Mom off a spaz ledge. When she was losing it—about a boss or coworker; about a weed that would not die in the garden; about her brother and the way he leeched off of her mother, or Aunt Rose or Uncle Neil; about me and my lack of desire to live up to my potential, or whatever else—only Dad's tone of voice could mollify her.

Mom didn't like to think she needed anyone. The proof of her independence was evident in her corporate climb. But still, even though she didn't technically need Dad's salary to clothe or feed herself, or maybe because of that very fact, he was her real partner. They'd already been married for 22 years. And the way he was looking at her now transformed her hysteria into a resigned sigh.

"Test prep and training," she said. They were words she could repeat to Rosalind Hickory's mom when she passed her house during her evening powerwalk. Rosalind was going to Brown for most of the summer and Middlebury before that. She'd considered sending me to these sorts of programs, but they were not free, and she was not totally on board with the idea of leaving her only child in a college dorm with strangers for weeks at a time. Ultimately, she'd decided against it, and then regretted it as soon as the deadlines passed, especially once she heard other moms talking about where their kids were going. But now Mom could just explain that Coach B had given me a fine-tuned summer training schedule, and since I was already number one in the class, the most important thing was to make sure I earned a 1600 on the SAT. Evoking the advice of Coach B and salt-and-peppering it with some test prep overrode the academic moms' college application grooming, where they strategically selected programs for their kids to be a part of in the hopes of having noteworthy experiences to humblebrag about in admissions essays. I didn't need to take courses in international affairs taught by poor graduate students. I was the golden goose. Mom didn't have to pay to take out a line of credit to send me to Brown for a summer program. I could run fast. That was something that money couldn't buy, so it was worth more.

Pressure aside, at least I truly liked to run. It felt good to let my body surrender itself to the drum of my sneakers against the pavement. I've heard singers say that they had to physically stop themselves from singing all day, that talking in a regular voice felt like being a dog on a leash. I could relate. And the fact that running was something I was good at—that it was something I could actually be celebrated and encouraged to do—was a relief to me.

"Remind me again what Burt wants you to do today?" Mom asked, referring to Coach B. She was rinsing a coffee cup and putting it in the dishwasher.

I ran upstairs and pulled the master schedule Coach had given Kelsey and me from the top drawer of my desk where I'd left it. I read from it as I reentered the kitchen.

"This week is just a strength and flexibility week. He said to go for relaxed runs but not more than two miles. He says to do yoga and have fun." I was only supposed to do one meet-up with Kelsey at the end of the week.

"Yoga?" she said.

"Maybe I can rent a yoga video at Absolute." Absolute was our video rental store downtown. We have ABSOLUTELY everything, they promised. I'd never taken out an exercise video before, but I'd studied their cases and laughed at the poofy-haired, skinny, spandex-wearing women advertising bodies that were "tight" or "solid" or "made of steel" alongside buzz-haired muscle men who looked like overgrown action figures. Usually, they were people I recognized from advertisements on television.

"I've always wanted to try yoga," Mom said, her calmer tone letting us know that she was done with her momentary outburst. "Maybe I'll do the video with you."

I laughed. Mom was famous for her enthusiasm for all the passing fads of video exercising. She was obsessed with being skinny. Somewhere in our alphabetized collection of VHS cassettes in the cabinet under our television was a copy of Richard Simmons's "Sweating to the Oldies," and Dad and I never let her forget it. If a

Temptations song came on the radio, my dad would pretend to be Simmons, doing squats while reaching his arms up to the sky. "Come on Frankie, you want to feel that burn!"

Dad couldn't resist the urge to tease her then. He whispered to me loud enough so that she could hear, "You know she's already thinking about a yoga outfit." I laughed.

"Ha, ha," Mom said. But we all knew it was true.

"20 bucks she comes back with outfits for all of us," I said.

"I'm not taking that bet," he said.

"Get your own yoga outfits, you hecklers! You guys are all going to be jealous of my yoga pants," she announced to us as she said goodbye. "I was actually just reading about them in *Lucky*." She turned and looked at me.

"I can't come back for lunch today. There's bread and turkey and cheese for sandwiches. Make sure you wipe the counter when you're done. Oh! And don't forget to put your cereal bowl in the dishwasher. "

"Yes, Mom."

"Bye sweetie, see you tonight," Dad said.

"Wait!" I said. "I need some money to rent the video." They looked at each other.

"I have cash," my dad said, extracting 10 bucks from his wallet. "Don't spend it all in one place."

"I won't. A rental is only 4 bucks!"

He laughed. And just like that they were both out the door. And I was alone, though it always took a minute or so to actually feel that way.

Our house was a place we all shared together, so my parents' auras easily lingered in the kitchen long after they left, their movements reverberating in my mind so strongly as I sat and finished my cereal it was almost as if I still saw and heard them. I soaked up this leftover energy like a dish towel collecting the milk splatters around my cereal bowl.

My parents weren't so bad. I mean, I guess they could have been worse. Yes, I was a teenager whom they still treated like a 12 year-old, but there was a part of me that enjoyed that consistency, especially in the morning when I still had on my pajamas and the reality of a new day hadn't actually sunk in yet. In those moments, there wasn't much difference between this day and one even ten years before, when my feet still dangled above the floor as I sat in the same spot and ate a similar breakfast. Sometimes it felt nice to forget that I had boobs and blood that burst out of me every 30-ish days.

But now it was just me, alone, living with the boobs in the woman's body, living with a heart that felt permanently slathered in Icy Hot, living with a brain cursed to broadcast shame on repeat every quiet moment of the day.

In my mind, I told myself that Doug had been genuinely interested in me. He'd asked me to go surfing with him, he'd invited me to the beach, and then even after what happened, he told me himself that he liked me. So why did he never talk to me again? I must have made a terrible mistake. What had I done wrong? What was wrong with me? Reviewing the footage in my mind led me down any number of avenues of self-loathing. I mean really, when it came to what was wrong with me, it was not actually a question of what, but where to start. It was a trap. Like cartoon quicksand.

There was only one way to cope. I had to leave the humiliation behind me in the dust. I put my bowl in the dishwasher, wiped the table, got dressed in running clothes, made my bed, put the ten dollar bill in the pocket of my shorts, and walked out my back door, locking it behind me and hiding my key under a pot along the deck so I didn't have to run with it in my hand.

The streets of Tonley passed in a familiar blur. My body was a well-oiled machine. The stress and pressure of my thoughts were released with every stride. My mind became comfortably blank, not in the dumb girl way I felt when I was with the older guys, but in a cumulative purr of thoughts that passed, like the breeze from a book when you fanned its pages.

When I looped back towards my house and knew I'd completed two and a quarter miles, I decided to slow to a walk and head to Deb's. Even though I had my issues with her because of everything that had been going down, I couldn't stop myself from doing what was familiar. It just made sense. Sometimes you just keep doing the same thing hoping that things get better.

Our backyards were actually kind of connected, even though they were like 10 acres apart. I could enter her house from mine by squeezing through a gap in the fence in my backyard along the shed, cutting through some tennis courts and a ball field, then walking along a woodsy path up a hill that opened to a soccer field which backed up to Deb's backyard.

Growing up, the Stevens' house was my nexus. It was everything I could dream of in one place: remote control cars, video games, a trampoline, pogo sticks and skateboard ramps and tons of blocks and building supplies, Barbie dream houses, My Little Ponies, baby dolls and carriages, a play kitchen, costumes, even a puppet theater. The combined forces of all these toys, plus the endlessly fascinating fact that she had older brothers, made her world way more interesting than my own. Barbies rode on skateboards that were "tour busses." Baby dolls were launched with slingshots across the backyard. We always had a blast.

Deb spent most of her life being bossed around by her brothers, which is why I guess she was bossy to me. If we were playing house, restaurant, or any other kind of make believe, she assigned the roles. I was who she told me to be. Mom did not like overhearing our play. "Why do you let her tell you what to do?" Mom would complain to me. "You know how to read already. She can't even identify all the letters in the alphabet." This difference held no weight in Deb's and my world. It still really didn't.

Maybe it bugged Mom because Mr. and Mrs. Stevens had both graduated from fancy colleges. Mr. Stevens had gone to Yale Law School. He'd been in the same class as Bill and Hillary Clinton. Now he ran his own law firm. Mrs. Stevens went to Bryn Mawr and worked part time for a bunch of organizations I could never keep straight. She'd grown up on a peach orchard near the shore. Her maiden name, Crecente, was literally on boxes of fruit in grocery stores all over the east coast, boxes that my mother's father used to drive around in a delivery truck as one of his many jobs before he died. Mr. Stevens could trace his ancestry to the Mayflower. In the historic little Quaker town where we lived, these details were important.

"They don't care if Deb does well in school," Mom said one time when we were arguing over why I had to stay up late working on an extra credit assignment when I knew Deb was home watching Christmas movies on TV. "She doesn't have to do well. She just has to be charming. She has an inheritance. You, I'm sorry, do not have that luxury, so don't let yourself be fooled by her life."

Still, that statement didn't really resonate fully until the summer between 4th and 5th grade when Deb's parents invited me on an overnight trip to New York City. Even though we lived just two hours away, I'd never been. My parents weren't big on going to cities. To them, cities were where robberies happened and people got shot. We vacationed at amusement parks or the Jersey shore. The idea of their daughter going to New York City terrified them. Mom didn't want me to go. "You're going to get homesick," she said, although she knew I'd be fine. I begged and pleaded and the Stevenses had to call the house and talk out the itinerary. I remember watching my dad talk to Mr. Stevens on the phone and seeing him pretend to know the names of the artists whose work was at the Guggenheim. I think the only reason my parents gave in on the trip was because they didn't want to look provincial. They'd scraped together everything they had and bought a house in Tonley so I could grow up in this world, so that I could appear more sophisticated, and in a way I guess they realized that the Stevens were sort of a model of what they hoped I'd be one day. So letting me go on that trip was a calculated risk. They wanted me to get some culture and they knew they couldn't really give it to me. I think they were nervous because they knew a trip like that might change me.

New York City is impossible to forget. The height of the buildings, the way the taxis look, the way city people walk the sidewalks with their faces set in the same determined way as South Jersey drivers on Route 70. It was the sort of trip that taught you more than just what you learned from the sites. Different families traveled differently. Since the Stevens' family had five people in it—and I made six—we had two hotel rooms. All the kids stayed in a two-room suite, and Mr. and Mrs. Stevens had a room of their own down the hall. Mr. Stevens gave Eric, Deb's oldest brother, his credit card. In the morning, the Stevens slept in, and we were allowed to travel down the elevator and to the diner at the corner all on our own. We could order whatever we wanted. I remember looking at the menu and knowing what my mother would make me get: oatmeal with honey, or scrambled eggs and an orange juice. I ordered chocolate chip pancakes and a Coke. Deb got French toast. I don't remember what the boys got to eat, but Eric ordered a cappuccino, which we all tried and agreed was gross. I was 9. Out the window of the restaurant, people walked their dogs towards Central Park. A disheveled man sat next to an overstuffed shopping cart covered with a blue tarp, an open shoebox full of change in front of him. Two kids walked together talking excitedly, toting instrument cases in their hands. Eric signed his dad's name across a credit card receipt. It was like he was Kevin in *Home Alone 2*.

Later that day we saw *Beauty and the Beast* on Broadway, and afterwards Deb and I linked arms and belted the lyrics to the songs like chorus girls as we walked through Central Park. Eric and Cody were horrified by us and kept quickening their pace so as to separate themselves from our hysteria. Normally, this would have made me stop—I valued Eric and Cody's approval—but I was possessed by a rush of silly joy. Deb and I were enjoying the harmony of our voices, the warm summer air, the seemingly endless expanse of park trails and New Yorkers who we thought of as an audience. I was daydreaming, imagining I lived in every apartment building that we could see towering around us from the outside of the park. I wondered what it would be like to have soccer practice here or go to birthday parties. I was lost in my own fantasy world, full of euphoria, and oblivious to the sibling war taking place between Deb and the boys.

Apparently, Eric and Cody's acting as if they were actual city kids who were appalled by us lame tourists struck a nerve in Deb. She'd stopped singing and her carefree smile darkened to a scowl. She yelled as loud as she could, "Everyone knows you don't live here. Everyone knows you don't know where you're going." Then she burst into tears. I was totally confused. It hadn't even occurred to me to feel uncool or rejected. Deb's parents had tried to smooth the whole thing over, but Deb pouted for hours that day, all through the park and our dinner. She was even mad at me for singing with her, as if I were the reason she'd acted like a nerd.

Though I guess her claim may have had some merit because the reason this memory came flashing back to me as I jogged up past the empty tennis court, where I stepped over a forgotten yellow ball that had lost its fuzz and a bit of its glow, was because I was humming the opening song of *Beauty and the Beast* to myself: "Little town / It's a quiet village / Every day / like the one before."

Maybe Tonley, I thought as I passed some kids and a mom setting up a little t-ball game at the baseball fields while on my way to my best friend's house—a girl I'd known forever— was a little bit like Belle's town. I thought of Cody at the church.

I climbed up the side of the sloped grassy hill along the soccer field and trudged across the Stevens yard, past the half moon of lounge chairs on the patio where Deb, Jenna, and I often gathered. Deb had left a magazine out overnight. A model smiled impishly in a little nightie from the cover. I picked it up to bring it inside but the pages felt soggy and warped from the morning dew. The wetness grossed me out, so I dropped it back on the lounger and walked up from the patio to the screened door of their covered porch, which led to a set of sliding doors that opened into their living room.

There was Mrs. Stevens, perched at the end of the couch with her coffee mug in hand, watching "Regis and Kathy Lee." She was wearing an oversized ruffled top and loose, drapey pants. "Mrs. Stevens always looks like she's wearing pajamas," my mother once said to me privately. It was true that she valued comfort. But what mom was really getting at was that Mrs. Stevens wasn't thin. She used half and half in her coffee. Ate hamburgers with fries. Had the audacity to put on a bathing suit at the beach and let her rolls happily fold over one another in her one piece, all which appalled my mother, the calorie counting queen. For Mom, it was a power thing. She didn't get to go to Bryn Mawr, but at least she was a size 2. But Mrs. Stevens seemed perfectly happy in her own skin as far as I could tell. To me, she looked how a mom was supposed to look. She just looked like a grown-up who wore clothes from the boring racks at the expensive stores and kept her hair shoulder length and slightly poofed.

Besides their olive complexions, she and Deb didn't really look alike in any specific way, but they did have certain mannerisms in common. For example, they both took unfathomably tiny sips of liquid from their cups, which Mrs. Stevens did right after saying hello.

"Debra's still sleeping," she told me. "You can wake her up!"

I took my time walking through the family room, dining room, and kitchen, then down the corridor towards the front door where the staircase was. The Stevens house was huge and airy with all kinds of fun fixtures to admire. It was built in the late 1800s, and I loved the feeling of my feet against the creaky stairs and the look of all the pictures in their antique frames—the one of Cody smiling with a missing tooth; the one with Deb holding a baby chick at her grandparents' farm, her hair still dirty blonde back then, before it turned a chocolaty brown.

Deb's room was the first door at the top of the stairs. I turned the old glass knob and pushed against the mound of clothes that prevented the door from opening all the way, squeezing through the crack. Her mess always struck me as a fire hazard. When I slept over, I always moved that heap to the side.

There she was in her bed, mouth open, still asleep, her breath coming through in wheezy snores. I sat on the edge of her mattress for a moment, laughing at the way her face looked when she slept, and then I threw myself across her legs crowing, "cockadoodledoo."

Eventually she opened one eye and looked at me. She wasn't at all surprised by my presence. "What time is it?" she groaned.

"I don't know. 10?" In fact it was 9:45. But who was really counting? "Want to walk downtown with me and get a donut? I need to rent a yoga video and my dad gave me ten bucks."

"Yoga video?"

"Coach B told me to just do little runs this week and focus on yoga and stretching."

"Yoga?" she said.

"Yoga," I repeated.

"I thought you were supposed to exercise with Kelsey Kramer."

"That starts next week."

She scratched her head. "Where do you want to get a donut?"

"McMillan's, obviously."

She nodded her head. I turned on the radio. I began reading the notes that people put in Deb's yearbook and she watched me from the bed.

"I wish Parker had signed it," she sighed.

"Oh wait!" I said, smiling. "Oh my god, you must have missed it. He did. Right here," I pointed at a page and cleared my throat. "My dearest Debra," I said in a breathy, romantic, old-timey voice, "I thank the heavens that we found each other on the beach—"

"No," Deb said.

I giggled. "Oops, I read it wrong. It actually says, 'Let's meet tonight on AIM to talk about our favorite episodes of *Seinfeld.*'"

She threw a pillow at me and I tossed it onto the pile of clothes on the floor and then rested against them. Then I tried a different voice, echoing this random Patrick Dempsey movie called *Happy Together* we'd been temporarily obsessed with a year or two before, where these two acting students keep looking into one another's eyes and practicing the same lines. The one says, "I want to be loved by you," and the other says soulfully, "I want you to be loved by me." I tried my best to imitate Parker as I repeated those lines.

"Ha," Deb said.

Now I threw a pillow at her. "Knew it!"

Deb brushed her teeth and then tried on a million outfits and pulled out her hair and brushed it, only to attempt to replicate the look she had when first waking up. For some reason, I enjoyed watching her sift through her wardrobe and put on makeup. I often did the same thing at home with my mother. They both loved scrutinizing themselves in front of the mirror and starving themselves. And they both had ridiculous mirror faces. My mom's was a little smile, and Deb's was a pouty, model's frown.

She frowned in the mirror for a minute straight as she examined the light yellow sundress with white and rose colored flowers she finally decided on. Then she slipped her feet into a pair of pink jellies and pursed her lips in front of the mirror.

"Ok," she said.

When we went downstairs, her mom was talking on the phone.

"We're going downtown," she said. Her mom nodded. "Can I have some money?" Her mom fished out a 20 and handed it to Deb. Deb slipped it in her bra and then blew her mom a kiss. Her mom mimed shock and then continued with her conversation.

"If Jenna calls, tell her I'll be back in like an hour," she whispered. Her mother nodded.

As we exited through the front door, I noticed there was a moving truck out front of the tiny, old house down the street where the old lady had used to live. "The toolshed" as Jenna had called it.

"Someone finally bought that place?" I asked, shocked.

"I know," Deb said. "Can you believe it? I wonder who they are."

I watched two movers negotiate an old, olive green, crazy-patterned couch down from the truck.

"Oh my god, that thing is hideous," Deb whispered.

I laughed.

We zigzagged down the wide, quiet sidewalks past historic, well-groomed homes, dodging sprinklers and bees that came too close as we made our way towards Main Street. On one end of the commercial strip there was a train station with a commuter line to Philadelphia, and on the other end there was the towering structure of our high school, newly empty thanks to summer.

The town was named for a Quaker family who were among the original white settlers in the area in the late 1600s. Half the town's shops and schools were named after them, the other half were named after George Washington because he'd apparently stayed in an old tavern-turned-museum on Main Street one night pre-Revolution. You could feel the history in this town. It was in the Georgian architecture. I liked that the trees were hundreds of years old and that some of the original streets were still cobblestoned and that on Main Street there were still hitching posts where people used to tie their horses.

Sometimes, I liked to imagine myself as a girl in a bonnet shitting in an outhouse, swatting at flies. Or the Disney version at least. It seemed so exotic, that a life like that had happened in this exact same place.

Ever since we were in fourth grade and our parents let us wander further than a few blocks down the street, all the kids in town would find their way to Main Street, a few crumpled dollars in their pockets. Usually this meant we'd go to the ice cream shop or the bakery or maybe the diner to eat some French fries. These places were where our crushes were born, where kids shaded off into alleys to kiss or smoke or fight, though actual fist fights happened very rarely. Tonley kids didn't really throw punches. They humiliated one another with cruel words while others watched or they just stole the other person's stuff. One time when I was probably 7, after an exchange of words by the gazebo, we'd watched Johnny Sherwin steal Eric Stevens' bike. The rest of the summer had been dedicated to somehow finding justice. I have no idea what Eric did to get his bike back, I just know that one time that summer when we were at the community pool and Johnny was there, I became possessed by my loyalty for Eric and picked up Johnny's towel and dropped it into the water when he wasn't looking. Now Johnny Sherwin was out of college like Eric. I'd seen him sitting at the bar drinking a beer last time I'd been at Connoley's for nachos with my dad. How was he a man that could order a drink? It was strange to me how far gone those days felt.

The streets were quiet. We both got a donut at the bakery. Mine was chocolate frosted. Deb's had rainbow sprinkles. We sat on the bench outside and watched the cars pass and the occasional person walk by with their baby or dog or briefcase.

"Parker called me last night," Deb said.

"What?!" I squealed. "You mean your relationship left the realm of the Instant Messenger screen?! And you're just telling me this now? We've been together for hours!"

"I know," she said. "I was worried my mom would hear me."

"Your house is huge!" I said. "Besides, why would she care?"

"You never know," she said. "She's crazy about Cody now that he has a girlfriend. She seems chill until she has a reason to decide not to be."

"That's safe," I said. Still, I felt alarmed by the fact that she'd waited so long to tell me. It almost seemed like she wasn't going to tell me at all, but then she ran out of things to say and so it popped out of her mouth.

"What did you guys talk about?"

She smiled. "Same old thing. Baseball. Phils beat the Devil Rays 7-0. There was a grand slam. He was there."

"Were you watching?"

"No. I was about to go to sleep, but I told him that my dad's office has box seats and that he should let me know next time he was going to a game, so that I could go too and we could meet up together."

"What did he say?"

"He said he was going in like a week or two. It's on a Friday. They're doing fireworks every Friday home game this season. Want to come?"

"Totally!"

"Cool! Jenna's going to come too."

Jenna. So she'd already told her. Which meant she'd called her after she'd hung up with Parker, and that it was like midnight or something, and Jenna had answered, and they'd had a whole chat about who-knows-what-else. Probably, they didn't even think to invite me at first. Doug will be there and that'd be weird, I could hear Jenna saying. If I hadn't shown up at Deb's house that morning, she might have never even told me. I took a deep breath and tried not to sound jealous.

"Awesome!" I said. "Hopefully Scott will be there too, for her."

"He will be. Parker said."

"Well, I don't have to go," I said, "If it's going to be like a double date or something."

"No! I think there will be more people," Deb said, with some uncertainty in her voice. More people meaning Doug, I wanted to ask, but for some reason felt like I couldn't. "Besides, you should totally come either way."

"I'll ask my parents," I said. There was a strange energy

rippling through the air. I wasn't sure I even wanted to go at this point.

I'd finished all of my donut and was licking the chocolate frosting from my fingers. Deb, meanwhile, had taken maybe two bites of hers. She stuck her finger in the icing and licked a bit of the rainbow sprinkles from her polished purple nail.

"I'm full," she said, standing up to deposit the donut in the trash can.

"Don't throw it out!" I said. "I'll eat it." I ripped a chunk off and shoved it in my mouth. She made a face at me.

"You are totally going to weigh a million pounds one day."

I flexed my arm to show her my muscles. "It will be a million pounds of muscle," I joked.

She frowned. "A million pounds of anything is a bad idea."

I was offended.

We ambled along, window shopping until we arrived at the front door of Absolute Video.

"Time to find your VHS guru," Deb said.

"VHS? This isn't 1993. I'm getting myself a DVD."

Deb attempted to whistle but failed. "You're fancy."

"Two donuts and a yoga DVD, a morning workout with Emily Banks," I said.

Deb laughed. "Patent that shit."

"Now we're going into bear claw pose," I said, pushing open the door. The store was in an old house and even on the front step, you could smell its mustiness. Deb wrinkled her nose. "It's so nice outside," she said. "You go and I'll wait here." She bent her leg and rested her right foot against the brick wall behind her, posing for the pedestrians and car traffic that went by.

"Suit yourself," I said, pushing the heavy door further so it jingled as I stepped up through the threshold. Then I did what I always did when I entered that store: sneezed. Maybe it was the AC units. Maybe their filters needed to be cleaned. Or perhaps there was just a layer of dust in that place that was never, ever cleaned. It had a smell to it, like an old bookstore, even though there were no paperbacks lining the aisles. Only VHS cassettes and DVDs.

As far as I could tell, I was the only customer. Maybe the place had just opened. Was it opened? The door had been unlocked. It was kind of dark inside. Were the lights on? I looked up and saw that they were. It was just the brightness from outside that made me feel slightly blinded by this windowless cave. I tried to remember if I'd ever been in a movie store before like 5 or 6. Noon didn't really seem like a prime time to rent a movie. In fact, I didn't even see anyone working behind the counter in the back. There was slow, creepy, classical music playing from the surround sound speakers that were hung along the ceiling in the corners of the room. What had I walked into? The set of a horror film? Was this some weird love scene? It was hard to tell. Usually, a movie was playing on the screen in the back, but the TV was blank. The notes on the piano felt too calm. I was definitely in a murder scene.

Maybe I was seeking a sense of safety when I went towards the children's section—I don't know—but somehow I ended up standing in front of the Disney films and there she was, Belle, my old friend from *Beauty and the Beast*. I picked up the case and looked at the picture on the cover, a girl in a golden dress with her hair swept back, staring lovingly into the eyes of a buffalo-man while surrounded by happy cutlery and smiling knickknacks.

"Stockholm syndrome," a voice said in my ear.

I screamed, terrified.

I turned and there was Jake Freelander, my old biology neighbor, the summer packet thief, smiling at me, pleasantly surprised with himself for delivering the scare.

"How the hell did you do that? I didn't even hear you!" I said, my eyes still roving in search of an explanation for my fright. Seeing him out of context confused me. "What the hell are you even doing here?" I asked.

He pulled at his Absolute Video t-shirt as if it would explain itself, but I guess he could tell from my expression that I needed further explanation. "I work here," he said.

"Here?!" I said, confused.

"Yeah. I started last week. It's the easiest money I've ever made. 11:30 to 5:30. Exactly the hours when like no one ever rents anything and maybe ten people return things. I'm allowed and encouraged to watch movies on the job. And I get paid eight bucks an hour."

"How many days a week?"

"Five."

I did that math. "That's good money!"

"I know!" he said. "I just lucked into it. I went through a Hitchcock phase last year and Mr. Magill, the owner, was here one night when I was returning one and taking out another. We started talking about cinematography and he recommended Fellini and then he offered me a summer job. Win."

"Fellini?"

"The greatest filmmaker of all time? Or do you consider that to be Walt Disney?"

I wrinkled my nose at this assumption, perhaps a little embarrassed by its truth. "I didn't know you liked old movies," I said, amazed that he used the word "cinematography."

"Banks," Jake said to me. "There's a lot about me that you don't know. I also like Hawaiian pizza."

"No," I said, horrified.

"Kidding," he assured me.

Then he looked at me earnestly, picked up the *Aladdin* case, looped around the shelf and did a dramatic leap across the aisle in front of me. "I could show you the world," he sang in a silly voice.

"Oh my god," I said. "No!" I tried to run into a different aisle.

He was clearly amused by his own performance. He met me on the other side, still singing the lyrics, "Tell me princess now, when did you last let your heart decide." He jumped on a little stool with wheels on it, trying to use it as a sort of skateboard, but then slipped so that he almost wiped out, catching himself at the last minute.

I covered my mouth as I laughed at the close call. "Be careful!" I said.

He stood up straight, then gave me a thoughtful glance. I thought he was going to laugh about his near wipeout, but then he continued singing. "I could open your eyes, take you wonder by wonder, over sideways and under on a magic carpet ride."

I sat down on the floor. "Stop," I pleaded, covering my eyes. "You're killing me."

I finally understood, years later, the magnitude of my nerdiness when belting the lyrics of *Beauty and the Beast* around Central Park. I kept my hands on my face but peeked at him through a crack in my fingers. He stopped and then spoke to an invisible audience, shaking his head as he returned the film to its place on the shelf. "So she doesn't like the *Aladdin* spoof."

I kept my hands over my face. "Not only does she hate the *Aladdin* spoof, she is also mortified and slightly concerned you might murder her because of this music."

"This?!" he demanded. "Don't you know what this is?"

"The soundtrack to *Silence of the Lambs*?"

"It's *Cosmos*!"

"*Cosmos*?"

"Banks, science star, future Yale graduate or whatever what's-her-face calls you, how in god's name are you going to blow Celestino's mind if you don't even know who Carl Sagan is?" He took my shoulders and steered me towards the documentaries. There was a ten disc collection of the entire Cosmos series that had been recently released. "I'm watching Season 1." According to the cover, the series aired in 1980, but everything about it had a 70s vibe. I picked up the DVD and inspected this Carl Sagan. His biography claimed he was "the author of *Contact*, a famed and celebrated astronomer, astrophysicist, cosmologist, and researcher of extraterrestrial life." He died in 1996. The picture on the back of the case was a still frame from the series. He had a shaggy swoop to his hair that grew down his neck and hit the top of his turtleneck. It was a lot like Jake's hair, actually, except that Jake had a little more curl and less of a receding hairline.

"Have you started stargazing?" I asked him.

"You mean keeping that journal or whatever?" he asked. "No."

"Do you still have that sheet?"

"You are so obsessed with that thing." He said. "I don't know. Probably."

Just then, the door tinkled. Another customer. It was Deb. I'd almost forgotten her. Immediately, like me, she sneezed.

"Bless you!" I said.

"What's taking you so long," she demanded. "I want to go home and eat lunch and then maybe get my mom to take us somewhere. Jenna was supposed to hang." She didn't even say hi to Jake. She just went to the new release wall and started picking up videos. There was one with some bowling pins and the dad from *Roseanne* holding a gun in the air. It was called *The Big Lebowski*. "My brothers keep telling me to see this movie," she said to me.

"Your brothers have good taste," Jake said. She ignored him. He looked at me and shrugged then went back to the desk in the back with the register, putting on a professional voice. "Let me know if I can assist you with anything," he said. We exchanged some silly eye contact. I could not suppress my smile.

"What are you laughing at?" Deb said.

"Nothing," I answered, noticing my smile fade.

The vibe had changed. It was time to go. I walked to the fitness section and spent about 30 seconds searching for a yoga video. There were only two. One had a long-haired Asian man standing on one leg in front of a tree. The other had a poofy-haired white woman in spandex promising to strengthen from the inside with power yoga. I chose the guy in front of the tree. The guy just looked more legit and serious. Perhaps he was the Fellini of yoga.

I was disappointed that Jake didn't even comment on my selection. I'm not sure he even realized what it was. He just looked my family's name up in the library card catalog-like organizer the store used, made note of my selection, took my four bucks, and told me when it was due.

"Have fun watching *Cosmos*," I said, as we turned to go.

"It's a personal voyage," he said back to me.

"What?" I asked.

"Never mind." he said.

I gave him one last smile and pushed the door open, making the little bells tinkle again. I wondered if Jake enjoyed that sound, if he welcomed the signal of a new arrival from the outside world the way Jodi Foster listened on her headphones for a ping in the static in the movie *Contact*. Jake probably didn't feel that way about the door, I decided. It was probably annoying to hear it. It meant you had to stop watching your movie and get up.

We entered back into the summer air. The sun was blinding.

I had to squint my eyes. "I think that kid's a vampire," Deb said. "It's so dark in there!"

I thought of what Ms. Celestino had said last week. That the sun, even though it allowed us to see what was directly in front of us, hid so much that lay beyond.

"I'm going to make my mom take me for a pedicure," Deb said. "Want to go? 100% Jenna's in."

"Sure, why not?" I said. What else was there to do? Except yoga later, of course, and memorizing at least 10 words from the SAT list and using them in a sentence. And 15 practice questions from the math section of the SAT book. And some reading comprehension questions. And searching the *TV Guide* to see if there were ever any reruns on of *Cosmos* or films by Fellini. "I just have to be back by like four-ish."

"Yay!" Deb said.

We linked arms like the little girls singing Disney songs in Central Park we once were, and together we made our way back through the sleepy streets of Tonley to her big and perfect Victorian house.

- 9 -

"Did you get your yoga video?" Mom asked. She was wiping her hands dry with a dish towel. The rice was ready, and the vegetables had been sauteed. Dad was carrying our skinless, marinated breasts of chicken out to the grill on the deck.

"That's going to take at least 20 minutes," she said. "Let's try it."

Mom was already dressed for yoga. The first thing she did when she got home from work was put on a cute-looking pair of sweatpants or spandex and a t-shirt for her after dinner walk. She liked to do chores and exercise in the evening. These were her "activity outfits." With Mom, everything was an outfit.

I threw the book I was reading onto the carpet and placed the DVD into its circular bed, then pushed the insert button and watched the player swallow it up. Then I got out the remote control and switched the input to the DVD player. We arranged ourselves on the carpet, an arm's length apart.

A brief FBI warning, threatening us with jail time or a hefty fine for attempting to reproduce this recording flashed onto the screen, then a tranquil scene emerged. The man in the center of the shot was on a mountain top. Behind him were two other people, a woman and a man arranged on either side. They were all sitting cross legged on their yoga mats. Trees and bramble were scattered around them. Below, you could see the sweeping expanse of a lake. There was the sound of a flute playing slow notes. The menu prompted you to select to either watch the introduction or to skip straight to the workout.

"Let's watch the introduction," I said.

"Ok," said Mom, sitting cross legged next to me. I pushed the button. The flute music began anew. The camera panned across the scenery and settled on the instructor's face. He looked calm. His long hair was pulled back into a low ponytail.

"Welcome," he said in a soft, soothing voice. "Today, we are going to put our never-ending to-do list to the side and occupy our bodies. We are going to feel our breath and how it connects us to the living ecosystem of the planet. Inside every person is a beating heart, and mind, and lungs, and blood that flows in a circle bringing us the oxygen we need to sustain life, connecting us to the living world outside of our bodies."

Mom groaned at the screen. "We only have 20 minutes till dinner. Let's skip this and go straight to the workout."

I obliged. I went back to the menu and selected the first workout. 60 minute Vinyasa.

"Vinyasa," the man said. We were off, bending over and then reaching up, and then hopping back into a backwards push-up and then pushing our arms straight and sticking our butts in the air. We weren't quitters, so we followed the man's directions to the best of our ability, our thighs wobbling and trembling as we settled into a series of lunges.

"This is hard," my mom said through clenched teeth. Her face was getting red and sweaty.

"Remember to breathe," said the man. We both audibly replied with an extra loud breath.

Dad opened the back door with a plate of chicken in his hand. That was the only signal Mom needed. She took her lunge a little deeper and grasped her hand around the remote, which was resting on the couch, and then hit stop, standing up tall and groaning out a stretch.

"Wooo!" she yelped. "Let's try again tomorrow. I'm hungry."

I pulled myself out of the pose, stretched my leg a little and joined my parents at the table, making sure to chug my glass of water while standing up so that I could refill it before I sat.

"I think I like step aerobics better," Mom said. "It feels more like dancing."

"I thought that was cool," I said. Not cool enough to delay dinner though.

After we'd cleaned up, loaded the dishwasher and set it to run, Mom went for her evening walk. This was her ritual. Every night, once all the chores were taken care of, whatever the season, she did a loop of about two miles, walking at a perfectly calculated speed, one she was certain burned calories and sustained an elevated heart rate but was slow enough so that she could scrutinize the neighbors' gardens. She was famous for taking note of every plant that thrived, and commenting excessively on every dry patch of grass, unsightly weed, or any planting that didn't meet her preferred aesthetic. Nothing bothered her more than a property that was not kept up. Tonley had laws that required your house to be painted a certain palette of colors, your fence to be made of only wrought iron or certain cuts of wood, and for your grass to not exceed a certain length. Mom had measured where that length fell on her calf, about midway up, and made sure to wade through the lawns of those who were known to let their yards go. "It affects everyone's property value," she'd always say before making an "anonymous" complaint to Borough Hall.

We were used to hearing her reports when she returned from her loop, though I never really found the content of them all that interesting.

I was sitting on the floor of the family room with a Sharpie, a dictionary, and a stack of index cards, choosing words at random from the printed-out SAT guide:

Despot (noun): dictator. Sentence: "Mom is a total despot when it comes to dinner. Fried food is always forbidden. Grouping:

politics. I left a note for myself: "Despots are actually evil leaders. (Was Hitler a despot?)"

Recalcitrant (adjective): stubborn. Sentence: "Deb was recalcitrant when it came to admitting that nail polish colors besides pink were cool."

I was admiring my own baby blue toe nails which I'd had done at the salon when Mom walked over to me. I looked up.

"Did you hear what I just said?" she asked. "That little house on Warren finally sold!"

She was talking about the tool shed on Deb's block.

"Oh yeah!" I said. "I saw a moving truck there. And an ugly couch."

A new family had moved in, Mom told us. A mother and daughter. And the mother had randomly been in Mom's high school class.

This was big news to Mom. It had been bothering her that the tiny house had taken so long to sell. She'd always been bothered by its existence. I'd had to listen to my parents debate about it countless times.

"Why doesn't someone just knock it down and build a bigger house?" Mom would complain. "No one wants something that little. Who can fit in a house like that? Where are the developers?"

"The lot is tiny," my dad would explain. "It's too small for a big house. A big house would take up the whole lot. Plus, you'd have to apply for a bunch of variances and the town might not approve."

But my mother wasn't one to bow to another's perspective once she'd settled into her own. "So what?" she'd say back. "Who needs a yard when it connects to a park! And besides, it's in the town's best interest to have a bigger, nicer house on the lot that will attract a wealthier family. It keeps the property values up."

Her indignation regarding the size and quality of the home must have come back to haunt her when she actually knew the person who moved in, though she didn't exactly admit this. I can only imagine how surprised my mother's face looked when she recognized Ceil, Cecilia Caputo, star of every school musical and love interest of every single one of her brothers and pretty much every other boy under 20 in Bronner when they were young. Suddenly that world Mom considered infinitely far, though it was really only 15 miles down the road, was right in front of her, calling her name from the yard.

Ceil, of course, hadn't moved straight to Tonley from Bronner—only Frances Banks could pull that off. Ceil—that's what she went by now, not Cici, she explained to my mother—had spent the last 20 years of her life in New York City, where she was first a dancer and then a choreographer and a long string of other things before she became a massage therapist and acupuncturist. Her daughter, Maeve, was four. And she was black. Mom was shocked by both of these facts.

"Four! Can you believe that? She had a baby at 41!"

I couldn't. It's not like I considered Mom to be old, but she seemed well beyond the childbearing years because, well, she was my mom, and I was a teenager.

Mom had me when she was 30, which to her was old, though Mrs. Stevens, Deb's mom, was older by two years. Mom had told me once it was hard for her to get pregnant and that I was a miracle she'd been waiting for all her life. I didn't know it at the time, but she'd had something like six miscarriages before me. She and my dad had tried to have a baby since they'd gotten married when she was 23 and he was 26.

"I prayed and prayed and prayed for you. You can see the worn spots on the rosary," she liked to tell me.

As for Maeve's blackness, Mom didn't quite know how to say it. It was like she was afraid to say the word out loud. Instead, she said, "Maeve is really pretty. She reminds me of the best friend from *Clueless*."

"You mean she's black?" I asked.

"Emily," mom said, as if I had spoken a bad word. "I didn't ask about the dad, but it's clear he isn't moving in. And I didn't see a ring."

"Anyway," Mom continued on her Ceil report, "She's still settling in and has to figure out how to fit her stuff into that terrible tiny house and set up work at this acupuncture and massage studio. Can you believe she sticks needles into people for a living?" Mom paused here to shudder. "I could never do that. Who does that? Why?"

I didn't provide an answer, not that she was expecting one.

"She told me Maeve is going to start in a preschool full time in September, but in the meantime, she needs someone to babysit three days a week, maybe more."

That was the point in the conversation where my mother apparently volunteered me for the position. "She said she'd pay you $150-200 dollars a week, depending on how many hours you agree to! That's a lot of money. I don't know how she can afford to give a high school kid that much, but you could use something to do." One look at my mom's face told me the decision had already been made, and that her stress over my summer stasis was finally put to rest. "We're meeting them tomorrow around the same time," she said. I could have argued, but I didn't. Honestly, babysitting didn't seem so bad. It meant less pedicures with Deb, but since she was so recalcitrant when it came to color selection, I could live with that. Besides, Ceil's house happened to be on the same block as Deb's, so I'd likely be seeing her anyway.

Plus, I was intrigued by the fact that Ceil had known Mom in high school. I'd never once met any of mom's childhood friends. The fact that she had ever been in high school seemed impossible. She wasn't one who displayed photographs of herself as a girl. It was as if she'd arrived on Earth as her present self, a woman with a constant agenda, in perpetual motion. Even her exercise outfit seemed like a business suit.

The next night, as she led me to Ceil's house along the sidewalks instead of the back way through the interlocking yards and the park, she gave me a quick summary of Ceil, from her perspective at least.

"Ceil just never had anyone to look out for her. Crazy as my life was, I had all my brothers and Nanny giving me heaps of work, so I just didn't have as much freedom. Her mom died when she was really young, like five, and her dad left before that, he lived in New York, so she was adopted by her great aunts, these two old maid Catholics who were like in their late 50s or 60s. They spoiled her rotten and loved her to pieces, but they were just too old to keep up with her by the time she was in high school, which is when things really went off track for her."

"Old maids?" I said, censuring her with my tone.

"You know, they couldn't find husbands, they never got married, so they had to live alone."

"What if they didn't want to find a man and get married?"

"Who doesn't want to get married?" Mom asked.

I was careful not to roll my eyes. "So...Ceil has a daughter but she isn't married. Does that make her an old maid?"

"Who are you calling old?" Mom said.

I laughed. "Not you."

"I don't know if you can be an old maid and also a mother.

All I know is that Ceil got herself into trouble our junior year and ended up running away and I never saw her again until I ran into her yesterday. I don't think she even graduated. Maybe she has her GED or something? Sounds like she went to college, so she must have finished one way or another. Anyway, she's not a bad person or anything. I can see that she's trying to get back on track."

"What? I'm babysitting for a high school runaway?!" This added a layer of excitement to the job.

"Hush," Mom said. "We'll talk about it later. There she is, on the step."

From afar, Cecelia Caputo almost looked like she was still in high school. She had a youthfulness to her posture, a suppleness to the way she lounged across the tiny stoop of the porch with a messy bun and a pair of black Converse All Stars and watched her daughter play in the driveway, like she was ready to spring into action at any moment if she had to, which she did as soon as she saw us approaching.

"Hello," she called in a sing-songy voice, walking towards us. Her face was pretty. She had large dark eyes and a wide smile. Both were lined with tiny wrinkles as you got closer but did nothing to detract from her allure. She wore no make-up. It made her look both younger and older than my mom. I felt disoriented by her vibe. It wasn't suburban. I didn't know grown women could dress and emanate the youthfulness of high school. I took her hand and said hello, then looked back at my mom, unsure.

"Ceil," Mom said. She pronounced the word slowly, like she was speaking the name of the animal—seal—and not comprehending how the woman standing in front of her was one. Ceil pounced on my mother with a loving hug, something my mother wouldn't usually even share with her own relatives, and I was surprised by the way she folded into it. The laugh that came from

Mom was full of affection. I found this sincerity alarming. It was strange to see her not putting on a show. "I keep wanting to call you Cici," she said.

"If it makes you feel better, do it," Ceil said. "Doris does."

Mom smiled. "Doris," she repeated, smiling, her eyes glazed in that way where you could tell she was looking into her own brain. Then she snapped out of it and grabbed my elbow, her usual stiff and well-mannered self intact again. "This is Emily," she declared, her voice laced with the firm, quiet pride she had for everything she considered her own. It was a simple sentence—three words—but I knew what it meant. This, do you see this? This girl. This girl with a 4.0 GPA who holds the state record for cross country. Do you see what I've made? I've made an Emily.

Ceil looked straight in my eyes and gave me an open smile. She also managed to acknowledge my mom's bragging at the same time by saying, "Your mom was telling me so much about you, I feel like we've already met!"

I gave a humble smirk. "I can imagine," I said, letting my eyes stray to the bags of potting soil stacked up by the front porch.

"She doesn't like it when I talk about her," Mom said.

"Me neither," said the little girl from the driveway, who was standing on the seat of a Strawberry Shortcake big wheel, attempting to balance on the seat and surf the wiggly waves of the wobbling front wheel as the bike slowly drifted down the drive. She succeeded for a second and then the bike flew out from under her and she crashed down on her butt.

"Oww," she screeched.

"I told you not to do that," Ceil said in a firm, pitiless voice. It added a dimension to the open, kind vibe I'd initially gotten from her. Like my mom, when it came to her daughter, she didn't take any shit. Maybe it was a Bronner thing. "Don't cry like that! You did this to yourself, just brush it off."

The girl gave another wail before she quieted down and stood up gingerly, brushing off the back of her shorts and assessing herself for damage. Mom was right, she was ridiculously cute. She put her hands on her hips and said, "No," defiantly to her mother, "you told me not to stand backwards on it."

Ceil shrugged. "Backwards, forwards, standing is a bad idea. Are you ok?"

Maeve nodded.

"Good," Ceil said, walking to her, wiping the tears from her cheek and then giving her a big hug. Maeve laughed. Then Ceil turned to me and smiled. "This," she said, squeezing Maeve's shoulders lovingly, "is the daredevil, princess, superhero, Maeve."

Maeve's eyes were sparkly and intelligent. She studied me carefully and said nothing.

I decided to make the first move.

"Hey," I said, giving her a little, uncertain wave, feeling as if I was applying for a job and she was my new potential boss. Apparently, that was all that the interview required. I was hired. "Hi!" she said back, walking up to me and putting her tiny hand around my arm. Then she pulled me, with impressive strength, towards the little shed/garage attached to the house, which seemed just barely big enough for a car. In any case, there was no room for a car at the moment because it was full of boxes.

"Uh," she grunted, as she attempted to push one box off of another.

"Let me help you with that," I said.

"All my toys are in these two boxes," she told me. "See, you can tell because Mommy drew a picture of a doll on them." She pointed at a sad looking stick figure with long marker lines for hair that I guess symbolized a doll.

"Cool," I said.

Once the box was eye-level, her little hands went straight to work, attempting to shred and peel the packing tape. She reminded me of a little squirrel hard at work on a nut. Her dimples revealed themselves as she celebrated getting a small section of the box flap free. She was assiduous and inventive in her techniques. I felt immediately that we were friends.

"I had to move," she said. "I had to move because Doris is sick and because Mommy says New York doesn't love her anymore."

"Why not?" I asked.

"Because there were bugs this big in our apartment," she said. She held her hand as wide as if she were holding a small dog. "And also, because she didn't get the fellship."

"The fellship?"

"Yeah." She shrugged and put her hands on her hips. "They gave her two interviews and then she didn't get it."

"Oh," I said, having no idea what she was talking about. Later, I'd learn that Ceil had been hoping for a two-year fellowship to work at Columbia University's School of Dance. The money would have allowed her to continue to dance and practice choreography while supporting Maeve and just doing massage and acupuncture once or twice a week. But the award had gone to someone else, another artist that she knew. One whose family had money, who lived in an apartment on the Upper East Side that had been purchased for her by her father. "It's all bullshit, the whole thing, no one cares about art, everything is always about money," she'd told Maeve, feeling bitter and depressed. She started making plans to go into massage and acupuncture full time, wondering if, even then, she'd ever be able to afford a place that wasn't full of bugs. Then, a few days later she got a call from a member of the congregation at Our Lady of Perpetual Hope in Bronner. Doris, her 93-year-old surviving great aunt, was starting to make a turn for the worse. "Sometimes decisions just make themselves," Ceil told me later. She wanted to be there for Doris as much as she could, but there was no way she was moving back to Bronner. That's when the smallest house in Tonley showed up on her search.

I bent over Maeve and was about to use one of my long thumb nails to slice the remaining packing tape she'd been slowly peeling, but she held me back.

"I got it," she said. And she did. A minute later the cardboard flaps gave way, revealing a treasure chest of half-dressed Barbie dolls.

"Barbies!" Maeve said with a mixture of joy and surprise, as if she'd accidentally run into old friends. She picked them up in a bundle by their hair and piled them on the seat of her big wheel. It reminded me of the way Deb and I used to put our dolls on Eric's skateboard and roll them down this very street. "Let's go for a ride!" Maeve said to her toys, pushing the big wheel down the hill of the driveway and then watching it swerve and ditch into the grass. Two of the Barbies clung on the seat for dear life. The other three were splayed across the lawn. Maeve didn't go to rescue the girls from their plight. She just smiled at the work she'd done. That was the point of the game it seemed. She ran to get the big wheel and piled more Barbies from the box on top. After all the Barbies had been scattered on the ground, she turned back to the box and began digging through its contents: a bouncy ball, a My Little Pony, a few princess costumes. She put on a cone-shaped pink satin hat with tulle spilling from the top. Then she fished out a lion's mask and handed it to me.

"Want to wear it?" she asked.

"No thanks," I told her.

She shrugged and put it on herself. Then she roared. "I'm a lion princess!" she said. "What animal do you want to be?" I didn't want to be any, but I pretended to be a lion too. I was the lion mommy. "That means you're the queen," Maeve declared.

While we played, I tried to listen to my mother and Ceil's conversation, but I could only pick up bits and pieces: Doris, home health care workers, the bakery that was still down the street, something about wanting to live in this town because of the schools.

Maeve took off the hat and mask and said, "Do you like star explosions?"

"Star explosions?" I said, not sure what she meant, and wondering if I was the only person who'd never heard of *Cosmos*. "You mean like in outer space?" I searched my mind, but could not retrieve the word. Supernova.

"What's your favorite color?"

"Color? Are they different colors? Could they be?" I pondered the question. Maybe she was right. Maybe stars did change color. They weren't all composed of the same elements, were they? Different substances made different colors when they burned, like fireworks. And didn't the horizon of the universe look red or something?

Maeve frowned. This was not the answer she was looking for. "Mom!" she called after Ceil. "Mom, Mom, Mom, Mom."

Ceil paused and looked over at Maeve. "You don't have to say my name so many times, Maeve. I can hear you."

"Emily says there aren't different colored star explosions."

Ceil laughed. "Go show her what a star explosion is."

Maeve ran into their little house through the door off the garage, then appeared with a package of Starbursts.

Ceil shrugged. "I don't know how we started calling them explosions," she said. "It just happened. And I've needed something to bribe her with during the last few weeks of moving and change."

We all laughed. Mom declined a Starburst, but I happily

took a pink one. Maeve had red. Ceil took a yellow. And while our mouths were exploding, we discussed when I would start, what the hours would be, the pay—all the stuff Mom had already told me. But hearing the job described by Ceil and knowing a little of Maeve, I was all in.

I swallowed my pink star explosion and felt the sweetness linger in my mouth.

"See you in a few days, Maeve," I said, giving her a high five.

"You are going to be a good influence on that little girl," Mom told me as we walked home, "Who knows who she's been hanging out with in that city. We just stood up there talking for almost an hour and she said nothing at all about the father. Where is he?"

Again, I tried not to roll my eyes.

- 10 -

The next day, I explained Ceil and Maeve to Deb and Jenna over a plate of fries at the diner. They were not at all interested in the subject.

"Did you go for a run with Kelsey yet?" Jenna asked.

"Yeah, we need your running buddy to run spy ops," Deb said.

Always happy to circumvent my pain, they wanted my "insider access" to their boy crush zone. Kelsey was part of the female sector of the "it" crowd and went to all the same parties as Parker and Scott and everyone else. Or at least we assumed she did because they were all part of the same high school royalty.

But Kelsey seemed to exist outside of the drama of being cool. It was impossible not to be intimidated by her effortless glamour. Her legs were perfectly skinny and long, not muscley like mine. Her face required zero makeup. Her hair didn't ever look tangled or unkempt. And she seemed to experience no self-consciousness whatsoever. She moved through the world without flashing her good looks. She was just beautiful. There was literally no way for her to even hide it. Gym shorts or a prom dress, it was all the same thing.

I had gone on my first "buddy" run with Kelsey the day before, but there was nothing really to report besides the fact that I was way faster than her, and that she'd made us stop at the Gladstone's house on our run because she was having a "bathroom emergency," whatever that meant. It was still confusing to me why Coach would pair the two of us together. We didn't really talk. We just met at the gazebo in the middle of town and then ran three miles and parted ways.

"It was just a run," I said.

"Why can't I be a cross country star?" Jenna said. "I'd get her gossiping in no time. I'd be like, dish girl, what does Parker say about Deb when he's high? Does he find the fact that she types in all lower case too mouse-like?" Jenna was making fun of me here—I was the one who found Deb's lack of capitalization confusing, like she was diminishing herself. But Deb said her brothers both did it, and it was cool.

Jenna hadn't taken a side during our original debate, a move I respected. She said her Minnesota boyfriend and she both capitalized their IMs. "But you East Coasters are always like a decade ahead, right?"

I side-eyed her diss. "Well, since I'm babysitting, we're going to start running later in the day, so maybe I'll get more intel about what's going on because I'll be running with her at night."

They high fived each other. "That's what I'm talking about," Deb said. "Hopefully nothing happens till after this week though." The 4th of July was coming up and there were vacations on the horizon. Deb was going back to her shore house for a little less than a week. Jenna was flying to her uncle's lake house. They were leaving Friday morning.

I was going nowhere special. A cookout with some of Dad's old friends. Deb put her hand on my shoulder and sighed. "I can't believe you're going to work in the tool shed."

"You know you don't just have to do it just because your mom says so," Jenna said. Deb stifled a laugh.

I shrugged. I knew what they were getting at. Having any sort of job made me different. Neither of them intended to or would be required to work until they were granted some sort of magic internship or graduated college. They would never scoop ice cream or babysit or bag groceries. Also, it was true, I did do everything my mom told me to. But so did they. Our moms were just different, so they directed us differently. The only thing I'd ever heard Deb's mom tell her to do was to be home by midnight. And she didn't even say that all the time!

"The little girl is really cute. You guys should totally stop by." But I could tell from their faces that they never would.

"Would we even fit?" Deb said.

"Don't be a snob," I said.

"I don't tell you not to be a scholar-athlete," Deb said. "Don't discourage me from doing what I'm good at!"

Jenna laughed in a shocked but delighted way.

"Oh, witty," I said, "Great topic for your college essay. You can choose the prompt, 'Describe something important about you the rest of your application may not express.'"

Deb smiled. "I love that I'm the one with two brothers in college, and you're the one who knows the essay prompts," she said. Burn.

I just let it go and rode the waves and let them guide me from the diner to the 7-11, where we sat on a cement slab in the parking lot sharing a Slurpee, waiting to see who would show up. We had a running commentary for every person we passed, whether we knew them or not. That girl's thighs were too big for those shorts. Ashley had rodent teeth. That lady definitely had stray cats living in her backyard. Alex liked to masturbate to the nature channel. It was our dialect. A learned language. It just happened, the same way that when you picked up a French fry, you stuck it in a glob of ketchup before guiding it to your mouth.

The schedule I had worked out with Ceil was to work Tuesdays, Wednesdays, and Thursdays from 10:30 to 5 or 5:30, with an occasional Monday or Friday thrown in if needed. It was a good schedule with the world's easiest commute. The first day, when I opened my eyes at 8:19, it was amazing to know I had over two hours to walk all of three minutes, so I did what any teenager would do under the circumstances: I stayed in bed, letting my mind drift down both happy and sad corridors. When I heard my parents' footsteps on the stairs as they made their way to my door, I pretended to be asleep.

"We're leaving. You should probably get up. Have a good day. We love you. Can't wait to hear how it goes." I pretended to stir, mumbling an ok. When I finally heard them drive away, I opened my eyes and returned to letting the minutes pass. 8:34 became 8:35, 36, 7. I was transfixed, always awaiting that transformational moment of one minute to the next, wishing to somehow ride the nanosecond between the collapse of one number and the creation of another. Time was important when you were a runner. You had to embody the difference.

On my bed, the shadow of my experience with Doug felt like a bruise on my ribs. I couldn't avoid the pain of it. I was reminded with every breath. But I would attempt to rise above it by encouraging my mind to wander elsewhere. I'd remember Jake singing that ridiculous *Aladdin* song. I'd wonder about the Middle East. What country did that story take place in? Then I'd think of the packet. Celestino. The stars. Ursula Minor. My grandfather and the car and the horror of my mother's childhood. Dreckford's class and her giraffe teeth. The Little Dipper as an actual pan. Then Doug, again—his dick blocking out the moon.

My stomach cramped. I was a horrible slut and I was ugly. I bit my nails without realizing it until they bled. I used my sheets to blot them. I tried to remember vocabulary words. Recalcitrant. I had to pee but couldn't summon the energy to stand. I relived the glory of winning the state championship. I thought of something funny someone wrote in my yearbook. The cycle repeated itself. There was

Doug.

It was hard to stay upbeat when I was alone. No matter how I woke up, once enough time passed, I'd become helplessly ensconced in a cloud of rejection. I became paranoid. There was something wrong with me. Everybody knew it. They were always discussing it behind my back. The Cranberries song "Linger" was all I could listen to. I pushed the repeat button on my CD player and moaned the opening hum along with Delores O'Riordan.

Eventually, I laced up my sneakers and ran.

I didn't wear any headphones. I didn't need to. My world in motion was like an alternate reality, a tunnel I could funnel myself through, an empty paper towel roll pressed tightly against one eye and focused on the furthest point. The familiar houses of neighbors went by in a blur of colors and smells: cut grass and hydrangea. I came home slick with sweat and suddenly in a rush. A two-second shower, new clothes and I was off, cutting through the park up the hill and approaching the front door of Ceil and Maeve's tiny house.

It really did look like a tool shed. Why did a house that small even exist on a lot that little?

"Originally, it was part of the adjacent property, the brick house," Ceil explained as I went between playing with Maeve and steadying a ladder as she attempted to install a ceiling fan. Part of my hours that first week just involved entertaining Maeve while Ceil dealt with home projects. "It was a servant's house, honestly. Back then, in 17-whatever, none of these other houses were here. The soccer field, all the houses on this side—probably even your house down the hill—all of that land was part of the same estate. When the family finally started to sell off pieces of the property, they gifted this little blip of land and the little house to the family that had been their groundskeepers for all those years. And the lady who I bought this place from was literally the great-great-great-granddaughter of that family. But when she died, she had no living relatives, and the house eventually went up for sale after sitting vacant for so long. Isn't that crazy? To be in the same family for so long?"

Inheritance was definitely crazy if you were Ceil, I guess, considering she was raised with no parents. Same with my mom, I realized. What would she inherit? Nanny's house? Uncle Tommy would obviously live there.

That Ceil was 45 and this was the first house she ever owned definitely made her different from every other adult I knew in Tonley. But if she was aware of this difference it didn't seem to bother her. I thought of Maura, Cody's girlfriend, and how she'd shamed me over Christmas about not knowing what a food desert was. I wondered if people would consider Bronner a food desert. Did that bakery Ceil and Mom said was still open count? There had to be some sort of fresh produce nearby, right? Then I thought of how the stuff Nanny was always offering me was from the freezer.

Ceil seemed satisfied with whatever she'd been fiddling with in the light fixture. She stepped down the ladder, went to the circuit box, flipped a breaker and then flicked the light switch on the wall to see if her handiwork was a success. The blades of the ceiling fan stood still. She waved a fist at them, sweat dripping down her brow. "I'll deal with you later," she said to them. "The realtor warned me it needed a gut renovation. But I figured it was just because they were soft suburbanites. You should have seen our old apartment. It was smaller than this and no dishwasher, no washer and dryer, nothing."

She sounded like she was spinning a tale from another era instead of a few weeks before.

It was inspiring to see Ceil do these maintenance projects and tell these stories of a world I didn't know. I'd never set foot in a laundromat. And I'd never seen my mother so much as pick up a screwdriver, let alone stand on a ladder and attempt to fix a fan. Those tasks were for Dad, or if he was unwilling or unable, a handyman that they hired.

"Maybe you should get an electrician or something," I suggested.

"And admit defeat? No way!" she said. She gestured towards a pile of manuals she had stacked on the couch. "I am studying! I will figure this out if it kills me. Which, I guess, zap," she pantomimed being electrocuted ,"I guess it probably could."

I laughed. "You're like a renegade electrician."

She gave a small, tight smile at the compliment, wiping some sweat from her forehead with the collar of her shirt. "More like a cheap idiot. I don't like paying for anything unless I really need to. I like to exhaust all options first before I empty my wallet."

"My mom would never do that. She'd make my dad call the electrician right away."

"Just one small example of how she is smarter than me. She's one of the smartest people I've ever met."

"My mom?" I said.

"She never let anything ever get in her way. Look at her awesome job! Look at her awesome house! Look at you! I can't imagine her being beat by a ceiling fan. Probably because she's just not stupid enough to try to fix it herself." I wanted to ask her to clarify, but then Maeve entered the room.

"Emmmmmily," Maeve sang. "Come playyyyyy."

Ceil turned off her Rosie the Riveter vibes and gave me one of her 1000-megawatt perfect teeth smiles. "Time to entertain the princess while I unpack these boxes."

Maeve was fun to play with. She had a passion for tea parties. She had me sit in a circle with her stuffed animals and she served me "bubble gum tea."

"When you're done," she told me, "you can blow a bubble."

"Awesome," I said, and pretended to blow an enormous one that she then pretended to pop.

Those first days went fast. Maeve and Ceil were chill and easy, like getting to know relatives you didn't know you had and were surprised to discover that you liked.

"Don't forget your money," Ceil said, chasing me down the block after I'd said goodbye on the last day of the first week, forcing a wad of bills into my hand. "Thank you so much! I can already tell Maeve loves you. And so do I! How lucky am I to run into your mom? Sometimes the universe just gives you little gifts to let you know that you're making the right moves. You're my gift! Thank you!" She gave me a tight hug full of the warm aroma of sweat, lavender, and whatever other herbs they put in hippie soap.

"Aw, shucks," I said, not really knowing what else to say.

Once I was farther down the block, I took the wad out and counted it. One hundred and fifty dollars. I could buy a plane ticket with that! It felt strange in my pocket. Potential energy all my own, untraceable to my parents, completely mine. What would I trade this cash for? What could it bring me?

It was a Friday. Ceil had been determined to get the house in order before she had to go to work the next week, but since she'd been home most of the time I'd been there, she let me off early. It wasn't even 4. I doubted Mom and Dad were home from work yet and I didn't want to be alone. Impulsively, I decided not to take the interconnected backyard way home through the park. Instead, I thought I would take a stroll along the street and soak up the vibes of my neighbors. But before I made it far, I noticed myself gazing at the warm, orangey-red shutters of Deb's house and the eyelet lace of her living room curtains. Then I realized that both of Deb's parents' cars were in the driveway. She mustn't have left yet for the shore. I hadn't talked to her or Jenna in a few days, and I'd assumed they'd have left town already for the July 4th weekend, so I felt elated seeing the cars in the driveway. I couldn't wait to show off my cold hard cash, to prove there were upsides to living the way I did, in sad compliance to my rising-middle-class parents' puritanical values.

I thought about doing my classic cut-through-the-back-door move, but I knew if Deb was home, she'd be in the living room in the front of the house where her family's computer was. I wondered how she was planning to survive being at the beach, where I knew her parents didn't have the internet.

I focused on the right corner window, looking for Deb's silhouette through the curtain, picturing her waiting for Parker to sign on.

Maybe she would need me to help her analyze one of his IMs, I thought, thinking of all the ways we'd poured over them like they were lines from *Leaves of Grass*—though it'd be a stretch to say they contained multitudes. I'd never get that hour back we'd spent deconstructing the meaning of the phrase, "If you want." Did that mean that he wanted to go to the party in the woods only if she wanted to? Did it mean he was planning to go to the party in the woods and would like her to come? Was this an invitation, or just an acknowledgement of her freedom to go to the party now that she knew it existed? Was I a fool to validate the agony Deb poured into this exercise by partaking in it?

If Deb was in there, I was planning to spook her. I felt giddy at the idea. I saw two people in the computer room through Deb's front windows. One was obviously Deb. The other, I realized with a jolt, was Jenna. They were hunched over the computer in a particular way. I felt alarmed by their obvious excitement. Something important was happening. I had somehow missed out. The money in my pocket, which moments ago had felt like a trophy, now felt like a paper representation of my mother's oppression.

My body seemed to hijack my mind full force. Without really knowing why, I was crouched underneath the window, behind a prickly hedge, trying to listen in on a conversation between my two best friends like a spy.

It was surprisingly easy to eavesdrop, I realized. The window was open, which was weird. Maybe the cleaning lady had done it. Or maybe, I thought, remembering Ceil's declaration from a few moments before, the universe had left it open for me.

"They're going to be there so much sooner," Deb whined.

"Not necessarily. They're leaving in 10 minutes and they're taking the train to the stadium. That could take at least an hour. They have to walk from his house! And then they have to transfer to the Septa line and walk from the station." Jenna's voice, which always had a cheerleader lilt, was almost trembling with spirit. "I love that they got us one strawberry and one watermelon Mad Dog because they know those are our favorite water ice flavors."

"Ha! I think that's probably a coincidence," Deb said, wisely.

Jenna didn't care either way. "Dare you to drink an entire bottle."

"Too bad we can't actually drink them because we can't actually hang out with them in the parking lot," Deb whined.

I realized they were going to the baseball game that Deb had halfheartedly invited me to the day we'd gone to get donuts. It seemed like she had conveniently forgotten she'd extended the invitation, since I'd heard nothing about it ever since, and thought she'd already left town.

My body was frozen, like I was a garden gnome or some sort of gargoyle carved out of stone. I didn't move a muscle. I'm not even sure I was breathing.

They were quiet for a minute, reading and tapping on the keyboard. Deb left the room, probably to go to the kitchen. I heard

Jenna make her signature huffing noise and call out to Deb like she was hyperventilating.

"Parker just IM'd you goodbye. It's so sweet! 'I wish your dad wasn't going! Too bad we can't hang in the lot. But don't forget, write it on your hand, Box 518, right next to third base. We have extra seats and Doug never gets carded so we'll get you some beers."

Deb sighed. "I wish my dad wasn't going too!"

Jenna smirked. "It could be worse."

"How?" she said dramatically. "How could it possibly be worse? The love of my life is going to be in the parking lot, and I'm going to be stuck in the stadium with my dad!"

"Em could be coming."

Hearing my name made my body tremble for just a second. It was as if the statue version of me had been pelted by an egg or a rock tossed by a vandal.

Deb rolled her eyes. "True." She covered her face as if she couldn't even bear the thought of picturing the scenario.

Jenna started to impersonate me, talking in a nerdy voice. "Um, um, um, don't look at me. Um, I'm so awkward. Um, I don't know how to talk."

"Uhhhh," Deb sighed. "What the fuck is her problem? Why hook up with Doug if you're never even going to talk to him again?" She said this as if it had been my choice. As if he hadn't ignored me.

"She's just too much of a weirdo," Jenna said. "She can't deal. It's....it's her mom's fault. She's a little Frankie. It's, like, disturbing. She's like a puppet or something. Oh my god, can you even imagine if her mom knew she'd been on the beach with them that night? She'd probably strap a chastity belt on her. She'd probably try to get your mom to put a chastity belt on you."

"What's a chastity belt?" Deb asked.

"It's some sort of medieval torture thing that is tied around your vag like a dog muzzle."

They were both dying in laughter on the floor. "Mrs., Mrs., Mrs." Deb attempted to speak through her laughter but could barely get it out. "Mrs. Banks would totally get one if she could buy it with her Macy's discount."

"She probably wouldn't need to, though, honestly," Jenna said. "Emily's face is her own chastity belt. Doug told me he liked her at the beach because she looked good in her bikini but once he saw her at school, he realized she was a butterface."

Butterface? It was a classic line I'd heard boys say to each other for years—her body is hot "but her face" is ugly. I thought of Jenna and her constant critiques of my teeth, how she said lipstick would draw attention to them. That was all I could take. In shock, I crept around the perimeter of the house and planned to dart through the park down the hill to my own backyard, but was surprised by the sight of Mrs. Stevens, who was watering plants on the back deck.

"Hi Em!" Mrs. Stevens said. "Are you going to the game? The girls are inside!"

My face felt hot. Clearly Mrs. Stevens had no idea what was going on in her living room. Just like she had no idea what went on that night on the beach when I was down the shore, or how sick I was the day after. She was being kind to me, but it was a clueless kindness. It felt disingenuous. Purposefully ignorant. My mom, my crazy-psycho-chastity-belt-buying (on a discount) mom was probably right when she complained that Mrs. Stevens was checked out and didn't care what happened at her house. But then again, nothing had happened at her house, or to her daughter. This wasn't even about Deb. It was about me. And I hated my mom for her paranoid overprotectiveness as much as I hated Mrs. Stevens right then for the opposite.

I felt my cheeks go splotchy as she looked at me, waiting for my response. What did she see? How much of my emotions was visible? I could tell I was going to stutter. "G-g-game? Um, um," I saw myself at that moment and understood clearly why Jenna was making fun of me. It was true. I acted exactly the way she said. "No," I said. "I have to get up early tomorrow to go to Pennsylvania. Have a good weekend!"

Then I took off down the hill at full blast, barely noticing any of my surroundings as I ran, too shocked to feel my heels hit the grass.

- 11 -

The trees made long slants of shade in the park. I darted through these patches with my head down, all business. I wanted to stay in the sun. There was a truth hiding in the shadows I was still trying to avoid. Even after hearing it just spoken aloud, I wanted to ignore it. I wanted to see if it was still possible to avoid, to still cling to the unanswerable motivation to move forward.

But there was nowhere to go and no one to go to and maybe that was the point.

The shaded grass under the trees could only be captured in a painting by coloring over the green with gray or black. It was a fact. I was alone. The teenage gloom of it gripped my throat.

But after acknowledging my aloneness all alone, in the privacy of my own head, I felt suddenly aware of the quiet trees and the squirrels and ants and birds that lived around and off of one another, and the sun, who fed us all, that not-so-distant, distant star. The sun was a star, I thought, with strange relief. Therefore, I could make a wish on it. So I wished for what everyone wishes for: love.

I saw my house from the backyard and knew it was still empty. A lonely planet on a crowded Earth. Better to be out here. I dropped to the ground and stretched out my skin on the grass, pressed life to life, connecting myself to the infinite mitochondria radiating outward, everywhere, from one organism to the next. Then I got tired of being bit by mosquitos.

Standing up brought back the sadness. The mosquitos had my blood. I entered the backdoor and greeted the family room furniture with my wad of cash.

It's not like I'd never been made fun of before. People called me a dork and a goody goody all the time. Even Deb, In fact, mostly Deb. Though usually, if she or Jenna delivered that sort of disparaging remark in my presence, I categorized it differently, like the way my dad teased my mom about shopping. I interpreted their teasing to mean, yes, you are obsessive compulsive about your grades and listening to your parents and being a perfect student, but we love you for who you are, so we're allowed to make fun of you for it. But now, after witnessing their exchange, I realized that their public pushbacks to my straightlaced behavior were actually the beginning of my exile.

I couldn't help but feel like this was all Jenna's fault. I'd never felt like she liked me. She made fun of the way I laughed ("Hee haw," she'd say if I was cracking up about something, sticking her teeth out and slapping her knees like I was a donkey, which always quickly took the joy out of whatever I was laughing over), the way I blew my nose ("That sounds like a fog horn"), the way I looked with lipstick on when I tried it at a sleepover ("Yeah, you definitely look better with a natural mouth. It's better not to accentuate your big teeth.") I'd told Deb before that I thought she hated me, but Deb always said that I was just being sensitive, that Jenna was like that to everyone, it was just her sense of humor. And besides, it wasn't like I hadn't said and thought awful things about her—about her sideburns and her fat toes and her accent.

But Deb wasn't innocent. She let her do it. She participated. She didn't defend me. It was like they only kept me around so they could mock me to feel superior. Even if it was true that they'd invented the joke about being hitmen hired to knock off Derek Gladstone so that I could maintain my number one ranking in the class, which I guess in a backwards way was supportive of me—at least in a public sense—I started to realize that even that could be interpreted as cloaked mockery.

Something about us as a threesome had always felt off. Maybe it was my fault. Maybe it was my only child syndrome. I didn't know how to share, and maybe Jenna sensed that from the start and so she went full attack mode on me. Or maybe she just couldn't bear to blossom into the sort of young woman she wanted to be with me as one of her sidekicks. I'd seen the pictures on her wall of her old friends from Minneapolis. They were beauty contest blondes with apple-colored cheeks who probably had huge jars of fancy makeup brushes on their vanities and Caboodles full of M.A.C. I didn't have a vanity. I had a desk.

So what. Whatever. Jenna got her wish. Deb was not my friend anymore. She actually seemed like a stranger all of a sudden. Nothing about her made sense. I suddenly saw the friendship from my mom's perspective: it just wasn't a match. It didn't matter that we'd traveled to New York City together or that we'd spent countless evenings catching lightning bugs and playing M.A.S.H. Or that we once made it to 52 playing numbers on a school bus, or that we had a dance routine to every song in Madonna's *Immaculate Collection,* or that I—and only I—knew that when she was in first grade, she'd said cat food was "a good snack" and used to eat it out of the bowl when her family wasn't looking. I'd never told anyone that. I'd kept that secret for years when it would have been so easy to throw that back at her. But who cared about that now? It was just something cute to laugh about from another time.

I had been replaced. What I'd seen coming a long way off had finally arrived. This was a divorce. I felt both stung and relieved. I flopped myself over the arm rest of the couch, my head hitting the center cushion like a brick, causing the entire piece of furniture to slide a little with my weight. On the fireplace mantel, there was a portrait of me in a white dress from my First Holy Communion, smiling for the camera with my undeniably oversized, freshly grown-in front teeth hovering above my lower lip like a rodent's incisors. Back then, it never occurred to me to care whether I was attractive.

Probably 15 minutes after that picture was taken, I was in my bathing suit in the backyard hitting the Slip 'n Slide.

But there was no going back. My breasts pressed against my bra. There was hair that persisted under my arms and between my legs. This was the body that contained me now.

"It's fine," I declared to the empty room. They weren't wrong. Their criticisms were valid. It was true I was a girl who did not like to wear revealing clothing. And I did clam up like a shy freak in the company of those guys. I couldn't help it. They set off an alarm in my nervous system. My body became flooded with mixed messages, and I didn't know how to act.

Those boys gave off a smug confidence that made me feel like I was the victim of a joke whose punchline I was living just by breathing air. I wondered if they even knew they were capable of this. Did they ask for this power? Did they study how to use it? Was it like some sort of golden ring bequeathed to them in some sort of ritual? What was the secret? There had to be one, right? Or was it instinct? An implicit understanding? Something imparted to you without ever using words?

What was confusing was the fact that even though my 15-year-old logical brain was capable of identifying asshole behavior, there was another, more powerful current in the air that seemed to distort my ability to process the signal. Like when I'd watched Doug hold the huge flame up to Rick's face and knew in my gut it wasn't right, but then laughed about it with him later. My body somehow ranked Doug's approval above my impulse to stop something I thought was wrong. His presence controlled and distorted my personality. And Deb's personality. And Jenna's. And probably even his own friends. And in a way those distortions had distorted the connection between Deb and me. Maybe it was inevitable. Maybe something had to give eventually. But ever since these guys had entered our lives, the way Deb and I talked to and about each other had changed.

There was a family picture on the mantel taken at a restaurant on Nanny's birthday the winter before. Why hadn't I just gone to her dumb Memorial Day party? Why hadn't it been Jenna who was there instead of me? Maybe Jenna would have done something differently.

I lay on the couch for a long time and just let my mind go in all the dark directions that it chose, punishing myself with my memory. The next thing I knew, Mom was standing over me.

"Are you asleep?" she said. There was drool on my hand and on the throw pillow where my head was resting.

"What time is it?"

"6. They must really tire you out up there!" she gave my hair a little comb through with her fingers.

I shook her hand off, shrugged and stretched. "I guess."

"Do you like the job now that you're a week in?"

"It's fun," I said, honestly. "Maeve is hilarious, and Ceil is really cool too."

Mom got strangely stiff in response to me calling Ceil cool, like she was threatened by my liking her. "I remember how she used to run out of school on Fridays and get picked up on a motorcycle by this macho Italian guy in all black leather. It was like that Aerosmith video with the girls in the uniforms. She'd go to New York City and then be back on Sundays for church. Nanny was always like, 'Who does that girl think she is taking Communion?' Everyone was always watching her and talking about how her aunties couldn't control her. All the girls thought she was trouble. But she was definitely popular with the boys." Mom's tone had an undercurrent. I decided not to take her bait.

"Were you friends with her?" I asked.

"A little," Mom said. "We were partners on a big history project. We were supposed to present it at Rutgers, but then she ran away, and everything went crazy at our school. I never ended up getting to present the paper."

"What was it about?" I asked.

"The atomic bomb," she said.

"Creepy," I said.

"It was Cici's idea. She believed in nuclear disarmament. I didn't even know what that meant. She'd met some activists in New York, and she was working with some choreographer on an interpretive dance or something. She had all kinds of crazy stories back then. We did some research on Oppenheimer's involvement and his reaction to Hiroshima. Anyway, our history teacher really liked the idea and encouraged us to enter this contest, and we did. We were finalists, but then she left and it all kind of fell apart. Long story." She looked at me and raised her eyebrows. "It's stupid to say, but I used to blame her running away for me not going to college. I always thought that if we'd gone to the college and presented the paper then we'd have gotten full scholarships or something. I know it doesn't really work that way. But I thought that maybe I'd meet somebody who would want to show me how to do it, who would encourage me to apply. Nobody was ever interested in helping me with anything. Nobody cared if I went to college. It was the opposite, actually. Not only did they not care, Nanny didn't want me to go. She thought of college as something uppity and snobby. It just wasn't an option for me. It was like, you can get married, or you can be a nun. But Mr. Burke liked Cici and Cici needed a partner for the project, so that's the closest I got."

"Couldn't you have presented the paper by yourself?"

"I mean, maybe. Technically it was supposed to be a group project, but I guess we could have said she was sick or something. But there was a lot of drama happening at the school. The teacher, Mr. Burke, couldn't take me. And Nanny wasn't going to take me. So I just skipped it."

"What was up with the school? Why couldn't Mr. Burke take you?"

She waved her hands at me. "Boring administrative stuff." But the way she said it, I could tell she was lying. But I also sensed I would get no more information from her. At least not tonight.

I'd never heard this story before, and I was quieted by the revelation of my mother as an ambitious high school student. I was suddenly so curious about the teenage version of her. But she sensed my piqued interest. Before I could frame a new question, she asked about Ceil's house and how all the unpacking was coming along. I told her about the electrical issue in the living room and all the boxes. "Renovating and unpacking at the same time? Poor woman! Such an impulsive person. See, I guess that's what happens."

The way she said it made it sound like Ceil was in a bad place. But I'd watched this same woman flip through electrical manuals and install custom shelves. She seemed perfectly in control and looked about as happy as any person her age seemed, perhaps even a little happier. It wasn't like Mom was always skipping through life. I mean, yes, I guess she was satisfied with herself, but who could possibly enjoy following rules so diligently? I watched her take a box of rice out of the pantry, observing her deliberate movements as she measured out some to cook. Thinking about Deb and Jenna's comments about how I was just like her, I suddenly felt prickly and defensive, irritated at my mom and them at the same time.

"I mean, it doesn't seem like she's suffering or anything," I said.

Mom lit the stove. "Ceil has to raise a kid all by herself. That is not a situation anyone wants to be in. She's not married. No one is responsible for Maeve but her."

Jenna's use of the word chastity belt echoed through me. Was this a cloaked "no sex before marriage" speech? I felt the urge to scream. "You can't speak for what everybody in the world wants. Everybody's experience doesn't have to be exactly the same. You don't know, maybe she likes raising her daughter alone. Maybe she prefers it. Or maybe she was married when she had Maeve and now she's divorced."

Mom's eyes popped widely at the way I challenged her read on the situation. She paused her knife above an onion before hacking it in half and letting out a cold, condescending laugh. "You just don't get it," she said. "But you should get it. Don't let it happen to you."

"Ceil is not a teenager. If it did happen to me, it wouldn't even be the same thing!"

"That is not the point, and you know it," she said back, looking at me, ready to take this conversation in a direction I didn't want to go.

I sighed loudly, annoyed with myself for even being baited into the argument. Obviously, Mom was going to say these things. There was no surprise here. The surprise was that for some reason I decided to try to change her mind, which I already knew was pointless. But at the same time, the way she was treating Ceil and Maeve's life was infuriating. Not only was it full of moral condescension, it was a flat-out lie. Why couldn't she see that there were different ways to be happy? She'd just said moments before that her own mother couldn't understand the importance of college. How was understanding that fact not enough to open herself up to the idea that maybe every mother had a blind spot?

But no, to her, it was not every mother who had a blind spot. It was just her mother. And the narrative that she chose to live by was that despite being raised by this deficient human, somehow she—

poor, dirty, Frances Reilly with the Catholic school uniform that didn't fit—had managed, with the help of the Virgin Mary, to pull herself out of her hole, become Frances Banks, give birth to me, and suddenly morph into the all-seeing, almighty Oz.

And I knew what would happen if I tried to push this subject further. I could see what waited down the road. Mom would just assume I was now interested in having kids out of wedlock, or that I was going to run away somewhere to become an artist or normalize some other part of Ceil's reality that she considered sinful and risky.

Mom's Catholic perspective of what made a person's life good made me realize that she probably thought allowing me to watch Maeve was some sort of charity work even though I was getting paid. But I couldn't flip out and yell at her for being small minded. That would only end badly for me. I tried to find a middle road before she told me I couldn't babysit anymore, and I was back to wallowing in my personal misery full-time with an SAT study guide as my only friend.

I took a deep breath and let the air sputter out of my lips, making the farty noise of a balloon as it deflates and flips wildly through a room. It was my final gesture of rebellion. Then I took a calmer breath. "I mean it's not like she's walking around saying she's so happy to be a single mom," although honestly, she had expressed that sentiment while hanging things on the wall and unpacking boxes, and I thought it was cool the way she was so self sufficient. But I knew what Mom wanted to hear. "She definitely seems like she has to work twice as hard. I'm just trying to say that her life isn't like terrible or anything."

"It really is a shame," she said. "She was going places. But she was just in too much of a rush. She was too fast. People can end up anywhere. You really have to look out for yourself from a young age."

Yeah, anywhere, I thought, like right around the corner from you, which doesn't seem so bad, does it? Though I guess there was the whole issue of the house being the size of a tool shed. But that only mattered to the kind of person who liked to make insensitive comments about the size of a person's home, which lately seemed to be everybody.

I kept my mouth shut.

- 12 -

After dinner, my dad turned on the Phillies game and stretched across the couch. Usually, I would sit next to him and perform my own sort of lazy, half-watch, which during the school year involved making and studying flashcards and during the summer consisted mostly of going back and forth between the kitchen and the living room to eat snacks and talk on the phone. But knowing that Deb and Jenna and Doug and Parker were all at the game, it was impossible to tear my eyes away from the screen. I wanted to see if any of the fan footage would pass over them, whether they'd be caught red handed on national TV having a night out without me—without even telling me!—after Deb had invited me!

That bitch!

A few times, a foul ball was knocked into the box seats that lined the bases. I couldn't remember if Parker's family's seats were on the first or third baseline. I thought I saw them a few times, but the camera panned past so quickly I couldn't be sure. The game was uneventful. One inning became the next. The Brewers had a rally in the 6th and scored 4 runs. It didn't look good for the Phils. Eventually I lost interest and decided to go to bed.

But there was no sleeping. No temporary forgetful cocoon. My brain ruffled with whys as the shadows of the curtains danced to the breeze of the air conditioning that came up from the vents on the floor. I heard my parents shuffle around in their room before a quiet settled over everything.

11:47 became 11:53. 11:58, 59. 11:59, 12:00.

The stroke of midnight. When proper ladies were supposed to turn into pumpkins. That's when I decided to break out. Not like out on the back of a leather clad man's motorcycle bound for New York City. Just out of the house and into the New Jersey night.

I wanted to surrender myself to the darkness. I had homework that demanded that I do this anyway—Ms. Celestino's star journal. I was supposed to contemplate infinity and the far-off galaxies. It was an assignment. I was an A plus student. Who could argue with that?

I grabbed my flip flops and tiptoed down the stairs. Maybe I could have just opened the front door and walked straight out, but that seemed too crazy. My parents' bedroom was right above the door. And even if they didn't hear me, what if a neighbor did? Instead, I used one of the windows in our family room that opened onto our back deck. It was the perfect escape, and it was surprisingly easy. The lock on the window was easy to undo and the window made no sound as I eased it up high enough to maneuver myself through, entering into the night air.

Freedom. Darkness. Humid air on my skin like the hot breath of the earth. The weight of my sadness, which felt like a crystalized shell I lived in, seemed to soften a bit, like the exterior of a chocolate dipped ice cream bar after it escapes the freezer. The gooey ice cream center of me came closer to the surface of the night. Even though I was alone, I felt like I had a companion with me, a friend. In fact, I even whispered, "what are we doing," out loud.

Maybe I wasn't alone. Maybe I had a spirit guide. "Footprints in the Sand" was framed in our bathroom. I'd read it countless times while sitting on the toilet. It was a poem about a person who had always seen two sets of footprints, theirs and God's I guess, on the metaphoric journey of their life, which they were somehow able to view from a bird's eye. The speaker of the poem asks God why there are only one set of footprints in the sand during the hardest moments of their life, when God had promised to always walk with them. God responds to the person that during those hard times it was Him, God, who'd actually been carrying the person, so the footprints in the sand were actually God's and not the person who thought they'd been abandoned.

"It wasn't me, Mom," I imagined myself explaining if I was caught outside. "It was God. He carried me out the window."

A shiver ran down my spine as my body adjusted to the heat of the summer night. I pushed the window closed and heard a rustle just behind me. I turned to see a raccoon scurrying out from under the deck back towards a tree in the yard. I almost screamed but caught myself, my heart hammering in my chest. I thought about going right back inside, but I knew nothing new was waiting for me in there. Better to face the unknown. Even if it was full of raccoons with scratchy little hands and sharp teeth and rabies.

I put my flip flops on and cut through the space in the fence by the shed, listening to the rhythm my shoes made as they smacked against my heels, hoping their sound would scare off whatever red-eyed nightcrawlers lurked in the brush. On the other side of our property was the blacktop behind the bleachers that surrounded the tennis courts. I ran along them until I hit the grove of trees with a trail through it that connected to the football field by Deb and Maeve's houses.

There was a chance, I figured, that Deb and Parker and Jenna and whoever else might be drinking or hanging out in the football field or in this little rim of woods that skirted the open grass, so I stayed on the path and moved fast, exiting the park at the first street. I thought I heard people laughing in the distance, and the idea of stumbling upon their party terrified me. I couldn't bear to be the butt of another joke.

I zigzagged down streets with my head down, focused on my flip-flopping feet and the shape my body cast against the sidewalk under the glow of street lamps. I was not one to amble. Even without sneakers on, I moved at a clip, close to breaking into a jog. My body had the nervous energy of a chipmunk scurrying in the yard at the sound of a car door.

It was only when I reached the top of the hill by the country club that I realized I'd forgotten to even look up and observe the stars. I stopped still at the entrance to the parking lot and craned my head skyward. I saw airplanes and satellites and beyond them, the faint glow of a few stars. I thought about entering the golf course, with its open green space, but the paved paths were dotted with lamp posts that illuminated the narrow roads the golf carts traveled. What was the purpose of keeping these lights on at night? Who golfed at this hour? The security lights were stealing the stars.

There was a little private road called Lane of Acres that cut along the perimeter of the golf course that I thought could possibly be a darker, easier place to stargaze. There were only houses on one side of the street. The other was about an acre thick with old trees that served as a buffer between the golf course and the hulking mansions that hid back there. The street had only five or six houses on it. I didn't know anyone who lived in any of them. My parents and I usually drove down this road at Christmas just to see the lights and decorations from the car, imagining what the people were like who lived inside these dreamscapes. My mom had heard a rumor that one of the people who owned all the malls in the Tri-state area lived back there. Dad always said they were probably professional athletes. Whoever they were, I wondered if they enjoyed seeing all the extra cars drive down their private road around the holidays. They had to know we were there just to gawk at their riches. The whole road, the way it was set back from all the other houses in our town, made venturing to it feel like a pilgrimage.

Walking down Lane of Acres, I felt a little like I was entering a movie set. There was no sidewalk and no streetlights and the narrow road I was walking on was darker than the others I'd traversed. The only visible lights were the ones that lit up the homes themselves. Porch lamps and spotlights were set in the grass of the front yards to illuminate the facades of these perfectly manicured homes. They looked like polished trophies. They made me feel small, like a beetle passing each one in a case.

I started to understand the name Lane of Acres. There were endless stretches between each home where there were no lights. These were the places where there was a hint of true darkness. I felt both called to those patches of grass and cautious. What was I doing? I was crazy. I should just turn around and go home. Still, something kept me walking onward, waiting for the perfect place to present itself.

Technically, I was committing a crime. There was a sign at the beginning of the road that said "No Trespassing." But it wasn't a sign I thought twice about because it wasn't one anyone obeyed. There was a shortcut to a good sledding hill off this road. And like I said, we all drove down here during the holidays. But it wasn't a snowy day. And there were no Christmas lights to revere. These facts, I guess, made me more of a trespasser. Though when you're a kid, it's hard to see something as private once it's been presented to you as public. It's not like I thought I had the right to walk into any of these people's homes. But I did feel entitled to their slice of sky. I just wanted to find a place that was dark enough, the same way we wanted the best hill to slide down when it snowed.

I sat at the edge of a sprawling lawn, on a sloped bit of grass close to the road.

It was dark enough, I conceded. Not true, true darkness. Not the kind that George Washington saw the night he spent the night in Tonley a million years ago, or even Walt Whitman's view 100ish years later when he was editing *Leaves of Grass* for the 1000th time, but still, it was darker than any other area I'd passed along the way. It was a space where I could at least come close to recording some honest observations from my own eyes instead of parroting my dad.

Would Celestino stop here? I pictured her on a rowboat in the middle of a lake in central Maine. Did she have kids? Grandkids? A husband? A wife? I couldn't see her in these parts for the summer. I opened my journal and scribbled blindly on the page: "Does the actual act of looking at stars and contemplating their location and brightness to one another change you? Does it make you good at blocking things out and ignoring the modern world, fleeing it, going off the grid?"

Why does any of this even matter? This assignment? This life? I didn't write those questions down.

My eyes were still adjusting and refocusing on the sky. The stars began to come out, which is to say that they revealed themselves. Actually neither of those verbs is correct. The stars were always there. To suggest that they were coming to me was missing the point. They weren't doing anything differently. They didn't even know the difference between day and night. They were just energy exploding into the sky, traveling lightyears in all directions.

I stretched supine on the grass and tried to conjure a feeling of oneness. All we are is dust in the wind dude. Dust. Wind. Dude. My mind saw strings. I was like a puppet, tied by beams of invisible dental floss to the sky. My hand raised on its own volition. Or was it something else? I've heard physicists don't believe in free will.

I shook my finger at the blinking lights of the airplanes making their descent into Philadelphia, like I'd seen Ceil shake hers at Maeve when she reached for a cookie from the jar on the shelf. "You're not stars," I admonished, wishing I could make them disappear for the sake of my homework, but then also feeling a witchy guilt for the impulse, as if wanting to erase the airplanes might somehow impact the people who were inside them. For a moment, I saw all those passengers up there in those blinking vehicles who were looking down at the lit-up grid of the city and thinking, "Finally, I'm home."

There would probably be another dark age. A future millennium when whatever humans managed to survive once again gleaned their purpose from these fire dots instead of their computer screens. I lay still and let my eyes grow wide and unfocused. The kind of thoughts that can be transcribed into sentences lost their footing and became something larger and less exact. My mind was skirting the rims of the atmosphere, like a helium filled balloon that escapes from your hand. Anyone was capable of this, seeing things they hadn't seen before. You just had to look. And then remember what you saw. I would draw them in a second, the dots behind the other dots, but I wanted to linger there in the stillness. Then out of nowhere a voice right behind my head said in a loud whisper, "Banks!"

I screamed. Like a blood curdling scream from a horror movie. I scrambled to stand up, but a hand clamped itself across my mouth and pulled me back down to the ground. Instinctively, I bit it.

"Ow!" the owner of the hand screamed, letting go. "What the fuck are you doing?" he said. "Do you want the cops to come?" My eyes focused on the assailant. Kneeling next to me was Jake Freelander in his Absolute Video t-shirt. I shoved him as hard as I could onto his back and then jumped on top of his legs and hit him in the stomach.

"Don't do that!" I yelled.

He laughed as he deflected my punch. "Thank God you hit like a girl."

I glared at him and picked up my star notebook from the grass and smacked him on the side of the ribs. "Are you asking me to hit you harder?" I said, shifting off of him and glaring at him from the grass, anger, alarm, and relief taking turns pulsing through me.

He scooted a few feet further away from me. "No, no, I'm good, it's cool."

I took a deep breath, taking him all in. Floppy hair unbrushed in straggly curls around his ears, skinny arms sticking out of his t-shirt, chain on his well-worn cut-offs, little athletic socks under his black All Stars, which were fraying along the toe line. His knees were bent up and his arms were extended behind him, lifting his chest so that I could see his face. His eyes, which were usually sparkling with the confidence of someone who was amused endlessly by his own thoughts, didn't have that look in them right then. He was searching my face in a way I'd seen my own mother look as she rushed to me after a bad fall, assessing to make sure there were no broken bones, that I was okay.

His sincere concern almost made me laugh, but I stopped myself because I was pissed and processing the situation. Still, those eyes and that face went straight to my gut. I knew instinctively that he would never hurt me. He was kind. My biology neighbor. I felt sorry for biting him and tried to show it by letting out a long sigh and crawling a little closer to him before collapsing in a heap on the grass.

"You are a feisty motherfucker," he said.

"I thought I was alone and you snuck up on me!"

"I just said your name and you screamed like you wanted to wake up the whole town!"

"I did want to wake up the whole town," I whisper-screamed at him. "I thought you were a murderer!"

"Well, the sad thing is, the whole town probably wouldn't even hear you because most of these fuckers aren't even home. They're like in the Poconos or at the shore or in Cape Cod or who knows where else, so maybe there's a chance that no one would even hear you, no matter how loud you screamed."

"Oh my god, shut up," I said, annoyed at him. "That's terrifying."

"But then again, even if someone heard you scream, they might not do anything about it. There was this incident in Queens where this woman got stabbed to death and like 40 of her neighbors heard her screaming and no one even called the cops."

"Where's Queens?" I asked.

He laughed. "You don't know where Queens is?"

"No," I said. "Is it in Canada?"

"It's a borough of New York City! It's where A Tribe Called Quest is from, and Seinfeld..." He seemed like he was going to go on, but I couldn't bear the list, so I stopped him.

"Like the show?"

"Yes, like the show. You don't know the boroughs of New York City?"

It made me feel embarrassed that I didn't know them. I thought New York City was just New York City. The Empire State Building and Broadway and Central Park. I'd been there. It'd felt big. But what did I know? It's not like we'd had a New York City unit in school. We lived outside Philadelphia. How was I supposed to know these things? Who was teaching him about Carl Sagan and Queens? I was the one who was first in my class! I don't think he was even in the top 10% of his!

"Stop making me feel dumb!" I said.

"How could you feel dumb? I'm genuinely surprised! Don't be so sensitive. Anyway, the point of my story is a woman got killed in a crowded place where a ton of people could hear her and no one did anything about it, so maybe it doesn't make a difference that we're here all alone."

"Well thank you for that comforting thought," I said. "I feel much safer with you all alone in the dark now that I know that if you were going to murder me, it doesn't really matter if anyone is home in these houses or not."

"Are you really afraid of being murdered?"

"Honestly, I'm more afraid of raccoons. I saw one when I was leaving my yard and it totally freaked me out. I don't like their eyes in the dark. They're red."

He nodded. "And those little hands!" He held up his hand and curled the ends of each finger, then made a little sucking sound with his teeth.

"Oh my god," I said. "Stop!" He stopped, and then he abruptly changed the subject. "Your yoga video is late!"

"What?" I said, my mind moving from raccoons to downward facing dog, and then remembering our weird moment in the movie store.

"It's two days late. Why haven't you returned it?"

"Are you keeping track or something?"

"I'm sitting in a store all day. I have to do something." Then he explained to me in detail the movie rental patterns of families in our town. Divorced dads, classmates who were obviously couples, dudes who seemed like they were renting movies just for the sex scenes.

"You know people probably don't want you reading into their choices so much. It's really not your business to pay attention and report all this in such detail," I said, feeling like a lawyer.

"That's fair," he said. "But I'm just one person. One day, they'll be tracking everything we do, like in *1984*, so a person like me who knows everything about a few people in a little town won't mean anything."

"Who are they and how will they do that?"

"Us," he sang, "and them—and after all, we're only ordinary

men." I said nothing. I recognized the song. I was pretty sure it was Pink Floyd, but I was afraid to make a mistake. He looked at me and smiled. "You know what?" he said. "You look a little tight around the shoulders. Maybe you should keep the video a few more days. Release all that tension."

I laughed a dry laugh in response, wondering if I had what it took to achieve the flexible serenity the video promised. I pictured the DVD on the shelf by the TV.

"I can't believe I forgot to return it," I said. "I don't think I've ever returned a video late in my whole life."

He shook his head. "Yeah," he said, "your whole life is turning to shit. First, you forgot to return a movie, and now here you are wandering down a dark, abandoned street at one in the morning looking to get murdered. What the hell's gotten into you?"

I pulled a clump of grass from the perfectly manicured lawn and tossed it at him. I thought of the baseball game, of Deb and Jenna and the stab of betrayal. If only I could answer that question honestly. I sighed and gestured upwards, to the sky. "I'm trying to stargaze," I said.

"Celestino?"

I nodded, then threw another clump at him. "Where's my packet?"

He gave me a look I didn't quite know how to unpack. "It's our packet."

"Whatever," I said, "You've kidnapped it."

Then he laughed at me and said, "You're right. Maybe we should arrange a joint custody agreement."

"Every other week?" I suggested.

"I was thinking every other weekend. I'm the primary caretaker."

I threw another clump of grass at him. "How can I trust that you're taking care of it? That's too long to be away! Are you feeding it enough vegetables? Is it watching too much TV?"

Jake brushed the grass off his shirt. "These people spend like hundreds of dollars on their lawn every week. They probably have video cameras recording us right now. If they see a patch in the grass, they're totally gonna review the surveillance film and make your parents pay for it."

This was not what I wanted to hear. My face must have become paralyzed in paranoia as I searched to see if a bare patch was visible, because he reached out and touched my arm.

"Hey," he said, "Just kidding. About making your parents pay for it at least. They will totally have their security people review the video if their yard's messed up. And if they see that it's high school kids fucking up their lawn, they will probably just get some guard dogs or something."

"I know," I said, defensively. "I'm not like freaked out or anything." I turned around and took in the house behind us, with its turret and its stone. "Who even lives here?" I asked.

"I don't know. Old people. A girl named Sara Jennings used to live there," he said, pointing to the stone house, "but she moved to Hershey, Pennsylvania. I heard her new house has its own landing strip for a plane. Her father is an amateur pilot."

"How do you know?" I asked, suspicious of his knowledge.

"I know because Travis lives next door and we used to play with her when we were little."

"Travis lives next door?" Travis, Jake's best friend, with the threadbare clothes and dumpy looking VW bus. "I didn't know that."

"Yeah. Did you think I was just taking a stroll down Lane of Acres at one in the morning like you? I'm on my way home. Travis was gonna drive me, but I just decided I wanted to walk," he said.

"And then here you are."

I ignored the happy idea of fate and said, "I just didn't expect Travis to live here."

Jake laughed. "Why? You think everyone who has money walks around in like seersucker suits?"

"I don't know," I said.

"Not everybody is like Deb's family, you know. They don't all buy their kids brand new Mercedes to induct them into the capitalist machine."

Capitalist machine? I recalled the rerun of a Kurt Cobain interview one night on MTV, but I didn't totally know what he meant then, and I wasn't entirely sure what Jake meant either, but I tried to respond as if I saw the whole picture. "Deb doesn't have a Mercedes," I said defensively. "She doesn't even have a driver's license." It was funny that I even bothered to defend her. I had to remind myself that she was no longer my friend.

"You know she will though," Jake said.

"I doubt it," I said. "They bought her brothers Jeeps or something. And besides, what's the difference? A VW bus from the 60s that still runs can't be that cheap."

His eyes opened wide as if I'd delivered a revelation. I felt proud. "That's true," he said. Then he shrugged. "But you have to admit, a VW bus is cooler." He gestured back towards the turret. "I have no doubt in my mind that Sara Jennings's parents have definitely bought her a Mercedes. In fact, the driving age in Pennsylvania is 16, so she's probably already crashed one and had it replaced."

"Ha!" We were back on Sara Jennings. I looked back at the stone house. It looked like something that had been built by peasants during medieval times, back in the mythical days of chastity belts. That window at the top of the turret had to have been Sara Jennings's old window. Was the tower she looked out of now in Hershey, Pennsylvania even grander? Did she have hair like Rapunzel? What was her deal? I gave Jake a skeptical look.

"Are you in love with Sara Jennings or something?"

"Why do you care?" he asked.

"I don't."

"Then why did you ask?"

"I don't know!" I replied. "To make conversation! You keep bringing her up, so..."

I was watching him, waiting for an answer. I figured it'd be snarky, like most of the stuff that came out of his mouth, but then he just kind of shrugged and shook his head. "There's like this seriousness in your face when you listen, like something with your eyebrow," he said. "I thought it was just the face you made in class, but you're doing it now and it's making me nervous."

Self-consciously, my hand moved towards my eyebrows. What were they doing wrong? How many parts of your body did you have to be aware of at one time to appear normal in this world? "Nervous?" I said, shocked. "You're the one who snuck up on me and put your hand over my mouth!"

"I was just trying to say hi! You screamed! I didn't want Travis's parents to hear!"

"What about the fact that you're always talking about stuff I have no idea about in a voice that acts totally shocked that I'm so ignorant? You don't think that makes me nervous?" I gave him a dirty look, suddenly overly conscious of my very serious eyebrows.

"What didn't you know?"

I couldn't tell if he was kidding or not. "You just made fun of me like two minutes ago for not knowing about that place in New York where Seinfeld is from."

He shrugged. "It's called Queens. It was just Queens!" he

said. "I just thought you'd know that. I thought everyone knew that."

"Well I didn't. I'm not as smart as you, alright?"

"Um, I'm sorry, can you repeat that into a tape recorder, please? I need to mail this to Dreckford."

"Oh my god, I'm leaving," I said. I started to stand up, but then he put his hand on my arm and I stopped.

"I haven't seen Sara Jennings since third grade. But she was, like, really good at hula hooping. And I do wonder about her every once in a while when I pass by her old house, so I think that you're probably right. Maybe I was in love with her, or whatever that means when you are in third grade. I mean I thought she was very pretty. Her mom was also very pretty actually."

I snorted.

"What?" he said. "It's true. I'm just stating facts."

"Okay..."

"Anyway, she moved. But I was quite fond of her back in elementary school, since you asked. But now she's gone. That's what happens when you're a kid. You just go wherever your parents take you."

For some reason, I didn't like this story. I looked up at the big house on the hill and tried to imagine a goldilocks with a hula hoop but kept conjuring the twins from *The Shining* instead.

Jake ripped out some grass and threw it at me this time. "Don't get jealous," he said. "She wasn't that good at hula hooping. You would have crushed her."

"Ha, ha," I said, inwardly frowning. I didn't have a bedroom with a turret. I was just a trespasser on the lawn. The best I could do was to "crush her." To win another meaningless contest. What a sham.

"Seriously, she was no Emily Banks."

I knew he was trying to be kind, that he was attempting to convey something mystic, but I wasn't entirely sure what it was and I didn't feel like figuring it out.

I dropped back and sprawled out across the grass and lifted my flip-flopped feet in the air, moving my heels so the soles moved back and forth. I felt his eyes on me. Maybe an hour passed. Maybe ten minutes. Maybe five seconds. It was unbearable, however long it was.

Somewhere in Hershey, Pennsylvania, in a house built of miniature chocolate bars, Sara Jennings was probably asleep on a featherbed with her face under a pink silk sleep mask. But for some reason Jake wanted me to know that she wasn't that cool.

"Also, she had a voice that sounded like an elf."

"Who?" I asked, confused for a minute.

"Sara Jennings!"

My face broke into a goofy smile as my image of Sara shifted from a princess to a child elf who'd moved to Hershey, Pennsylvania to work at the chocolate factory. "I'm picturing an Oompa Loompa for some reason. They're like chocolate-making elves, right?"

"They aren't elves," Jake said. "No way, they are totally their own thing, but her mom was sort of orange-y. I'd always figured it was fake tanner."

"So you're into fake tanner," I said.

"That was a non sequitur!"

"You said her mom was hot!"

He shrugged. "I didn't say she was my style."

A laugh escaped my throat. Now there was an Oompa Loompa in a bikini in my mind's eye. Everything was suddenly silly.

"What does an elf even sound like?" I asked. I rolled onto my stomach, my elbows bent and my chin resting in the palms of my hands. He was sitting cross legged next to me. From my angle, I had a view of his nostrils. Because it was nighttime, I couldn't see inside them, but I noticed that they were wide and round, much larger than my own. The skin on each side of them seemed to flare a second as he considered the question, then it relaxed as his face stretched into a smile. It was that same mischievous, crooked-toothed grin from bio. We'd shared these sorts of laughs in science a million times, but here, on this grass at this hour of the night, all alone, it caused a tingle to travel from my crown down my spine. It was the same sensation I got when a friend in elementary school would braid my hair from her desk behind me. I felt like a cat who'd been pet exactly how she liked.

Mirthfully, I considered an elf. I imagined the tiny vocal chords of a playful, tiny, almost-human taking shape in my throat, and then I took a deep inhale and attempted to speak. "Is this what an elf sounds like?" I said in a squeak. But my voice cracked.

Jake giggled. This laughter sent another tingly wave across my skin. "No," he said, in his own cracked squeak of a voice. "That's a munchkin. An elf sounds like this."

"No," I said in an even higher pitch. "I think I got it. I think this is an elf."

"Ding ding," he said. He offered me a hand and I gave him a high five. "I think you may have just become semi-possessed by the spirit of Sara Jennings."

"At least the third grade version," I said. "Who knows? Maybe puberty and all that fake tanner gave her a deep, sultry voice." I tried to make my voice as scratchy and deep as possible. "Hey, Jake," I said, holding in my laughter by pausing to take a deep breath. "Wanna hula hoop?"

We devolved into hysterics. Through our laughter and tears, we kept adding to the joke.

"But she's not like a kid anymore," Jake managed.

"She's like an old lady," I added.

"With like a cigarette, like one of Marge's sisters."

We laughed until our faces hurt and then breathed ourselves back to sanity.

He pulled a cigarette out of his pocket and lit one. I guess the mention of Marge's sisters somehow awoke a nicotine urge. I watched him tilt his head to one side and shield the end from the breeze with his left hand as he flicked the lighter with the other. It made my hands feel useless.

"Can I have one of those?" I asked, impulsively.

"You don't smoke," he said. "State champions don't smoke cigarettes."

"School's out. I'm not a state champion."

"You're the reigning champion. Until someone beats you, that's just how it goes."

I glared at him and then reached out and pulled his cigarette right out of his mouth.

"Well, if I can't have one then you can't either," I said, standing up, holding the brown filtered side of the stick while watching the other end burn. I froze, considering whether I should smoke it, hearing Jenna's voice in my ears and the way she mimed me being such a nerd. What did she know? I frowned at Jake. "Why do you even smoke these things? They're disgusting." But then, before waiting for an answer, I held the end up to my mouth and sucked on it like it was a straw in a slushie. Immediately my mouth filled up with the taste of dirt. I hacked out a cloud.

This image of me must have been more than Jake could bear. He jumped to his feet and ripped the cigarette from my hand, tossing it off in the yard somewhere.

I controlled my strangled cough. "Aren't you supposed to put it out first? It could start a fire."

"Isn't your butt wet from sitting here? They water this lawn all the time."

"Still," I said.

"You find it," he told me. "You're the one who stole it."

So I ran off in the direction he'd tossed it, and spent a few minutes kicking through the grass. But the lawn was too thick and shadowed. I couldn't really see. I came back empty handed, but as I strolled towards him, I noticed a twinkling directly above him.

"Hey look!" I said, delighted, pointing up at the sky. "Look at that star! It's like actually bright. You can see it. What is it? Is it the North Star?"

"Polaris," he said, standing up next to me.

"What?" He was standing so close that our arms were touching.

"It's the other name of the North Star."

"Polaris," I said, feeling delighted. "We found the North Star!"

"No. We didn't. That's not Polaris. Or, maybe it is, I don't know. I just know that Polaris is the name of the North Star."

I looked up at him with a smirk. "Did Carl Sagan teach you that?"

"No," he said. "I can't remember where I learned it. Sometimes you just know something and you don't know how."

"True," I said. We smiled at each other. Something was sealed in that moment. Whatever happened, however long this life lasted, it was impossible to ignore that we were linked.

"What's something that you know like that?" he said. He looked genuinely curious.

"You can't just ask someone something like that," I said. "I know stuff, but I can't remember what I know." I fixed my eyes on the sky. Above us that no-name, possibly-not-North star revealed another star, and another. Jake felt like the only other person in the universe, like it was just us, Adam and Eve, on an abandoned planet of darkened houses, wet lawns, golf courses, and parked cars. The crickets chirped the same song they always played, but to me they were suddenly playing the *Cosmos* theme.

Jake just stood there. He didn't appear to be in any sort of rush. Maybe he was expecting me to go on. I wanted to tell him something. I just didn't know what. It was as if all the locked chambers inside me were rushing to reveal their hidden codes. But just at that moment, when the truth seemed to be so close to words, my awareness of this sensation to open up turned into self-consciousness. Immediately, all the safes inside me were again slammed tight, their codes promptly forgotten.

I sighed at the sky, but really I was directing my energy towards him. "Asking me what I know is a trick question," I said. "You know that I know nothing. I'm just one of those perfectionists who studies for the test and then immediately forgets everything."

He laughed. "I'm not grading you on your response, you know. And besides, being a perfectionist is something you know how to do that I don't."

"It's not something you know how to do," I said. "It's an affliction."

"Spoken like a person who has never gotten anything less than an A." It was true. I'd literally never gotten a B. When I was younger, it'd been a source of pride, but now I realized how embarrassing it also was. I was incapable of ignoring an assignment. Grades and awards, hoops that I jumped through instead of hula-ed, were what defined me.

"We need to figure out what that star's called," I said. "We need a starfinder."

"You don't have one with you? I thought you were stargazing."

"I guess I forgot," I said. Then I yawned, realizing it was probably two in the morning, and remembering the world I'd escaped with my room and empty bed and sleeping parents. Were they still asleep? Did they know?

"I need to go," I said. "If my parents wake up, I'm dead."

"But we were just starting to stargaze!"

"Don't you have a curfew?" I asked.

"Not really."

"Let's do it another time," I said. "I'll make my dad drive me to Edmund Scientific so I can get the finder thing."

"Fine," he said. "I'll bring our packet."

"My packet."

"I thought we already went over this." He was right. We had. He pointed at my notebook, still resting on the grass. "You should at least sketch the sky in that notebook you brought," he suggested, "so that you can remember where the stars were so you can figure out what they're called later."

It was a good suggestion. I sat back down and started drawing on the heavily shadowed page.

Instead of joining me, he started walking towards the road.

"Where are you going?" I asked him.

"Stay right there," he said. Then he disappeared behind a grove of trees back towards Travis's house. I thought maybe he had to pee, but he returned a few minutes later with a bike.

"I borrowed Trav's cruiser from the shed. I'll ride you home," he said.

"How?" I asked, confused.

"On the handlebars!"

"Are you kidding me?"

"Come on. It's easy."

I walked up to the bike and straddled the front wheel.

"Don't worry," he said. "I'll hold the frame. I'm not gonna let you fall."

I looked down at his fingers that were gripping the handlebars tightly and saw the speckles of my teeth marks. I jumped up and made sure my legs were spread wide enough that they didn't rub against the wheel.

"Ready," Jake said. "One, two—" on three we were gliding down the darkened road. It was an incredible feeling. I was a little breathless for a second.

"I live on Hillcrest," I said, trying to control the ebullience in my voice.

"I know," he said, his voice cracking a little, probably because it was hard to pedal with all my weight. "By the tennis courts."

"How?" I asked.

"Everyone knows where everyone lives."

"I didn't know that Travis lived up here."

"Once again, Banks, you are the exception."

He said this directly in my ear. Not on purpose, really, but because of proximity, considering the way I sat on the handlebars and the fact that he had to stand a little to push harder on the pedals. It gave me a rush of adrenaline. I let out a giggle as we coasted down the slope of Lane of Acres and made a right onto the even steeper decline of Winding Way.

We entered the more crowded streets of big, old, nice houses with smaller yards, packed closer together. On these streets, we didn't even whisper. I don't know if this was for fear a light would turn on in someone's house and they would look out their window, or if it was just the energy of our bodies so close together that caused the hush.

The ride was mostly downhill. Jake pedaled backwards for most of the journey to put some friction on the brake, making sure we didn't go too fast, but even still, the speed flew my hair backwards. I felt the happy thrill that only coasting down a hill on the handlebars of a bike at two in the morning can provide.

He stopped at the corner, near the entrance to the tennis courts. I hopped off, pulling my shorts down where they'd ridden up my thigh.

I didn't know what to say. I was afraid to look too closely at him, so I just whispered, "Bye," and then darted behind the bleachers along the fence to the little hole that led to my backyard.

Suddenly I was alone again in the same place I'd been earlier that day, when I'd felt plagued by my exile. I looked up at the sky and found that star. There it was, gazing down, the maybe-not-North Star.

Once I was through the window, inside, upstairs in my room, I opened up the notebook and cleaned up the lines of my night-sky sketch, writing "Maybe-Not-North-Star?" on the one we'd debated. Secretly, I thought of it as "The Jake Star." But I was afraid to write that down. His name in my handwriting felt too much like a wish.

- 13 -

I collapsed into a deep, dark, dreamless sort of velvet sleep, only to open my eyes at 8:56AM to discover that my bed sheets were covered in blood.

I'd gotten my period. Everywhere. It was like a murder scene. And I was supposed to spend the day in Pennsylvania with a bunch of my dad's high school friends and their families.

In the shower, I watched the red turn pink and swirl down the drain, my vulva pulsing in pain.

"Make sure you drink water," Mom said. "Staying hydrated helps."

"I have cramps," I whined. "They kill." It felt as if there was a chainsaw in my abdomen. I was half bent over in the doorway of my parents' bedroom, asking my mom for a pad. The bathroom closet was empty.

She retrieved a few from a bag.

"Do I have to go to Benji's party?" I moaned. Benji was Dad's best friend from growing up. The party was an annual event, the sort of thing where the grownups delighted in each other's presence so much that they forgot that none of their kids were really friends, and so the younger crowd was forced to forge friendships that lasted for one day a year.

"Oh honey, yes, I think so, but I'll tell them you're not feeling well and maybe you can just sit downstairs and watch TV."

At the party, though, I did manage to find the strength to smile and socialize. I played card games with the other kids, Spoons and Spit and Crazy 8s, and helped myself to Cheetos and Doritos and two hot dogs with spicy mustard and relish. I even drank a can of blackberry soda. Mom didn't chastise me about these choices like she normally would. She always tried to seem less like a nutrition psycho in public, although she only ate from the fruit bowl.

My cramps were ever present, but there were stretches of time when I managed to ignore them. What I couldn't ignore was the wet feeling in my underwear. The fear that my pad was leaking led me to visit the bathroom like 700 times. Most of the partygoers were using the powder room that was downstairs off of the kitchen, so I kept walking up the stairs to the full bathroom in the hall. It was awkward to figure out ways to excuse myself and to sneak the pink plastic wrapper of a maxi pad into my pocket from my mother's purse in the living room. Sitting on the toilet, using basically a whole roll of Benji's double-ply Charmin every time I went upstairs, I wondered why I couldn't just tell everyone. Why they couldn't just escort me to a cozy cave with a wad of towels or something and maybe the entire first season of *Cosmos*, so I could deconstruct Carl Sagan/Jake Freelander's mind while I suffered? Why was everyone always talking about man caves? I was the one who needed a cave. Right now. This cushioned toilet seat that I had to keep wiping down after I stood up in this foreign house was just not cutting it.

I couldn't believe this was going to happen to me for like 30 or more years. Was I really going to have to bleed like this like 350 more times? What bullshit!

"Did you know human females are the only mammals who menstruate every 28 days?" That was Ceil's response to my report on my weekend, when I arrived to babysit after the holiday. She was telling me this from the top of a ladder, where she was again fiddling with the electric, this time using a screwdriver to reattach the fan.

"We are?" I said. "Why?"

"Can you hand me that big screw right there?" she asked me.

"This one?" I asked, holding up the biggest screw that was resting inside an upside-down plastic frisbee, which was resting on the seat of the recliner, which was shoved up against the wall below some old framed black and white photos, one of which featured a mustachioed man on a motorcycle. I recognized the man. There were other pictures of him around the place. This must be the man that she ran away with to the city. One of the pictures was of Ceil, looking the same, except a little scrawnier and more childlike, wearing a weird-looking toga thing in front of a store that had it's metal gate down over the windows. The sign above her said, "Caputo's Meats." Ceil's body was twisted and spinning, her hands in the air, in the middle of a dance routine, I guessed. I looked up at her as I offered her the screw. The fine lines of her still-beautiful face revealed themselves as she frowned in concentration.

"You know women are connected to the ocean, which is the source of all life, and the ocean is controlled by the moon. And 28 days is a moon cycle. We're all walking mermaids. But nobody wants to tell you that, because the patriarchy spent like 300,000 years suppressing our power."

"So what are we supposed to do?" I asked.

She beamed a straight-toothed, supermodel smile at me that made me feel both a little dumb, and also loved. "Oh, my dear Emily, where do I begin?" She climbed down the ladder and then put her hands on each of my shoulders, her posture still perfect from all her years of dance. Then she swayed back and forth with me for a moment, like we were slow dancing. After that, she stopped swaying, squeezed my shoulders and wobbled them back and forth. My blood felt like it was dancing in my veins. Whatever she had just done was magic.

"The most important part is to love yourself," she said. "And to let your love of yourself tell you what rules to obey and which to rebel against. Because this reality we're functioning inside is held together by scotch tape and cardboard. It doesn't mean shit." She folded up the ladder. "Are you ready?" she asked, smiling.

"For what?"

"For the moment we've all been waiting for. Maeve!" she called. "Maeve! Get out here."

Maeve came out of her room pushing a baby stroller that was stuffed with three teddy bears that were wearing pairs of her underwear. "Look at their outfits!" she said.

"They look great!" Ceil gave her a kiss on the head as she walked to the light switch and pointed to the fan.

"You fixed it?!" Maeve was pumped and ready to celebrate.

"We'll see in a second." Ceil said. "Ready?" Her hand hovered over the switch.

"Turn it on!" Maeve said.

"Give me a drumroll," Ceil said. It was like *National Lampoon's Christmas Vacation*.

"Rat, tat, tat, tat, dum, dum, dum," Maeve said.

I rolled my tongue against the top of my mouth.

"I need more than that, people," Ceil said. "I want to hear you in the back."

Maeve and I both upped our volume. I started clapping my hands. She started jumping.

"I'm every woman," Ceil sang dramatically, waving her arms, "It's all in me..."

She flipped the switch.

Our eyes all stared overhead. The blades took off in a swirl.

"Wee," Maeve said. She stuck her hands out like the blades of the fan and started spinning wildly in circles. Ceil joined her and then so did I, the three of us spinning in crazy circles in the tiny living room, bumping against each other with each swirl until we collapsed on the floor, giggling and dizzy.

"Feel that breeze," Ceil said. It felt wonderful. It was drying the sweat on our faces and breathing new life into the room.

"You did it, Mama," Maeve said.

Ceil pulled her onto her lap and gave her tickles and kisses. Then she quickly got dressed and hurried out the door. But the fan blades continued to spin all day. They were a reminder of the fact that time was passing and that things were possible, that good things could happen if you just kept trying.

The more I ran with Kelsey, the chattier she became. Like Deb, she was the youngest, but she had five older siblings instead of two. Her oldest brother had just had a baby and she was already an aunt.

"Mandy says I'm baby obsessed," Kelsey said. "She acts like just because I love my niece I want to get knocked up."

"No way," I said.

"Right? But I'm not on the pill. Are you?"

This question was hilarious to me. That Kelsey would assume there was even a chance that I could potentially get pregnant showed how little she considered my reality. Or maybe she'd heard the story about Doug and I and assumed that was like a weekly sort of ritual for me.

"No," I replied, kind of confused.

"Kate was on them last year," she said, referring to one of her friends, "not because she was being like a crazy slut or anything but because she had a lot of pimples and her cycle was weird. The doctor said that maybe it was a hormone thing, but it made her have crazy PMS rage. She threw a ham sandwich at me once for saying I didn't like *Dawson's Creek*! If that isn't certifiably psycho, I don't know what is."

I found all of this information riveting.

We also talked about the beach. Her family vacationed in North Carolina, but her uncle had a house at the shore near Deb's.

"Doug's family has one there too," she said. I didn't know if she said this because she knew what happened and was trying to get me to talk about it, or if this was just random chit-chat. Either way, I tried to stay cool and just didn't say anything. But then of course she questioned me about it.

"I heard you guys all hung out one night down there over Memorial Day."

"Yeah."

"Mandy and I are always teasing Parker because he's obsessed with IMing your friend."

I thought it was funny that she said "your friend" instead of Deb. She obviously knew her name. Still, I was relieved that the conversation was taking a turn away from me. "Yeah. She like lives next to her computer these days."

"Did they hook up at the game the other night?"

"Honestly, I don't know. I haven't talked to her in a few days. She called me, but she wasn't home when I called back."

The truth was I'd been avoiding them. I just let the phone ring and ring when my parents were at work, and then listened to the answering machine. If it was Mom or Dad, I picked up, pretending to be just out of the shower. Jenna never left messages on our family answering machine. She always just hung up. But Deb did. She would greet each member of our family, and she did this a few times, the last time, saying, "Em, don't like poof and disappear. I know you're all important with your summer training and your job, but your lowly best friend needs you. Call me! Please!"

Oh, how that message needled me. The disdainful tone when describing me as "important" and the reverse psychology of referring to herself as "lowly." But at the same time, I knew there was also truth in it. She'd always been intimidated by my grades and my athleticism, just like I was intimidated by her wealth and beauty.

Maybe she did actually need me. Maybe something happened at the baseball game that I should know about. Maybe Kelsey was acting like she was curious about something, but she actually already knew.

Still, I was pissed and hurt and my pride would not allow me to enter into a conversation with someone who threw her longest friendship under the bus so easily. If she wanted to talk about whatever happened, she had Jenna. Or all of her countless friends on IM. What did she need me for anyway? She was probably just bored. Why else would she bother reaching out to a "butter face" like me? I pushed the delete button as soon as she finished her message. I didn't want my parents asking questions. But it was also out of spite. I felt a rush of adrenaline from silencing her voice.

Ignoring Deb and avoiding Jenna wasn't just an act of defiance, it was also a way to push the entire experience with Doug to the far corners of my consciousness. Hanging with them in the weeks after Memorial Day, I had to constantly relive the details of that night, roiling in the lingering rejection. Not having to watch Deb agonize over every single one of Parker's typos, or Jenna validate her obsession, was a vacation from my pain. Of course, it was still present, like a deep bruise. But without anyone actively poking it, there were moments when I could pretend it wasn't there.

They were not the only human beings on planet Earth anyway. They weren't even the only human beings in Tonley. I had other friends. I played mini golf with Jamie Markles and Brigid Elmore. They were alright. Still, it wasn't a perfect match. I was a free agent. Thankfully, it was summer, so it was perfectly acceptable to eat lunch all alone.

Even though Jake told me I could keep it, I eventually returned the yoga video. It was an impulsive decision. It was my day off from babysitting, and I had slept in, done a few flashcards, and lazed about the house in the morning before realizing it was already

1pm. I was afraid my mom might show up with food to share a late lunch with me—sometimes she surprised me when she had a morning site visit to a mall before going to her office—and I didn't want her commenting on my slothful morning, so I quickly tidied the house, got dressed, scrawled a note, and set off for my run. Before I was heading out the door, I realized that the TV was still on. The *Price is Right* was airing to an empty room. The prize was a brand new set of kayaks, complete with life vests and a weekend trip to a scenic lake somewhere in New Hampshire. "2,000," one man said. "10,000," said another. "What do you think those kayaks are made with? Gold?!" I asked the guy through the television set. "1 dollar," said the remaining contestant. The price was $4,500. I turned off the TV. Maybe the kayaks were made of gold. Before closing the TV cabinet, my eye caught the yoga video peeking out from the shelf below. So I grabbed it and clutched it in my hand for the whole 3.5 mile run, feeling it become slick inside my sweating palm. It was only when I ended my run in front of the store and walked into the cool, darkened cave of the interior—where again, I immediately sneezed—that I suddenly felt self-conscious and smelly. I was covered in sweat. What was I thinking? I spied Jake immediately. As the door was still opening, I saw him behind the counter, focused on whatever film was on the little set on the shelf in the back. I went into cardiac arrest, or at least the teenage version of it. My legs told me to run away, but I didn't have a chance to act on the impulse. The bells at the front door had caused him to turn his head faster than I could flee.

I saw his eyes light up. He fumbled the remote control and hit the pause button.

"Banks," he said. Could it have been possible that he, too, could think of nothing to say?

"Freelander," I said in return. I made no moves towards or

away from him. I was still standing right next to the door. We were speaking across the empty void of the store. I thought of flinging the DVD across the space between us and bolting, but my body became anchored, unwilling to give in to my cowardly desire.

Since I had no words, I just held up the video. He smiled. I took a few tentative steps towards the back counter, my eyes scanning the new arrivals, desperate for something to latch onto for conversation. I wondered if he was watching one of the films I saw displayed on the shelf.

"You've achieved Zen already?" he said at the exact same second that I asked, "What are you watching?"

"Not really," I answered him as he said, "*Breakfast at Tiffany's.*"

I knew pretty much nothing about *Breakfast at Tiffany's*. Only that it was a movie that had a song about it on the radio. I didn't know it starred Audrey Hepburn. I didn't know that it was based on a Truman Capote book. I didn't even know who Truman Capote was then. But I had been to the Tiffany's on 5th Avenue with Deb during that vacation to New York a million lightyears ago. It'd felt like a museum, but Mrs. Stevens had said a trip to New York wasn't complete unless you visited Tiffany's. She had tried on a $5,000 diamond necklace and waggled her eyebrows at Mr. Stevens. "We have an anniversary coming up," she'd said, to which he'd snorted in reply, "In three more months."

"As I recall, I think, we both kinda liked it," I said, quoting the song that basically encapsulated the bulk of my knowledge about *Breakfast at Tiffany's*. Then I cringed at my own lameness.

"The film is way better than that one hit wonder," he said as he put a library card thing into the back of the yoga video and tossed it into a pile of returns to be shelved. There were probably like 25 videos in the laundry-basket-ish container. "I still have to put those all away," he said. "It's my least favorite part of the job."

"Yeah," I said. "Doesn't sound nearly as interesting as searching through rental archives and playing town detective."

"Speaking of which," he said. "I think Mr. Dubelton has a Reese Witherspoon fetish. That or he's a sociopath who might kill people in his basement. He returned *Cruel Intentions* three weeks late and just told me how much he loved *American Psycho.*"

"I don't know who Mr. Dubelton is," I said.

"Good," Jake said. "You're safe. For now. He's like a super-jacked, finance dude who works half of the week in Philly and half the week on Wall Street. I mean, he doesn't come in that often, I'm sure he just does Pay-Per-View most of the time. He's divorced. His kids are little. He brings them in every once in a while."

"How do you know so much about him?"

He pointed to his ears. "People will tell you anything," he said. "You just have to listen. That's what he babbled to me when he brought back the video three weeks late."

"Has he taken out *Election*?" I asked.

"Good point," Jake said. "That will definitely let us know whether his creepiness tends towards Reese specifically, or if he just gets off on rich, male cruelty and violence."

I put my hands on my face and groaned, "Oh my god."

"What?" he said.

"Don't you think it's kind of disturbing that our conversations always stray towards murdering and violence?"

"You're right. It's fucked up. But it's not me. I'm a pacifist. And a vegan. No meat, no leather, nothing."

"What's a vegan?" I asked.

"It's like a vegetarian on crack. No cheese, no eggs, no honey, no byproduct of a living creature."

"But plants are alive."

"True, but we are not as in touch with the way they experience pain. And also, factory farming is insane. Talk about psycho killers." He pulled out Mr. Dubelton's rental history and then exclaimed, "No *Election*! Someone call the FBI."

"I guess I should feel comforted that you are watching *Breakfast at Tiffany's* when I surprise you."

Jake laughed.

"I've never seen it though, so I don't know if there's like a crazy murder scene in it," I told him.

"There's not. But full disclosure, I do enjoy a Hitchcock every now and then, but more for the camera angles than the killing." He pointed to the TV on pause. "I just started it like 5 minutes before you came in. Want to watch it with me?"

"Now?" I said. "Aren't you working?"

"Technically, yes, but I can pull up a stool. No one will care." He looked around the store. "Does anyone care if Emily watches this movie with me?" Of course there was no one in the store, so no one responded. He turned and smiled at me. "See?"

I looked at the clock. It was 2:13. I mean, there was no reason that I couldn't stay. I had nowhere to be. I shrugged. "Sure. Why not?"

"For the record," I said as I stuck my butt against the counter and swung my legs to the other side, feeling my knee brush against Jake's elbow. "I don't really like that "Breakfast at Tiffany's" song."

He raised an eyebrow at me. "I don't believe that for a second," he said. I didn't want him to know he was right. I didn't own the CD or anything. But it's true that I'd sung the lyrics alone in my room before. Still, he didn't know that. I stuck my tongue out at him and settled into the other side of the counter, helping myself to a wax-lined paper cone of Deer Park water from the cooler I saw hidden behind a cabinet.

"We need snacks," I said.

Jake pulled a huge plastic tub of peanut butter crackers out from a shelf. "These have been here since I started and I have no idea how long they've been here, but they're only actually like medium-stale."

I reached into the container and tried one. They were passable. I helped myself to like five more.

Jake restarted the film and a quiet settled over us. Our eyes were directed towards the television, but my focus wasn't all there. It volleyed between the movie itself and the boy I was watching it with. I was distracted by his physical presence, by his reactions, and by what he thought of Audrey Hepburn, who was a gorgeous, perfect twig who didn't seem to produce a single bead of sweat.

But though she was perfect-looking, she wasn't perfect. I liked how she was a total mess and how she refused to name her cat because she didn't think she had a right to name him and how she said she suffered from the mean reds, which were when "you were suddenly afraid, but didn't know what you were afraid of." I knew the mean reds, though I'd have called them blue.

And, of course, there was the love story between Holly and Paul. At one point, I stopped sitting on the stool. I paced a little bit back and forth, and then I decided to sit, cross legged, my head tilted up towards the screen, my back leaning against Jake's shins. He put his hand on the top of my head. It made me jump.

"You want to sit in this chair?" Jake asked.

"What if your boss walks in? Won't he think it's weird?" Jake scooted himself over so that half of the chair was available.

"Let's just share it," he said. I positioned myself on the available patch of the seat, my legs and arms all brushed against Jake's. Did I smell? I hoped not. In the movie, Paul had published his story. He was writing again. Everything was possible. My hand was resting on my thigh. Jake took his and sort of linked his pinkie against mine. We were almost holding hands. I let it happen. I liked that it was happening.

Holly and Paul were in Tiffany's negotiating getting the Cracker Jack ring engraved when the bells over the door jingled. Jake and I's pinkies unlinked. I bent down a little and rested my elbows on my knees and my head in my chin, hoping to hide a little behind Jake's frame. I couldn't see the person who'd entered, but when I heard him speak, I recognized his voice. It was Scott. He was with a girl—his younger sister I assumed. "Mom said we could each pick a movie. You can pick out both if you don't tell her that my friends come over." I knew his sister. Her name was Ramona. She'd been a kindergartener when I was in 4th grade. Now I think she was going into 7th. I felt my face go beat red, but I didn't move. There was nowhere to go. Besides, the movie was so good. They finally kissed.

"What's up Freelander?" I heard Scott greet Jake from somewhere in the store.

Jake stood up from the chair and stretched his hand out. They did like a high five handshake thing while Jake nodded back, "What's up?" he said.

I wondered if Jake detected my sense of alarm. Was he embarrassed to be spotted with me? If he was, he didn't show it. He played it so cool that I felt myself relax. Who gave a shit who saw us watching a movie together? What was wrong with watching a movie together anyway?

I felt Scott see me, but he did not say hi. I didn't look at him and offered no hello in return. Ramona walked up with some movies. "I'm ready," she said.

"No way," Scott said. "You cannot get that movie. It's rated R and you're going to be screaming like a crazy person and never sleep again and Mom will kill me."

It was *The Exorcist*.

"Just tell her you picked it out," Ramona said.

"You're not going to tell her anyone came over?" he asked.

"No," she said. "But you're going to let me pick where we order food from, right?"

"I don't care," he said. I was trying to focus on the movie. Paul couldn't find Holly anywhere. He was looking for her all over the city. He broke up with the married lady who'd been paying his rent.

Then Paul finally found Holly at the library. I was standing in front of the TV now. Jake was checking Scott and Ramona out. I refused to look in their direction. This was probably a stupid thing to do. It's not like not looking at them made them cease to exist. But I was embarrassed and shy and still reeling and humiliated by the term "butter face" on top of everything else. Scott had witnessed a night I'd have rather never lived. And besides, he'd never made me feel all that comfortable or included when I was on his turf anyway. I didn't owe it to him to acknowledge his existence. I stayed sucked into the movie.

When the bells above the door tinkled and we knew they were gone, Holly was engaged to the Brazilian. Jake settled back down onto his half of the seat and took up my pinkie again, actually this time he also scooped my ring finger. He leaned his shoulder into mine a little and said, "I like how you gave Scott a straight diss."

I tried to play like I had no idea what he was talking about, as if I'd only been present in the vacuum of the screen. I just shrugged at him, afraid that he'd see through me if I said anything. He'd know.

He didn't press the issue. The movie was too good. We watched the rest in silence, and then the cat was in the rain and they rescued it and it was over. How much time had passed? It was like waking from a night of sleep and realizing that you've grown.

"One day, I'm gonna live in New York City," I said.

Jake smiled at me. "Me too."

There was a silence. Inside the silence was a future. And a hormone rush. It was time to flee.

I took another stale peanut butter cracker from the huge plastic tub. "This was fun," I told him.

"No," he said. "Don't leave me."

"I have to go home."

"But then I'll be bored."

"But you still have to put away all those movies."

"You could help me."

I laughed. "Um, I think letting you copy my homework all last year was helping you enough. I'm not doing your job for you. Anyway, I have SAT workbooks to study and my parents are going to be home from work soon."

"I get off at 5. I could walk you home." It was 4:30. It sounded nice, in theory, to stroll the leafy streets with Jake in the daylight, when there were actual people standing in their actual yards and cars drove by on the street. But what would happen if he tried to hold my hand again? Like my whole hand? Would my entire body become some sort of puddle on the sidewalk? Who would see us? Would we kiss?

"I can't. My mom checks my work when she gets home, so I have to hurry so I can finish a few pages."

We looked at each other in a way that is hard to report. It was meaningful.

"Fine," he said.

I reached my hand out to him like Scott did and forced him to go through an awkward and slow, bro-doggish hand slap.

"See you around," I said.

- 14 -

It turned out that *Cosmos* still did air on network television. I stumbled upon it one night at around 1am when I'd walked downstairs for a glass of water and capitulated to the pull of the remote control. I was barely even looking at the channels, just lost in the rhythm of button flicking, enjoying the way my brain barely processed each network's world before it vanished and made way for the next channel. Sports documentaries became infomercials, infomercials became MTV, until all of a sudden there was Sagan sitting at a weird desk holding an object he called a tesseract.

There are easy explanations for why Carl Sagan was on the television in the middle of the night, of course. His show was celebrating an anniversary, and they had just released a box set. Maybe they were showing reruns to pique interest in its purchase. He was an astronomer. People who like astronomy are likely to be awake in the middle of the night. But to me, it was just a big old sign. All I thought about was Jake.

Sagan was talking about the fourth dimension and how, when you live in a three dimensional world like us, you can only experience the next dimension in impressions.

Maybe the fourth dimension was love. When the show was over, I opened the back door and sat for a few minutes on the floor of the deck searching for the star Jake and I had contemplated the other night. When I found it, I connected it to other planets and stars and glowing things, making the handlebars of a bicycle. I sat my soul on top of them and relived the story of that crazy night, of Jake appearing out of nowhere.

Then the backdoor opened and my mom was standing there in her pajamas.

"What are you doing out here?" she said.

"I woke up and was thirsty, then I decided to do some star homework."

"See anything new?"

"That one," I said, pointing out a pinprick of light directly overhead. "But I don't know what it's called because I don't have a starfinder."

"Doesn't that defeat the purpose?" Mom asked.

"I mean it would be helpful to have one, but the rules are vague," I told her. "I think the point is to just start really thinking about how we are on one tiny planet in an inconceivably large universe."

"It is crazy, isn't it?" Mom said. "I honestly never really thought about it until you had this project. In fact, I'm really just thinking about it right now. It's kind of freaky."

"And we just live in this tiny little part of this tiny little ball. It's even freakier."

"But is it really better anywhere else?"

"I guess you never know unless you go and see for yourself."

"True," she said.

"Do you ever wish you left New Jersey? Like, that you moved somewhere different? Like California or Montana or Florida or New York City? Or Paris?"

"To me," Mom said, "Moving to Tonley was moving somewhere. My mom moved from South Philly to Bronner and that was something too. I know you can drive between them in 20 minutes or so, but those moves meant something. I'm not like Ceil. I wasn't running from anything, so I didn't need to risk everything to start over. The moves weren't far, but they mattered."

I thought it was funny that she suddenly brought up Ceil. That wasn't even what we were talking about. "What was Ceil running from?"

"Oh, I don't want to get into that," Mom said. "A lot of things. But it's not really my story to tell."

"But you're always half-telling it, so you might as well just tell the whole thing."

Mom exhaled a long breath. "You know how I told you about that contest and the college?"

"Yeah."

"And how the teacher was helping us with the project?"

"Yeah."

"Well, the teacher's wife came to the school one day and started screaming all kinds of things at Ceil when she left the building. Ceil was apparently having an affair with the teacher. People say she went to the city to have an abortion." Mom gave herself the sign of the cross after she said those words.

"Poor Ceil," I said.

"The poor teacher's wife," Mom said. "She had a two-year-old and was pregnant herself!"

The stars kept their poker face and watched without judgement overhead. I wondered what an alien would think of this conversation. Who was wrong? What was right? A silence extended over us as I thought of Ceil running away from all the nasty words the teacher's wife and probably everyone else slung at her after whatever went down. Mom was looking at me carefully, but I didn't return her stare.

"I guess if I left here, I'd be interested in living in the Poconos," she said.

"The Poconos?" I said, surprised. "Really? Why?"

"They seem quiet. And I like country decor. All those old Dutch style houses. They just seem like they should smell like apple pie."

Mom didn't even eat pie. She only took tiny bites from other people's plates.

We ran out of things to say outside and retreated inside. The clock said three in the morning. "We need to go back to sleep!" Mom said. On our way up the stairs she asked, "Are you going to share your observations with your science partner?"

I sighed. Jake had left a message on the answering machine that I didn't get a chance to delete before my parents heard it. He said he was my science partner and was checking in about the project. Since then, Mom and Dad were constantly asking me about him, trying to make sure I was staying on top of my summer assignments.

"Definitely," I told her, "but not now. It's way too late." Though as I got back into my bed, I wondered if maybe he was awake, and if maybe he was thinking of me.

Still, I didn't call him back. He left another message with my dad. A week or so went by. I avoided Main Street and Absolute Video. I avoided Jenna and Deb too. I even avoided walking by Deb's house when I left Maeve and Ceil's, walking the other way down the street and looping around an extra three blocks. I didn't want to think or process things that were beyond my control. I just wanted to cross things off my checklists. I just wanted to perfect my practice exams. I liked problems that stayed neatly within the confines of a Scantron sheet.

Dad bought me a starfinder. One night, he drove me down the White Horse Pike near the edge of the Pine Barrens where my grandfather used to go so we could get some dark sky. We even got out of the car and sat on the hood. Of course the first star I saw was the not-North one—Jake's one—but I pretended like I had no idea what it was. "What's that super bright one, right there?" I asked my dad. We moved the concentric circles of the starfinder to align with the date and time and then positioned it according to the cardinal points. We both agreed that it was Vega. It was apparently part of the constellation Lyra, though I couldn't really make out the rest of the stars.

"Do you think Mom didn't want to come because this is where her dad used to go?" I asked.

"Maybe," Dad said.

"Do you know where he died?"

"I know it was out here somewhere," Dad said, "but I honestly have no idea. Probably farther down."

I could tell he didn't really want to talk about it, and I realized I didn't really want to either. It was like inviting in a ghost neither of us had ever met. We knew this guy was part of us, but how? Maybe we were there to find out. Maybe my grandfather's spirit was with us. A few times, I imagined him helping my hands move the starfinder just so, conveying his knowledge to me through the instruments available.

As we stargazed, Dad and I talked about all the cool forgotten parts of New Jersey he'd discovered over the years from his coworkers—the abandoned mental hospitals, ghost towns, interesting places to canoe. On a normal day, I didn't feel one way or another about New Jersey. It was just the place where I lived. But that night it felt like where I was from. I felt like part of its story. And that didn't necessarily seem like a bad thing. It was probably just as good as anywhere else.

The days continued to pass uneventfully. The only person I really hung out with, strangely, was Kelsey Kramer.

If Coach had paired me with a rising freshman as a running buddy, things would have been so different. I could have just remained a nerdy hermit. But the problem with my plan to disappear was that Kelsey Kramer became less of a Barbie doll with each run.

She was actually fucking hilarious. It only took a week or so for me to learn why she was always insisting that we stop at her friends' houses on our runs. The truth was that she was incapable of holding in her poop. If she had to go, she had to go. And on long runs, her bowels liked to be emptied. Usually, we made it to a friendly toilet in time. But there was once when we were deep into the loop around Lander's Pond that she had no choice but to crouch down behind a tree and use leaves to wipe herself.

That moment bonded us for life. We were in tears, we were laughing so hard. I hid behind a tree far enough away that I could be a lookout—and also avoid seeing or smelling anything.

"You need to bury that!" I'd demanded.

She'd dug a hole with a stick.

On another run, we were passing the scene of the crime on the trail when out of nowhere she said, "So are you and Jake Freelander a thing?"

"What?" I said as I exhaled.

"Like, are you guys hooking up?"

"No!" I said. He'd left another message with my parents that I'd avoided, which made for a total of three. I knew I needed to do something soon. I just couldn't force myself to act.

But then I became worried that she was asking because he was hooking up with someone else and wanted to make sure I didn't think Jake and I were an item before she gave me the bad news, so I asked, "Why?"

"Scott had a party a few weeks ago, and he told me he saw you with him at Absolute. I meant to ask you before and kept forgetting. But then I went there last night to rent a movie and saw him and thought of you."

"Oh," I said. "Yeah, I went there to return a movie one day and we just started talking and ended up watching a movie together."

"Ramona said you were sitting on his lap."

"Sitting on his lap!?" I said. "No way!"

Kelsey gave me a look. "Do you like him?"

Maybe I should have been honest with her. She was surprisingly honest with me. I knew all kinds of things about upperclassmen guys and demands for blow jobs and how she'd only actually given one once, but that one of her friends—she wouldn't say who because she didn't think that was fair—loved to give them to whoever asked her. The friend called it "practice."

But despite all this unsolicited information, I couldn't bring myself to confess.

"No!" I said defensively. "We're just friends. We sat near each other in Biology all year."

"And then you decided, why sit in two chairs, when you can just share one?" she said, coyly. "Makes total sense."

"Whatever. There was only one chair. The other thing to sit on was a weird, uncomfortable stool. We were watching a movie."

"What movie?"

"*Breakfast at Tiffany's*."

"Oh my god," Kelsey shouted, giving me a little shove. "It was totally a date."

"It was not a date," I said.

"I think he's cute," Kelsey said. "If you don't like him, maybe I'll date him." I looked up at her with a bit of worry and saw a triumphant smugness in her expression. My eyes had done the confessing. Shit.

I upped my pace so that she couldn't keep up, trying not to think about the fact that if they were gossiping about me hanging out with Jake, there was no way Kelsey didn't know about Doug.

At least babysitting was chill. I got to be the big sister I never was. Usually Maeve was hiding when I arrived. Ceil would pretend not to know where she was, shrug, and then go to her car and leave for work. Once we were alone, I would pretend to look in every corner but the one Maeve was obviously hiding in (usually the closet.) The game would end when Maeve jumped out of her hiding spot and yelled, "Boo!" at the top of her lungs. I would feign terror and tears, she would comfort me with a hug, and our day together would begin.

We personified everything: peas, pieces of trash, mosquitos. We read every *Berenstain Bears* they had at the library. We debated which Crayola crayon was best for drawing the sky—cobalt or blue or aquamarine.

When it was time to nap, she liked me to lay with her in her bed until she got settled. One time, when I thought she was already asleep, she spun around spontaneously, put her hand on my cheek and then kissed me on the nose.

"I love you, you silly ragamuffin," she said. It filled my heart with joy.

One morning, I walked into their house and all of Maeve's toys were strewn about the living room. It was impossible to take a step without making contact with some plastic figure. But she wasn't really playing with them, just aggressively tossing them around.

"We went to the city this weekend," Ceil said as an explanation.

"The city?" I asked, confused, thinking she meant Philly. I tried to sound fake happy, like grown ups do when they talk to sad kids. "Did you go to the Franklin Institute?"

"We were in Manhattan," Ceil said. "Her best friend Ramile had a birthday party at the park."

"Oh," I said, suddenly sympathizing. I felt her pain. I knew what it was like to pine for another time.

After a few hours, the memories of Manhattan seemed less

poignant. I was spraying the hose into a mist and we were marveling at the rainbows it made while Maeve danced. I noticed Deb walking towards the house from her backyard. She had on an oversized pair of aviators and a beach cover up with flip flops. She gave an enthusiastic wave. Maeve didn't even notice. It would have been crazy to make her stop her fun and retreat into the house, so I just stood there with the hose, waved back, and waited to see what would happen.

"Hi!" she said in an overly happy voice to Maeve, who had paused suspiciously at her arrival.

Maeve looked over at me. "Who's that?"

My first instinct was to ignore Deb, but I didn't have the energy for drama.

"This is Deb," I said to Maeve. "She's my friend."

"We're besties," Deb said, linking my arm. Her skin was cold from her central AC. It felt like something from the morgue. "Do you know what that means?"

Maeve wrinkled her nose and nodded.

"We've been best friends since we were little like you," Deb said in her sing-songy voice. I winced at her declaration, feeling the way it was trying to reach towards me, looking for me to bend in her direction in some way. But my heart felt hard and cold in my chest, like a pebble. I wanted to spit on the ground.

"I'm not little," Maeve said.

I laughed. "It's true," I told Deb. "She's big." I handed Maeve the hose and told her she could spray it into the baby pool. As Deb watched her play, she gushed. "Oh my god, I need to marry a rich black man. I want a baby who looks like that." She looked at me and said, "Is that racist to say?"

I just gave her a look. I didn't know where to start.

"What? I'm being serious."

"I know you are," I said, "and yes, you're right, she's insanely gorgeous. She's also super smart. She can write her name! She's my new best friend and I love her." I didn't realize until it was too late how pathetic it sounded to call a four year old my "new best friend" when I was actually talking to my old best friend, but whatever. I tried to change the subject. "So is Parker officially your boyfriend now? Are you, like, in love?"

Her face told me that this was the question she'd walked over here so that I would ask. But before she could report, she had to chide me. "Where have you been? I've been trying to call you to tell you about everything." Even though the burn from the baseball game and all the rest had left a permanent scar, I felt myself soften a little. She had walked over without any pretenses. She was just being her regular old self. An even more guarded version actually. She knew I was upset about something, and considering what I overheard, I can only imagine how many different ways she'd actually betrayed me. She had plenty to feel guilty about.

I refused to look her in the eyes or give her a real smile. "Sorry I missed the game." I tried to say it with no emotion, "otherwise, you wouldn't have to fill me in." I couldn't hide the wobble in my voice.

"Uh," she groaned. "I know, it sucks. I'm sorry. I just told Jenna she could go first and then Dad wanted to bring his friend and we only had four tickets."

I thought this was probably a lie, but I didn't want to press it. I squinted at the lawn for a second, not looking at her, the anger and hurt of the words I overheard resurfacing in a way I couldn't easily ignore. I took a deep breath and tried to keep the tears from bursting out of me.

Maeve was splashing around. She had a shovel and was leaning over the side of the baby pool, dropping clods of dirt into the pool, watching the particles float and spread. It didn't bother me that she was soaking in a dirty pool. She was occupied. I looked at Deb's face. She looked different. It's hard to explain exactly how. She could see that I was trying not to cry.

"Tell me what happened," I said.

"It's a long story. First, we got there and my dad and Joe, his friend, wanted to buy us a bunch of food, so we were like stuck there eating hot dogs and popcorn until the fourth inning."

"You ate a hot dog?" I asked. This was very unlike her.

"Ha!" she said. "Actually, no, but Dad bought them. He knew we were going to meet up with some boys. I was like, oh my god, we have to go! But he kept wanting us to stay to watch Lieberthal's next at bat. I was like, give me a break. Then Lieberthal hit a double and started a rally and there was no way we were able to leave then. Finally, he was like, ok, go meet your friends, but you have to be back by the top of the 9th, because if it isn't close, we're leaving. So we split and found the guys, but by then they were pretty wasted. They had smuggled in the plastic bladder from a box of wine. Doug taped it to his chest! They'd each bought a big soda, dumped it and were drinking wine on ice. Jenna and I shared a cup and I was feeling pretty buzzed. Then Parker was like, we should go on a walk. I was like, ok. He could barely walk straight. His face was kinda droopy like a puppy, but he was still cute. But he was like, all over me. I was afraid Dad or Joe would be like coming back from the bathroom or something and was like you cannot touch me here. Anyway, we walked up to the 700 level, and there was like no one there, and we sat in the furthest seats. Like the highest you can go. Everyone looked like ants. Then he started kissing me and we like hooked up for a really long time. He even," she looked at Maeve and then mouthed the words, put his hand up my shirt, while moving her hand up and down in the air.

"Wow," I said. I had no other words. I wondered where I would have been when that went down and felt a little glad for being excluded. I would have hated being left with Doug and Scott and Jenna while Parker and Deb disappeared. "So, what now?"

"I don't know. I'm freaking out. We were supposed to go to a movie last week, but then my mom made me go to this dumb dinner on the same night. Then we went to this other party, and we hooked up again. But it's awkward."

"Awkward how?"

"I don't know. I just don't know what to say. When we IM from home, everything is normal. We talk about baseball and other random stuff. You know, you've seen it. But then when we're together, we don't like talk or anything."

"Like when you hook up?"

"He just doesn't really talk to me when we're together. Or he does but it's not the same."

A shout from Maeve interrupted us. "Look, look, look, look at this look at this, hurry, hurry, Emily right now! A worm, a worm, a worm!" Maeve was standing in the middle of the pool gesticulating wildly, her eyes fixed on the wriggly creature as it slowly sank. The pool was now a murky brown. There were pieces of grass and other lawn bits stuck to her legs and arms.

"Maeve!" I said. "You're going to kill it!"

"No, no, no," she said, "look, it's swimming. It likes the water. It's not dying."

I considered its movements. I didn't know that much about worms. I only knew that they liked to come out onto the sidewalks when it rained.

"Let's just let it go back home into the ground," I said. "Look, you're all dirty. We should clean off and eat lunch. You can help me dump the pool."

"Can I have Doritos?" she asked.

"Only if you help me dump the pool." Doritos were our secret snack. Both our moms forbid them, so I had a secret grab bag of them that I bought from the CVS that I used for bribery purposes when needed. Maeve complied in under a second.

"Ready?" I said, standing at the side of the pool, "on the count of three. One, two," on three we dumped the water onto the lawn and watched the fat worm flop into a puddle in the grass. "Now I have to hose the dirt off of you," I said, spraying her. "Do a dance," I said. "Do the rainbow dance." I managed to get about half the dirt off her. It seemed passable.

"You are like Maryanne from *The Babysitter's Club* or something," Deb said, impressed.

"I feel like I'm more of a Kristie." Kristie was the jock; Maryanne was the smart, obedient one. The two of them were best friends.

"You're like a Kristie meets Maryanne," she said.

"Then who are you?" I asked.

She smiled haughtily. "I'm Stacey," she said. Stacey was the stylish New Yorker who was forced to live in the suburbs.

"You wish!" I said, spraying the hose near her.

"Ah," she screamed. "Will you come over after you're done babysitting?"

"I can't," I said. "Nanny's coming over for dinner tonight."

"Can you come when she goes home? My parents left this morning to go to Vermont for a long weekend and Cody and Maura are at the house "babysitting" me. Mom doesn't know Maura is here, obviously. We may have a few people over. Come!"

So that was why she was over here. Because Cody was asking about me.

I shrugged. "I'll see if I can."

"You should just sleepover!"

"Is Jenna?"

"I think so," she said. "Come on! We miss you!"

"I'll ask."

"Yay!" She clapped her hands and started running back to her house. "Nice to meet you Maevey Wavy Gravy," she yelled.

Maeve just wrinkled her nose again.

- 15 -

I probably would never have entered Absolute Video again if my mom hadn't made me.

It was all part of her Nanny plan. We were going to have ham and cabbage—my least favorite meal, but Nanny's favorite. An Irish Sunday staple. But we were having it on a Wednesday because Nanny always had coffee and breakfast with a bunch of other seniors at a Denny's on Route 38 on Sundays after Mass.

Mom worked from home on her Blackberry so that she could cook the raw cut of pork she'd bought from a special butcher. Apparently, it was impossible to get uncooked hams at regular grocery stores, and so I had to endure the smells of this enormous pink piece of flesh boiling in apple cider before I left to babysit. I thought about Jake and how he was a vegan. He would have been horrified.

I couldn't help but hold my nose as I walked into the kitchen.

"You're the one who wanted Nanny to come," she said.

"We could have ordered pizza."

"I wanted to honor her with her favorite dinner that she never bothers to cook correctly. It was her mother who taught me how to do this. I'm sick of those Christmas cop-out Heavenly Hams. You know I like a challenge."

"We should get a photographer in here," I said. "You could make your next home decor display about different cultural traditions. There could be a bunch of different dining room tables set in the kitchenware area, with like recipe books and stuff."

Mom clapped her hands, which were covered in pork fat and cloves. I almost gagged, but she was too delighted by my idea to notice her slippery fingers. "That's genius!" She said, "I love it! If my hands weren't dirty, I'd call Marketing right now."

She was flitting around the kitchen with an extra bounce in her step. She didn't need to consult a cookbook—this recipe had been handed down from woman to woman for who knows how many generations, stretching somewhere backwards towards County Clare on the mother isle. After the meat was boiled, she covered it in mustard and cloves and brown sugar, then baked it. While it was in the oven, she made a vile-looking sauce that was all white, with milk and butter and flour and parsley.

By the time I got home from babysitting, the ham was out of the oven. The transformation was epic. It actually looked kind of good. Mom said it needed to "rest."

"Go take a shower and put on the dress I laid out on your bed."

"Why do I have to wear a dress?" I said. "Why does this have to be so fancy?"

"Because I made a ham," Mom said. She was already wearing a nice pair of plaid capris and a black scoop neck top. I rolled my eyes, bit my tongue, and went to take a shower. I knew what she was doing, and I didn't like it. I mean we all knew if this party was at Nanny's house, it would be a grocery store ham and an Entemann's cake for dessert and we'd all be wearing shorts with elastic waistbands and t-shirts. But I had no choice but to go along with the whole thing.

The dress was a halter, and it still had the tags. It was form fitting in the chest and flared a little below the waist. My mom put out little flats for me to wear with it. I took my hair down and put a little product in to help calm my waves out of their frizz. I had to admit I looked pretty good, even for a butterface. My teeth weren't that large, I noticed. My ears were normal sized. The high neckline of the dress made the shape of my poofy hair even look sort of stylish.

Perhaps even Doug would rethink his insults if he could see me in an outfit like this. It's sad to say, but that's actually where my rejected brain went.

"Come on," Mom yelled from the bottom of the stairs. Nanny didn't drive. For some reason, Mom thought it was important that I come along with her to pick her up. I didn't understand why she couldn't go herself, but I didn't really have anything else to do.

Riding shotgun in the car as we made the rote turns towards the highway, my brain was already powering down into rest mode, preparing for a chill 20-minute ride, when Mom suddenly veered over by Absolute and put on her flashers. She reached into her pocketbook and handed me five bucks. I looked at her, confused.

"Can you go in there and grab that Meg Ryan and Tom Hanks movie about the email if they have it? Nanny said she wanted to watch it with us. Tonight's theme is 'Dinner and a Movie.'"

"*You've Got Mail*?" I said.

I looked at the clock. It was 4:45. Jake was still working. There was no reason for her to understand the teenage crisis this placed me in. How the hell was I going to walk into the video store all dressed up? I felt absurd.

"Come in with me!" I said.

"Why?"

"I don't know. I just don't feel like looking for it alone. What if I can't find it?"

Mom looked at me like I was an inept employee. Then she turned the car off and jumped out. "This isn't technically a legal parking spot," she said, "So we have to be quick." Fine with me.

It occurred to me when we got to the door that I could have probably made the argument to wait in the car, but it was too late now. She pulled on the handle, and I heard the familiar tinkling of the bells. Then I sneezed. Jake was checking out someone's video and there were a few other customers in the shop. He looked up from the register at the sound of the door. We made eye contact. He raised his eyebrows at me and nodded his head. My heart thundered in my ears.

"Romantic comedies," Mom said, scanning the rows for *You've Got Mail*. There was *Breakfast at Tiffany's*. Mom found what she was looking for, and we walked to the back to pay.

"Hey, Emily," Jake said as he took the film and pulled the checkout card from the back to record our names and stamp the return date. I noticed he called me Emily instead of Banks. Probably because of my mom. He handed us the stamped receipt. I liked that Absolute Video had no computer system. No barcodes to scan. A relic of another time.

"Hey," I said, feeling myself blush.

"Who's this?" Mom asked, recognizing him as a person for the first time.

"This is Jake," I said. "He's a friend from school."

"We're science partners," Jake said. He gave her an easygoing smile, clearly unaware of how hard she was to please.

This information made Mom light up. "Oh!" she said. "Right. You're that Jake. Nice to meet you. Have you guys exchanged notes yet?"

That Jake. I wanted to crawl to whatever dusty corner in the back was hiding those semi-stale peanut butter crackers and die.

"I'm still waiting on Emily to get back to me," he said. His eyes were hard to read. Was he mad at me? I looked at the floor. I'd never noticed how ugly and sad the faded red rug was.

"You guys need to make a plan," she said. "Maybe you can come over one day after work and work on it together at our house."

I was mortified.

"Sure," he said. He handed the movie to my mom. "Meg

Ryan," he said. "America's Sweetheart."

"Is it good?" Mom asked.

"I watched it with my mom," Jake said. "As I recall, we both kinda liked it. Which is rare." I had never seen Jake's mom. "Though I don't really agree with the whole premise. It would be like the owner of this place falling in love with the heir to Blockbuster." His review piqued my interest. Also, I liked the idea of him watching a movie with his mom.

"Oh good," Mom said. "We're having a special party with Emily's grandmother and she requested it. She saw Meg Ryan on Oprah like a year ago and has been telling me she wants to watch it ever since."

"Three generations. Sounds fun," Jake said. He handed the movie to my mom and gave her a friendly look that seemed foreign to me, sincere but also not his true self, a kind of filtered version of his aura devised specifically for customers and grown ups he needed to impress. I didn't know he was capable of that sort of charm. I guess Dreckford never earned it. "Have a good time," he said. Our eyes locked for an instant, and it was like our bodies were transmitting messages through our irises and pupils that my conscious mind couldn't translate. "See you," he said. I had trouble turning away. I nodded in reply.

I looked up at my mom as we walked to the door. She didn't seem to have picked up on a thing.

"He seems like a nice boy. That seems like a pretty good summer job," Mom said as we got in the car. "You don't want to leave that project until the last minute. Make sure you guys pick a time to work on it."

"Ok," I said, hoping she would forget this conversation ever happened and knowing that she wouldn't.

But at least for the time being, that was the end of that.

We pulled into Nanny's driveway. Uncle Tommy was watching TV in the living room. You could see the blue glow through the curtains. Nanny was waiting at the kitchen table and opened the door as soon as we pulled up. I got out of the car to move to the backseat.

"Who is this woman?" she said to me, stopping for a moment like she was taking me in. She was wearing what she called a house dress, but what most people would refer to as a nightgown. It had tiny pink roses on it and hung to about her calves. Her feet were in plasticky sandals. Her hair was done though. You could tell she'd put it in curlers earlier. And she had lipstick on.

"Who is this woman?" I said in return. We gave each other a big hug, and she left a big lip print on my cheek, which she tried to rub away like she'd been doing my whole life.

The three generations had fun in the car. The oldies station was on. It wasn't a song I recognized, but the men's voices were harmonizing and talking about a girl they wanted to approach.

"Tommy wants me to get an email address," Nanny said.

"An email address?" Mom said, "Why?"

"He says I can get in touch with people I used to know."

"Is that why you want to watch *You've Got Mail*?" I said.

Nanny laughed. "Maybe you're onto something."

We joked about Nanny getting into chat rooms looking for other single people in their 70s.

"Uh oh, Margaret's here," Dad said when we walked in. He turned off the television and stood up to give her a hug. "Lock up the whiskey," he said to Mom. Nanny laughed. She never drank a drop of anything, unless it was Pepsi or root beer, but for some reason this was a running joke between her and my dad.

Mom had set the table out back on the deck. Ham and cabbage wasn't really a summer meal—or a meal for any season, as far as I was concerned—but she lightened and brightened the table with a colorful garden salad and some San Pellegrino with lemon on ice.

I'd thought that all of Mom's extravagances for this dinner were going to be offensive to Nanny, but she seemed to appreciate them. I even noticed that Mom was on her best behavior when she spoke to her. She didn't act like Nanny was a burden or dumb. She really treated her like the guest of honor. Maybe cooking the ham had put her into some sort of Irish trance. I was baffled. Everyone ate enthusiastically.

"Franny, this tastes just like Bobo's," Nanny said, referring to her own mother, who was nicknamed Bobo for reasons never explained to me.

"I went to Caputo's for the meat," Mom said.

"Bertolas," Nanny said.

"I don't know why I always call it Caputo's," Mom said.

"It's been Bertola's for 30 years! You still lived at home when he sold the place!" Nanny laughed. "Not as good as they used to be, but they're still the best around. The prices are crazy though. I just go to the store." "The store" was Acme, our local South Jersey grocery chain.

"Do you mean Caputo's, like Ceil?" I said.

"Yes!" Mom said, excited by my observation. "Actually I do!" She looked at Nanny. "I haven't told you this yet. Guess who moved around the corner? Cici Caputo!"

Nanny made some va-voom, sort of sexy moves in her chair, like she was in Madonna's "Vogue" video, I guess in reference to Ceil's reputation for being a hottie. "Maryanne told me in church that Cici was in Tonley. I forgot to ask you."

Mom shook her head. "It was crazy seeing her after all these years. It was like seeing a ghost."

"It's like *A Christmas Carol*," Nanny laughed. "The ghost of

Bronner past."

Mom laughed along. "Except she can't really haunt me."

"What about the college thing though?" I asked.

Nanny looked at me, but Mom just rolled her eyes. "She goes by Seal these days, like the animal."

"You mean like that Black singer who married the supermodel?" Nanny stayed up to date with celebrity news.

"She doesn't spell it that way though," I said. "She spells it C-E-I-L."

Nanny shrugged. "It's probably some New York thing." She gave herself the Vogue face again and whispered, "Ceil."

As much as I loved Ceil, I couldn't help but laugh at Nanny in her house dress with her brownish teeth mocking Ceil's glamour.

Nanny's face got serious. "We were saying prayers for Doris in Mass last Sunday. She can't leave the house anymore. Father Mike goes to visit. It's a shame."

"She moved back to help with Doris," I said, offering the bit of information I could to the conversation.

"That, and to get out of the city," Mom said, "so Maeve could go to a good school."

"I never heard her say that," I said.

"It's obvious," Mom said.

"Why was the butchers named Caputo's?" I asked. "Did her dad own it?"

Nanny cleared her throat. "Her dad helped open it—well not that one, but the one in the Italian Market. It was her uncle's store. Her dad's side of the family are all butchers from Italy and when they came here, they cured meat and sold it to delis in New York. Cici's uncle moved to Philly to start a business down here and her father came down sometimes to help him get it started. That was before she was even born though. Oh, her poor mother! Cici's dad was a rat. One of those Sinatra mobster guys with his hair always just right. Handsome, but too handsome. He had big wads of cash. I saw him once by Bobo's on 15th and Tasker when she still used to have those big family Sunday lunches, and I couldn't believe how much cash he had in his pocket. Imagine trying to fold an entire stack of napkins, then try sticking it in your pants. He was buying ice creams for all the kids on the street. They acted like they were being visited by Jesus Christ himself. It was disgusting. He never even married Filomena."

"Who's Filomena?"

"Cecelia's mother. Got her pregnant and then left her to raise that child all by herself, living with that aunt of hers that wasn't even her aunt. Poor thing died of a broken heart."

"A broken heart?" I said.

"Lots of people die from broken hearts," Nanny said. "Your grandfather died of a broken heart. It was more common back then."

"I thought that was a thing that happened in fairy tales," I said. I gave a confused look to Mom and Dad. Was Nanny losing it?

Dad said, "They were depressed. You know, depressed people don't really take care of themselves and then they develop health conditions or addictions."

"So they killed themselves?"

Nanny winced. "Taking your life is a sin, and I know for sure that Patrick is in heaven because he has visited me and told me so." She crossed herself then and then closed her eyes and rocked back and forth in her seat, taking my mom's hand. Mom was quiet. They were remembering a person we'd never see or know.

"Let's pray it's the same for Filomena, rest her soul, that poor little child. She was so young. Only, what, sixteen? Seventeen when she had Cecelia? And an orphan on top of that. Found on a doorstep on Salter. God strike me dead if I'm lying. I was eleven years old when it happened and I heard the nuns talking about it at school."

God did not strike. We were all quiet. Dad peeled a piece of ham from the serving tray and ate it. Mom gave him a dirty look. Whether it was because she thought he'd already eaten too much, or if she just thought it was in bad taste to eat at that exact moment, I couldn't tell.

The silence extended for a few beats. I could hear the click of Dad's jaw as he chewed. Some of the kids down the street were playing tag on their lawn. "I caught you," one was saying to the other. "You're It now." "No you didn't," the other kid said back. "I didn't feel anything."

So Ceil's mom had died of a broken heart, just like Mom's dad. I tried to imagine one of my parents suddenly dying, their lives so heavy with grief that they could not find the strength to go on.

Nanny sighed. "She had it tough, little Cici. So pretty and all alone in that house with Doris and Grace. What a strange place to grow up. I always felt bad for her. She was always a little weird. All the nuns hated her at Our Lady of Perpetual Hope. The girls too."

"All the girls hated me too," Mom said.

"No they didn't," Nanny said. "You just had an attitude. You didn't like them."

"I didn't have an attitude," Mom said.

Based on the way she said it, I didn't believe her; based on the way Nanny looked at her, I could tell she didn't either.

"You just knew you weren't going to live there forever, Frances. I can't blame you. And I can't blame Cecelia either for running away with that boy on the bike."

"Excuse me a minute. I have to use the bathroom," I said. I was sick of the family talk. When could we just watch the movie? I sat on the toilet seat and stared at the framed picture of "Footprints in the Sand."

The window to the bathroom was open. As I sat there wasting time, I could hear bits and pieces of the conversation on the deck.

"....black girl," Mom said.

"Father's probably in jail," Dad said.

I put my face in my hands and groaned, annoyed that they'd waited for me to exit the table before espousing their racist theories about Maeve's father to Nanny, who they knew would agree. We were in a new goddamn millennium, and yet this was really the way they talked. I didn't know why they did it. It made me feel lonely. Maybe that's what Ceil felt like in that house with the two old maids. Not old maids, I corrected myself. Sisters. And not the kind of sisters who were nuns. Just two unmarried ladies from the same family who stuck together and took care of each other. That was nice. I didn't have a sister. Mom did, but she lived in Arizona because she married a man in the Air Force and they only ever sent Christmas cards. The chances of Mom and her sister being old together were slim.

I washed my hands and sat back down on the closed toilet seat just staring out into space, absorbing the ebb and flow of their conversation as it drifted back towards the food on the table and how it was prepared, and how Bobo used to make it, and all the brothers and sisters and cousins that used to be in Philadelphia, but were scattered all over the place now. Dad talked a little about his own family. His stories were always interesting in a different way. He'd grown up way more comfortably. His relatives were all college educated doctors and lawyers and corporate executives who'd purchased second homes or nice boats or went somewhere expensive on vacation.

I heard Mom clearing the table, so I stood up and left the bathroom. The sun was setting. We watched *You've Got Mail*. In the opening sequence, when Meg Ryan prances around, waiting for her boyfriend to leave the apartment before checking her email, I noticed the music was similar to *Breakfast at Tiffany's*, the plucking of a cello. And so I could do nothing but fret over my feelings for Jake. Were we friends? What about our pinkies? What about the way I always felt like I was going to turn into a frothing pile of mush?

As Nanny struggled to understand the concept of email and how you could hide your identity with a username, I understood what Jake was getting at in his review. There was something ethically problematic about the plotline. But it was really just a remake of *Pride and Prejudice*. Which was kind of a retelling of *Taming of the Shrew*. And if you just told the same story again and again, there was no room for revolution. Or evolution. Or both.

I went along for the ride to take Nanny home. After we dropped her off, I said to Mom, "That story about Ceil's mom is crazy."

"Yeah," she said. "I told you. She didn't have anyone looking out for her when she was growing up. Her poor mother. Ceil is honestly lucky that her life turned out as well as it did."

"I guess it shows how smart she is. She managed to pull herself out of a bad situation and become who she wanted to be."

Mom was quiet for a minute, changing lanes on the highway. "It's weird to think of it that way," she said. "I can't help but see her and think of all the stuff she ran away from, but I guess you're right, she did have to leave in order to become herself. Though she had to kill an unborn child in the process." Mom's judgment sucked the air out of the car. I took a deep breath.

"How do you even know that's true?"

"What?"

"That she had an abortion? Or that she was even pregnant?"

"That's what everyone said."

"She could have given up the baby for adoption. Or had a miscarriage. Or maybe she was never pregnant at all. The wife could have just made that up. Maybe she was jealous."

"Of a high school student?"

"You all say everyone was obsessed with Ceil's looks."

"Well, she didn't have to flaunt them so much."

I contained my impulse to groan. "Well, since you think she did have an abortion, let's assume she did. If you think that's so terrible, why do you let me associate with her? Why is it ok?"

"Because I believe in forgiveness," Mom said.

"But why is it your job to forgive her?"

Mom was quiet a moment and then she said, "You're right. It's not my job. It's God's."

"So why do you care so much?"

Mom was quiet again for a few moments and I realized that she was choked up. "You don't realize how hard it was to have you," she said. "I lost so many babies. You are the miracle of my life, truly. I am so grateful. I can't help but feel angry when I hear that someone else gave up the chance. I thought of her sometimes when I found out I lost a pregnancy."

She had to keep her eyes on the road, so we couldn't really look at each other, but I felt her jealousy and also her crushing love for me. I loved her back, as confused as I was by my whole existence, or anyone's existence at all. Fucking Earth! What a strange fever dream of a place! Still, Mom and Dad raised me to be a levelheaded person, and I felt the need to stand up for Ceil.

"Mom, you never even asked her for her side. You just believed that she was having an affair with the teacher. You don't know the story. What if he did something to her she didn't want him to?"

Mom considered the question as we paused at the familiar

traffic light by the Burger King. She made a noise like she was going to speak, but then she didn't. Then the light turned green, the car moved forward, and she said, "Whatever happened, you're right that Mr. Burke was also to blame. But as they say, it takes two to tango."

I wanted to say that she had no proof about anything, that it was all speculation and therefore unfair to assume anything. I wanted to say that Ceil was a teenager and he was a teacher. That even when two people were tangoing, someone took the lead, and there were tangos that went awry. Sometimes a partner could just get dragged across the floor, feet stepped on, a total mess. I wanted to say that maybe someone could think they wanted to tango until they started tangoing, and then realize that they didn't want to, but since they didn't realize they didn't want to until they already started, they didn't know how to stop the dance until the music came to an end.

We traveled three more traffic lights in silence. Then a left, a stop sign, two more streets and a left into the driveway of our house.

"I'm really tired," I said, unbuckling my seatbelt.

Mom looked at me and laughed. The sound of it unnerved me. Sometimes I could predict exactly what was on her mind, but this wasn't one of those moments. She pushed her car door closed and walked towards the front door.

"Me too," she said.

- 16 -

I'd totally forgotten about Deb's sleepover invitation. I just went to bed and woke up to a steady pitter patter of rain at 7:06. By the time I cracked my eyes open again at 8:37, it seemed to have stopped. Or at least it was taking a break. I stayed under my covers until after Mom and Dad visited me in my bed to say their goodbyes. Then I crept downstairs and turned on the television just as the morning meteorologist was giving the forecast. Rain. Every day for like a week. Potentially longer. The radar was all green with yellow specks.

But it wasn't raining right that second. The conversations from the night before were weighing on my chest, and I felt an antsiness in my bones. So I set out on a spontaneous seven-mile run. I was due for a long one, and my body just decided this course on its own, taking me down a strange maze of roads from my house. After the first three miles—when I was about as far from home as I could be—the clouds began to drizzle. It didn't take long for the drizzle to turn into something more. But I didn't care.

It felt exciting to be in the rain. A few neighbors drove by and tapped their horns as a hello from their cars as they passed. I was surprised by what an ego boost I got from these greetings—it was like I was completing a lap to the cheers of my team. I kept up my pace and let my feet pound out my teenage thoughts: Deb's party. Shit, I missed Cody, Was he still there? Maybe I could stop by after babysitting. I felt the anxiety of missing something and wondering who was there. But I left those feelings behind me as quickly as they came. They were like raindrops bouncing off me, beading up and dripping down my leg.

I was as Zen as I'd ever been. I felt a glow inside of me. The stress was incinerated. Fuck all the friendship drama, the boys, the pressure. I could just do this. Feet, legs, arms, breath. When I ran alone, I felt power and freedom. My body was not really a body. It was a collection of photons, a quasar speeding through galaxies after being super-compressed by a black hole. Water and light. This was my truest form.

The rain came down in sheets. I became euphoric. I wanted to dance, and I sort of did. It was a runner dance. I skipped up a little with each step with a huge perma-smile spread across my face.

I was soaked. Like the level of wet you get if someone picks you up in your clothes and tosses you directly into a pool. I hadn't considered the fact that I could possibly end up this wet when I'd gotten dressed to go. My clothes were clingy and see-through, but I wasn't even thinking about the way that I looked. I only saw visions of inspiration, the pictures of soaked people smiling during an especially wet Boston Marathon I'd seen in an old copy of *Runner's World*.

So it took me a second to even realize that a driver had slowed down and was lurking at my pace, his window rolled down. I heard a yell from someone and looked over. It was a guy around my dad's age. I didn't recognize him or his car. He wasn't a neighbor-friend.

"What?" I yelled. I could barely hear him over the sound of the rain and his car. I slowed my run and moved closer to the curb where he'd pulled over. I figured he needed directions.

His hair was slightly gray. He had a bit of stubble on his chin. But it was his eyes that I noticed immediately. They had a strange energy to them. I felt both drawn to them and wary. He had a big smile of nice, straight teeth. "Would you like to get in? It's nice and dry in here. I can drive you home," he said louder. "Do you want to come in and dry off?"

Immediately I felt repulsed. Was this one of those dudes

who offers little girls candy that you hear about? He was driving an expensive-looking SUV though. It wasn't a van.

"No, thank you!" I said, and then I returned to the sidewalk, keeping my pace, but he did not drive away. He lingered, driving at my pace and staring at me through the window. The cars behind him didn't stop or honk, they just went around him. He rolled down his window again and gestured at me. We were on a residential street, but the lawns were large and the houses were set back from the road. I was on an old highway from before they built the Interstate, and I didn't know anyone personally on this block. Panic swelled inside me.

I ran straight up the driveway of the next house and around the perimeter of their fence, zigzagging, jumping and ducking between yards like a robber being chased by the cops until I came out on a narrow one-way road that ran along the commuter train tracks. There was no way the guy would look for me here. Still, I ran like a lunatic, like it was the last race of my life. The sodden earth along the sidewalk squished beneath me. Earlier it had felt like a spring—now it felt like a sinkhole. This little road delivered me onto Main Street and the first thing I saw was Absolute Video. Jake! I wanted to crawl inside that dark, musty cave of VHS tapes like a wet bear in search of a warm den to cuddle inside, but the door was locked and the lights were out. It wasn't 11 yet, and the store wasn't open. I pushed my face against the door but didn't see a light on in the back. I pressed on and ran back to my house, hopping over puddles and looking over my shoulder, scared the man was tracking me and looking for where I lived. I'd left the backdoor unlocked. Once I was inside, I locked the door and took a hot shower.

Dry, safe, and wearing fresh clothes, I wondered if I'd overreacted, but I didn't know who to tell. Certainly not my mother or father, who'd just respond by revoking more of my freedom as if

I was little and fragile and incapable of caring for myself. Not Deb, she'd just use it as fodder for her IMs with Parker. Then who? Ceil? The digital clock on my microwave said 10:40. I'd have to leave to walk to her house in 10 minutes anyway. I could leave now and catch her before she had to run out the door. But then she might feel obligated to tell my mom, and Mom would tell Dad and neither one of them would know how to approach me and before I knew it, it'd be the scene at Umberto's where they freaked out about the noose in my yearbook all over again. It wasn't worth the risk. Impulsively I picked up my phone and dialed the number for Absolute video.

I decided that if Jake answered I would tell him what happened, and if someone else answered, I would just hang up.

"Absolute Video," Jake said. It was funny hearing him speak the name of the video store. It was like when I directly called my dad or mom at work and they didn't know it was me and answered, "This is Nathan" or "Frances Banks, House and Home."

I froze. It felt stupid to tell him what happened to me. I didn't know how to explain it. What should I do?

"Absolute Video," Jake said. "Hello?"

Still, I didn't say anything, waiting for him to hang up.

"Banks," he said. "Are you there? You know the store has caller I.D. right?"

I let the air I was holding in explode out of me. "Are you kidding me?" I said. "Oh my god, I'm so busted."

"Totally busted. But it was exciting to hear the phone ring. No one ever calls here this early."

"What are you watching? *Cosmos*?" I asked.

"Not yet," he said. "Right now I am just rewinding the VHS cassettes of those who were not kind enough to rewind them themselves and reshelving all the DVDs."

"Wow," I said, thinking of the bucket of unshelved videos

from our *Breakfast at Tiffany's* day. "You're really getting right to work this morning."

"I have to keep moving or I may just collapse. I drank like six Icehouses last night."

"Ouch," I said.

"Where were you?"

"What do you mean?"

"Last night."

"You saw me. At the store, remember. *You've Got Mail*?"

"Yeah, I mean, why weren't you at Deb's?"

"You were there?" I asked, surprised.

"Me and pretty much every other person who has a Tonley zip code. I was hoping to hear your spirited analysis of the film, but then I just had to sit in a room and listen to Anais read Deb's diary."

"What!" I said. "Anais was there?" Anais was a super hippie, impossibly beautiful, weed smoking chick who did everything with her boyfriend Jaron. They both had hair to their waist and usually just whispered in each other's ears.

"There were a lot of people there. Her brother was pissed."

"Wow," I said. "It's probably a good thing I couldn't go then." I was still picturing an onslaught of teenagers raiding the Stevens' house, thinking about Cody freaking out and the fact that Ceil and Maeve might have heard the whole thing from their house if it was super wild. I hadn't even processed the fact that Anais was reading Deb's diary when Jake said, "I didn't think you were the kind of girl who fell for popular guy stuff."

The way he said it made my entire body sting.

"What's that supposed to mean?" I said. But there was a pit in my stomach. I knew what it meant. I knew what must have been in that diary. I could've died at that moment. I wanted to. I thought of all the ones before me and their broken hearts.

"You know how Doug talks about girls right?"

"Jake—"

"He describes everything he does with chicks."

"I have no idea what she wrote—"

"I've heard him at parties before. I smoked a bowl with him once and he told me a lot of things about girls in our school that I'm sure they'd rather not be repeated."

"But—"

"I mean, for all you know you he could be carrying a disease—"

"Shut the fuck up! Fuck you! It's none of your business!" I screamed as I hung up the phone. It was a primal sound. It even scared me when it left my throat.

The silence of the house afterwards was deafening. A minute went by and then the phone started to ring. I went upstairs and sat next to the answering machine in my parents' room and listened to Mom's voice say, "You've reached the Banks family. Doug, Frances, and Emily can't come to the phone right now, please leave us a message and we'll get back to you." Beep. Then the caller hung up. Two seconds later, the phone started ringing again.

I knew that it was Jake. I gave the telephone the middle finger and went into my room. I took off the lazy babysitting outfit I had thrown on after my shower and replaced it with a long skirt and a tank top that I liked. The phone kept ringing and ringing. I adjusted my hair in my parents' mirror. My mother's make-up bag was resting on top of her dresser. I unzipped it and took out a tube of lipstick and smeared it across my mouth. My teeth looked large and intimidating, like they could saw through reeds along the shoreline. I was a sexy muskrat. I hated everyone. I kissed a piece of toilet paper and examined the many lines that cracked and curved to make my mouth. Then I wadded it up, flushed it down the toilet, found an umbrella in the closet, and walked out the door.

- 17 -

It was pouring rain, and I had no fucks left to give, so I skipped the whole walking an extra 20 minutes to avoid Deb's house. There was her porch. There was the window to her living room. There was the bush I'd creepily lurked behind.

It was like passing Chernobyl. The inner Geiger counter of my soul was beeping off the charts.

Had Cody heard the diary entry? Had Doug been there? Did he smirk and say something nasty about the shape of my breasts?

Something brave inside me suddenly emerged. I kept my head high. I had nothing to be ashamed of. I was a good person. I worked hard.

I opened the screen door to Ceil and Maeve's house and walked inside, leaning my umbrella in the corner near the door. Something felt different. For a second, I thought it was just me. But the air smelled a little smoky. I could hear The Velvet Underground playing on the record player in the living room.

"Baby be good, do what you should /You know it will work alright." It was the first time I ever heard Lou Reed's voice.

Ceil had so many pictures on her walls. I noticed more every time I arrived. They were in frames of all shapes and sizes. None of them matched, and they covered every inch of the hallway. Some were paintings, some were newspaper clippings, some were black and white photographs. Others were of the last few years, of her and Maeve standing various places, in playgrounds and the woods. There was a Black man in a few of them. In one, Maeve was a newborn baby, and the man was holding Maeve, looking at the camera with proud dad eyes. In another, he and Ceil and Maeve were standing together under a waterfall.

None of them were like the portrait studio pictures that were displayed in my house, where our outfits had been arranged ahead of time and our hair was set and styled exactly the way my mother envisioned. The pictures on Ceil's wall were spontaneous. They were little worlds unto themselves. Group shots of friends at cafe tables or on the beach. Maeve running through a fire hydrant in the summer. I found myself fixated on a black and white shot of the guy with the mustache, the motorcycle man.

Ceil appeared from the living room. She was holding a smoking plate of grass and had a feather in her hand.

"I thought I heard the door," she said, smiling. She saw me looking at the smoking plate. "Oh, I was just saging the house. Here," she walked over to me and then waved the smoke in my direction with the help of the feather. She walked to the door and did the same thing. Then she turned and went back into the living room. Maybe I should have followed her, but I was frozen in place, looking at the photographs. She came back after a second without the plate.

"Is that Maeve's dad?" I asked, pointing at the picture of a man holding a baby.

"Richie Cooper, the man, the myth, the legend," she said.

"Where is he?" I asked.

"Now?"

I nodded.

"Berlin," she said.

"Germany?"

"Yeah. He's an artist. All of a sudden he's famous. He wants us to come there. Who knows, maybe we will one day."

"Are you guys...married?"

She looked at me and laughed. "Who's asking," she said, "You or your mom?"

I gave her a side smile. She'd made her point. I decided to change the subject. I pointed at the picture of the motorcycle guy laughing on the wall. “I like this picture,” I said. “Was he your... boyfriend?”

Why was I taking these liberties with her? I was unhinged. The words were just coming out of my mouth. She laughed a loud laugh that made me feel a little stupid and embarrassed for asking, then she realized the effect of her outburst. “No, no, sorry, don’t feel bad,” she said. “It’s just...I’m in a weird space this morning. It’s just weird that you’ve been coming here for weeks and now is the day you’re asking me about this stuff.

“Maeve and I talked to Richie on the phone last night. It was the first time since we’ve moved,” she said, “and now you’re asking about Joey.” She held up her arm and showed me the hair that was standing up. “See,” she said, “I have goosebumps.” She suddenly sat down on the floor cross-legged with her elbows resting on her inner thighs and her chin resting in her palm.

Suddenly I was looking down at her. “Why?” I asked. I had the impulse to sit next to her, but I held back. It seemed too weird, the two of us on the floor right here when there was a couch in the other room. But she must have known that I wanted to sit next to her. She looked up at me and gestured with her hands. I obeyed.

We were quiet. I watched her braid a small clump of her hair then twirl it around her finger. I could hear Maeve in the other room, moving things around and talking to herself. She didn’t know I was here, or if she did, she was too engrossed in her play to care.

“It’s his birthday today,” Ceil said. “He should be 48.” She did the sign of the cross. I didn’t know if this was a Catholic reflex she couldn’t shake or if it was something she just did spontaneously this one time.

“What happened?”

“AIDS,” she said. Then she sang along with Lou for a second, “Down for you is up.” It reminded me of the way I sang to the Cranberries. Or the Beatles. Or Janet Jackson.

She gestured towards the picture. "Joey was my cousin and my best friend in the whole world. I met him when I was 14 at a family reunion. He was 16. I can still remember him pouring us both enormous cups of wine on Fire Island. I had felt so out of place. I don't know how much your mom has told you, but Doris isn't my mom. I was adopted by her. My dad was from New York. He lived in Long Island, and for some reason, he invited me to this reunion. I went, but I was feeling so crazy and shy, like I didn't know any of these people. My dad pretty much never did anything but send me money. I didn't even know why he invited me, but I just went because I could. I just wanted to go to New York, and well, anyway, there was Joey and it was like, oh, ok, I'm not the only freak in the world. We were both just weirdos. I danced, he just drew on every surface he could find. We did what we did and we laughed and laughed. He used to drive down here on that freaking motorcycle from the Lower East Side just to pick me up to take me back to the city to go on adventures. I have gone up and down the New Jersey Turnpike on a motorcycle so many times. Don't ever do it! It sucks!"

The way she looked at me, I believed her, and I guess whatever expression I offered back was enough because she took it as an invitation to continue.

"It's all a long story and it all feels like it happened a million years ago, but it's only been 10 years since we lost him. I don't want to burden you with it. I can't really describe it anyway. I'm just so glad you asked me about him right now. It just feels like magic. When I was talking to Maeve's dad last night, he kept asking me if I was going to be okay. He knew Joey. We were all friends. 'I'm going to be fine,' I told him, but I woke up and it was all gray outside, and I don't have any friends in this town, and I was like, what am I doing here? And then you asked me about him and I feel like he's saying hi to me because here I was walking around with that freaking sage in my hand, playing a Velvet Underground vinyl and, poof," Her eyes were a little wet with tears, but none of them escaped to her cheeks. "He was just—he's just right here," she gestured to the empty space in front of her as if he was sitting with us. "You would have loved him. Everybody loved him." She looked at me and I looked up to meet her eyes. She could tell I was really listening.

"You're like the age I was when I met him," she said. "Sometimes, you just meet people and know they're going to help you get to the next version of who you are." She gave me a wise sort of grimace that became a grin. "I have this theory," she said, making sure that I was following along, "that everyone gets a person. Like, at any moment in time, there's always someone. I feel like it's not always the same person. You know, it can change over time, depending on where you're at. It's not like a romantic thing. Or it doesn't have to be, at least. But he was my person then."

"Who's your person now?" I asked. Then I felt bad for asking. Maybe it was supposed to be Richie but then he went to Germany. It wasn't any of my business.

She laughed. "That's easy," she said. "Maeve." Then she leaned over and gave me a hug. She smelled like vanilla and sage. When she pulled back, she gave me one of her classic smiles, but then it became wobbly. "Thank you so much for listening to me," she said. Then the tears came. They were silent, but they fell in a steady stream. I felt frozen by them. My mother never cried. But Ceil kept on weeping and wiping the tears to the side, snorting and laughing through them at points, while I stared on, wishing I had the power to be more openly empathetic. Once her tears slowed down, she smiled at me. "And thank you so much for helping our family. I'm not sure we could have pulled off this move without you." She wiped her cheeks again, like the final swipe of the windshield wipers after the passing of a storm. She leaned her weight against mine, giving me a shoulder bump. "You make me doubt myself less," she said.

"Me?" I said.

She laughed as she stood up and offered her hand to help pull me back up. "Yes you, you scholar-athlete, warmhearted, babysitting embodiment of grace," she said. "Also," she looked at me with genuine encouragement, "I like your lipstick."

I felt embarrassed for a moment. I'd forgotten I was wearing it. Normally I didn't like compliments, but I couldn't help but smile then. "Thanks," I said.

Her kind words were a buoy for me to cling to. They lifted me up just enough to keep moving through the day.

It rained and rained and we never went outside. Maeve and I completed two 100-piece puzzles. It took all day. We ate carrots and made messes and danced to songs she made up while I guided her towards matches and we fit the pieces together. And it occurred to me that the entire process of putting a puzzle together was too clean. In real life, you could never complete a puzzle all the way. There were always pieces missing. There was always someone questioning whether the pieces fit together at all.

When I came home after babysitting, Mom was in the kitchen getting dinner together. She said that Deb had called.

"Ok," I said. "I'll call her back in a minute." I didn't really have any intention of calling her back, but I didn't want my mom to know that.

"Also," Mom said. "There's a message for you on the answering machine."

"Ok," I said. I ran up the stairs two at a time to my parents' bedroom. My dad wasn't home from work yet. I kneeled next to the bed and pushed the button on the machine.

"Hi, Emily, it's Jake, your science partner. I, um, wanted to talk about our project. Please call me back." I scowled at the machine and pushed the delete button.

"That's the boy from the video store, right?" Mom asked. I hadn't noticed that she'd come in behind me.

"Absolute," I said. "Yeah."

"You should let him know if you don't want to work with him."

"I told you, there aren't any partners really. We don't have to work together," I said. "He's kidding."

"Then why is he calling you?"

Like I was going to answer that question. "Because we said we were going to work together."

"Ok, see, that's where I'm confused," Mom said. "This poor boy is trying to get his homework done." It was hard not to release a cold, hard, cynical laugh at the words, "poor boy."

I threw my arms up in the air and rolled my eyes at her. "Mom, he can do it himself. You can work with somebody if you want to. It's not mandatory. We can do it on our own."

"Just tell him you want to do it by yourself," she said. "Just call him back so I don't have to field his phone calls and ask myself whether I should feel bad for him or annoyed."

"Fine, I'll call him back," I said, "Right now." I grabbed the cordless phone and walked towards my bedroom.

"Dinner is in a half hour," Mom said.

"What is it?"

"Salmon."

"Fine," I said. I would have preferred a greasy pizza. As she was walking down the stairs, I asked, "Did that teacher who Ceil had the thing with keep teaching at the school after she ran away?"

"I was wondering if you were going to bring that back up,"

Mom said.

"Like did you have him as a teacher after that?"

"I did. It was a small school. There were only two history teachers for the whole school, and he taught the juniors and seniors."

"Did Ceil's name ever come up after she left?"

"Only when we would accuse each other of flirting to get what we wanted," she said. "We used to call it a Caputo."

"That's mean!" I said.

"I know. You're right. But you asked if her name came up and that's the truth."

"I'm happy she ran away," I said. As the words left my mouth, they felt like a challenge. I was daring Mom to tell me that it would have been better for her to stay. But maybe our conversation from the night before had an impact. She let the topic drop.

"I hope your father is back soon. There's a bad thunderstorm coming through," she said as she walked down the stairs.

Then, as if on cue, there was an enormous crack of thunder. I was scared for a second, like a little kid. I thought of Maeve and hoped she was ok.

I pushed the talk button on the phone and was greeted by the sound of the dial tone. I dialed the first six numbers of Deb's line but couldn't bring myself to push the seventh. I let the phone hang like that in limbo until it started making the beep beep sound that let you know that it was off the hook. I repeated this a few times.

I heard Dad come in, commenting on the weather. The news was on when I walked down the stairs.

"That poor girl," Mom was saying.

"Crazy," Dad said.

Apparently, the lighting had been particularly bad in Pennsylvania. There was a 16-year-old girl who'd been struck by lightning and was in critical condition. She'd been working at a summer camp in the Poconos, and she was in the middle of pulling a metal row boat back to the shore when a bolt of lightning came down on the boat and threw her 30 feet—luckily in the direction of the shore and not the water. She was being treated for third-degree burns and head trauma.

I couldn't help but wonder whether my parents were thinking the same thing I was: that would totally happen to me. I was totally the type-A one who, when torn between the fear of getting struck by lightning and the fear of getting yelled at for disobeying my boss, would make the choice that compromised my safety.

We ate our dinner with the news on. People were dying. Economy. Rain. Afterwards I went upstairs and almost called Jake. I looked up his number in our high school directory. I remembered the feeling of his breath against my neck as he pedaled me home on Travis's bike. I thought of the judgy way he'd scolded me for what happened with Doug. Then I threw the book across the room and listened to the second disc of *The White Album* while flipping through a book, *The Amateur Astronomer*, which I'd bought with my dad at Barnes & Noble the week before.

There was a section where lifelong stargazers discussed their favorite telescopes, places to stargaze, and moments that inspired them. Almost every single astronomer said that the thing that got them addicted to the night sky was seeing Saturn's rings through a telescope for the first time. I thought about Saturn out there. I'd been drawing it for years with a crayon.

I looked out my window, which reflected my image back to me. This is what it was like to be in the artificial light of the night. Indoors, when the sun was down, windows were mirrors, inflicting their own sort of blindness.

I loved reading *The Amateur Astronomer*. The way they agonized over equipment resonated deeply with me.

Deb called me the next day when my mom was home, so I was forced to take the phone.

"Why didn't you come the other night?" she asked me. "Oh my god Cody hates me. He says he's going to tell my parents."

"I honestly forgot. Nanny stayed later than I thought she would and by the time we got home, I was tired and I just went to bed."

"It was nuts. There were a lot of people here."

"Like who?" I said. I wanted to see how she would paint the event.

"Well Jenna and me and Park—" she'd taken to calling Parker "Park"—"and, I don't know, Doug, Scott, um, pretty much the entire future senior class? Some juniors? There were a lot of people. Too many people. Our patio table got broken."

"Oh no!" I said. I tried to sound genuinely upset about it. I just wasn't. I could barely summon the air to form words.

She told me she'd gotten really drunk. That she'd given "Park" a hand job in her bathroom and that he'd fingered her. That they'd decided they were boyfriend and girlfriend. Oh, and that Doug and Jenna were now hooking up. Or at least they had hooked up. On her parents' bed.

I didn't say anything. I didn't care if Jenna and Doug wanted to hook up. Of course, it hurt on some level and felt like betrayal on another, but at this point, it didn't really surprise me. I did wonder if Jenna's experience was similar to my own. Despite my lingering anger over her cruel words, I worried about her. But what I cared about the most was that Anais had read whatever bullshit Deb had scrawled in her diary about me out loud to a room full of people.

"Are you mad?" Deb said.

"About what?"

"About Jenna and Doug."

"No. Why would I be?"

"Because you're not saying anything."

"I don't know. I just don't know what to say anymore. Good for her?"

"So you're not into him anymore?"

"I don't know if I ever was."

"That's not what you used to say," she said.

"I didn't know what I was talking about. I still don't. I don't think you can say that you actually like someone until you know them."

"Well, you definitely knew him, and you still liked him."

"Ok..."

"What?"

"I just don't feel like we're having a real conversation. Congratulations on getting a boyfriend." I hung up the phone. I knew she would think that I was jealous. I didn't care. Let her think whatever she wanted.

The rainy days persisted. On the schedule, Coach Burt had arranged for us to check in at Landers Pond to do a run together, but he called to reschedule.

"Let's meet in the weight room," he said. "It says scattered showers and another chance of a thunderstorm," he told me over the phone in the morning. "I'd prefer for us to run outside, but since everyone is freaking out about that girl and they say there may be lightning, we'll meet inside. Just to be safe."

That girl was in a coma now. It wasn't looking good.

Normally, I'd have walked to the school for practice with an umbrella, but because of the lightning scare, Dad left work early and volunteered to drive me.

"Should I just wait out here in the car?" Dad said as we approached the school. "How long do you think the practice will be?"

"No!" I said, thinking about how embarrassing it would be if someone saw my dad hanging out in a car outside of the school. "It's going to be long. At least an hour. I think Burt wants to walk us through a new strength training program."

"I just don't want to get home, get comfortable, and then have to get right back up and turn around to get you."

"I promise it will be at least an hour. Go watch a rerun of *Star Trek* or something."

He fished around in one of the cupholders between the driver's and passenger's seats where he kept loose change and handed me two quarters for the payphone in the hallway by the gym.

"You should just buy me a cell phone," I said.

He snorted. "You can buy one yourself with your babysitting money."

"Maybe I will," I said.

As I ran into the school entrance, I met Kelsey, her car keys in her hand.

"Hey!" she said, "Oh my god, I'm so dumb, I totally should have picked you up! Duh! I can give you a ride home."

"Perfect," I said.

The school smelled differently during the summertime, a combination of cleaning products, cardboard and new paint. Only half of the lights were turned on. We walked through the empty gym towards the weight room, where we could hear the sound of rap music.

It was mostly football players who used the gym, but sometimes other athletes came in. Coach B was obsessed with strength training. I understood that it was important. I just hated being in the same room as all of the guys.

"This sucks," Kelsey said as we walked through the open doors. "Like I feel like running on a treadmill."

Boy sweat assaulted my nostrils before we even stepped inside. I noticed, with a flash of alarm, that Doug Ryan was bent over a bench doing arm reps, the horseshoe of his tricep pressing against the surface of his skin each time he straightened his elbow. Outkast sang from a speaker: "Never meant to make your daughter cry / I apologize a trillion times / I'm sorry Ms. Jackson / I am for real."

Coach B was already there waiting for us, lording over the only two treadmills in the place to make sure no one else claimed them.

"I already set the course on each of these to match your needs," he said. "It's a 30-minute workout." He looked at his watch. "I need to go to the athletic office to make a phone call real quick," he said. "I'll be back before you're done."

We pressed go on our machines and started to run. I hated treadmills. Running in place was not my thing, not to mention the fact that they always seemed to be situated near mirrors, which meant I was forced to either scrutinize or avoid my appearance. Kelsey didn't seem to have this problem. I noticed that she did a special little bounce, just to watch her ponytail sway back and forth behind her head like a pendulum. Doug noticed. Everyone did. We were the only two girls in the gym. Usually, when I was outside, I kept my head up as I ran and gazed straight ahead, but here I looked at the digital numbers on the panel in front of me. Looking straight ahead would mean staring both at Doug Ryan doing reps in the foreground and at my own reflection in the mirror behind him. It was strange seeing myself reflected next to Kelsey. She seemed so slight next to me, so feminine. I was taller and more muscular. My thicker, puffy hair didn't bounce the same way. I felt like Tanya Harding next to Nancy Kerrigan.

Kelsey looked at me. "Shit your arms are so muscular. Mine look like chopsticks. I wish I was buff."

"No you don't," I whispered back, "People like chopsticks, not man arms."

Her laugh was high-pitched, like a bird making a mating call, and it sent all the boys eyes back over to us again. We ran silently until they went back to their workouts. Then she whispered to me. "You do not have man arms."

I assumed she didn't mean this.

We tried to keep it low key, but dudes still came over to say hi. I got nods and 'sups mostly. Really, everyone wanted to gossip with Kelsey. Did she hear that Rick had gotten busted with weed by his mom and that she called the cops on all of them?

Poor Rick, I thought, remembering him buried in the sand on Memorial Day weekend, the torch of Doug's lighter threatening his eyebrows as it approached his cigarette.

Kelsey pushed the down button on her treadmill to slow down the speed enough so that she could talk, and nodded along to the stuff they were saying.

Eventually, Doug took his turn sauntering up. He was wearing a bright green Heineken t-shirt. The sleeves had been cut off, so the armholes hung wide, revealing glimpses of his armpit hair and chest. The shirt was old, and the print was beginning to flake off in places, but you could still make out the message: *Grab a Heiny!* He clasped his arms behind him so that his chest puffed out. Then he brought them in front of him, grasping each of his elbows, stretching after the rep.

"Banks!" he said, shouting my name like he was greeting a teammate before a game in the locker room.

I opened my eyes wide at him and said nothing. He shook his head at me, like he understood my psychology better than I did and was disappointed but not surprised.

Doug turned to Kelsey, and I noticed she didn't turn the speed back down to talk to him.

"Some of Gordy's friends from school are in town and he said we could all hang in his basement," he said. Gordy was a guy who didn't go to our high school. He went to boarding school in north Jersey, but a lot of people were friends with him from way back. His house was out in the super mansion land, near Travis, and his basement was a legendary den of teenage debauchery that I had never pierced. It was the kind of event Deb and Jenna would jump at the chance to attend.

He smiled at Kelsey. "You going out tonight?"

Her face stayed completely neutral. "I'm not sure."

"We're gonna play quarters." Quarters was a drinking game—I knew that much from Eric and Cody and pieces of conversations overheard in the cafeteria and gym— that involved bouncing quarters off of countertops into cups and making people chug beer.

"I'll see what everyone's doing tonight," she said, noncommittally. "Maybe." I felt her eyes dart towards me, searching to see if I was listening. "Who's going?"

I tried to pretend that I wasn't listening, but Doug saw Kelsey's eyes stray and took that as an invitation to include me in the conversation. He moved from the far side of her treadmill to directly in front of mine, looking straight at me with that same all-knowing smile on his face.

"Hopefully Banks is going to come," he said.

He did a push up against the front of my treadmill. I saw the muscles in his arms contract and release. I saw his fingers and thought about how my hands had touched those hands, how my mouth had touched that mouth, how his body had rubbed against my body, and how even though afterwards I'd felt humiliation and regret, I had also somehow longed for him to stand this close to me to help me make sense of what had occurred, to make me feel something more than ugly and invisible. Now all I wanted was a way to disappear. He was searching my face. I reluctantly met his eyes.

The terrain program Coach B had put on the treadmill was in the process of shifting into a steep incline. It felt like I was trying to run into his chest. My legs felt like jelly. I wasn't sure if it was because of him or the speed or the slope, but I forced myself forward. It was a strange sensation. I kept expecting to barrel right into him like a bull into a matador, but there was nothing, just the showdown of our faces and the puffing rhythm of my breath and the groan of the machine and the rap music behind it. The humidity of the day coupled with the moisture of so many sweaty bodies felt too thick. Was it possible to suffocate on a treadmill in a gym? Because it had recently been proven that you could maybe die from pulling a boat onto shore during a lightning storm, and this felt just as risky.

Doug lunged uncomfortably forward, making it impossible not to meet his eyes. "Your friends are coming," he said to me. "You should come too."

My friends? I had to think about who my friends even were before I realized he was talking about Jenna and Deb.

"If you go, I'll go," Kelsey said to me.

"Awesome," Doug said.

Just then, Coach came bouncing in like he was Billy Blanks in a tae bo video. We all looked at him baffled, collectively remembering that we were in a school, and that he was the adult in charge.

As Kelsey and I were walking out of the gym together,

she said, "Seriously, I'll take you out tonight if you want. Just tell your parents it's a bonding thing for cross country. You can even sleepover. It'll be fun. I'm sure Mandy and Kate will want to go to Gordy's anyway. I'm the one who's the homebody." It felt absurd that this was happening. As absurd as the moment when Doug had invited us to party on the beach.

Outside, the rain was more like a heavy mist. Kelsey unlocked the doors to her car and I hopped in, tasting the chemical scent of her strawberry air freshener. She turned on the car and the album she had been listening to sprang to life through the speakers, Beyonce singing: "Say my name, say my name."

"This is going to be awesome," Kelsey said.

"There's no way my mom and dad will say yes," I said.

"Oh please," Kelsey said, "Let me do the talking."

I shrugged. It was worth a try.

I saw from the driveway that my mom's car was still out. It was only my dad who was home. If anyone could be convinced, it would be him. He'd played football and basketball in high school and loved team spirit. Just a few weeks ago, he had been lamenting this subject on the way home from Benji's barbeque. "I wish you got to experience the joy of being on a team. It's just not the same in track." I'd tried to remind him that Cross Country and Track and Field were, in fact, team sports, that we were scored as a team and that we won as a team, but because there was no ball being passed, he insisted it was different. I got that to a degree, but it annoyed me how he tried to suggest that my chosen sport was lacking.

But now, here was an opportunity to use this idea to my favor and sell the night as a rare team bonding event.

"Actually, let me do the talking," I said to her as we were getting out of the car.

"Sounds good," she said.

My dad was sitting at the computer in our living room.

"What?" he said, obviously surprised by my arrival. "I've been waiting by the phone over here."

"Kelsey gave me a ride. Dad, Kelsey; Kelsey, this is my dad."

"Hi, Mr. Banks," she said.

"Hello," he said in his friendly dad voice.

I addressed him in my no nonsense, please-be-cool voice. "What are you doing?"

"I'm reading the minutes from the Tonley community board meeting on the website. There's a proposal to add lights to the football field back behind Deb's house. That's a terrible idea."

"Why?" Kelsey asked.

"Because it will bring a ton of people to this area all the time and there will be lots of noise and cars parked all over the place and the games will light up this whole area at night!" he said. "The lights will shine right into Emily's windows."

"Light pollution," I said, knowingly.

"Celestino," Kelsey laughed.

"Did you have her?" I asked.

"No, but my sister did. She loved the class."

Dad snapped his fingers. "You know, that's a good angle for opposing this. You girls should come to the next community board meeting to voice your concerns about light pollution before the vote happens. Em, you can use your research. They'll probably listen to you over me."

Dad didn't seem to care that Kelsey hadn't even taken the class. He was lost in his vision of a perfect defense. We nodded our heads, making noncommittal promises to participate.

"Dad, can I sleep over Kelsey's tonight?"

"A bunch of girls from the team are coming over," Kelsey said, picking up the metaphoric baton and launching into her explanation about the team bonding event.

"That sounds nice," he said. He looked at me. "Do you have to babysit tomorrow?"

"Tomorrow's Saturday, Dad."

"Oh right," he said. "Duh." His use of 'duh' made me give him another be-cool look.

"Hopefully, the rain will be done by then," he said. "It's supposed to clear up tonight."

We left Kelsey's number on a post-it by the refrigerator, then we went up to my room, where I tossed a few things in a bag.

"We've gotta get out of here before my mom gets home," I said. "Or we are definitely going to have problems."

"Oh my God," Kelsey said. "Your room is sooo cute." She was looking at the trophies that my mother had displayed.

"Please, don't even look at anything in here," I said, mortified. "Close your eyes."

"You're hilarious," she said.

"No I'm not. I'm just being real. This is not my room. This is my mother's representation of what my room should look like. I would never put my trophies on display."

"Why not?"

"Because who wants to look at their trophies?"

She shrugged. "I don't have any trophies," she said. "So I have no idea what I'd do with them."

- 18 -

Kelsey's house was a big old Victorian, even bigger than Deb's, with multiple staircases and a huge front porch. Her parents looked like senior citizens compared to mine. She was the youngest of six.

Her dad was watching television in the living room and her mother was back in the kitchen talking on the phone. Neither one of them seemed concerned that a child who had never entered their home before was carrying an overnight bag.

We took the back set of stairs off the kitchen. On the way up, she reached into a pantry and extracted a bag of pretzels and took the Brita pitcher by the sink.

Kelsey's bedroom looked like the set to a television show. It was huge and full of fluffy pillows, some with yarn-like fringe. Pictures of silly moments were haphazardly scotch taped on the walls. Makeup littered the top of her dresser. There was a pink dusting of blush over the chipped white varnish. It felt like what a teenager was supposed to live in. Also, it had its own balcony. It was built for some sort of *Romeo and Juliet* romance.

I couldn't help but catalog every item in her popular girl dreamscape. I was dazzled by everything, especially by the fact that I was there. But she didn't act as if my visit was an act of charity. I felt truly invited. We ate pretzels and talked about sneaker brands.

Her friends Kate and Mandy arrived one by one. As each of them entered, I felt newly intimidated by their presence. Kate gave me a stiff smile. Mandy made sure to let me know that I had beaten her brother for first in the class. The many fringy pillows in the room were put to use. We lounged in various corners. They talked. I was quiet as a mouse. I listened. I noticed that Mandy was pretty smart herself. I had no idea what her class rank was though. Kate was harder to read. She had a general vibe of discontent. I couldn't tell if it was because of me.

It had stopped raining outside, but I was too busy laying across Kelsey's bed, paging through her collection of CDs to fully take note of it.

"Put on anything you want," she said to me.

"Not anything you want," Mandy fired back. "No Tori before we go out. Those are the rules."

"Tori?" I asked.

"Amos?" Kelsey asked me back.

I gave her a blank stare. "Emily, you are like made to be her fan." She grabbed the CD book out of my hand and handed me *Boys for Pele*. "Listen to this later," she said. "Best enjoyed alone."

"Tori Amos is too depressing," Kate declared. "I don't even understand what she's talking about."

"Kate just says that because she doesn't like to reflect on her own sadness," Mandy said. It seemed like a half-serious comment. Kelsey's eyes looked amused. Kate's looked annoyed.

"She's not for everybody," Kelsey agreed, "But Emily is going to love her."

I put *The Miseducation of Lauryn Hill* on the stereo to universal approval.

Kate high-fived me. "This is so exciting!" she said. "We're partying with Emily Banks tonight! Celebrity spotting!"

I didn't know how to respond. I just shrugged. I was no celebrity; we all knew that. Kate opened the door to the balcony and sat in the doorway, lighting up a cigarette.

"I don't want the smoke coming in here," Kelsey said. "Smoke it outside."

"It's soggy out there," Kate said.

"Just stand up."

Kate sighed, "Fine," she said, walking out onto the balcony but leaving the door open. It was fascinating to me that smoking a cigarette on the balcony was so pedestrian. This sort of thing would not even fly at Deb's.

Kelsey had her own computer, which was set up on her desk and connected to the internet. She was signed into AOL and started tapping away furiously to several different people.

"Oh my god," she said. "Fucking gross."

"What?" we all asked.

"This guy. I don't know who he is. Read this."

We all gathered around to read the conversation on the screen.

Trees420: You going to the party tonight?

KelseyGirl313: Not sure.

Trees420: Are you mad because your tits are smaller than Mandy's?

KelseyGirl313: Wtf?

Trees420: I heard you like to kiss girls.

KelseyGirl313: Who is this?

Trees420: Can I watch?

Mandy made a face. "Dudes are so stupid. I'm mad because my tits are bigger than yours."

"Scumbag," Kate said.

"Ew," Kelsey said, covering her ears, "please don't say tits. I hate that word."

"We should tell him we'll show him our tits," Mandy said. "Then when he reveals himself to us, we should cut off his dick, Lorena Bobbitt style."

"I said to stop using that word," Kelsey said.

Mandy stuck her tongue out and shook her chest in Kelsey's face saying, "Titties, titties, titties, titties, tits, tits, tits." Then she looked at the screen. "Probably just one of the idiot guys in our grade. They are probably all at Gordy's house." She rolled her eyes.

"I hate this shit," Kelsey said. "Now I don't even want to go."

Mandy disagreed. "Oh, come on. You know they're just trying to show off in front of Gordy's friends."

"Well, I'm not impressed," Kelsey shot back.

"They're just fucking with you because you gave them shit the other night," Kate said.

Everyone was quiet. I could tell it was something they didn't want to discuss in front of me.

"Just tell her," Mandy said.

"Mand," Kelsey said. "Shut up."

"She deserves to know!"

"What?" I said, trying to sound flippant and brave. "That Anais read Deb's diary at her party last week and that everyone knows about that night with me and Doug?"

"Anais read Deb's diary at that party?" Kate said.

"She is such a bitch," Mandy said.

"She doesn't give a shit about anyone," Kelsey agreed. "She just takes bong hits and laughs at us all like we're idiots."

"Ok, so that's not it," I said. I was worried. If it wasn't that, then what was it?

"Doug was just drunk talking shit," Kelsey said, "And I threw a beer bottle at his head. It missed though. Unfortunately."

"And I had to clean it all up, but that's another story," Kate said.

"Shit about me?" I said. "What did he say?"

"You don't want to know," Kate said.

"I do want to know," I said. I felt an anger licking inside me.

"He said that you begged him to put it inside, but that he didn't want his dick to smell, so he didn't do it." Mandy said, straight-faced.

"Mandy!" Kelsey said.

"That's what he said," Mandy said.

I was shaking. My entire body was trembling. My teeth chattered so hard I thought they might break. Kelsey protectively put her arms around my shoulders. "What is wrong with you," she said to Mandy.

"I don't think it's fair to pretend like people aren't saying crazy shit. People have said crazy shit about me before, Doug included, and I personally think it is better to know."

I wasn't sure I agreed with Mandy, though I appreciated the sentiment. I thought about how lucky it was for Ceil that she could run away. If there had been a person named Joey with a magic motorcycle to whisk me to a rat-infested apartment on the Lower East Side, I would have mounted it in an instant.

Nobody said anything. Mandy opened her duffle bag and extracted a bottle of red wine. It was a twist off. She opened it and took out a sleeve of paper cups, filling one for each of us. She came up next to me and put her arm around me. I could smell Bath and Body Works products. Watermelon and Cucumber. I took the cup she offered me and she knocked hers against mine.

"Drink this down in one enormous gulp," she said. "And then forget about that fuck face. One day, someone is going to launch a beer bottle at his face and hit him straight on, and it will be a win for the entire human race."

I wanted to believe Mandy, but there was a part of me that doubted anything of consequence would ever hit Doug Ryan. Still, I did as instructed. Or at least the first part. The wine warmed my body and went straight to my head. I reached across the bed to grab one of the fringy pillows. I pet the mustard-colored yarn for a minute, rubbing little tendrils between my fingers, and then I picked it up and held it tight against my face and screamed bloody murder and said every curse word you could think of. I probably made some up. Then I dropped the pillow on the bed, exhausted.

Mandy laughed and then poured me another cup of wine. I drank it down again in one gulp.

"You really are a fucking force," she said. "I like it."

Kate and Kelsey looked unsure what to do. I didn't want them to worry at my expense.

"Can I borrow some lipstick?" I asked.

"Yes!" Kelsey said. She unzipped a little bag and dumped all her tubes on the bed. I chose a dark, purple kind of black. I was going goth tonight.

"Please let me line your lids," Mandy begged.

I declined. We refilled our cups one more time, emptying the bottle, and things started to feel better. We were just getting ready to go when the phone rang.

Kelsey answered it. "House of hookers, Madam speaking."

It was my mom. Of course. Kelsey turned down the music and the girls all watched me while I picked up the phone.

"Who is that girl? Are her parents home?"

"It was a joke, Mom. Yes, her parents are home, do you want to talk to them?"

Kelsey shook her head no, pretending to slit her throat with her finger. I bit my lip and prayed my mom wouldn't do what I assumed she would do, which is say yes. She sighed. "I wanted to get up early and go on a canoe trip in the Pine Barrens. Will you come back for breakfast in the morning?"

"What time?"

"8?"

"That's way too early."

"Well, when were you thinking?"

"I'll be home by 10. I promise." I said.

"Ok, fine," she said. "Just behave yourself."

I was worried she could tell I was a little buzzed. And then I made it worse for myself by saying, "Don't worry, I'm no Caputo." I don't know why I said it. I don't even know if I meant it maliciously, or what. It just came out of my mouth.

"What?" she said sharply.

"See?" I said. "It isn't a nice thing to say."

"No. It's not."

I thought I should continue talking. That way I would appear less crazy or drunk. "You know that guy with the motorcycle?" I said. "Who drove Ceil away to New York?"

"Yeah?"

"His name was Joey. He died of AIDS and it was his birthday the other day. He would have been 48."

"That's sad," Mom said.

"I meant to tell you that but I forgot."

"Wow," Mom said.

"Anyway, I should go. Try to survive a night without me."

"I'm sorry I missed seeing you and Kelsey. Dad said she was really nice. Make sure you behave yourself tonight. No more house of hookers."

"I promise," I said. I hung up and we all breathed a sigh of relief.

- 19 -

Gordy's was like a half hour walk from Kelsey's, but she didn't want to drive her car because she was already feeling tipsy, so we walked in a pack down the Tonley sidewalks. The air was full of dahlias and begonias and other flowers I couldn't identify. Thankfully, the bees had gone back to their hives for the night. There were only crickets and tree frogs to serenade us on our stroll.

Kate kept talking herself in circles about a guy named Jeff, who was a friend of Gordy's from school who she had hooked up with the last time they'd gone to a party at Gordy's place over winter break.

"I don't care if he's there. Really. He's cute, but he's really not that smart. He just goes to boarding school because his parents don't want to deal with how dumb he is and they can like afford to build a gymnasium."

"Uh huh, he's dumb and uninteresting, that's why you can't stop changing your hair every five seconds," Kelsey said.

"It's the humidity," Kate said, defensively. "It makes my hair look slick."

"It does the opposite to mine," I said, pressing against the poof.

"I bet he's Trees420, the guy who typed the titty messages," Mandy said.

"Please god, don't let that be true," Kate said, alarmed. Then, in the middle of trying to coax her hair into a ponytail, she touched the annoying flyaways near her forehead. "I'm going to get my bangs cut tomorrow."

"Don't cut them!" Kelsey screeched, stopping in her tracks, wheeling around and putting both of her hands on Kate's shoulders with a dead serious look on her face. I could tell she was feeling the wine. "Remember, you made me promise that I would intervene at this moment. I will help you stay strong. You can do this! Grow out your bangs."

Kate groaned like an addict, "Scissors. Scissors. I need scissors."

"No!" Mandy declared, playing along and trying to grab Kate's arms. "No scissors Kate. Scissors bad."

Kate rolled her eyes, obviously enjoying the passion of her friends' intervention. "Fine," she said, "but does anybody have a barrette or bobby pin or something? They keep getting in my face and I can't promise that I won't chop them if I run across a blade."

"Just own the swoop tonight," Mandy said.

"I think they look kind of mysterious," I said. "I always wanted to be the kind of cartoon character who only had one visible eye at a time."

Everyone thought this was funny.

Kelsey gave me a little hip bump. "You were born too late. You're in the wrong grade."

"Maybe I can skip a few," I said. It was possible to graduate from high school early, wasn't it?

"If anyone could pull it off, it's you," she said.

The conversation went to why Gordy's house was available for partying in the first place. "There is some party this weekend in Atlantic City," Mandy said. "It's like a pre-game for the Republican National Convention, which starts Monday in Philly."

"I heard the RNC paid to demolish all the strip clubs on Admiral Wilson Boulevard so that the rich donors didn't have to pass them on their way from AC to Philly," Kate said.

"Everyone in this town is a goddamn Republican," Kate sighed, shaking her fists at the sky.

"Yes, yes, everyone is evil and racist here, it's true," Mandy said, "except for your parents, who are academics who for some reason want to raise their child in an almost all-white town, even though they're not racist at all."

"It's the train access," Kate said.

Mandy laughed. "Probably," she said.

"It's true," I said. "Well, I don't know your parents, but I think it's true that, like, people are racist. Maybe not evil. At least not on purpose." Then I attempted to explain the long story of Ceil, Maeve, and the things my parents said about Maeve's dad without any evidence, even though he was an artist who lived in a different country. But either I didn't tell it fast enough, or I wasn't compelling enough, or they were all just in their own heads. I didn't get a response. Literally I heard crickets.

"My parents are voting for Gore," Kate said.

"Nobody can even vote yet," Kelsey said.

"Everyone has already made up their minds," Kate said back.

"Isn't it crazy that that's true?" I said. "I feel like it shouldn't be that easy."

"Yeah, like you should really stew over it," Mandy said, rolling her eyes. "Like pizza or nachos."

"But I never know which of those I want," I said.

Mandy put her hand on her head and then flailed out her fingers, miming an explosion. "Exactly," she said.

All this time, we'd been walking a strangely similar course to the one I'd walked that night weeks ago when I'd run into Jake.

Gordy and Travis, I realized, were only a few houses apart. We passed the "No Trespassing" sign on the private road. Everyone just strolled past it. No big deal.

I couldn't help but look at the sky. Even though the rain

had stopped, the clouds still acted as a chastity belt. The heavens were locked away.

We could hear the sounds of voices spilling out of the windows of the unfathomably, stupid-huge house. I realized I wasn't ready for it. I didn't want to go in. Mandy sensed this first.

"Ready?" she said, linking arms with me. "Let's find Parker. He said he got us a case."

"Parker?" I said, nervously.

She waved her hand at me. "To Deb, he's like a god. To me, he's my beer wench."

"I think I'll just stay here," I said, unlinking arms with Mandy.

"Like hell you will," Kelsey said. She and Kate and Mandy made a circle around me with their arms, and then they dove in and embraced me.

"Group hug!" Kelsey said.

Their collective presence sent a pulse of warmth through me. We were all feeling it.

"Women loving each other out here," Mandy shouted.

"Trees420 don't come close, or you'll be smote by our coven," Kate yelled.

The tears in my eyes felt silly. I tried my best to blink them back.

Kelsey squeezed my arms. "Running buddy, you're coming into this party."

"If I shit my pants, will you bury it?" I asked.

"You act like I have a choice," she said.

Mandy gave a loud laugh.

We followed stepping stones around to the backyard and then walked up a few steps to a door that opened onto a mudroom.

I followed everyone through a door to a darkened hallway where I noticed a few people stray towards another doorway that I think led into a kitchen. Kelsey knew where she was going though. She went straight down the stairs. We squeezed past others on their way up.

The basement was enormous. It was like a pool hall. A very glamorous man cave. Gordy's father must have had it custom designed. It was the kind of thing rich dads had on TV. There were framed baseball and football jerseys on the wall and trophies and plaques and pictures of sports celebrities behind a case.

"Gordy's dad is an exec at the NFL," Kate told me. "That's him." She pointed to a picture of a fit, gray-haired man smiling next to Jeffrey Lorrie, the owner of the Eagles, then she turned and saw some guys walking down the stairs. She pulled my arm and nudged in the direction of the stairs. "That's Gordy," she said in an excited whisper. "He's the guy with the blond hair and popped collar. But don't look, fuck, he's talking to Jeff."

I looked. I couldn't help it. Gordy was on the taller side, thin with a slightly grown out preppy haircut, like an honorary Culkin brother. Jeff, on the other hand, had a thick set of eyebrows that seemed to waggle up and down with every breath that entered his body. Whatever he and Gordy were talking about must have been hilarious. His eyebrows practically leapt off his face while they gasped for breath. Maybe they were just high.

"I said don't look!" Kate said. "Do you think he's cute?"

"Gordy?"

"No! Jeff!"

I didn't. But what did I know? "Definitely," I said. "He looks like he's funny too."

Mandy appeared with four beers.

"I don't want to drink this shit," Kelsey said.

Mandy shrugged. "Go tell Gordy. I'm sure he'll give you a shot of something."

Kelsey walked away. I opened my can of beer and took a sip. It tasted like the gluey side of an envelope when you lick it, but with bubbles. Thanks to the wine buzz, it went down easy. People moved from one side of the room to the other and then back again. It seemed like the main goal of this event was just to rub against as many other humans as possible while yelling nonsense at unfathomable decibels. The busybodiedness of others caused a contrarian stillness inside of me. Mandy and Kate got called in one direction or the other, but I was cemented to my place in the middle of the room, near a group of kids playing a vintage pinball game. An alarmed, orange cat appeared between my legs, meowing and looking at me insistently. I finished my beer and bent down to scratch this timid beast behind the ears. "Hello cat," I whispered scooping him up and rubbing my cheek against the top of his head. "I know how you feel," I told him. "It's too crazy down here." I carried him up the stairs and deposited him by the doorway that led to the kitchen. As I was walking back down, I passed Gordy. We made eye contact. He smiled.

"Emily Banks," he said to me.

"Gordan Chandler," I said back.

"I see you and Pumpkin have been acquainted," he smiled, referring to his cat. I felt like I was talking to Gatsby. He was so charming. I had the urge to start calling him "old sport."

"He told me his name was Mr. Pumpkin," I said, thinking I was funny.

"So he was being formal with you, huh? He can be a little stuffy." I was impressed by his ability to run with my joke.

I made a show of waving off the comment. "I'm used to that," I said.

He got that I was joking and laughed. Then he looked at me seriously. "Do me a favor. If you see him by any of the doors to the outside, can you scare him away? He's really not supposed to be outside. There are some mean raccoons out there."

"Tell me about it," I said.

"My mom got him declawed a few years ago because he was tearing up the furniture, but now he's defenseless."

"Poor guy," I said.

Then Gordy was gone. I walked down the stairs feeling proud of our exchange. I'd actually spoken real words. I liked how he didn't pretend to not know me. He didn't try to act too cool. Maybe boarding school kids were more civilized. They were forced to live in community with one another for extended periods of time, after all, and they weren't infantilized by growing into adults in their childhood bedrooms like us. I looked around at all the kids I didn't know and admired them for what I imagined to be their sophistication. How had they even all arrived here? Had they chartered some sort of party bus?

I asked this question to an energetic Indian guy from Gordy's boarding school named Ray, a super tall dude who seemed to enjoy explaining every aspect of everything to me—including who I was and everything about my cross country statistics. "You only beat the girl from Our Lady of Grace in Morris by a fraction of a second in that first match with her back in September," he said.

"Rosaria Esposito, you mean. I know. She's really good, but luckily it wasn't a photo finish at states," I said. I'd beaten her by a full three seconds. She'd thrown her shoes. Ray laughed when I told him that. But she was only going into her junior year; she'd be back out there in the fall, hot on my heels. And there was a freshman in Newark named Noemi Baker that people were already talking about. All at once, I felt overwhelmed by the tasks that lay ahead in the fall. But I didn't want to discuss that with this guy. I'd started this conversation to get real information.

I motioned my hands around the party. "But wait, you never answered my question. How did everyone from your school get here?"

"Some took the train from Princeton to Trenton or Philly and transferred. Some drove. A lot of us are doing a summer session and we got our parents to sign waivers for weekend trips. We just all sort of concocted different stories and wrote letters on behalf of each other's parents." He started pointing at people in the room and explaining the confusing overlay of alibis.

"Wow," I said. "Amazing."

I wanted that sort of autonomy. Not necessarily in this man cave. I just liked the idea of being somewhere no adult could find for an extended period of time without the pressure of knowing they'd be looking for me.

Ray did his thing, enjoying the sound of his own voice as he deconstructed an episode of *The Simpsons* that was muted on the screen. I half pretended to listen as my eyes searched for Jake. Surely he would come, wouldn't he? Travis's place was right down the road. How could they miss this?

I needed to see him.

I needed whatever would happen when that happened to occur. I just wanted to know if he was still my science partner. If he understood why I couldn't return the calls. Why I couldn't pick up. Why I needed to hide.

My beer was empty and I had to pee.

"I'll be back," I told Ray, though I knew I probably wouldn't return, and I doubted he'd be waiting for me.

I didn't know where Kelsey, Kate, and Mandy were, but I found that my buzz—along with the surprising comfort I felt around these prep school kids—meant I actually didn't care. I just kind of floated from one space to the next like some sort of content ghost.

I joined the long line to the bathroom in the basement. People were talking about all kinds of things: brands of jeans, the best places to go swimming on Martha's Vineyard, whether or not the American water supply was in danger from unregulated pollutants or if that was a socialist conspiracy, if George W. Bush was really in Skull and Bones—one person claimed somebody there's dad was in it and had confirmed that Bush was in it too, which dude had a boner that was visible in his pants. It all blended into one conversation.

At points, people offered bits of conversation in my direction. I offered bits in return. I couldn't commit to any sort of real exchange of information. I just really had to pee. Plus, this party was a sensory overload. Finally, I was next. I watched the person in front of me open the door and enter. When he closed it, I turned to look behind me and there was Deb.

Her hair was in a strangely high ponytail, and her shirt was new. It was a collared sleeveless Izod. She was wearing a khaki skirt with Birkenstocks on her feet and she'd gotten a French mani pedi. She looked like she was trying to be a Ralph Lauren model or like she was auditioning to be an extra in *Dead Poet's Society*.

"You're here!" she said when she saw me, as if she had searched for me everywhere and taken me for dead. Again, she was so easy and casual about seeing me. It's like she thought that no matter what she said about me, I would never stop being her sidekick. But at the same time, I realized that she was relieved. For a flash, I understood the balance of our friendship. She confidently took me places I'd never go, and I was her companion on the journey. Also, as a bonus, most of the time I truly thought her jokes were funny and that her hair looked cool, which gave her confidence. We both liked certain TV shows.

And, of course, we'd been babies together at the same time and place. But listing it that way in my head made me realize that maybe this was just as far as a friendship like that goes. Still, it was hard not to feel bitter.

"What a coinkydink meeting you here," I said in a crazy happy voice, just as the guy in front of me was exiting the bathroom. "I have to pee," I said, grabbing her arm. "Come with." I pulled her into the bathroom, locked the door and plopped on the toilet, deciding to ignore the wet sensation of someone else's urine on the seat.

I gave her a crooked, potentially mocking smile. "Does 'Park' have a matching polo shirt?" I asked her.

"What's that supposed to mean?" she asked.

"It means I like your shirt."

"Did you see him? Is he here?"

"Park-er?"

"Yeah."

"I figured you'd know that," I said.

"How did you get here?" she asked me. I wasn't sure what she was trying to imply. I was offended.

"Well obviously not through you," I said, standing up and flushing. "You wouldn't want to bring a butter face with you to an event like this." When I'd thought up the line in my mind a second before I said it, it'd felt strong and defiant, but as I spoke the words, I felt my lower lip tremble. It looked especially dramatic seeing that it was painted a corpse-colored purple, something I'd forgotten about until I saw myself in the mirror as I washed my hands. I was shocked by this vision of myself. I grabbed a wad of toilet paper and tried to rub the color away. It was lighter now, but they were still stained, and I was still radiating revenge vibes from *The Craft*.

Maybe Deb was thinking the same thing when she gave me

her worried face. "What are you talking about?" she said.

We looked at each other, her eyes searching mine in a kind and nervous way, full of love for me, even regret and worry for being exposed for her hypocrisy. Mine felt cold and dead. I'd already gone through the pain. Part of me was on the other side. I wanted to answer her question, but I realized that I'd never actually be able to explain to her the depths with which I felt betrayed. It was just over.

"You used to be my person," I said, "but you're just not anymore."

I felt the strength that comes with stating the truth. I opened the door and left in a hurry, taking the basement stairs two at a time. On my way up I ran into Mandy coming down.

"Slow down there, champ," she said. She had two beers in her hand. She handed me one. "If my brother knew I was standing with you on the top of these stairs, he'd be mad at me for not shoving you."

I opened the beer, took a sip and said, "Go ahead and shove me. It'll take more than that to kill me. Tell your brother to get used to it. He's number two."

She choked on her beer and followed me back up the stairs.

In the kitchen, there was a crowd of upperclassmen gathered around a table. Doug was playing quarters with Parker against two other guys from our high school. "We've got next," Mandy said.

"I don't want to play," I said to Mandy. "I don't know how."

"You don't need to know," she said. Clearly she didn't understand that I was incapable of playing a game without playing to win.

I tried to watch them bounce quarters to get a sense of the

rules, but though my eyes were focused on the game, I was mostly suffocating under the toxic aura of Doug's presence. Where were Jenna and Deb? Didn't they want to play against their boyfriends? Doug and Parker won. Now it was Mandy and my turn to go against them. Doug came over and put his hands on the backs of both of our necks. His fingers were warm. All the hairs on my body stood up. The fact that he'd hooked up with both of us before was something I think we all were aware of. I felt repulsed by this fact.

"Ready?" he said.

"Bring it on," Mandy said.

Doug refilled the cups of beer. All around us, the party was hitting peak insanity. There was all kinds of action in the kitchen. People were opening and closing cabinets. A random sleeve of thin mints was excavated from the freezer to cheers.

I think in her mind, Mandy thought that our playing these guys in a game of quarters was some sort of act of retribution. That by having to stare at me from across the table, these guys would have to come to terms with the person they'd wronged, or at least acknowledge my humanity. But as much as I'd come to love her in the last few hours, I just couldn't get on board with Mandy's logic. I didn't want to play Doug's games. The rules were rigged.

First of all, there was no chance in hell we could win against them at quarters, and the thought of being forced to guzzle down beer in front of them—just the image of it in my mind—felt like a flashback to that night on the beach. Doug's body, his smell, his easy confidence—everything that had once seemed attractive to me now made me feel ill. Everything about him—his eyes, his muscular build, his natural leadership, even his intelligence—seemed dangerous. My entire body rejected the notion of being across the table from him.

Playing this game would be like saying everything that

had happened between us was ok, that I had put it behind me, that nothing that had taken place had been wrong. That seemed to be the message Doug got from every other woman. I had no idea whether he'd gyrated and came all over all of us, or if I was just the lucky winner, but I refused to signal any sort of peace.

The shame that had lived inside me suddenly shifted. This repulsion I felt from being near him gave me a new sense of power.

There would be no stand-off. I wasn't going to tell him off. Nothing I could say right then would ever hurt him anyway. He had alcohol and his cadre of bro-dogs to validate his every utterance, not to mention decades of cinema and glossy magazines to reinforce the narrative of his god-like existence. It would take time to dismantle these structures. To redefine the rules and the game itself.

In the meantime, I had to live my life. And the best way to start that was to get the hell out of that kitchen. But first, I directed the deepest loathing of my soul straight at Doug, hoping my ire would leave a mark on some part of his more enlightened being, the part that would stick with him long past his high school glory days. Though I admit it was wishful thinking.

"Sorry, Mandy. I just can't," I said. But there was no time for my exit to make any dramatic effect.

"I'll play," said a girl who I'd never seen before.

Mandy shrugged, "Ok."

I retreated from the kitchen and wandered down a hallway to the front of the house, where there was a living room and a dining room and a big staircase that led upstairs. Kate and Kelsey were sitting on a couch in the living room.

"Do you want a tequila shot?" Kate said when she saw me.

"I think I'm good," I told her. I knew I was good. I already felt like my face was a little rubbery. I walked up the stairs to the next level, letting my fingers trace the wallpapered wall, feeling for the seams. I wondered what my mother would think of this place. Most of it seemed plucked from a Macy's showroom, though maybe Macy's was too pedestrian. Maybe they bought the furniture from Neiman Marcus or Saks. Mom would definitely have opinions on all of it—especially the plush of the carpet and the salmon-colored curtains. She'd be able to tell me how much every item in the place cost. She'd probably know the brands of furniture and would have something to say about the shade of the wood stain on the entertainment shelf. And the way the hall closet doors were all mirrored. I hated them. I was not into mirrors really. But maybe Mom would defend them. We did not have the same taste.

At the top of the stairs was a hallway that stretched to the left and right and a series of shut doors on both sides. The second one on the left was a bathroom. The toilet seat was pale pink. The toilet paper was three-ply. I had a delightful time just sitting there long after I'd finished peeing, listening to the muted sounds of the others below, letting my heart beat and the air enter and exit my body.

This is my life, I thought to myself. I am drunk inside a mansion. I wondered if Nanny was ever in a mansion. Probably not unless she was hired to clean it or something. Would she feel proud to know I was here? In one of the houses we used to drive by to look at their Christmas lights? I think she'd consider it an accomplishment. So would Mom. Dad too. And the thing was, a mansion was just a house with more bathrooms. It had the same stuff inside it, just more of it. They kept their thin mints in the freezer too.

When I finally decided to stand and flush, I saw that there were little soaps by the sink in a dish that were in the shape of seashells. I picked them up and smelled them. They smelled sweet, like candy. As I put them back into their dish, I caught my eye in the mirror and pantomimed a series of faces—sexy, serious, super happy, engaged. My lipstick had faded to a good level now. I liked it. For the time being, alone in the bathroom, I felt pleased with myself.

"Is there a different party going on over there?" I asked the girl in the mirror. She asked me the same question. Neither one of us replied.

Outside the door, I heard the sounds of people walking. Maybe the others were looking for me, I thought suddenly. I shouldn't stay in here too long. That'd be creepy. I unlocked the door and opened it into the hallway. Ray, the guy from the couch, was waiting by the door. His brown eyes were glazed and he had a loose smile on his face.

"Well, there you are," he said. "I thought I'd lost you forever and you'd just be a face I saw on the TV one day, winning a gold medal in the Olympics." He looked at me like I was a beautiful gemstone that he was delighted to recover. I was flattered. It seemed sincere and I liked feeling pretty and seen.

"Here I am," I said. I wanted go downstairs and look for Kelsey, but Ray was standing between me and the stairs. Any step in that direction was a step closer to him, and the way he was looking at me made me afraid to give him too much of an invitation. Not that I thought he'd do anything terrible to me or anything. I just didn't want to have to deal with him getting too close. So I turned the other way, further down the hallway of closed doors. That was when I saw Travis walking into a door.

Travis! I didn't think at all. I just followed right behind him and walked in. There was Jake, sitting on the floor next to Jaron, who was sitting at a desk rolling a joint. Anais, his girlfriend, was sitting on the bed. They were all talking peacefully like they always gathered in other people's bedrooms to roll joints and hang out. Which, maybe they did. As soon as I saw Jaron and Anais, my impulse was to run. I was still mortified by the idea of her reading my personal business from Deb's diary. They all turned and looked at me, and I basically just pivoted on my feet and did a complete 180 and found myself back in the hall. Ray was in the bathroom, I guess. Or maybe he'd gone back downstairs. I started walking towards the stairs, then paused. I didn't know what to do. I waited for Jake to come out. I wanted him to follow me, but he didn't. I tried to will my feet to walk back in, but they wouldn't move. So I did what Ceil did that morning when I saw her with the sage. I just sat there in the middle of the hallway. The rug felt soft. I stretched my legs out, staring at the ceiling.

"A mansion is just a house with a lot of bathrooms," I imagined myself explaining to my Nanny. "And fluffy rugs that feel like beds."

Maybe I was starting to fall asleep I heard someone walking up the steps again, so I quickly sat back up. It was Ray. He was with Mandy and some other people.

"You gotta see this," Ray was saying to everyone. "It's hilarious. I'm telling you."

"What are you doing up here, weirdo?" Mandy asked when she saw me.

"Where are Kelsey and Kate?"

"They are down in the basement playing Mario Kart with your favorite people." She could have meant Parker and Doug or Jenna and Deb. Or maybe she meant all four. She offered her hand and pulled me to my feet. We walked back into the bedroom where Jake was.

Ray clearly didn't know anyone was in there. "Oh shit," he said, "it's dank in here."

Jaron passed him the lit joint. He took a puff, and it began going around the room. Ray walked over to a backpack that I guess was his and extracted a large CD booklet.

"First, we need music." He started paging through the book while he was talking, explaining why some specific studio in Memphis was super important to the legacy of American rock music and how this guy he was talking to had to check out this album. But then he turned the page and pulled a different one out. "I burned this mix for a moment just like this," he said with authority. I didn't know until later that Ray prided himself on being the resident DJ of their dorm at school. I had to give him credit. The room transformed. The sound of The Beastie Boys brought momentum to the space.

This room was clearly Gordy's. There was a pennant with the name of his boarding school over his bed and a *Sports Illustrated* poster of Heidi Klum covered in sand wearing a nude colored bathing suit with her boobs bursting out was tacked up to one of the walls. Anais was paging through a yearbook. I guess she couldn't locate any diaries. I felt a primal urge to pull her hair.

My entire body was in an overjoyed panic to find itself so close to Jake. He wasn't wearing an Absolute Video t-shirt. It was a light blue t-shirt with art from Built to Spill's *Keep it Like a Secret*. I was in a state of mind where I truly believed that every detail of my existence was delivering me a message. I tried to decipher what it could mean that those words were speaking to me from the chest of this person who seemed to be made with magnets, so strong was the force I felt behind every one of his tiny gestures.

Was I losing my mind? Was I delusional? Was I just drunk enough to think I was telepathic?

I wasn't making this stuff up, was I? It was all real, right?

I knew that he knew I was there. But he was with his people and I was with mine and somehow everything had gone sideways into strange territory. Was it possible to just walk up to him and say, "Hi"? Is that what I should say? "Hi?" Or "Yo." Or, "Whattup." Or, "I'm sorry I'm an idiot." Or, "fuck you for judging me."

We were on opposite sides of the bed. And the bed had like five people sitting on it. Through the moving limbs and shouting, we suddenly caught each other's eyes. They were like Lego pieces coming together. Snap. So seamlessly connected that once they were joined, they were impossible to pull apart. A surge rippled across the invisible cord that bound us. Our faces exploded into smiles. I felt a lump surge so quickly into my throat I'm shocked that I didn't gag and puke on the floor.

A boy I did not know handed me the joint. It was a little soggy on the sucking side. The fire side was smoking wildly. I tried to accept this gift and handle it casually. I was deliberating how to bring it to my lips when Jake was suddenly right next to me, his familiar smell causing a thrill to start at the base of my spine and fuzz up towards my neck. It was loud in there. He spoke close to my ear.

"You don't have to smoke it if you don't want to," he said.

"I just want to try a little," I said.

"Well, then don't pull on it as hard as you did that cigarette," he said. "It's strong. I don't want you to bug out." His eyes were bloodshot. Maybe he was bugging out.

I did as instructed. It was easier to smoke than the cigarette I'd stolen out of his mouth a month or so ago, but still the smoke didn't leave my mouth in a professional looking line, instead it poured out of me like a cloud, as if my tonsils had suddenly combusted. I passed the joint onward. A few minutes later I realized that one little puff had indeed done the trick. My heart was beating a little faster. My smile felt a little more permanent. Time dissolved. I became absorbed in my own thoughts and had to keep reminding myself of the people around me. Jake and I said nothing to each other, but he stayed right next to me, and I didn't want him to go. Even though no words were exchanged, we were deeply engaged in a conversation. There was no doubt in my mind anymore about whether it was real. It was the truest thing in the room. That thought arrived to me as an absolute truth, the way absolute truths sometimes strike you when you're stoned.

Mandy broke the spell by sauntering over with a clear fizzy beverage in a coffee mug that said Best Mom Ever.

"Oh, look who found each other," she said smiling.

I gave her a look that said please, don't.

Jake gave her a stoner smile. She offered him a pound. "Freelander," she said.

"Gladstone," he replied as their fists collided.

"Drink this," she said to me, offering me her drink. "You gotta stay in the game."

"What's in it?" I asked.

"Tequila and Sprite," she said. "I had one already downstairs. If I have another, I'll feel sick."

I took a few big gulps. It was sweet but I could feel the liquor Ray walked into the closet and chose a jacket from a rack. It was plaid. "Look at how many suitcoats this kid has," Ray said, pointing to an entire rack's worth of jackets. "It's ridiculous. Where is he going?"

Ray started displaying them one by one. It was hilarious. After he held up like three of them, he started looking for a place to unload the ones in his hands. I offered to take them. Then I did the next thing that occurred to me. I took one off the hanger and tried it on. It was too big for me. The bottom of it hung lower than my shorts and tickled my legs. Ray was delighted by this. He put one on too. Gordy was tall, but Ray was taller. He was well over 6 feet. Gordy's sleeves ended short of Ray's wrists. He celebrated the strange fit by doing the running man and flailing his arms all around. The spectators cheered. I helped Mandy into one. Jake passed them out but didn't put one on. Soon, almost everyone had a blazer on.

The song "Kiss" by Prince came on. People were bouncing on the bed in Gordy's blazers screaming, "You don't have to be rich, to be my girl, you don't have to be cool, to rule my world." Mandy took my hand and spun me in a circle, then pulled me up on the bed. Ray stayed by the stereo, flailing like one of those windsock guys on top of auto parts stores on the highway. Travis did the robot. Anais unbuttoned the bottom half of her shirt and tied it underneath her bra so she could show off her stomach. Jake was doing his own hippie/robot sort of thing. Mandy shook her booty. I had a shoulder shimmy thing going on. We were all laughing and yelling things about the board meeting commencing.

Prince became Modest Mouse's "Tiny Cities Made of Ashes." Everyone screamed along. "We're drinking, drinking, drinking, drinking coca coca cola." Ray opened his arms in front of Mandy, and she jumped into them. Then they started making out against the wall. It seemed like a good moment to hop down from the bed.

Gordy's closet continued to be ransacked. Ties were worn on heads. Someone came into the room with one of Gordy's mom or sister's bras on over his shirt. Things were getting wild, and I liked it. Gordy had shown up and didn't seem to mind the chaos at all. In fact, he left and returned in a sexy lace and silk nightgown he must have purloined from his mother's closet.

I was standing by a window that looked out onto the back patio, which was lit up, the chairs all pulled askance, though no one was sitting on the furniture anymore. There were flowers blooming from huge pots at each corner of the lounge area. I was admiring them and wondering what they were when I saw Mr. Pumpkin dodge from behind a pot out into the shadows of the yard.

"Oh no!" I said, remembering Gordy telling me about how he was declawed and supposed to stay indoors. I turned around to tell him, but he was in the middle of performing an absurd strip tease and didn't look like he should be interrupted.

I needed air anyway. I weaved my way out of the bedroom, down the stairs, and outside. The party had thinned out. I didn't hear any noise from the basement. I wondered where Kelsey and Kate were. I opened the door and stepped outside. The night was still. The crickets were still deep into their nighttime performance. I could hear the sounds from Gordy's bedroom upstairs. Whoops and cheers. But they weren't as loud as I'd imagined they'd be. If the neighbors were home, they probably wouldn't even hear.

"Mr. Pumpkin," I whispered, creeping back towards where I saw the cat run. "Mr. Pumpkin."

I crept and poked and called but came up with nothing. The poor cat. Maybe he was just waiting for everyone to leave before he snuck back in. I realized I was tired and also dying of thirst. I took a deep breath and exhaled and sat on a patio chair. Beyond the flowerpots, I noticed a vegetable garden off the far corner of the patio. There were zucchinis and eggplants and carrot flowers and other sorts of squash on one side and a row of wire cylinders surrounding each tomato plant on the other, helping each to grow tall. My stomach growled. I spied one round red ripe tomato on a vine. The other plants were full of green ones. Without thinking, I just plucked it off, rubbed it against my t-shirt, and took a bite of it, squirting red juice all over myself and into the air.

"Fuck," I said. But I continued to devour it. It was delicious. Sweet and earthy and hydrating too. Say what you want about Jersey. The tomato hype is real.

The door opened, and I turned to see Jake. There was no way to conceal my garden thievery. I was covered in tomato juice, the red pulpy innards dripping down my arm. I looked at him guiltily. He started giggling at me.

"You are like some kind of vegan vampire," he said.

I shoved the remainder of the tomato into my mouth and attempted to dry my arms and face using my skin and t-shirt and, yes, I'm sorry to admit, the sleeve of Gordy's suit jacket. I swallowed it down and then said, "It was about the size of a human heart."

"I'm never going to forget the way you look right now," he said. "I'm going to remember finding you out here eating a stolen tomato for my entire life."

"You don't know what you'll remember," I said. "Life is long."

"It's my favorite thing I've ever seen," he said.

"Even better than *Cosmos*?"

"Even better than *Breakfast at Tiffany's*."

"You know, I came out here looking for a cat."

"Like hell you did, you tomato thief."

"I swear!" The tomato had lightened the mood between us, but now that the quiet of the night became so noticeable and clear, I could feel Jake wanting to apologize. But I'd already forgiven him. He pulled a chair right next to me and looked at me seriously. Too seriously. I didn't like it. I wanted to linger in the wild silliness of upstairs, not wallow in whatever this was.

"I'm sorry about the way I brought up the diary thing—"

I had to interrupt him. "Stop it!"

He tried again, "While we were on the phone—"

Again, I interrupted him. "Bah! Bah!"

"I should have asked you about it. I shouldn't have just acted like I knew how it went down—"

"I said stop it. Can you please just listen to me? I don't want to talk about it."

"Why?"

"Because. I don't. I want to live my life and have fun."

"I just don't want you to think that hearing that stuff changed the way I feel about you."

"But it did!"

"No, it didn't!"

"Yes," I said emphatically, "it did."

I stood up from the chair. I thought about going back inside, but I didn't have the energy. I thought about running home, but there was the tricky fact that I was supposed to be somewhere else. I didn't know what I should do. I just started walking towards Sara Jennings' lawn.

"Where are you going?"

I didn't respond. I just walked until I got to about where he scared me that day and I bit him, then I collapsed into the grass.

There were so many things we didn't know about each other. I didn't know his dad lived in the Florida Everglades. He didn't know about Nanny, or Uncle Tommy, or my crazy mom, or the rest of her siblings. I didn't know that he could build things, that he and his dad and his sister had built a cabin in the swamp, just the three of them, or that his dad was remarried and that his stepmom was pregnant and that soon he'd have a much younger brother. How could I have had any idea that I would meet that younger brother? That I would learn how to knit him a very tiny pair of socks?

He was still under the illusion that my class rank was commensurate with my self-confidence. He didn't know I was forever paralyzed by a feeling of doubt. That the only thing I ever really wanted was to not do something wrong, which of course prevented me a million times from doing what was right. He didn't know that I'd never been on an airplane. Or that I'd never tried an avocado. Or that whatever the status of our connection, however many years from now, in the middle of Times Square subway station I would be able to pick him out of a crowded platform waiting for an uptown 2 train. It was the way he boarded the car. That goofy, bouncy gait he never grew out of.

And of course, 9/11 hadn't happened yet. A year hadn't passed. We hadn't drifted apart and not spoken for three months because of some stupid fight we could never even remember who started. The news of the towers hadn't traveled through the school yet. We hadn't locked eyes in the hall before even realizing that we had been looking for each other. We hadn't walked out of school together into the woods, where, instead of staring at the television like the rest of the world, we sat in a tree for most of the day playing a game we invented called "Would you come find me?"

Would you come find me if World War 3 started?

Would you come find me if you found out I was in a horrible accident?

If I was dying of cancer?

Would you help me escape if I was a political prisoner?

Would you know I was innocent?

Yes, yes, yes, we promised, no matter what. No matter how much time had passed. As if we understood what anything meant, or that we were reciting some sort of strange vows.

How could I have known right then that one night in the not-too-distant future I would say I was sleeping at Kelsey's when he was alone at his house and we would sleep next to each other, fully clothed, all night, side by side on his couch with *Back to the Future* on repeat the entire night, the automatic replay function cuing it up again and again?

From then on, the sound of Huey Lewis's voice would be a hilarious portal to this moment in my life.

"Better remember / Lightning never strikes twice."

The girl who got struck by lightning and was in the coma eventually woke up. It took her two years before she could speak again. Her memory had been wiped clean. She had to start again from zero.

Keep it like a secret, Jake's t-shirt told me. Why are the most important things always the most impossible to explain?

Lying on the grass right then, tomato on my shirt, waiting for it all to start, it felt like it had already happened. I only felt it as the energy that would transcend time. The light that would be released into the galaxy.

How would Fellini tell the story?

Disney?

John Hughes?

Sylvia Plath?

I guess the way you understand something is entirely dependent upon the angle from which it is approached. The way the light from one galaxy enters into another.

Space, time, symbols for math I hadn't gotten to yet. Calculus I didn't understand.

I felt our future. I'd always felt it, now I could see.

Could it be that just discovering the potential for something to exist made it burst into being?

Like a book that hadn't been written yet?

What had Carl Sagan said? "To bake an apple pie from scratch, you must first invent the universe." Mom said the Poconos smelled like apple pie. I wanted to ask Jake what he thought of that.

Could I erase Doug Ryan from existence? Could I live in a different world where I didn't have to feel like everything was a race with a trophy at stake? But without all of that, would Jake be gone too?

The grass was long. Perhaps past the borough's agreed-upon length. The week's worth of rain had really sent it sprouting. Someone alert Frances Banks.

As I laid back into it, I felt it squish into my shorts.

"Do you want me to follow you or not?" Jake called.

"It's too late to ask that question," I said.

He came and laid down next to me in the grass and took my hand with both of his and sort of started massaging my fingers. The clouds had all but disappeared. It was dark enough right there across from the thick trees that hid the golf course, far enough from the party and the lights from the patio where Mr. Pumpkin crouched. Aliens could maybe land here. E.T.'s ship might foolishly think that it was safe.

The constellations fought against the suburban Philadelphia glow, but if you weren't aware of it, you just might not know. You just might think there were only like 25 or so stars up there. And yes, this was a travesty, but right then, it was enough.

Because there was Vega, its bright beam like a beacon, like a sparkly tomato. Something I'd never forget. I giggled at it like it was an old friend, then I took the hand that Jake was holding and pointed it to the sky.

"Look," I said. "It's our star."

Acknowledgements

Writing a book is an impossible thing to do alone, even though we imagine it to be just one person in a room. Thank you to my husband, Brian Russ, for always believing in me and encouraging me and being my person every day: I love you and could not have ever done any of the things I've done in the last 20 years without you. There is nobody better to be a grown up with. Let's make art forever! Thank you to Barbara Belski, my amazing mother, for always encouraging me and also for helping me realize my artistic vision by watching my kids so I could begin writing this book. And thanks to my father, Ed Belski, for modeling creativity every day of my life, and also for always going on the crazy water slides with me. Thank you Scott Adkins and Erin Courtney, for providing me with a desk at the Brooklyn Writers' Space so I could actually have the mental space to write this book. Thank you Kimberly Schwab, the greatest science teacher of all time and an amazing friend and coworker, whose summer assignment inspired me to reshape an earlier draft of this book. Thank you Heidi Diehl, Caeli Widger, Stephen Aubrey, and Judson Merrill for being my early readers and giving me feedback and encouragement on my journey. Thank you to my agent, Arielle Datz, and Julia Kenny at Dunow, Carlson & Lerner for believing in my book. Thank you Jenny Offill, CJ Hauser, and Helen Phillips for being friends and champions of my work since the beginning. And thank you to Vedra Chandler, my share-a-brain bestie, who sent me pictures of the South Jersey night sky throughout my writing of this book from her backyard in Camden, NJ.

Thank you to Loni Gaghan for designing the cover of my

book and for always being a creative force in my life. I love you so much!

And if you, reader, are still reading this page, thank you! I am truly grateful. <3

Lauren Belski lives, writes, and works in New York City with her husband, musician and writer Brian Russ, and their two children. A graduate of the Brooklyn College MFA program and the author of the short story collection *Whatever Used to Grow Around Here* (Crumpled Press), her short fiction, poetry, essays and criticism have appeared in *Make*, *StoryQuarterly*, *Avidly*, and many other pockets of the world. She almost died in 2020 when a tree branch fell on her car while she was driving. Every day is a gift.